Heliacle Rising

By C.C. Davie

First published in New Zealand in 2022 by C. C Davie

Copyright © C. C Davie 2022

The right of C. C Davie to be identified as the
Author of the Work has been asserted by her in accordance
with the Copyright, Designs and Patents Act 1988.

All rights reserved. No part of this publication may be reproduced,
Stored in a retrieval system, or transmitted, in any form or by any means
without prior written permission of the Author, nor be otherwise circulated
in any form of binding or cover other than that in which it is published
and without a similar condition being imposed on the subsequent purchaser.

All characters in this publication are fictitious and any resemblance
to real persons, living or dead is purely coincidental.

A catalogue record for this title is available from the
National Library of New Zealand.

Cover design by Grady Earls
Illustrations, map, and formatting
by Etheric Tales & Edits
etherictalesnedits.com

Trade paperback ISBN 978 1 99 116580 0
Hardback ISBN 978 1 99 116581 7
eBook ISBN 978 1 99 116582 4

Pronunciation guide

Characters:

Amylia Sylvers: *A-mee-lee-ah Sil-vers*

Rayvn Sylvers: *Ray-ven Sil-vers*

Lylith: *lil-lith*

Cecily Wynter: *Sess-ily Win-ter*

Gryffon Wynter: *Griff-on Win-ter*

Lyrik Damaris: *Li-ric Da-ma-ris*

Rogue Salvador: *Row-g Sal-va-door*

Ingryd Galyspie: *In-grid Gal-iss-pee*

Mica Drakon: *Me-ka Dray-con*

Ulric Drakon: *Ul-rick Dray-con*

Calypso: *Cal-lip-so*

Freyja: *Frey-ya*

Asspyn: *Ass-pin*

Falkyn: *Fal-ken*

Places:

Lylican: *Lil-lik-an*

Asteryn: *Ass-ter-in*

Perregrin: *Pear-eh-grin*

Credence: *Cree-dence*

Ateraxya: *At-ah-rax-ia*

Solos: *So-loss*

Eilysh: *Eye-lish*

Attica: *At-i-ka*

Calibyre: *Cal-i-burr*

Other:

Sylkies: *Sil-kees*

Druka: *Drew-ka*

Sabyre: *Say-burr*

Dyre wolves: *Dire-wolves*

Heliacle: *Huh-lie-uckle*

They say it takes a village to raise a baby.
Well… it took a village to write this book.
Firstly I would like to thank my mother, who did my initial run through and thoroughly ignored my plea for her to skip the spicy bits.
I would like to thank my partner, who put up with me ignoring the world to write and gave me the support to do so.
I would like to thank Violet, for the many midnight brainstorm sessions, and finally, I would like to thank Wes, my editor, who took my raw manuscript and polished it into a gem.

I am eternally grateful for my village.

xxx

LABRYNTH

CHAPTER 1

"Cyrus! The west wing is on fire! If Milly is burning those lessons again, the Gods save her," Addelyn yelled, appearing from her study pale and harassed. A small face peeped out from the folds of her skirts, looking wide-eyed at his father as Addelyn tried to pry his fingers from the cloth. "Rayvn, please let go for a moment."

Cyrus chuckled, laying a hand on her shoulder. "I will go, darling. Go rest. You still look peaky."

Addelyn ran a hand through her dark locks and glared at her husband, her jade eyes sparking, and he raised his hands in protest.

"Still beautiful, just... peaky." He grinned, tweaking his son's nose as he backed away with a wink at her. "I will go wrangle our little fire-starter."

He found the culprit quickly, the smoke billowing from the small lavatory a beacon to her whereabouts. He leaned against the stone wall with a bemused look on his face for a while, watching his daughter angrily rip out the pages of her workbook and shove them down the flaming toilet with angry grunts, muttering under her breath.

He straightened to his full, impressive height and leaned over her shoulder silently, peering into the blue flames that fast engulfed the wooden seat and climbed slowly across the carved wooden basin next to it.

"Hm, I can still see a bit of the number lessons to the right there. Needs a bit more fire, sweetheart."

The tattered remains of the book flew upwards as she jumped, and he caught it deftly as Amylia squeaked in surprise and spun to face him.

"I... I wasn't... well, I was, but it's all Kestrel's fault, Father. She's just so mean." Amylia's small nose wrinkled, her dark brows descending in a scowl. The miniature of her mother, except for the stunning blue eyes with silver highlights that glowed softly as if backlit, her father's eyes. She stamped, glaring at him and he chuckled, nodding soberly at her.

"Cranky nursemaids and number lessons. I sympathise entirely," he said, pulling her away slightly as the blue flames licked higher and singed the edge of a hanging tapestry. "But… I would really appreciate it if from now on you took your anger out on them in the lower-level lavatories, sweetheart. Now we have to traipse all the way downstairs until this is fixed." He raised a brow at her.

Amylia looked at her feet, shuffling under his gaze. "Sorry, Father… I just got so mad."

He grinned, reaching a hand around her. Frost snaked out across the burning wood, smothering the flames as it passed them, and then guttered, whispering out as the flames reclaimed their space. Cyrus frowned, sighing, and stepped around Amylia to reach for the faucet and pour water into the bowl of the basin and quickly splashed it with his large hands over the fire, putting it out with a hiss. He turned and picked Amylia up with a grunt, flinging the book out the open window with a flourish, and winked at her.

"I didn't see any lesson books, did you?"

Amylia shook her head vehemently, her black curls cascading around her, and then frowned, taking his palm, and squinting at it. "What happened to your gift? It didn't work right."

"I'm just a bit tired, sweetheart," he smiled at her. "Never too tired for this, though." He cupped a hand over her small one and she grinned, wriggling slightly in anticipation until he lifted it again. A tiny ice figurine lay in her palm, exquisite in its detail, before melting away from the heat of her hand.

"What was that one?" Amylia breathed, still looking at the puddle in her palm. "We haven't got one of those here."

"That, sweetheart, was a Sylkie," he rumbled, kissing the top of her head, and placing her gently down by the huge front doors. "A long time ago, I fought in a war where our kind soared high above the clouds on them. Beautiful beasts. I will tell you and Rayvn all about them tonight at bedtime… but right now, your mother needs a nice strong cup of tea and a foot rub. Why don't you run along to the pool and once I have done that, I will bring Rayvn out and we will go for a swim. Yes?"

"Oh, yes." Amylia nodded eagerly, hugging his leg quickly. "You won't be too long?"

"I will be right there." He smiled and squeezed her shoulder. "Now run along. If Mother sees you before I can get some tea into her, we will both be in trouble."

The sun warmed Amylia's skin as she lay in the crook of the huge tree that overhung their pool, watching the huge golden fish that lazily swam in the clear blue water. She yawned widely and rubbed her eyes, tired from the long morning of lessons. Blinking sleepily, she let the warmth settle over her, muzzy as the sounds of the slight breeze in the branches and the crickets faded away and she slipped into sleep.

Amylia shivered, starting awake and sitting up quickly. She baulked as she realised where she was and gripped the bark beneath her as she scanned the glade below.

"Father?" she called, her brows knotting as she noted the sun dipping low in the sky. She slid down the large tree, barking her knee on the rough surface and hissing under her breath. Licking her thumb, she cleaned the small scrape before picking her way back through the woods.

It took her a while to notice the creeping silence around her and she paused, listening for the birds that had been singing moments before, but now fell silent, as if they too strained to hear something.

A distant scream carried through the air, and her arms prickled, the fine hairs there rising. Coldness filled her belly as she scanned the trees. She knew that scream, except it wasn't full of its usual laughter and happiness. Her eyes scanned the surrounding trees wildly.

"Rayvn? Rayvn, what's wrong?" A pause and then crashing steps broken with sobs grew louder as he got closer. A thud sounded followed by a rustle as his small body tripped over something. He whimpered from amid the brush and then suddenly he was there, tripping over his feet in his haste to reach her with tears running down his face.

"Mm-mylia," he sobbed, clutching her dress, and burying his face in it. He trembled, sobs wracking his little body as she knelt in front of him.

Voice trembling, she asked again, "Rayvn, what's wrong?"

She tried in vain to pry his face away from the fabric of her skirt. The cold feeling spread over her whole body like ice. Losing patience, she gripped him by the arm, hauling him up to look at her.

Blood… there was blood on his face. The smell of it hit her a second later, metallic and warm on the air. Her heart stopped as she scanned him over, looking for a wound… but there was none.

"M-mumma," he moaned.

"What's wrong with Mother?" Amylia asked, her voice hitching as she got to her feet, pulling him up onto his little legs again, but he only shook his head, face white.

She gripped his hand and turned towards home, moving as fast as she could, while dragging Rayvn with her. They ran, tripping over roots and stones, Rayvn's breath coming in pants and sobs as he struggled to keep up with her, the small keep in the distance growing bigger with every step.

Smoke curled through the air, coming from not just the keep but the small township further behind it and the air… the air filled with the scent, of blood and smoke. And another odour she didn't recognise, like the kitchens before dinner roast was set out, but not the same — wrong, she knew it was very, very wrong.

They ran through the front gates into utter chaos. Mounted riders in silver and red armour milled around in the yard. The beautiful lawn had been reduced to mud. By the trees, one of her father's favourite hounds lay, a massive slash down its side… utterly still. The foreign men yelled to each other in a cacophony of noise that overwhelmed everything. Rayvn started crying, dragging his weight against her as he tried to back up… to get away from the large horses that were so close to them.

Suddenly, a large man, his silver armour glinting in the sunlight, stood in front of her, shielding them from the chaos and noise, herding them backwards into the shadow of the keep wall with gentle hands. He pulled off his cloak and threw it around both of them, pulling them together and tight against his body. Amylia turned her face to him, confusion and panic coursing through her.

"Mother? Where are Mother and Father?"

His face softened. "Child… Amylia, yes? And Rayvn, I believe?" His eyes turned to her brother, who still clung to her skirt. "I'm sorry. We were looking for you… we hoped… We… we didn't get here in time. I learnt of the attack too late, and I could not stop it. We chased off the last of them as we got here, but your parents… we were too late… I'm sorry." He looked at them, soot smeared across his face and a cut on his temple oozing blood slowly.

Amylia stared at him in confusion.

"Too late for what? Where are Mother and Father?" She looked over his shoulder to the entranceway of the keep as he shifted uncomfortably.

"Too late to save them, Amylia. I'm sorry… but they are no longer among the living." He glanced at Rayvn uneasily, as if waiting to see if he understood.

Heat built inside her, the hot burn of it curling through her belly and heating her flesh. Rayvn's skin felt cool against hers.

It hit her, like a blow to the gut. Mother... Gone. Father. Both of them. She couldn't breathe, couldn't take this, no... No! This must be a mistake. Father would be here any minute to laugh and tell her this was wrong, this was all wrong. Panting as she struggled to catch her breath. Rayvn started crying again, sobbing into her skirts. She didn't think he even understood what had happened and was likely just responding to her own distress.

She wrapped her arms around him protectively as steam rose from her skin, the tears on her face evaporating as soon as they fell. Feeling a tickle on her arms, she glanced down. Flames licked their way around them, over Rayvn, not burning but forming a wall, slowly encasing her and her brother entirely as her ears rang. Her head spun as she searched for a face she knew, vaguely noting the fear growing in the man's eyes as the flames raged around them.

The panic in her rose with the heat as it swelled inside her. She moved backwards, pressing her back against the cold stone behind her, clutching Rayvn to her as the flames sparked, shooting out towards the man, keeping him — keeping them all — away. A sudden movement to her side made her jump just as a sharp pain erupted behind her ear and then... nothing.

A blinding pain pulsed behind her left ear, and her arm throbbed with a steady ache, just above her elbow. She must be lying on something. Amylia whimpered, cracking her eyelids open and wincing at the blinding light that pierced through them. She tried to catch her bearings.

A wagon, she was in a wagon, and... fur? Was that fur she was lying on? She could scent the faint musty odour of the wolf it had once been. Soft and comforting, she dug her fingers into the pelt as her head swam, blinking slowly as she raised herself up onto her knees and looked blearily around.

Her eyes snapped to Rayvn's small form, curled into a tight ball in the furs next to her, tear tracks marked down his grubby face and thumb in his mouth. She lunged for him, ignoring the violent stab of pain in her head and gripped his arm.

"Rayvn," she whispered hoarsely, shaking him.

His eyes fluttered open, red rimmed and puffy. Instantly his bottom lip wobbled around his thumb as he looked at her before launching up to wrap his little arms around her neck. The rough scratch of a bandage around his arm brushed her neck. She clutched him tight as she looked around the covered cart. They sat in a pile of furs, rocking slowly with the movement of the white canvas-covered wagon. The steady beat of hooves around them and murmuring of men told her there were riders surrounding the cart.

Rayvn's muffled voice came from her lap. "Your arm sore?"

She looked down as his sticky finger traced down her arm, tugging at the surrounding bandage before he quickly shoved his thumb back in his mouth.

Voice wavering, she replied, "I... I think so."

The wagon slowed and halted. It jostled as the driver hopped off, his shoes crunching on the dirt road before the sound stopped at the back of the wagon for a moment. An older man with greying hair pulled back the outer sheet, looking in carefully. The man from the keep looked sadly at them.

"My dears, are you feeling ok?" Amylia eyed him with mistrust as he extended a hand to her. "Please, come sit up front with me. Rayvn, too. You have been asleep for a long while. I was beginning to worry." He kept his hand out, smiling gently as she stared at him. "I am Lord Drakon, Lord Ulric Drakon. I... I was a friend of your parents.' Your mother Addelyn and I knew each other well." His face creased in sadness as he looked down at his hand for a moment. "I will mourn her loss. The loss of both of them." He glanced up again, flexing the offered hand.

Numbness crept over Amylia at his words, and she blindly reached out to grasp his hand, feeling helpless. She slowly pried Rayvn's hand off her skirt with her free hand as she stumbled toward Lord Drakon and into the sunlight. Drakon lifted her down carefully and set her on the ground, Rayvn settling beside her moments later.

"How old are you child? It's been a while since I last saw you," Drakon rumbled.

Amylia searched through the fog of grief in her mind, trying to remember anything, think of anything besides her father's face the last time she had seen him that morning, smiling down at her as he carried her, safe and secure in his arms.

"Eight, my lord," she whispered, reaching down and clasping Rayvn's sticky hand.

Drakon smiled. "I have a son, Mica, he is not much older than you at eleven. I'm sure you two will become good friends. I'm taking you back to my keep, it's the least I can do for... for Addelyn." A look of pain washed over his face. "I promise you that I will keep you safe there."

Amylia nodded mutely, lurching towards the front of the wagon.

Clambering up onto the steps, her stomach dropped again. "But... our nurse, Kestrel, and our dog, Namira? Are they coming with us?"

"I'm sorry, child," Drakon grunted, heaving Rayvn up next to her and himself up after him. "No one survived the raid on the keep. There is no one left. I have… left men behind to make sure every person gets the respect they deserve."

The wagon lurched forward, guards falling in around them, providing a protective circle to the wagon and its occupants. Her head throbbed, her arm hurt. Rayvn gripped her arm, squeezing the sore area, but she was too tired to push him off.

Gripping the side of the seat, she twisted to look back behind them, searching for any sign of home, land she recognised, but it was alien to her. A guard caught her eye as she turned back, he was staring at her… right at her, nothing nice in his gaze as he surveyed her face coldly. And then he grinned, a wolfish, feral expression that ran an icy finger of terror down her spine.

Twisting back to Rayvn, she hugged the little boy to her and shut her eyes.

Chapter 2
11 years later

It was snowing. Again.

Amylia tugged her cloak tighter around her shoulders, breath misting out in front of her as she leaned out over the balcony railing and took a deep breath of the frostbitten air.

It smelled of pine and faintly of the rich cooking smells coming from the kitchens below.

At a clunk behind her, she turned to see the red face of her maid, Harriet, as she put the heavy washbasin down on the chest by her bed.

"It's warm, m'lady, if you use it quick like. Lord knows, it's cold out there at the moment and this will freeze solid if you keep those doors open." Harriet huffed, wiping her brow with the back of her sleeve.

Smiling, Amylia stepped back into the warmth of the room, closing the tall glass panes behind her with a click as the maid bustled across to the armoire and started rummaging through it.

"Thank you, Harry." She dropped a washcloth into the steaming water and bent over the bowl, pressing the cloth to her face. The warmth seeped into her skin where the wind had chilled it moments before.

The water ran in tendrils of heat down her neck and chest before soaking into the fabric of the clothes she still wore. Shrugging off her outer layers and stripping to her shift, she ran the cloth over her neck, and down her arms, sighing as her body stole the heat back into itself.

Harriet's small frame appeared next to her, a gown resting across her arms.

"The royal blue one tonight?" The maid frowned, a crease forming between her warm brown eyes as she studied the fabric before gazing up at Amylia. "No, no, the silver one. It will bring out your eyes," she muttered, sweeping the gown out of Amylia's reaching hand and disappearing back into the depths of the cupboard again.

Amylia chuckled and shook her head as she picked up the waiting towel. "Honestly, I don't even know why I'm to be there tonight. It's just another trade alliance meeting, isn't it?"

Harriet shrugged, placing an ornate silver gown carefully down on the bed. The tips of the sleeves and hems were midnight black, fading into silver through the rest of the low-backed dress.

Amylia cringed. It was so… fitted, and feminine. A far cry from her preferred loose dresses that let her move easily. She had only worn it once before, at the betrothal ceremony for her and Mica six months ago.

It was gorgeous if you were impartial to breathing… or eating… anything… at all. But everyone had complimented it, and Mica's eyes had glowed with pride when he had seen her wear it, saying it made her look as if she were a goddess.

She blushed at the memory.

"The maids are being run ragged down in the kitchens and the hall preparing," Harriet said, picking up a brush and enthusiastically setting herself to tackling Amylia's hair. "Whoever they are, Lord Drakon wants to impress them and isn't taking any chances." She paused. "Down or up?" She held a handful of Amylia's dark curls and eyed the reflection in the mirror. "Down," she said, nodding to herself and not waiting for an answer. "And that pretty necklace Lord Mica gave to you will finish it nicely."

Amylia watched her maid fondly as the small woman, a veritable walking tornado, swept through the room and back.

"Do you ever stop moving, Harry?" she teased.

She was very fond of Harriet. Not much older than Amylia herself, she had been assigned to care for Amylia since her arrival at the keep.

Only thirteen, Harriet had been her playmate and confidant, and slowly coaxed Amylia out of the shell of grief that had wrapped around her in those first months.

Eleven years had passed, and Amylia had requested for her to remain with her even after the maid had married.

Harriet's husband Raol, captain of the keep's warriors, had moved to the keep's staff quarters as well. He oversaw weapons-training for her brother Rayvn, who had grown into a handsome fourteen-year-old.

Amylia's hair glistened by the time Harriet grunted in satisfaction, stepping back with her hands on her small hips to survey her handiwork.

"Well, I know where everyone will be looking tonight, m'lady, and it's not at any trade agreements." Harriet grinned before carefully picking the dress up and holding it for Amylia to step into.

Amylia groaned, rolling her eyes heavenward, and prayed to the Gods for the patience to get through the night. She sighed and stepped into the glistening material.

The great hall was a bustling hive of activity and Amylia grimaced, slipping into the bustle of it as she breathed in the delicious smells of roasting meats and spiced wines. She scanned the gathering crowd for the tell-tale black mop of her brother who, as usual, towered over the other guests.

She smiled when she saw him, animatedly talking with a group of young men. Catching his eye, she winked. Rayvn's broad shoulders and height hinted at the strength he would grow into one day. He was graceful and lithe. His skill with the sword that hung so casually from his belt was already unmatched by any warrior in Drakon's army, save perhaps Raol himself.

Harriet let go of her gown's lengthy train, cast a last look over her, and gave her a wink.

"I'll go ask Cook to set aside a plate and send it up to your room, m'lady." She grinned.

Amylia grimaced and rolled her eyes. "Whatever would I do without you, Harry?"

"Starve. Not to mention look like you had been in a tavern brawl most the time, hay sticking out your hair and whatnot," came the tart reply, Harriet's grin turning impish. With a swirl of skirts, she was gone, disappearing into the scurry of maids.

A hand fell gently on her back and made her startle. A low voice whispered into her ear, "You look absolutely ravishing tonight, my love."

Turning, a smile on her lips, she was met with beautiful hazel eyes flecked with green. Mica leaned in, brushing a kiss to her cheek. "Mmmmmm, and is that?" He sniffed her neck. "Jasmine?"

Amylia smiled back at him. "That is entirely Harry's doing," she whispered. "The woman is a miracle-worker."

"I think you underestimate yourself." He chuckled. "I will need to place guards on you tonight, looking like the Jewel of Lylican."

His gaze lowered to her diamond necklace, a look of approval entering his eyes before he brushed a finger against her cheek and gave her a small smile.

Mica led her towards the throng of people gathering around the giant table set in pride of place in the centre of the room.

A roaring fire in a hearth the size of a carriage crackled and popped happily, filling the room with warmth, and bathed the guests in a golden light.

When the light hit Amylia's dress, the fabric shimmered, drawing jealous looks from some of the female guests as she passed. None, however, with the level of intensity that came from a pair of green eyes that caught her gaze.

A beautiful woman with blond hair stared at her in stony silence, her full mouth set in a hard line.

Lylith, daughter of a wealthy merchant and friend to Lord Drakon, who had been lost at sea when Lylith was still in swaddling. She had been taken under Drakon's care when her mother passed away, arriving at Lylican at age five, not long after Amylia and Rayvn, and had been raised alongside them.

Amylia had thought they were friends, until it became obvious that Lord Drakon wished Amylia and Mica to be betrothed. Things became strained between the girls when Mica's feelings for Amylia had grown obvious and their friendship slowly turned to love.

Amylia looked away, irritation grating at her. First the dress and now having to sit next to Lylith. She turned to Mica.

"Who are we meeting tonight for this trade agreement?"

"Two parties," he answered, eyes scanning the guests, "though Father is more interested in one than the other. They don't seem to be here right now. Some from Perregrin in the West, Lord Umber, I think his name is." He gestured to a portly, bearded man standing by the large fireplace with a sweet-faced woman on his arm. "And from the North, Asteryn. Lord and Lady Wynter are powerful allies if we can negotiate terms, though that will be tomorrow and between them. Tonight is just about showing them who we are." He smiled down at her, chucking her under the chin. "And showing them we are united with the lower territories—your people, my jewel. Wine?" He passed her a glass of heated wine, the spices filling her senses as it steamed up to her. Taking a sip, it warmed her core and she moaned softly in approval.

A soft gust of cool air and a grate of wood on rock announced the opening of the large entry doors. Lord Drakon swept into the room, followed by a small party of guests.

"Ah, good," murmured Mica. "Now they are here, Father will relax."

Amylia turned, scanning the newcomers, and paused as the rest of the guests, also silenced briefly, surveyed the new arrivals.

They were different, she could feel it. They felt… strange.

Four in total, in the lead stood a tall handsome man, muscular and tan, dark brown hair tied up in a bun and eyes such a light brown they looked amber. He wore leather pants with a loose white shirt open at the front, revealing a broad chest. Next to him stood a short, slightly built, beautiful woman. Golden hair tied in a thick braid hung nearly to her waist. The woman wore a gorgeous, fitted gown in dark red with a plunging neckline, and moved like a wildcat. Her deep brown eyes, slightly slanted and rimmed with thick lashes, seemed to take in everything as she surveyed the hall. Then she stepped to the side to make way for the couple coming up behind them.

Amylia's breath hitched when they came into view.

She had never seen anyone like them. The man, tall and solidly built, had eyes of a tawny gold that glowed as if backlit by burning fire. Predator's eyes. And his face... She wanted to say it was beautiful, but that didn't feel right. Handsome didn't feel enough. He had a ragged scar under his eye, two points ending in a V midway down his cheek, one point cutting through his brow and down, the other starting under his eye. It did nothing to detract from his looks.

His hair—even though he was young, maybe late twenties—was so grey it was nearly white, the top half tied back from his face.

The woman on his arm was devastatingly beautiful. A turquoise dress, cut daringly low, fitted snugly to her slender frame. Her pale blond hair flowed down her back, held away from her face by a tiara of silver and diamonds. Her face—Amylia had never seen a woman so perfect—with fine features and eyes that shone in the same eerie way the grey-haired man's did, in shades of sky blue.

She had intricate, delicate, silver tattoos in marks Amylia had never seen, running across the bridge of her nose and across her high cheekbones that caught the light as she moved. There were similar tattoos on her fingers, glinting when the woman gestured as she talked to the smaller blonde woman.

When the woman turned slightly to look at the man with whom she had entered, Amylia noticed the tips of her ears were slightly pointed and tattooed silver as well.

The other three members of their party also had those slightly pointed tips, though none had the tattoos. Cold bloomed through her belly as she heard the shocked whisper from somewhere behind her.

"Wytchling."

Amylia's focus snapped to Mica, who did not seem at all surprised at who the new guests were.

Shock permeating her voice, she whispered, "You knew they were Sylvyns?"

"Oh, of course." He smiled at her, placing a hand on her back, and guided her towards the group. "Father." Mica inclined his head in greeting to Lord Drakon as they approached.

"Mica." His father smiled warmly in return before he turned to the couple. "Lord Gryffon Wynter and Lady Cecily Wynter. Allow me to introduce my son, Lord Mica, and his betrothed, Lady Amylia Sylvers."

Lord Wynter inclined his head to Mica. "On behalf of Asteryn, I am honoured," he said, his voice deep and husky, as if he had just woken up. Lord Wynter's eyes flicked to Amylia, and he held out his hand. "Lady Sylvers."

She took it, heart beating so loud she thought everyone would hear it clearly, and he brushed a kiss to the back of her hand, never breaking eye-contact. Mica stiffened beside her, clearing his throat subtly and Lord Wynter let her hand go with an amused look.

He looked towards Lady Wynter, who had not taken her eyes from Amylia's face, elegant brows arched over her piercing eyes.

"A pleasure to meet you, Lady Sylvers," she said, in a voice that was liquid and honey. "And Lord Mica, of course." She inclined her head to Mica in the way her husband had. "And please let me introduce our court. Our Second, and Captain of the Sylkie riders, Lyrik Damaris."

All eyes turned to the tall man standing to their right who, with a small smile, stepped out of the way for the small blonde woman behind him to come forward.

"My Lords," she purred, her voice smooth and steel together, "and Lady." Lyrik looked up at Amylia. Her depthless brown eyes glowed slightly, too, though not as noticeably as the Wynters'.

"And our Third, and Captain of our armies, Rogue Salvador," Lady Wynter said, eyes still fixed on Amylia.

Rogue smiled, the amused expression still on his face as he bowed to the men and took Amylia's hand in his own, kissing it gently. His hand was as warm as Lord Wynter's had been, almost hot, his smooth skin heavily calloused across both palms. They reminded her of the wolves that prowled the forests, predatory and powerful, in a room of lambs.

Wytchling. Her skin prickled.

Amylia looked to Lady Wynter, who had now turned her gaze to her Lord Wynter as he bent to whisper something to her. The power that flowed from them, surrounded them, was unmistakeable. The two Wynters were definitely

Sylvyn, part of the ancient Gifted race who had joined with humans centuries past and, in some cases, merged bloodlines, creating Demi Sylvyns.

The Gifts from their ancestors faded out slowly through the generations as the lines grew murkier over time.

The other two, she was not so certain. Were they Sylvyn? Or Demi Sylvyn? The strength she sensed emanating from them made even the strongest warriors in the keep seem like untrained adolescents.

Amylia turned. Mica kept his hand firmly on her lower back as they made their way to the table and took their place to the right of the head. Mica sat closest to his father, who took the centre seat of honour.

Lord Wynter escorted Lady Wynter to the seat opposite Amylia, holding the chair as she gracefully sank into it, her hand brushing softly over his where it rested against her shoulder before he turned and took his seat opposite Mica.

Dinner was a long, tedious affair, especially when she couldn't eat. Amylia pushed her food around her plate, her stomach rumbling painfully. She took small bites at intervals and listened to the conversation. She felt as if she sat next to a wall of ice. Lylith, to her right, sat in stony silence, refusing to acknowledge Amylia's presence and the hound on the floor before Lylith growled menacingly whenever Amylia moved her feet.

On her other side, Mica engaged in animated conversation between his father, Lord Wynter, and Rogue, who had brought a seat up next to his lord to answer questions about the training of their men.

Amylia stole glances at Lady Wynter when she could. She lounged back in her chair, listening to Lord Wynter speak. One hand drew idle circles on the back of his hand where it rested on the table, the other held her glass loosely as she sipped from the ruby liquid.

Her eyes slid from watching Lady Wynter's hand up to her face and she froze when their gazes locked. Lady Wynter's eyes were piercing, as if she could see through to Amylia's soul, but also oddly tender as she returned Amylia's study with one of her own.

She was young, younger than Amylia had first thought. Maybe mid-twenties? Her face was completely unlined, her skin showing no sign of sun damage or stress. Amylia started, realising she had been staring, and blushed, feeling flustered.

Leaning in towards Mica, she tried to refocus on the conversation, which had moved to the accommodation of the Wynters' Court.

"With thanks," Lord Wynter said, "we will stay in our own lodging. It's not far from here. Being… who we are, we tend to make those who are not of our kind… uncomfortable. I think you can appreciate that it is hard to truly relax in those circumstances."

"Of course," Lord Drakon replied, though his face showed distaste. "Though, if any of my servants have made you feel unwelcome, I wi—"

"No, of course they haven't," Lady Wynter interrupted. "Please do not take it that way. We just prefer not to intrude."

Lord Drakon leaned back in his chair and nodded.

"As you wish," he sighed, his irritation at being interrupted evident. "But please allow me to send you back with some of my guards later. The streets down in the town proper have been reporting too many disturbances recently. We have had people arriving from Oryx and causing… issues."

Rogue grinned. "I would want to see them try. Lyrik has been getting irritable the last few days. She needs a good scrap to settle her down."

"I wouldn't let her hear you say that, Rogue. You know what happened last time you baited her," Lady Wynter said, eyeing him over the rim of her glass.

"Oh, we all remember what happened to him the last time he baited her," Lord Wynter chuckled, smiling wickedly at Rogue, who shifted in his seat and flashed a grin back at his lord.

Amylia glanced at the small woman a few seats down in quiet conversation with Raol and Lord Umber, her blonde head close to theirs, looking at the sketch Lord Umber was drawing on a piece of parchment as he explained something.

She looked… so small. Yet both Rogue and Lord Wynter looked at her with such respect.

Amylia excused herself. Refilling her wine, she slipped out the side doors into the night air of the patio. Looking out over the gardens to the winking lights of the town in the distance, she watched her breath curling in dancing mist.

A soft voice came from behind her. "The views here are almost as good as ours."

Amylia jumped, spinning around as Lady Wynter appeared next to her, an apologetic expression on her beautiful face. "I'm sorry, you didn't hear me coming?" Her eyes met Amylia's, that piercing sensation again, as if she was searching for something. Something in Amylia.

She laughed nervously. "No… I… Sorry, my mind must have been drifting. The wine — I needed a breath."

Lady Wynter nodded, looking out over the dark landscape, and leaning up against the marble. "I don't blame you. I'm feeling a tad light-headed myself." She laughed softly.

An alluring scent surrounded her, as beautiful as she was, fragrant with hints of vanilla and wildflowers. Breathing it in, Amylia let it fill her senses, felt it twine itself into her being.

"Your necklace is gorgeous," Lady Wynter said. "I was admiring it during dinner, could I have a closer look? The diamond looks like it was mined from Nymaria, my old homeland."

Lady Wynter stepped towards her, her beautiful eyes studying Amylia's face.

Amylia flushed. Reaching for the clasp, and slipping it off, she handed it to the lady.

"Thank you, my lady. It was a gift from Lord Mica."

Lady Wynter scooped it up, her hand warm when it brushed Amylia's and she cocked a delicate eyebrow at Amylia.

"Please, call me Cecily," she said, her smile sending butterflies skittering down Amylia's spine.

Cecily took a step back into a shaft of light to admire the gem with an appreciative sigh, the soft light glinting off the tiara on her head.

Amylia studied the woman, feeling as if a magnet was moving away, fighting the near irresistible urge her body had to get closer. She subtly took a deep breath of the cold air, centering herself with a little internal shake as Cecily moved back to her. With one end of the necklace in each hand, she motioned for Amylia to hold her hair out of the way.

She came closer, reaching gracefully around to clip the delicate ends together as her breath tickled Amylia's ear, sending a shiver running down her spine as warm hands grazed the sides of her neck. Her skin tingled where her hands had touched and they locked eyes again as Cecily pulled away, a mischievous smile playing across her lips.

"Almost as beautiful as its owner," she murmured, winking at her before turning with a whisper of her skirts back into the great hall.

Chapter 3

The negotiations of the courts started immediately.

Gryffon fought to keep a straight face as he noticed the looks of adoration Lord Umber was throwing Lyrik, seated to his left and feigning ignorance.

Lord Umber, who ruled over Perregrin, a small keep with vast lands rich with crops, left after the second day, taking his leave from the Sylvyns with a prolonged, wet kiss to Lyrik's hand. Much to her disgust and Gryffon's eternal amusement.

Lord Umber's negotiations had been simple enough and he was content with his harvest trades in place for Lylican and a new trade alliance with Asteryn for a herd of breeding livestock. These were set to be driven up the east coast and through the Dead Forest yearly under the protection of Lyrik's Sylkie riders as an extra food source for Asteryn's growing Sylkie colony.

Sylkies were beautiful creatures, living in the far northern mountains above Asteryn. Once, they were all but extinct after the Great War just over a century ago, between mortals of Labrynth and the Sylvyn kingdom of Attica. The war had been sparked by Attica's despicable treatment of mortals, taking away lands, food sources, and even people at will. Turning them into slaves. Families had been ripped apart, the men sent to the Attican mines and labour camps while the women and children had been sent to the city to serve there.

A great number of Sylvyns from Labrynth and Calibyre had fought alongside them, denouncing Attica's ways, and it had seen the country obtain national sovereignty, removing itself from Attica entirely.

Labrynth had divided into eight territories after the war; each had their own lord to manage them. The lingering Sylvyns gradually drifted to Asteryn or returned to Calibyre, freeing up territory as greater numbers of stricken mortals immigrated to the rich lands, now free of Sylvyn tyranny, and gradually, the Sylvyns that had given so much to aid the mortals were forgotten.

The Sylkies, after being so decimated, had been carefully nurtured through Lyrik's breeding program and had once again grown into a strong colony.

Lyrik had described them for Lord Drakon, whose eyes had gleamed as she formed an image of the beasts. Larger than the biggest stallion in Lylican's stables, the back half the body of a lion, with a long, muscled tail. The front had claws and wings like an eagle with a wicked spike at the joints, long feathered ears, and a deadly curved beak.

They could sprint on land or soar through the sky, easily holding the weight of a rider or two.

Drakon coveted the Sylkies, trying again and again to include some cubs into the agreements, his frustration growing at Asteryn's flat refusals.

"They are dangerous when not trained and handled correctly," Lyrik stated firmly.

Gryffon could hear the strain in her voice as she struggled to control her temper.

"I will not have one killing its handler and getting free to run wild. It wouldn't stop at livestock if they were hungry. They are intelligent and would attack villages looking for food. They could even take children. I will not have that on my conscience."

Drakon looked to argue yet again. She challenged him with a glare.

"My riders are trained to handle these beasts. From the time they walk, they are taught to ride. No one here has the ability to do the same."

Gryffon put a firm hand on her shoulder. "Lyrik, I'm not asking you to give up any cubs," he said softly. Turning to Drakon, he said, "I cannot include our cubs in any negotiations. Lyrik is right, they need to be trained and not just by our riders, but by the mature Sylkies, who teach them manners that even we cannot. But I can offer an alliance that would come with protection from our Sylkie riders, and our army, if called to aid, in return for the same."

Gryffon paused, trying to gauge Drakon's reaction. "Your forces are the largest in these lands that I know of, besides my own. We all know what has been happening recently in the southern territories, especially Solos and Eilysh. There have been similar attacks to some of my smaller villages in the north and we have reason to believe it's coming from Attica." His face darkened. "The fire. There is never any trace of who attacked. No ships or armies seen. The only thing that can cause such damage and get away unseen are the beasts they wield, a mixed-blood mongrel of wyvern and sea dragon, fast, intelligent, and able to breath fire. They call these beasts Druka." Gryffon paused, his gaze moving to Lyrik's. "We fought them in the Great War." He turned looking to Drakon. "And your great-great grandfather did as well. Trust me when I say that we do not hold a chance, separated as we are, if they decide to attack again."

Drakon sucked in a breath, looking between Gryffon and Lyrik, then to Mica's pale face.

"Druka," he said in a low voice. "The Gods save us all if they bring those beasts here."

Getting up, he strode to the window, looking out across the coastline in the direction to which Attica lay and shook his head with a sigh, turning to give Gryffon a long look.

"I accept your terms of alliance, and of trade. On the condition that you will take a small group of my men back to Asteryn and into training with your men. I will have them know the ways of those they could be fighting alongside. I will have the treaty drawn up tonight for you to view tomorrow if this is to your satisfaction."

Lyrik opened her mouth, but Gryffon silenced her with a look. He straightened, running a hand through his hair, eyeing her in contemplation.

"We will take six men, or women, willing to take part in the training. However, the standards will be the same as what we expect from our people and, if they do not pass the training, they will be sent back immediately," he said, raising his chin to look directly at Drakon.

Drakon ran a hand over his beard, seeming to consider for a moment. "Agreed." He nodded.

Lyrik clenched her jaw, sparks flying from her eyes as she nodded curtly and left the room.

Gryffon chuckled softly. "Oh, this is going to hurt badly."

He stood with a sigh, picked up his overcoat, and inclined his head to Drakon. "We will be back in the morning for the final settlement. If I'm still alive by then." Nodding to Mica he strode off in the direction the irate woman had disappeared in.

Amylia nudged her mare with a heel as she guided her through the trees and was rewarded with a disgruntled squeal. She whipped her boot back just in time as teeth snapped the air where it had been moments before. "And we were getting along so well today, Shadow." She grinned.

The mare was a powerhouse, all fury and muscle and Amylia loved every fiery inch of her.

Riding was the one thing she and Mica disagreed on. He chastised her 'total disregard for life' as he put it, always pleading with her to take one of the quieter geldings broken to side-saddle if she must ride.

Amylia couldn't stand them, plodding along with no spark.

Instead, she had steadfastly stuck to her Shadow, wearing a pair of riding leathers she had traded from the stableboys, in exchange for her silence that none of them were brave enough to go near the irascible mare.

Every member of the stable staff had been bitten, kicked, or generally traumatised by the horse, leaving her entirely to Amylia. Each morning at dawn, she slipped out and turned Shadow out, returning at sundown after dinner to turn in, groom, and stable the irritable mare.

Today, she had needed to ride, needed to breathe, after being stuck in the keep for days after a heavy snow only just beginning to melt.

They had picked their way down the short forest path to the coast. Shadow danced all the way, throwing in a buck when Amylia gave her the slightest bit of slack on the reins, the energy from being stabled too long turning the mare into a coiled spring of fury.

Arriving at the long golden beach that stretched on the west side of the keep, Amylia dropped low in the saddle and gave Shadow her head. She felt the powerful muscles bunch underneath her as the mare launched herself, hooves flying, neck stretched out, dashing at breakneck speed down the beach. Shadow's inky black mane whipped in the icy wind and tangled with Amylia's hair as it lashed around her face.

After horse and rider had thoroughly exhausted themselves, Amylia walked Shadow back through the surf, cold waves lapping at Shadow's belly, cooling the mare's temper along with her body. Amylia's feet dragged in the tops of the waves, the icy water a sharp kiss against her hot skin.

She breathed in the cold, salty air in big, long breaths, content to let the mare pick her way back home. Watching the huge sea birds wheeling across the water, searching for food for the fuzzy chicks in the cliffs beyond, she lost herself in thoughts of her upcoming wedding.

Planned for spring, only three months away, she cringed at the thought of how many people would be there. The list grew every month with people she barely knew from all the territories and Lord Drakon was sparing no expense, it seemed.

Heliacle Rising

Pushing away the nerve-wracking idea of being the centre of attention to so many people, she tried to focus on what would come of it. Mica... her Mica... becoming his wife, the children they would have. Their future at Lylican.

A tendril of dread crept into her stomach. Not because of Mica, but of the thought of her destiny being mapped out ahead of her, for her. Seeing the road of her life all the way to the end, she wasn't sure she liked it. Wasn't sure it was everything she wanted. Or needed.

She shook her head, clearing the images away and noticed how far Shadow had brought her. The road to the keep was up ahead through the trees.

Amylia snorted with amusement as Shadow picked up her pace, ears flicked forward as she, too, saw the familiar road to the keep, knowing her oats were close as they pushed through the overhanging branches onto it.

Faint shouting in the distance reached her. A woman's voice. Farmers often yelled at their stock in this area and she ignored it, settling into a calm walk. Shadow's ears flicked every direction, taking in the sounds as a rumbling came faintly from the direction of the keep.

Amylia's brows knitted as Shadow tossed her head, ears pricked towards the noise, the rumbling turning to hoof beats.

Two horses. Concern grew in her as they approached rapidly and she was startled suddenly by a man's voice, yelling.

"For the love of the Gods, would you just listen for once, Lyrik!"

Shadow snorted, ears pinned back and eyes rolling as she danced and kicked on the spot.

"Woah, girl, settle." Amylia tried to soothe her, kicking her feet out of the stirrups, readying to jump down and grab her head.

A grey horse burst round the corner at a full gallop, a woman on its back, and as the horse sped past, Shadow flung herself back and reared up, throwing Amylia out of the saddle.

Twisting as she fell, Amylia landed on her feet and rolled backwards into the brush behind her. Her ankle gave on the uneven ground and a bolt of pain shot up through it.

Shadow whirled, bolting away from the scuffle of hoof beats, and away from the keep, galloping after the grey horse.

Amylia groaned, running her hand across her face. She grabbed a sapling beside her and used it to pull herself up, hearing the second rider slow to a halt in front of her.

She looked up into golden eyes and froze as Lord Wynter vaulted off his horse and strode over. "Are you hurt?" he asked, his face lined with concern.

"No, I'm okay." She put her foot down to step forward. White-hot pain flashed up her leg and she cried out, falling forward.

He lunged to grab her, catching her neatly by the waist.

"My ankle," she said quietly. "I... think I twisted it. My horse. Did you see where she went?"

Lord Wynter bent, hooking an arm behind her knees and the other behind her shoulders, and lifted her as if she weighed nothing.

"She followed Lyrik, I think," he said as he walked back to his horse. "I'm sorry, we were not thinking of others coming up the road. Lyrik... Lyrik has a bit of a temper," he said apologetically. "And I've really pushed her this time."

He lifted Amylia onto his stallion gently. "Would you like me to take you back to the keep?" He asked as he vaulted up behind her, "Or go for your mare?"

"Mare," she said quickly. "She's dangerous to anyone who tries to touch her."

He chuckled. "Oh, I'm well used to dealing with that sort. We will find her. Don't worry."

They rode slowly towards the town, Lord Wynter careful not to bump her ankle too badly. His arm around her waist held her gently, but she could feel the power behind it, muscles moving beneath the skin as they rocked to the horse's smooth gait.

His other arm reached around her, holding the reins in a feather-light grip as he guided his stallion.

He leaned forward and looked down at her leg, his voice rumbling next to her ear, "How bad is it, do you think?"

She took a deep breath, and his scent made her head swim slightly. He smelt amazing.

She straightened, her head bumping gently against his collarbone. "Not too bad, I don't think, though it's swelling. I think I need to take my boot off soon. Thank you, Lord Wynter."

He nodded and huffed a laugh. "Please, call me Gryffon. Lord Wynter was my father. I only use it for formal occasions." She could hear the smile in his voice.

They rounded a corner, the town coming into view. Amylia spotted a dark shape in the distance walking back towards them.

"There she is." Gryffon nudged his stallion to pick the pace up a bit. The jostling sent little pins of pain shooting up her leg and she bit her lip, bracing against it.

Relief washed over her. Shadow showed no sign of injury, but apparently, she had thrown a shoe somewhere. "Damn," she muttered, leaning forward to hook the trailing reins.

Shadow pinned her ears and snapped towards Gryffon's leg as she sidled up alongside. Amylia jerked the reins and hauled Shadow's head around. "I'll be having none of that after your display," she scolded, holding her arm out to give the mare space between them.

"I see what you mean," he muttered darkly, scanning the road ahead and back over his shoulder towards the keep. "We are close to where I'm staying. You can't ride with your ankle like that, Cec — Lady Wynter is gifted in healing. Let me take you to her and get that looked at."

Amylia tensed, throwing him a cautious look. "I — I'm sure the physicians at the keep can check it. I don't want to impose." She twisted to glance up at him.

Those golden eyes looked down at her, amusement flitting across his features, and this close, she could see the scar on his face was lighter than the rest of his skin, but flat. No pulling or bunching from what must have been a deep cut.

"Oh, this is partially for my own benefit, too. Lyrik is less likely to behead me if there are multiple witnesses." He paused. "Plus, it's not every day I have a beautiful woman riding with me, leading a beast sent from the dark-lands themselves."

Amylia flushed, staring at him in horror. "You are jesting... about your Second?"

Another dark chuckle from him. "I wouldn't put it past her in the mood she's in. I'm hoping the ride cooled her off a bit."

He nudged his horse forward, glaring at Shadow. "Behave!" he said sternly as the mare fell in step next to them, ears pinned flat to her head and lip curled back.

The rest of the ride was fairly uneventful, with Shadow only trying once more for a mouthful of Gryffon's leg, earning her a swift slap from Amylia, followed by a hiss as the movement jolted her ankle. Gryffon seemingly noticed her discomfort and slowed his horse slightly, never taking a cautious eye off the mare beside him.

They rode up to a large stone house on the outskirts of town. In the small stables adjacent to the building, she could her the thunk of tack being hung up harshly behind the grey horse, already unsaddled, rubbed down, and cooling off under a blanket.

Gryffon slid down as Cecily appeared in the entrance to the house, wearing a flowing white top tucked into grey pants, her hair pulled into a loose bun.

A short pause was the only surprise she showed as her eyes fell on Amylia before giving her a warm smile.

"What did you do to Lyrik, Gryff?" she asked, amusement in her voice.

He glanced at the stables. "I've saddled her with six of Drakon's men to train as part of our new alliance." He sighed, looking cautiously at Amylia as if gauging her reaction to his words.

"Ah." Cecily smirked. "That explains a lot." She glanced up at Amylia. "Where are you hurt?" she asked gently, blue eyes glowing as they scanned over her body. Amylia started in alarm. "M-my ankle." She flushed.

"Lyrik spooked Lady Sylvers's charming little mare here." Gryffon said, gesturing towards Shadow and snatching his hand back when she lunged for him, teeth snapping.

Cecily laughed and reached for the horse. "I'll take her and put her in the stables for now." She caught the loose rein hanging across Shadow's neck. "Hello, wee beastie," she crooned.

"No!" Amylia cried, lunging for the reins, ready to pull Shadow around, but she stopped dead, mouth hanging open.

Shadow, ears forward, sniffed Cecily as she scratched her softly on the cheek with her free hand.

Cecily winked at her before she turned and walked away, chatting softly to the mare who followed meekly along beside her.

Gryffon chuckled and reached up to lift her off the horse. "She has a way with difficult spirits." He gave a marked look towards the banging still coming from the stables.

The warmth of the house rushed out to meet them as they entered.

Amylia looked around the simple but comfortable lodgings as Gryffon gently set her down on a huge seat covered in a soft mattress and fur.

"I've never been to this part of the township," she admitted, looking up at him. "This is lovely."

"We paid a merchant for the use of it during our stay here," he replied, waving his hand towards the room beyond. "There are not many of us staying here, so it does the job we need and puts your servants at ease."

Her eyes went to his ears, the tip just pointing out of his hair, and he laughed softly.

"Yes, because of that."

She looked away quickly, as he chuckled, excusing himself and heading for the door. He passed Cecily as she came in and she gave him a sympathetic smile. "Good luck," she said softly.

Walking to the counter, Cecily poured a glass of water from a copper jug and handed it to Amylia. "Do you mind if I take a look?" she asked.

Amylia took the glass nervously, her eyes lingering on the tattoos across Cecily's fingers. "Thank you. And no, but I'm not sure if I can get my boot off. Though, how — how did you know I was injured?"

Cecily sat gracefully on the other end of the seat, folding her legs until she was resting cross legged and picked up Amylia's foot gently, putting it into her lap.

"I can feel it. I could feel you were hurting. I can't tell where, just that you are," she said softly, gently wiggling the boot until it slowly slid off.

Both of them sucked in a breath at the sight of her ankle, purple and swelling fast.

Cecily rested her warm hand on Amylia's ankle and her eyes seemed to glow brighter as she focused on the area. "It's broken," she said quietly and placed her other hand on the opposite side of Amylia's foot.

The relief was instant; the aching receded until it vanished entirely. Amylia watched wide-eyed as the purple slowly faded to blues, reds, and then, finally, pink.

Cecily ran her thumb gently across Amylia's ankle, as if checking nothing more was left, as shouting started up from the stables. Gryffon's voice now joining Lyrik's.

Rolling her eyes, Cecily placed the ankle carefully back down again and stood up. Walking quickly to the door, she shut it with a click, muffling the rapidly growing noise from outside.

"Give it a minute before you try to stand on it," Cecily said softly just as Amylia cautiously put her foot on the ground. There was nothing, no pain at all.

"How did you do that?" she questioned, her face blank.

"My Gift is healing. It came from my mother, and her mother before that." Cecily's face held caution and her eyes searched Amylia's face as she spoke.

The shouting picked up in tempo outdoors, followed by a crash. Amylia jumped and glanced toward the window, asking in alarm, "Should someone stop them?"

"Not if you want to walk away from it," a male voice said, then laughed. "We learned a very long time ago not to get in between those two when they lose their tempers."

The huge, dark haired Sylvyn walked into the room from the hallway grinning. "Lady Sylvers." He bowed slightly.

Amylia remembered him vaguely from the Wynters' introduction. "They won't hurt each other?" she asked.

"Not fatally," he said in amusement. "Nothing Cess can't patch up. Those two are too evenly matched to cause any real damage unless Lyrik loses her shit entirely, and then we're all screwed anyway."

Cecily shook her head, glancing out the window and wincing at whatever she saw there as Amylia heard another crash.

"Half a crown on Gryff, Cess. He's been training more than her recently." Rogue grinned, putting his hand in his pocket and jingling it.

Cecily eyed him from across the room, brow raised. "One crown on Lyrik, and you cook tonight." A slow, wicked grin spread across her face.

Rogue snorted. "Done."

Amylia stared at them, amazed at the casual ease they had with each other. This was not how her court interacted. It seemed familiar, in an odd way, as if it were prodding a vague memory that flickered in the recesses of her mind.

A final bellow and crash came from outside before it went quiet. Everyone paused, looking to the door as footsteps sounded. It swung open and Lyrik stalked in, blood running from her nose and a deep cut across her brow.

Rogue sighed, reached into his pocket, and pulled out a gold piece, flicking it with a ping across the room to Cecily, who caught it deftly with one hand.

Lyrik glared at Rogue. "Really, Rogue? Against me?"

Cecily laughed. "It cost him dinner duties, too. Don't worry, he's suffering."

Lyrik huffed, picked up a cloth and dipped it into a cup of water before holding it to her brow. Scathingly, she said, "He's out cold, Cess. He might need... assistance."

Cecily sighed, grabbed a cloth, and hurried out the door, muttering something Amylia couldn't hear.

Rogue strolled casually to the window and looked out. "Well, at least the stables are still standing." He chuckled. "I was worried I would have to rebuild them before we left."

Lyrik shot him a grim look. "Six of them Rogue, six humans. You are going to be training them, too, you realise?"

"Oh, but you are so much better at it than I am." He smiled sweetly at her.

She picked up a carving knife off the table, pointing it in the vague direction of his balls with a pointed glare before turning and meeting Amylia's eyes. "I'm sorry, Lady Sylvers, for spooking your mare. I didn't see you before it was too late. If it makes you feel any better, that black beastie of yours caught up and let me know what she thought of me." She grinned then turned slightly and used the knife to flip back a flap of torn fabric to show her thigh.

A large, double crescent of purple showed through the tear. Shadow's signature bite mark.

Rogue roared with laughter. "Remind me to stay on that mare's good side. I've never seen a Sylkie land a scratch on you, and a horse did that!"

"I don't think Shadow has a good side to get on," Amylia said wryly. She looked at Lyrik apologetically. "I apologize for my mare. She's difficult at the best of times."

A snort came from the entrance. "Don't apologize for that," Gryffon said, walking slowly through the door, rubbing his temple and eyeing Lyrik reproachfully. "It's about time she came up against a female with the same temper as hers."

He ducked quickly as the knife Lyrik had been holding moments before sailed through the air, narrowly missed his head, and embedded deep into the door frame.

Cecily appeared behind him, calmly stepping around the quivering blade with a raised eyebrow at Gryffon. "If you get injured again, I'll leave you to suffer." She stopped in front of Lyrik, taking the cloth away from her brow and inspecting the wound.

She gently ran a thumb along the split, pink skin shining as it sealed behind her finger. Just a smudge of blood was left behind. Next, she ran her thumbs slowly down Lyrik's nose. The redness disappeared from it and the puffiness beneath her eyes vanished.

Lyrik sighed softly. "Thanks, Cess," she breathed and blinked rapidly.

Wiping her hands on the cloth, Cecily turned to Amylia. "Did you want to dine with us? Rogue is a fine cook." She smirked at him. "I'm sure he would love a chance to show off his talents to someone new."

Amylia ducked her head. "Thank you, but I probably shouldn't. Mica will worry that I've not come back. He doesn't particularly enjoy the fact I ride Shadow."

Gryffon snorted. "I can't possibly think of why. Such a charming beast."

Amylia grinned. "She may be, but not one horse in that keep can best her speed, or her heart."

"I'd like to take you up on that bet one day." Lyrik laughed. "My Freyja to your Shadow."

"Oh, how is that fair?" Rogue interrupted, "Freyja has wings!"

"On land, fool," Lyrik quipped. "She has outrun horses on land before."

"My father told me about Sylkies as a child," Amylia said softly. "The way he described them ... They must be beautiful. I'd love to see one, one day."

"I'm not sure I'd call them beautiful." Rogue snorted, earning a glare from Lyrik. "But they are fearsome beasts, similar to their trainer here." He grinned at Lyrik who rolled her eyes at him.

"Your father knew of the Sylkies?" Cecily sat at the large table in front of the fire, leaning her head against Gryffon who stood behind her, arm draped casually over her shoulder.

Amylia couldn't help but look at them. They were a stunning couple. "He did. And about the Wytchlings. Mother did, too."

"Are your parents Sylvyn?" Cecily asked. Again, her eyes searched Amylia's. Looking for that light Amylia realised, that glow the others gave off.

Amylia looked down at her hands. "Father was Sylvyn. I don't know if Mother was. It was a long time ago… and I can't remember much of my old life. I used to have lessons, I think. My brother was too young. Oryx — our lands — and our keep were attacked when I was eight. My parents were murdered, and the village burned. Since then, I've lost whatever Gifts I had."

She smiled ruefully. "I know I had something, I can remember Father telling me he was proud of me… it can't have been much, though, and Rayvn doesn't have anything." She looked up to sympathetic eyes. "I have not met others since then. There are no Sylvyns at the keep. Lord Drakon was a friend of my mother's, and he took us in after the attack. We had nowhere else to go and he has looked after us all these years and now… I'm to marry Mica."

Cecily inclined her head, eyes sad. "I'm sorry for your loss. That is a young age to lose your parents."

Rogue hummed in agreement, moving to sit at the table, pulling the chair next to him out for Lyrik.

"We have heard of similar attacks recently. Sometimes small, a cottage or a farm. Other times, entire keeps are lost, like your family's. It's why we're here," Gryffon rumbled.

"It's becoming more frequent. We needed to see if it was happening here, too, you being closer to Attica, where we believe it's coming from. An alliance between us, being the two largest courts in the continent, might give us a better chance if these attacks turn into something bigger."

Amylia paled slightly. "I hope that day never comes."

Chapter 4

Mica was clearly fuming when Amylia got back.

The sun had all but disappeared by the time Amylia rode back through the gates, accompanied by the small Second from Asteryn who took her leave quietly with a nod to Amylia when Mica strode towards the stables, face like thunder.

"Where on earth were you?" He roared, "I was about to send guards after you!" He stood a healthy distance away from the mare, glowering at Amylia. She was taken aback, Mica never raised his voice to her.

Slowly, she slipped off and started unbuckling the saddle. "I'm sorry," she said, eyes wide. "Shadow got a fright and ran away from me towards town. I had to go get her and Lyrik Damaris offered to accompany me back to the keep, as it was late."

He sighed and dragged his hand over his face, eyeing the mare as Amylia wiped her down. "That horse needs to go to the war-horse trainers. She's too much for you." Voice calming, he said, "Amylia, I was so afraid you had been injured."

"Shadow wouldn't hurt me," Amylia soothed, giving him a small smile.

A stable boy approached them cautiously, a horse blanket in his hands, wide eyes fixed on Shadow and reached a reluctant hand for the lead Amylia held. She hesitated, though, flicking an eye towards Mica and then at Shadow, before finally handing the lead over.

"No oats if you kill him," she whispered, patting the mare on the neck, and glaring her in the eye before stepping out the way for the terrified boy to lead her away.

She grimaced in sympathy, watching him over Mica's shoulder as he valiantly attempted to dodge a nip that took him on his upper arm, and sighed.

She stepped towards Mica. "It wasn't her fault. Another horse spooked her, and I was just about to get off. It was just bad luck."

He sighed again, taking her by the shoulders and looking her over critically. "I just can't stand the thought of you getting hurt and no one knowing. If you go for a ride, please take a guard with you at least, if you insist on riding that thing." He looked at the retreating mare, disdain on his face.

"I don't think any of them would keep up." She laughed and twined her fingers with his as they walked towards the keep.

They took the long way around the beautiful gardens, hand in hand. Amylia admired the small blue flowers pushing their way up through the cold ground. Mica pulled her against his side to keep her warm as they walked in amicable silence. The discomfort of their minor rift melted away.

When they paused at the small pond, watching the white fish darting around in it, they stood close together, breath merging in the crisp air, and he turned her to him and kissed her deeply.

"I'm sorry," he murmured, holding the front of her coat, and pressing his forehead to hers.

She smiled up at him. "Forgiven."

Mica glanced down at her clothes and grimaced. "How about you go and get dressed into… anything else… and I'll ask Harriet to bring up a dinner to the day lounge. We can dine there." A soft smile lit his face.

She nodded, feeling guilty. "Sounds lovely."

Amylia worried that telling him she had ended up dining with the Wynters would just irritate him further, and she was tired, longing for the warmth of the fire and to take her boots off.

Rogue's food had been good. Really good, in fact. The smell of it cooking, as well as the need to learn more about the people her family had come from, had enticed her to stay far longer than she should have.

She could still taste the beautifully roasted quail on her tongue. They had been stuffed with their own eggs and served on a pretty bed of greens. She wondered absently if Mica could taste it on her, too.

"I will go wash and meet you there." She kissed him on the cheek and hurried away towards the wing designated for the lord's family.

They dined, Amylia picking at her food, still full from her earlier meal, then chatted well into the night, content in each other's company. The warm fire crackled away in the fireplace of the small lounge that served as a dining room. Once a playroom, as they grew up, it had been repurposed into opulent glory.

Rayvn strolled in later in the evening, covered in mud and bruises with a huge grin on his face, informing them he had finally been given a war-horse to replace his gelding, and Raol had given him a crash course in cavalry combat... literally. He earned a clap on the back from Mica, who wryly commented about both siblings turning him prematurely grey. And Rayvn then stumbled off to find a hot bath and his bed.

Mica sat back on the long seat in front of the fire and tucked a leg up. Taking Amylia's hand, he massaged it softly, his thumb pressing into her palm.

She smiled at him sleepily and stifled a yawn.

"Will we turn this into our living room once we're married?" she asked, looking around the room.

"No." He shook his head. "It wouldn't be fair to Lylith or Rayvn. They use this space, too. Not that I've seen much of Lylith recently." He frowned. After a moment, he continued, "Father said we can take over the west wing. It needs some work but there are a few bedrooms in it, and a dining room a bit bigger than this." He glanced at her. "I... I've already got the servants cleaning it out for us. I was going to surprise you with it but maybe you would like to come and see where you want everything to be?"

Amylia flushed slightly. "I'd like that." She smiled.

"It has a few extra bedrooms there. For our children... when they come." He looked at their hands nervously and squeezed hers gently.

Her stomach fluttered. She wasn't sure if it was excitement, dread, or both, but she smiled again anyway, returned the squeeze, and leaned in to give him a soft kiss.

She pulled away when he reached for her, though. With a grin, she murmured, "It's getting late." She looked up at him through her lashes. He was watching her, slight disappointment still showing in his eyes. "We will be married soon. You know what your father said."

He nodded, squeezing her hand again, and stood up, pulling her with him into an embrace.

"Well, then... good night, my jewel," he said softly against her lips.

Amylia couldn't sleep. Instead, she lay in her bed gazing up at the canopy, the day playing back in her mind.

The stunning blue of Cecily's eyes, and the way they had watched her all afternoon. The softness of her hands on her ankle. She remembered, too, the feel of Gryffon's chest pressed against her on the horse and the graze of his arm across her stomach.

She wondered if it felt the same when he kissed Cecily as when Mica kissed her.

It had been a shock the first time Mica had. She had been seventeen, Mica twenty. She had seen him kissing others before. Even Lylith once, though one of the cooks had seen them and reported it to Drakon who had been furious. He had punished both Lylith and Mica far harsher than Amylia thought fair.

There were no other eligible boys in the keep. The stable lads knew it was risking Drakon's wrath if they went near either of his wards and kept well clear of the girls.

With no mother figure, as Mica's mother had died birthing him, Amylia had not known what to expect, other than what Harriet had told her, whispering, and giggling about a boy she had been seeing in town.

Lord Drakon himself was an attentive foster father, always seeing the needs of Lylith and Amylia were met. They never wanted for anything. However, he was emotionally aloof, saving his brief displays of affection for Mica and Rayvn.

He had taken over the Sylvers' estate and Oryx territory, repaired it from the raid damage and settled a wealthy merchant family there to run it in the Sylvers' name. He had also built up the trade town and the smaller villages and farming communities surrounding the keep, to be taken over by Rayvn when he came of age at twenty.

Amylia had inherited a large dowry from the estate, which he also kept for her.

As they got older, Drakon had made it known that a match between Mica and Amylia would please him. It had become an unspoken assumption that Amylia was the future Lady of Lylican.

The alliance this created between Lylican and Oryx strengthened them into a formidable pair, Oryx being the capital of trade and Lylican an army base, training warriors for both, and with the future lords of the two territories under Lylican's roof.

Amylia drowsily ran her hand up her arm, tracing a finger over the small scar above her elbow, and back down, feeling the tiny bumps raise on her skin against the touch. She had watched surreptitiously as Cecily's delicate hand had reached across and rested on Gryffon's leg as they sat after dinner, in front of the fire, drinking hot peppermint tea. Her thumb had rubbed gently over the soft fabric and the looks that had passed between them were full of heat and love.

Amylia wondered if it would be like that for her and Mica. They had kissed and sometimes Mica tried for more, running a hand up under her clothing or pushing himself against her, but no more than that.

Her thoughts wandered back to Cecily, the first Wytchling she had met since her childhood when others had come to her parents' keep as guests. Beautiful people with eyes that glowed bright in different hues, with powers that danced across their skin as they moved, little wisps getting away from them as if they bubbled over slightly.

Wytchlings were Sylvyns, born Gifted. Their powers manifested in many ways, most of which were unknown to Amylia. She did know the power usually ran strongest through the females of the Immortal race, though in recent decades it had been watered down as more mortal blood mixed with Sylvyn, creating Demi Sylvyns and eventually most were just mortals with traces of the ancient power, or who lived lifespans far greater than they should have.

Wytchlings were still out there, and mostly kept to themselves in their own lands. Some were known as Elementyls, powerful Wytchlings who could harness the elements. Others were healer Wytchlings, like Cecily, rare and Gifted with powers to sense and treat illness and injury.

As a child her parents had told her stories of the Heliacles, the rarest of the Sylvyn Wytchlings. Heliacles were gone now, however, with only bedtime stories to remember them. The Wynters had backed this up, confirming they had not come across any in their lifetime, except maybe the Queen of Attica, though information about her was limited and murky, as closed-off as Attica was.

She could still vaguely remember her father using some of his fire magic around her, the feeling of warmth when he wrapped her in his Gift when she was cold. She remembered the small animals he would make dance out of the water in the garden fountain, her brother's chubby hand reaching for them as he squealed with delight, the small water bird sitting on his hand briefly before melting back into the pool.

Of her mother, there was nothing. She remembered only her warm voice, laughing at Father, teasing him about something, remembered arms reaching around to cuddle Amylia as she sat in their bed.

But no Gifts. Mother had been mortal.

Amylia mused over the Wynters again. Cecily was a Wytchling healer but what was Gryffon? His eyes showed he had Gifts, but was he just Wytchling, or Elementyl?

His eyes floated through her mind, golden and intense as they looked at her and she felt warmth curling through her belly as she thought about him.

She shook herself, guilt creeping over her. Quickly, she brought an image of Mica's face into her mind, the way he had looked at her, his smile as they had danced through the hall together at their betrothal. But she couldn't shake the nagging thoughts of his explosion of temper.

It unnerved her, but then, hadn't he just been worried? Shouldn't she allow him that?

Shutting her eyes with a sigh, Amylia pushed the Wynters away and let her mind wander into the darkness.

Chapter 5

Only Gryffon returned the next day to meet with Lord Drakon and Mica. "Glad to see you are still among the living," Mica said under his breath to Gryffon as they walked towards the meeting chambers.

"Oh, it was close." He laughed.

Mica paused, studying his face. "Why do you allow your Second to challenge you like that? Especially a female? Do your warriors not lose respect seeing her act like that towards you?" He faltered. "I mean no disrespect; I'm asking more out of curiosity than judgement."

Gryffon stopped and looked at him, "Lyrik and I have been together a very long time, however, she came from a very different situation than mine. I watched her claw out a place for herself, earn the respect of the men and women on and off the training fields." He snorted. "Some of it by terrifying them, I'll admit. But I have never met a better fighter than her, both physically and mentally. I value her and her opinions, even when they clash with my own, and if there is one bit of advice I can give you, it's to never cross a woman who can hand you your ass in three hundred different ways without breaking a sweat." He grinned. "That, and I trust her with my life… when she's not trying to kill me herself." He strode on, Mica staring at his retreating back.

"Sylvyns," he muttered. "They are all raving mad." He shook his head and followed.

Drakon had the contracts ready when they got there, pouring glasses of wine for all of them. When he sat down, he waved a hand at the thick stacks of paperwork.

"We had better make a start on these or we will be here until next year," he muttered, sighing as he leafed through the pages.

They worked for hours, going page by page of the contract, discussing and omitting clauses, adding others.

"We agreed six, not ten," Gryffon said irritably when they arrived at the pertinent clause.

Drakon sighed, leaning back in his chair, and eyeing him. "I have ten men who have volunteered. You yourself said odds are against them; isn't it likely that most won't make it anyway?" he asked.

"Six caused enough issues with my court. I will not make the situation worse by raising that number," Gryffon snapped back.

Drakon paused. Finally, he asked, "Would you consider eight, then? Only two more. And out of good faith, I will gift you four mares and a stallion out of my war-horses. They are great bloodlines and will make a good start to your own herd."

Gryffon sighed, eyeing Drakon reproachfully. "I will accept eight, if your son is one of them, to lead his own people through the training."

Mica blanched, "I don't thi—"

Drakon interrupted, "Done."

Mica glared at his father. "I don't get a choice in this??"

Drakon cocked a brow at him, "Not when it's not you going… Rayvn will go."

"Rayvn's not even fourteen!" Mica spat. "What if he doesn't come back? Amylia has lost enough!"

"He's Am… you're betrothed's brother?" Gryffon asked, a confused look on his face.

"My foster son," Drakon clarified. "Both Amylia and Rayvn have been my wards for the last eleven years, and Rayvn," he looked markedly at Mica, "is one of our best swordsmen in training. If anyone will pass the tests, it's him."

Mica fell silent, tapping his finger on the table irritably.

"It's done then." Drakon added the final bit to his contract, Mica and Gryffon doing the same, signing them before standing and thrusting his hand out for Gryffon to clasp. "Take your copy back for your court to look over. I will send you the horses, and we will prepare the men to leave, unless you plan to stay awhile?"

Gryffon took his hand. "Only a couple of days. Lyrik will be needing to return to the colony soon."

Drakon nodded. "That is fine, it gives us time to prepare and get supplies together for the men."

They shook hands and parted, Gryffon winking at Mica as he left.

"I don't like him," Mica said once they were alone. He rounded on his father. "Rayvn, Father?"

"Yes," his father said simply.

"I know he's a good fighter, but why agree to send 'one of your sons' in the first place?" Mica snapped.

"Because," Drakon said calmly, "your priority is to marry and give me the heir I need, and aside from you, he's the only one I trust to destroy that contract."

Mica sat down. "What do you mean?"

"I mean that if Lord Wynter's copy is destroyed, which is slightly different to our copies, we have the only other two signed copies right here." He patted the papers. "And these say we just bartered five of our war-horses for five of their Sylkie cubs to return home with our warriors who by then will be trained in how to manage them."

He grinned deviously. "If there is no other copy of it, they have to honour these contracts or risk the alliance he's so worried about." He sat back, a pleased look on his face.

Mica was stunned, but a slow smile spread over his face. "Praise the Gods," he said quietly. "I know the perfect mare to send as well."

Amylia was brushing Shadow when Mica found her, slipping his arm around her, and kissing the back of her head. "Had a good day, my love?" he asked, picking an errant bit of straw out of her hair.

"I have." She turned, smiling up at him. "Yourself?"

He winced. "Few hours going over contracts with Lord Wynter that I could have done without, but better, now I've seen you." He patted her rear.

"Have they left now, then?" she asked, trying not to show too much interest in the answer.

Mica laughed. "No, in a couple of days. They are taking eight men now, so we are sending supplies with them. And your brother is going for training as well."

She started. "Rayvn? Why?"

"It was one of Lord Wynter's requests, that if it were eight, that one of them be Father's son. Since our marriage is so close, Father is sending Rayvn." He cringed. "I tried to go myself, my jewel, but Father was having none of it."

"He's a child." She gasped. "Why did he agree to this?"

Her face felt both cold and hot in patches over her cheekbones, like they had as a child when her temper had run away with her.

"He will be fine, Amylia. Lord Wynter is not going to let the son of his newest alliance come to any harm, I promise you," he soothed.

Shadow tossed her head and kicked the floor, sparks flying off her metal shoe as it hit, agitated at the distress in her mistress's voice. Amylia put a soothing hand on her neck and leaned against her. Shadow flattened her ears towards Mica.

He eyed the mare with a frown, his displeasure at the horse evident. "Leave the horse to the stable boys, my love. Come up and have dinner with me. I would like you to be there when I tell Rayvn."

Shadow was still glaring at Mica. Amylia gave her a subtle poke, getting her an outraged squeal from the mare that made her chuckle.

"Such dramatics, wee beastie," she scolded, putting the brush down and catching the eye of the nearest boy who reluctantly walked towards them.

Amylia giving him an apologetic grin as she passed him. She would bring the lad down a pastry from Cook tomorrow. He already had two big bite marks from the mare and no doubt a third was coming shortly.

When Mica broke the news to him at dinner that night, Rayvn's eyes sparkled. "The Sylkies! I will get to work with the Sylkies?"

Mica nodded. "I know that I don't have to say this, but you will be leading our men there. I expect you to show those Asterynians what we are capable of."

Rayvn's chest swelled noticeably, and Amylia felt a rush of love for him, reaching to touch his hand. "I believe in you, Rayvn," she murmured. "If anyone is going to do well, it will be you."

Rayvn swallowed hard, looking down, then met her gaze with a fierce look and nodded. "I won't let you down, Milly. I won't let either of you down." His gaze flicked to Mica who nodded at the boy, clapping him hard on the shoulder.

A huff sounded in the corner where Lylith sat, reclining on a long couch in front of the window, a book resting in her hand as she glared at them, disdain on her face. Two of the keep cats were draped around her, vying for the space on her lap, and she stroked them absently. "Who says we can trust them," she snapped. "Sending our men into that viper's den of Sylvyns."

Amylia was shocked and her gaze shot to her brother to see his reaction. Mica, too, blanched and slid his hand over hers, resting it on her knee. "Father knows what he's doing. He would not risk Rayvn if he didn't think Rayvn could handle it." He glared at Lylith, and she looked away, blushing slightly.

"I just don't trust them, any of them," she muttered softly.

"They have given us no cause not to trust them," Amylia snapped at her.

Mica's hand tightened on hers, and she turned to see him watching her. She pulled her hand from his grip, feeling defensive. "They seem like very reasonab —" A soft knock interrupted them.

"Enter," Mica called, frowning slightly.

A young boy peered around the large door, eyes like saucers.

"L-Lady Sylvers," he stammered, looking at his feet, "I'm… I'm s-sorry to interrupt your evening, m'lady."

"What is it, boy?" Mica demanded, stern gaze eyeing the boy.

"It's Shadow m'lady. She's chased old Ren up into the lofts and none of us can tempt her out of the stables to let him down."

Amylia cringed and looked at Mica, whose expression turned forbidding.

"I'll go, it won't take long." She rose, brushing her skirts off.

"No," he said, catching her arm. "You are the future Lady of Lylican. This is why we have men in the stables. To look after the beasts in there. You do not go and do common work." He turned to the boy. "If you cannot get one simple mare in line, you should not hold a position in those stables, boy. I suggest you go and find someone in there capable before you find yourself unemployed."

The boy's face lost all colour, and he withdrew suddenly. His running footsteps could be heard echoing down the hallway.

Amylia glared at Mica. "Mica. It won't take long. She's jus —"

He held up a hand. "No, I mean it, Amylia. That horse is dangerous. She's not appropriate as your mount. I've given her time to settle as she's aged. But if anything, she's gotten worse. And now she has thrown you, which ended up with you in the hands of those Sylvyns. Anything could have happened to you."

"Mica, I was fine. It was not her fault!" Amylia's voice raised as she felt a flush of anger rising up her neck.

"I'm going to go sort her out," she said shortly, trying to pull her arm out of his grip.

"You are not!" he snarled. A vein pulsed in his temple as he bellowed at her, the grip on her arm tight enough to bruise.

"I will not have you putting yourself at risk for that mare any longer. This will stop! What if you're carrying my child once we wed? Are you going to risk my child's life? Just because you want to satisfy your fancy of riding an animal that is far out of your skill?"

Amylia rocked back as if she had been slapped. "Is that what I am to be, Mica? Just the mother of your children and that is it? I'm to have no life of my own anymore?"

"You will be the mother of my children... the Lady of Lylican. I expect you to act like one," he spat back at her. "And as for that mare, it's not going to be an issue. She leaves the day after tomorrow with the trade herd going to Asteryn."

"What?" Her voice came out weakly as she stared at him, anger cooling to a sudden chill of disbelief. "You traded Shadow? You traded my Shadow? No!" She shook her head and tears filled her eyes.

Mica looked suddenly ashamed, running a hand through his hair as he stepped back. "I'm sorry. It was not my intention to tell you like this. She is dangerous, Amylia. I mean it. Father agrees. It's either the trade agreement or she gets placed with the training war-horses. I thought, of the two, this would be better."

He looked at her, then took her shoulders gently. "I have a lovely mare for you. I was going to surprise you with her tomorrow to take the sting away from Shadow leaving. I honestly did not mean to tell you like this."

Amylia shook her head and backed away from him towards the door. "How could you?" she whispered, tears running down her cheeks. Turning, she fled, catching sight of Lylith as she did, her hard gaze fixed on Mica. It was the first time she had ever seen the woman look at him with anything other than adoration. She ran for the stables, not caring that her dress swept the ground, catching and trailing through the wet grass.

The grooms vanished as she arrived, shocked looks on their faces at seeing her as she was, panting from the run, dress wet at the hems and tears staining her face.

She ran straight to the mare circling under the hay loft like a shark and threw herself around Shadow's neck. Sobbing, she clutched the mare's mane and buried her face into her warm neck.

Shadow's head came down and pressed against her back as the beast leaned against her mistress, sensing her distress.

Amylia vaguely heard scuffling as the old stablemaster threw himself down the ladder of the hayloft and raced for safety. Grief wrapped around Amylia. The old feelings of loss tore at the scars in her heart, still so fresh after all these years.

Heliacle Rising

Dashing the tears away from her face, anger propelled her away from Shadow. She grabbed a bridle, putting it on the huge mare who, for once, stood like a lamb, letting her mistress buckle her in. Amylia tucked her damp skirts up and vaulted onto the mare's bare back, feeling the powerful muscles under her move and flex as she turned her out into the night.

To fly together in the dark one last time.

Chapter 6

The sun had barely risen the next morning when there was a knock at the door. Gryffon opened it to Amylia and noticed the sadness on her face immediately.

"I'm sorry for turning up like this," she said quietly. "Your horses are due tomorrow, but I wanted to bring one personally." She glanced at the stables. Gryffon followed her gaze to see the recalcitrant mare from the other day tied to a post.

"Shadow? She's been included? Is she not your mare?"

Amylia looked skyward and he saw her swallow before dropping her head and nodding. "She is... was... Mica... He does not want me riding her after we marry. He thinks she's too much for me to handle and if we have children..." She paused and Gryffon watched the war of emotions cross her face. Finally, she said, "When we have children. He says she is too dangerous." She looked towards the mare and back to Gryffon. "I was wondering if I could speak to Cecily?"

"I'm here," Cecily said softly, walking up behind Gryffon and slipping her arm through his. "Is everything okay?" Her face tightened as she took in Amylia's expression and the mare behind her.

"Shadow is joining your trade herd," Amylia said, and her voice shook. "It's either here, or the war-horses. She... she will get herself killed there. They would break her." She looked at Cecily. "She likes you. Would you please look after her for me? I-I know I have no right asking this bu —"

"I'll take her personally," Cecily interrupted, expression softening. "If it's truly what you want?"

Amylia barely nodded. "I'd like knowing if she's not with me that she's safe, and I think she will be with you."

"Of course she will be," Cecily nodded. "Gryffon's safety, however, I'm not so sure about, with two females now with a price on his head…" She smiled gently. "But Shadow will be fine, I promise." Stepping back into the house, Cecily gestured. "Please, come in. We leave tomorrow, and we have wine that needs drinking."

Lyrik strolled in from the back rooms, nodding in welcome to Amylia.

"Ah… perfect." Gryffon grinned. "Lyrik, there is a friend for you in the stables. If you could be so kind as to go and not die while you stable her."

Lyrik glanced out the window and grunted in amusement. "Don't tell me you fear the black dragon, Gryff?"

He snorted. "I wouldn't call it fear, but more a healthy respect for life and limb." Lyrik raised an eyebrow at him and walked out the door towards the stables. Through the window, Gryffon could see her chatting amicably to Shadow who pinned her ears and snorted at her.

"If nothing else, those two will finally have found a match for each other," he muttered as Lyrik whipped her arm away from snapping teeth.

Amylia stayed late into the afternoon. The thought of returning to the keep and seeing Mica after the tension of the previous night's argument set a lead weight in her stomach.

Reluctantly, she bid her farewells as the sun made its way to the horizon, the extra horse she had brought with her saddled and waiting.

She eyed it with distaste and sighed. "Look after Shadow, and my brother," she said with a sad smile, looking at Cecily.

Cecily stepped forward and hugged her, catching her off guard. "I will, sweetling," she murmured into her ear.

Amylia nodded and hesitantly brought her arms up around her, returning the hug as the woman's scent washed over. She felt the woman suddenly stiffen, her whole body going rigid under her arms before Cecily cried out and threw herself backwards and away. Eyes wide, she scanned Amylia's body.

Amylia stared at her. "Wha —?" she started.

"What was that?" Cecily snapped, her face drained of colour.

"What was what?" Amylia asked, confused.

Cecily grabbed her arm, running a hand up the inside of it until she got to the small scar, pausing. She gingerly traced a finger over it, hissed, and yanked her hand away.

"What — what's wrong?" Amylia asked. A touch of fear curled in her stomach.

Cecily glanced towards Gryffon. He moved over and took Amylia's arm gently, turning it to the light and inspecting it.

"Where did you get this scar from?" he asked cautiously.

"It's… it's nothing. It was from the attack on my home. I… we took some wounds. But it was bandaged, and it healed, okay?" Defensively, she pulled her arm back and bent over it slightly, protecting it.

Cecily took a breath. "I'm sorry, I didn't mean to scare you. It's just… Can I see your arm again?"

Amylia hesitated, but nodded and slowly held out her arm, peering at the scar.

Cecily carefully cupped a hand over it, her eyes glowing a noticeably brighter blue before she pulled away again and wiped her hand on her pants, a shiver rippling over her.

"There's something in your arm," she said. "It's not part of you. It feels like… I can't describe it. Like a void. Where my Gifts touch it, they vanish. As if they are sucked into it." She shuddered.

"What?" Amylia's voice wavered as she glanced down at it. "Can you get it out?"

Again, Cecily looked at Gryffon who held his hand out for Amylia's arm. He took it and pushed warm, cautious fingers over the scar, pressing down into it and rolling it side to side.

"I can feel something small just under the scar," he said carefully. "I can remove it, but it's going to hurt. We have no medicines on us to help with that." He looked at Amylia, clearly giving her the choice.

Slightly hesitant, but steady, she nodded and held her arm out to him again. "Take it out now… please," she whispered.

Taking a small, sharp knife from his boot, Gryffon strode to the fire and passed the blade through the flames until the tip glowed red. He waved it in the air to cool and walked back.

With gentle but firm hands, he held her arm, the tip of the blade just touching her skin.

"Ready?" he asked, eyes flicking up to hers. She nodded and hissed as the blade nicked in and across, fast and neat.

Blood welled as he turned the blade, using the spine to swipe through the cut. Amylia felt it grate against something hard.

They both froze. He flicked a small jet black stone into his palm, then promptly dropped it onto the ground, swearing under his breath as it touched his skin.

Cecily cupped a hand over the wound, healing it instantly, leaving only a small smudge of blood and the old scar, a line of unblemished skin in the centre of it.

Gryffon ripped a bit of his sleeve off and scooped up the object. "It feels… wrong," he said and opened his hand to peer into the cloth.

Cecily touched the cloth with a careful finger. "It looks like stone." she mused.

Amylia felt nauseous. Odd. As if she had been sitting on her leg too long and the blood now rushed back into it. But everywhere. It flowed through her as her heart started racing.

"Cecily," she murmured. Her head swam and she reached out to steady herself.

Other hands grasped her. Anxious blue eyes stared into hers, no… staring at her eyes.

Gryffon swore softly and called for Lyrik. Hands helped her sit down on a reassuringly sturdy ledge.

Cecily knelt between her knees, cool hands on her face, calling her name, soothing her.

"Amylia, breathe. It's okay. Look at me. Just breathe. You're okay."

Loud footsteps sounded and she looked up as Lyrik ran in, followed by Rogue.

They both stopped dead when they saw her. Lyrik's face went pale.

His voice hard, Gryffon said, "This was in her arm." He passed the cloth to Lyrik. "Have you seen it before?"

Lyrik looked down at it and growled, dropping it onto the table. "Helix," she said quietly, staring at Amylia. "It's so rare that I haven't come across it in centuries, and even then, it was just a fleck of it, in a ring."

Amylia started, looking at the women. She must have heard her wrong. Centuries?

"It binds or dulls powers when worn on the person themselves. Just a tiny sliver helped with Heliacles and Elementyls learning control. That much… Amylia, that much should have killed you."

"Does that surprise you, Lyrik?" Cecily asked quietly. Her soft hands continued holding Amylia's and her thumb rubbed soothing lines down her wrists as she gave her a sad smile. "Look at her eyes."

Chapter 7

Panic swept through her in waves. Shutting her eyes, she concentrated on breathing, feeling like all her senses were in overdrive.

Cecily's voice was calm, filtering through her overpowered senses. "Amylia, just breathe, sweetling. Open your eyes and look at me."

She took a breath and centred her focus on the voice in front of her. Her skin prickled still, and her heart raced. It pounded in her ears, drowning out the voice she so desperately clung to as the room dipped and spun around her.

"Amylia!" Hands shook her shoulders. Slowly, she opened her eyes, meeting Cecily's worried gaze.

Cecily cupped her cheek and then flinched and drew back. Her palm was red, a blister already forming on the fleshy part of the heel of her hand. She rocked back and cupped it to her chest. "Gryffon?" she called, her voice unsteady.

Amylia's stomach curled at that note of worry, pulling her slightly out of the spiral she was teetering on the edge of.

Gryffon grabbed Cecily and pulled her away from Amylia, then behind himself. They argued rapidly, Cecily's voice tight and Gryffon's low.

Yellow eyes emerged into her vision. No, not yellow. Amber. Flecks of burnt orange were scattered through them. They focused on her.

Rogue.

He took her hands, the muscles in his neck bunching as the heat that radiated from her bit into him.

He pulled her hands up in front of them, into her line of sight. Detachedly, she noticed blue flames licked over them and swirled over Rogue's hands delicately, singeing the cuffs of his white shirt.

Heliacle Rising

The flames felt... familiar. Comfortable. As if an old friend had come back and filled a space in her that she had not, until this moment, realised had been empty.

"Amylia," he gritted, "pull it back into yourself. I know you want to avoid hurting anyone here." He squeezed her hand painfully. She shook herself, gaze focusing, and the ringing faded.

Looking over his shoulder to Lyrik, she found the warrior wearing a wary expression and she had placed herself between Amylia and the Wynters. Cecily leaned towards her in Gryffon's tight grip and cradled her burned hand.

Cold swept through her. She had hurt Cecily. She had... burned her.

A small cry came from her lips, and she started upright, lurching for Cecily, but a tight grip on her hands stopped her.

"I need you to pull this back in, Amylia." Her focus snapped back to Rogue, and she followed his gaze down to her hands. "I-I don't know... how," she whispered.

"Breathe," he coaxed. "Deep breaths. Feel it where it is escaping. Follow those threads and pull it back into your core."

She took a deep breath and reached.

It was there, an odd fullness that felt comforting, yet alien to her. And there — there were the tendrils of it, reaching down her arms, white-hot and flowing over her skin.

She hauled on them, pulling them back from Rogue onto her own skin and away from his.

Rogue sighed. The muscles in his neck loosened, but he did not release her. "Good, that's it. Keep pulling it back until you have it all there in the centre of yourself."

She did, slowly clawing it back piece by piece into that space inside herself until she had it, all of it, and hugged it to her with protective arms.

"Let go, Gryff. She has control of it," Cecily murmured softly. Then a soft hand cupped her chin again.

"Look at me, Amylia."

She did, tears welling. "Cecily, I'm so sorry I didn —"

"Hush," Cecily soothed. "I know, it wasn't your fault. None of us blame you. Look. It's healing already."

Amylia looked at the hand Cecily offered her, the bright pink now fading to normal colour.

"What... what is this?" she whispered, looking at her hands.

"Someone bound you," Gryffon gritted out. He looked furious, his eyes burning as he watched where Cecily's hands stroked hers.

She started shaking her head. "No. This is a mistake, I'm not... I don't have Gifts. I lost them."

"You have had Gifts all along. They were just bound... asleep," Cecily disagreed softly. "Amylia... your eyes... You are a Wytchling, but I've never seen eyes like yours before."

Rogue stepped forward and passed a small object to Amylia. She took it mutely, still staring at Cecily in bewilderment. Dropping her gaze to the small bit of glass in her hand, she gasped.

Ice blue and silver eyes stared out at her, the colours swirling as if burning embers lit them, so similar to what had looked back at her the last nineteen years. But where the colours had been mute, these were alive and burning, as if a window down to a fire in her core.

She thrust the glass back towards Rogue and lurched out of the seat, bracing herself with a hand against the wall and sucking in ragged breaths.

Utter silence fell behind her, but she felt four sets of eyes watching her intently. "How?" she asked flatly.

She wanted to scream, to rip the house apart, and run until she couldn't walk, but she couldn't move a step further.

"I thought maybe you had something, passed down from your father. You mentioned he had Gifts," Cecily said carefully. "I felt... something from you, but I couldn't see anything. I thought maybe it was just minimal. A trace from a few generations back. I never contemplated that it was bound power I could sense, though. I'm so sorry."

Amylia shuddered. "But... how?" she breathed again and turned to look at them. "I'm nineteen. How could I not know... that this was inside me?" She waved her hands at them.

Lyrik stepped forward. "What I want to know is... how are you even still alive? That much Helix — in a ring it would have drained most Wytchlings completely. That was inside you!"

Lyrik looked at Gryffon, her face a picture of shock. "She's not just a Wytchling, Gryff. She's an Elementyl. And I have never come across an Elementyl with as much power as she must have."

Rogue sucked in a breath. "Well... I guess there's one more female I get to be terrified of." He smirked at Lyrik. "How does it feel not to be the deadliest in the room for a change?"

Lyrik gave him a withering look.

"Too soon?" he teased.

Gryffon silenced both of them with a hard look. "Do you know who would have done this?" he asked calmly, the stern look on his face softening as he looked to her. "Drakon?"

Amylia shook her head. "I… no, I don't know. Why would he do that?" Gryffon was silent as he continued to study her. "He wouldn't," she said, defensively. "He saved us. He took us i —" She blanched, feeling the blood rush from her face. "Oh, Gods… Rayvn."

She sank down the wall to the floor, her hands coming to a rest in her lap as she stared at them. "Does this mean Rayvn is like me?" She raised pleading eyes to Gryffon.

"For you to be an… Elementyl," Cecily said, her voice shaking slightly, "your mother must have been a Wytchling, and your father, too, or Elementyl himself. So, yes, sweetling, your brother will have Gifts, too. And if neither of you knew about this, you were bound at a young age. Gifts start to emerge at about seven years of age." Cecily bit her lip looking to Gryffon. "Gryff, what do we do? We can't leave her with this. There are no other Sylvyn here."

He shook his head. "I think we need to know why she was bound before we can do anything else. You don't remember anything?" he asked quietly, eyes soft.

Amylia shuddered. "No. How do I go home? And Mica. What will Mica think? And Rayvn? How do I tell him what we are?"

She shook her head, a small cry of distress coming from her as she stared at her hands again.

"I can help," Lyrik said softly. "The Helix, I can make it into something for you to wear. You will be in control. You can take it off at any moment, but it will bind your powers again, making you look as you were, while you decide what you want to do. It might make it easier for you to talk to the people you need to, if they are not screaming about your heritage at the same time," she said with a wry smile.

Amylia huffed a small laugh, then took a shuddering breath and nodded. "Please," she said softly, nodding to Lyrik.

Lyrik squeezed her hand, wrapped the small stone into the cloth, and headed for the exit, grabbing Rogue roughly as she passed and hauling him out behind her.

"I'm not sure telling anyone is the best idea," Gryffon said softly. He held out a hand to Amylia, pulling her to her feet. "We don't know why you were bound. I think we need to find out why." He glanced at Cecily, and they exchanged a look before Cecily nodded slightly. He turned back to Amylia. "We will stay here for a while longer. Lyrik and Rogue can take the trade herd and the men back to Asteryn. Cecily and I will stay with you while we figure this out."

Gryffon ran a hand over his face. "I have some questions for Lord Drakon." His voice hardened at the name.

Amylia looked at him. "He's a good man, Gryffon, he can't have known." Her voice shook. "Or he would never have promised me to his son, he doesn't care much for… for Sylvyns. He has said in the past that my mother was too good for my Sylvyn father."

Gryffon's face was sad when he looked back at her. He squeezed her arm lightly. "I hope for your sake… and for his… that you are right."

Chapter 8

"It's not going to hold for a long time, but it will do for now." Lyrik studied the anklet she had just wrapped around Amylia's leg.

The stone had been intricately woven into the material, slightly poking through the threads enough to keep constant contact with skin.

Amylia sucked in a breath at the sudden hollow feeling. The powers, so briefly back in her possession, had been ripped from her again.

Picking up the glass Rogue had given her, she gazed into it. Her eyes, ice blue and grey, looked normal once again.

Cecily pushed a cup of warm, spiced wine into her hands. The heat seeped through the cup and up her arms and the heady aroma filled her senses. She gave Cecily a grateful smile and took a sip. The warmth trickled down the back of her throat, slowly filling that now empty space inside her.

How had she not noticed its absence before?

"We need to discuss the next few days." Gryffon sighed, leaning against the table. "For the sake of the alliance, we need to approach this carefully. Lyrik, are you okay to lead the men from Lylican back with Rogue? He will have the trade herd to deal with, but with the extra men there will be plenty of hands."

Lyrik nodded, face unreadable.

"What about Rayvn?" Amylia asked, her voice muffled by the steaming cup in front of her mouth.

"I don't think we should tell him just yet," Cecily said quietly. "Not until Gryff and I have had a chance to catch up. If he loses control…" She drifted off, the sentence unfinished. "You had remarkable control for one who has not touched her Gifts in eleven years. Rayvn was only three when you left Oryx?" Cecily raised an eyebrow in question.

Amylia nodded miserably.

"We have to assume you were both bound then… or before," she said quickly, raising her hands placatingly as Amylia went to object.

"That was well before his Gifts would have started to manifest. When released, they could be anything, and he will need help to control them. On the road surrounded by strangers is not the place for that."

She smiled encouragingly. "We can help him, Amylia, but you need to trust us."

Amylia stared at the steam rising from her cup and gave a slight nod. "And what about me?" she asked quietly.

Gryffon crouched in front of her, waiting until her gaze met his. "You are welcome to join us if you wish. We will stay while you get past this initial part, but after… We can teach you how to control your Gifts if you come to Asteryn."

Amylia stared at him aghast. "I'm betrothed to Mica… I… I can't just leave. Everything I know is here!"

Gryffon nodded. "The offer is open, long term. We cannot stay away from our lands too long, but if you decide in the future that you want to learn from your own kind, we have a place for you at Asteryn, should you want… or need it, Amylia." Standing, he squeezed her knee gently.

The ride home was subdued, bumping slowly along on the quiet mare Mica had purchased for her, a kind-eyed bay, unremarkable, but stolid.

Gryffon had offered to accompany her, but she had refused, insisting that she wanted the time to compose herself before getting back to the keep.

Lost in her thoughts, she let the mare pick her way back home as she idly rubbed the scar on her arm with its new, odd little mark. That little spot that had so drastically changed everything.

She tried to remember that day her world had come crashing down, but after so many years of trying to forget, the memories faded into murky shadows. Only the echo of fear and pain remained. She tried to remember her parents using their Gifts. She could remember her father, his little animals he made when telling her stories but… nothing like what had been streaming from her. The fire that rushed unchecked from her as if in wild happiness at being let out.

A young stable hand rushed out to meet her when she got back, guiding her mare into the quiet warmth of the stables, Amylia busied herself untacking, waving him away. The boy's eyes were wide as he took off his dirty cap and wrung it between his hands.

"Please, m'lady, we will look after her nicely. Go on back to the keep. Lord Mica will see me gone if ye get caught 'ere settlin' your own mare again."

Amylia sighed and rubbed a tense spot between her eyes as a headache loomed behind it. "Right… of course… I won't stay."

Silently, she slipped through the servants' entrance to the keep, making her way to the domestic wing. She breathed a sigh of relief once she made it inside her room without bumping into anyone.

Leaning against the door, eyes closed, she let the peace of the room melt into her before crossing to the bed and collapsing onto it. Only then did she give way to the tears of anger and pain which gripped her soul.

She felt lost, as if the carpet had been ripped out from under her. Her brother was leaving for the Gods knew how long. Shadow was lost to her and now… even her very self had been irrevocably changed forever.

Though she longed for someone to hold her, at the same time she couldn't stand the thought of it. There was no one here she could call. Mica would still be angry at her, and she did not have the energy to deal with that conversation.

She wanted her mother.

Some time later, a gentle shake woke her. "M'lady, wake up. You missed dinner so I brought some up… and you're filthy!"

Amylia opened her eyes, unfocused, the thump of her headache making her squint as she tried to make out the person in front of her. Instantly, she relaxed as Harriet's face swam into view. Looking down at herself, she saw what bothered Harriet so much. Dust from the road streaked her hands and arms and singe marks marred her sleeves.

The maid's soft brown eyes were full of sympathy. "I'm sorry, m'lady. I know that mare meant a lot to you. Here, drink this. It will help."

A warm cup was pushed into her hands and the smell of peppermint washed over her. Gratefully, she took a sip.

"Here," the maid said, "drink that up. I'll get some hot water and draw you up a nice bath."

The maid bustled back and forth, filling the tub until the copper monstrosity sat in the middle of the room, steam rising from the water's surface.

"Come now." Harriet took her cup. "Let's get you undressed and in that water. A good soak fixes everything."

Amylia raised her arms, letting Harriet pull off the soft shirt she wore, then stood, untying her pants, letting them fall to the floor. Groaning, she unlaced the back of the tight breastband she always wore for riding, running her hand over the slight ribbing raised from the tightness of the band and sighing deeply.

"Oh, wait," Harriet muttered. "That anklet, too. It will get ruined in that water."

Amylia shrank away as Harriet stooped to untie it.

"No!" She shook her head and quickly tempered her voice when she saw Harriet's shocked look. "No… it's okay, leave it on."

"But, m'lady, it will get all waterlogged and nasty."

"That's fine. I… can't… take it off. Just leave it, please." She quickly stepped into the tub, submerging the offending foot in water. The rest of her followed soon after, and she groaned in appreciation as the water lapped up her body and the stress of the day receded slightly.

Harriet grabbed a brush and pulled up a seat behind her. Unbraiding the thick plait Amylia had tied her hair into, she ran her fingers through the dark curls, gently unsnagging small knots here and there as she went.

Amylia leaned her head against Harriet's knees and sighed.

"When I came to the castle… at the start… did you notice anything different about me?" she asked quietly. The fingers paused in her hair briefly before carrying on, making long sweeps through it with the brush until the black strands gleamed in the candlelight.

"I don't know what you mean, m'lady?" Harriet sounded puzzled. "You were grieving, very quiet, but… I was young myself. I remember thinking how pretty you were."

"Please, Harry, call me Amylia. We have discussed this." She sighed.

"You know I can't do that." Harriet chuckled. "Me… a maid… calling the lady of Lylican by her first name." She huffed. "Get away with ye, I would be out on the streets by dawn if either of the lords heard."

Amylia sighed in exasperation, sitting up and swinging herself around to face the maid. Water sloshed over the side of the tub onto the floor.

"Please, Harry, think. Did I say or do anything… odd? Anything you thought wasn't normal?"

Harriet eyed her warily. "How much of that wine did you drink, m'lad—"

"Harry!" Amylia begged.

The maid threw her hands up. "I don't know! It was eleven years ago. You barely spoke for weeks. Lord Drakon would come around every day asking if you had eaten or slept, but no… there was nothing else. Why are you asking this now?"

Hearing Harriet's rising concern, Amylia opened her mouth to speak but didn't know what to say, so she closed it again and flopped back into the tub. Another tidal wave surged over the side.

"M'lady... Amylia..." Harriet skirted the side of the tub and knelt next to it. "What is this about? Is it the wedding?"

Amylia huffed, looking at the ceiling. "Gods, I wish it were." She looked at the maid then. "I'm not what everyone thinks I am... I'm..." She hesitated, but Gods, she had to tell someone. "I'm... like Lord and Lady Wynter."

Harriet stared at her in confused silence. "What do you mean?"

Amylia groaned, looking at her hands. "I'm... I'm not like you. I'm Sylvyn."

Harriet guffawed. "What on earth are you talking about?"

Frustration surged through Amylia as she struggled to find the words, and then she glanced at her ankle, anxiety rippling through her. As Harriet chuckled, Amylia fumbled with the anklet, the wet cloth frustratingly refusing to unknot.

"Of course not, pet, don't be si—"

The anklet gave suddenly, and a rush of energy coursed through her body again. Focusing on that hollow space as it filled, she only just registered Harriet's gasp as she struggled to keep the tendrils of the Gift safely tucked into herself.

The brush dropped with a bang and Harriet's soft brown eyes grew huge. The maid stepped back, a hand over her throat as she stared, mouth hanging open.

"What... what... Amylia, what is this? What have they done to you?" She sobbed, falling to her knees next to the tub.

Amylia glanced at the mirror and noticed, yes, her eyes had shifted to a silver glow. "They didn't do anything." She shook her head with a sigh. "Except remove this from inside my arm." She tossed the anklet to the floor next to Harriet. It landed with a small, wet, thunk.

Harriet picked it up with a shaking hand and peered at it. "What is this?"

"It's a stone. Inside that strap. Called Helix? I think? It... binds powers. This is me, Harry. I've always had this, been this. I just didn't know. How could I not know?"

A small sob escaped her. Harriet's face was a mix of caution and sympathy. The maid reached out, hand still shaking slightly, and rested it on Amylia's.

"But how did they know..." Her voice trailed off as she looked back at the anklet.

"Cecily... Lady Wynter. Her Gift is healing," Amylia said, her voice thick. "She felt it when she touched my arm, and Lord Wynter cut it out when I asked him to."

Harriet gasped and her eyes darted over Amylia's arms, as if looking for a wound.

"No... I'm okay," Amylia assured her quickly, her hand running absently over her arm. "Cecily healed it again afterwards."

Harriet stumbled to her feet before sinking onto the padded seat next to the window and dragging her hands across her face. "Oh, dear me," she mumbled through her fingers.

Amylia stood and stepped out of the tub, pulling a towel around her as she did. Stooping, she gently took the anklet from Harriet and retied it securely around her ankle.

The hollowness instantly took over. It felt worse this time, as if her body protested the sudden emptiness. She shuddered slightly, the hairs on the back of her arms rising.

They talked late into the night. Amylia told her everything, feeling a sense of relief as Harriet slipped back into the easy way they usually spoke.

"I'm not sure what to do," she said softly. "I need to talk to Lord Drakon. Lord Wynter wants to see him, too, but he's given me time to decide how I'm going to talk to him first. I wish I knew what Mica will think. We had a horrible argument yesterday about Shadow, and now there's this."

"I'm sure Lord Drakon will know what to do," Harriet soothed, patting her hand gently. "And... and you have that anklet... it makes it go away?"

Amylia nodded, looking at the small strip of woven cloth on her ankle.

"You need sleep for now, m'lady. You shouldn't do anything on no sleep, and you look worn out. Why don't you hop into bed for a few hours? I'll come back and wake you in time to see your brother off."

Amylia winced, reminded she would be saying goodbye to him today. "Please, Harry... Don't say anything to anyone about this. Especially Rayvn. Not until I've had time to think."

Harriet held the covers back as Amylia fell into them, then she tucked them gently around her. "Of course I won't pet." Smiling, she blew out the candles. Pausing at the door, she gazed worriedly back at Amylia before slipping silently out.

Chapter 9

It was daybreak far too fast. Amylia heard Harriet's familiar light footsteps before the maid bustled in the door. Dark circles shadowed her eyes and stray wisps of hair had escaped the neat bun she usually kept it in.

"I'm so sorry, Harry. You look exhausted. I should have told you to go home far earlier," Amylia groaned as shame heated her cheeks.

"I'll be fine, m'lady." Harriet ducked her head and set down the tray of food on Amylia's lap.

Fresh bread with melted butter started Amylia's mouth watering, though her stomach still churned with anxiety. She pushed it away with a sigh and reached for the steaming cup of tea, warming her hands around the mug.

Harriet flitted around the room, readying her clothes, and tidying as she went. She realized the maid was avoiding eye contact with her. An air of tension existed between them. Amylia sighed inwardly. This was what Gryffon had warned her about: mortals grew anxious around Wytchlings, instinctively distancing themselves from harm.

Glancing towards the mirror, Amylia noted with relief that her eyes looked normal as she sipped on the scalding liquid in her cup. It burned comfortably down to her stomach, but she frowned at the cup, noticing a slightly different taste.

"This is new?" she asked, nodding to the cup as the maid came towards her with a fresh gown.

"Chamomile, m'lady… with the peppermint… I thought today would be a rough one for you. It might help a bit."

Harriet gave her a hesitant smile and Amylia echoed it. Passing the mug to the maid she took the dress Harriet handed to her. "I appreciate it, Harry. And thank you… for… for just being here."

Harriet looked up from the mug and met her eyes. "I know I'm only your maid, m'lady. But you have been good to me. And no matter what you... you are now, you're still Amylia... and still my friend." She smiled again and squeezed Amylia's shoulder gently before disappearing from the room to let her dress in peace.

The court of Asteryn arrived at the keep at noon. Cecily sat astride Shadow, who received a wide berth from everyone.

Amylia watched them longingly, her chest restricting as she gazed at the mare, though she received a soft smile from Cecily as she soothingly petted Shadow's neck, the mare's ears flat to her skull as she glared at everything.

She didn't miss the look Mica gave her as he saw that the mare was already in the Wynters' possession, either. Shifting uncomfortably under his reproachful look, she guessed from Gryffon's stiff posture that he had seen it, too.

Gryffon dismounted, handing his reins to Rogue, watching Shadow darkly as he passed her. Cecily looked amused as he went by and Amylia noticed an almost imperceptible tightening on her reins, a warning to Shadow to behave as her mate came within reach of the velvet mouth.

Gryffon bowed to Amylia as he approached, looking her over surreptitiously. His gaze lingered on her skirts hiding her ankle.

"Lady Sylvers," he said softly. He then turned to Mica and Drakon, greeting them casually. "Lords."

Lord Drakon gestured towards the trade horses milling in the yard, held by the stable staff. All were gorgeous animals of prime breeding age. The stallion was a giant beast, proud neck arched as he pawed the ground. Two stable boys struggled to keep him separate from the herd as they hung off the lead ropes.

"My side of the agreement is fulfilled, Lord Wynter. These are all part of my prime breeding herd," he said proudly. "And the men have all been handpicked as some of our best."

Gryffon nodded, surveying them critically. "They have a fair ride ahead of them. We were due to meet with the Sylkies on the far side of the Dead Forest, but with the herd and the recruits, we will have to ride the distance hard. Are they prepared for that?"

Drakon nodded. "They all have decent provisions and there are packs to be loaded onto the herd, too. And all the men can hunt to boost their diet on the way. Rest assured, Lord Wynter, my men will manage."

Gryffon nodded grimly. "They will leave directly, then."

Amylia glanced between the men, relieved to see none looked at her.

Subtly, she stepped back, picking up a small leather-wrapped bundle, and left the group talking. She slipped towards the waiting men and looked up with a sad smile at her brother sitting atop his new war-horse.

"I'll miss you, little brother," she said. He grinned down at her. "You make sure you don't get eaten by one of those beasts and come home."

He grinned wider. "Sylkies, Milly! I'll write and tell you all about them. Drakon said there are trade ships being set up between the ports now directly through here. I'll send one with the first ship."

Leaning down, he hugged her tightly, almost pulling her off her feet, and as he let her go, she slipped the parcel into his hands.

"A treat for the road." She smiled. "You have the fur cloak I got you?"

Rayvn rolled his eyes. "Yes, I do." He glanced at the men. "Now stop, before I get chuff for you clucking over me."

Amylia grinned wickedly at him. "I love you, little bother," she said loudly. He groaned and some of the men nearby chuckled.

Amylia squeezed his knee with a wink and slapped his horse on the rump, sending it back to the milling men.

Lyrik, dressed in her formal fighting leathers and a thick fur cloak, looked over her new recruits, nodding to Rayvn as she touched two fingers to her forehead.

He bowed low in the saddle to her. "It is an honour, Lady Damaris, to be entering your training programme."

She snorted. "It's Lyrik, Lord Sylvers. I'm no lady, and I doubt you will be feeling the same in a few weeks."

She cast him a wicked grin and turned her horse, walking slowly in front of the line of waiting soldiers. "Okay, men. We leave at high noon. Take this time to water your mounts, say your goodbyes, and check your packs. Make sure you have as many supplies as your mounts can comfortably carry. Leave your arms free as we will need some of you to help with leading the trade herd."

Pausing and turning her horse to face them, she scanned the line of men, her face impassive. "If you have forgotten your tents, you will be sleeping in the snow. If you have forgotten warm clothing, you are going to have a miserable few weeks, as that is how long the return journey could be if we have to take the detour. Especially if we hit bad weather. Do I make myself clear?"

The men nodded and turned to follow her orders, busily checking canteens and straps.

A tall blond man sneered as she passed. "The fuck does she think she is," he muttered under his breath to the soldier next to him who chuckled nervously, throwing a glance at her.

It happened faster than Amylia could follow. Lyrik swung her mare about, ploughing into the man's horse and knocking him clean out of his saddle, the small woman leaping nimbly off her horse before he had even hit the ground.

The blonde man rolled as he hit the dirt but came up fast with a knife fisted in his large hand. Lyrik's fist smashed into his face, the knife flying from his grip as he reeled back.

He shook his head as if to clear his vision as her knee came up under his chin and snapped his jaw together with a load crack.

Amylia winced at the noise as he crumpled into the dirt, unconscious.

Lyrik paused for a moment, looked down at him, disgust on her face, then eyed the rest of the men as if daring them to say anything. A few had pale faces as they looked at their comrade motionless on the ground.

"I suggest the rest of you learn some respect, real quick, if you share the same thoughts as this man," she snarled as the man at her feet stirred. Reaching down, she grabbed him by the ear, eliciting an outraged cry from him as she hauled him across the courtyard. The man scrabbled, trying to take the pressure off his ear until Lyrik threw him at the feet of Lord Drakon.

He didn't look at the man but met her gaze as she glared up at him. "He is one of our best in hand-to-hand combat," he said coldly.

"If that's the case, I doubt many will make it the first week," she retorted, her face unreadable.

The man at her feet attempted to stand, but she grabbed him by the back of the neck and shoved him face first back down into the cold dirt.

"No man is going to last long in my training that does not know how to show simple respect," she snarled. Her eyes never left Drakon's. "I suggest you replace him with someone who values his testicles a bit more. The next one who shows this level of ignorance loses them."

The blond man growled as he wiped his face with the back of his hand and spat blood onto the dirt, and she stepped back slightly to give him room to rise. Standing and staggering slightly, he whirled towards Lyrik, raising his hand to strike.

Drakon opened his mouth to snap at the soldier just as the man was hauled off his feet by a hand on his collar. "That is enough, you fool. You disgrace yourself and our men," Rayvn snarled. "Get back to the barracks. You are relieved of duty, and I will see Raol hears about this."

Heliacle Rising

Amylia masked the surprise she felt at the speed and silence with which Rayvn had appeared next to Lyrik. She saw the huge Sylvyn soldier, still mounted next to Cecily, eyeing her brother with interest, no worry for the small Second on his face.

The man bared his teeth, but wisely stayed silent as he straightened his crumpled jacket and whirled to stalk off.

"Please accept my apologies, Lyrik," Rayvn said stonily. "Joharren does not represent the rest of our men." He glanced at Drakon who shifted slightly, irritation written across his features.

"Can I suggest Silas as his replacement, my lord? He only just missed out on the draft, and I know he was disappointed."

Lord Drakon nodded curtly, waving a young boy over. "Go fetch him, boy. Immediately." He turned back to Lyrik. "I hope this is to your approval, Damaris?" His voice dripped with sarcasm.

She nodded, giving him an insolent smile as she touched her forehead in a mocking salute. "Much appreciated, my lord."

Walking back to her waiting mount, she vaulted lightly to its back as Rayvn drew his mount up next to hers, adjusting himself in the saddle and nodding to her.

"I will go collect Silas and then ride to catch up immediately. Joharren's lapse in judgement need not delay our departure."

Lyrik nodded and motioned for him to go, watching as he whirled his horse, headed for the barracks.

The entire party moved out as one, falling into step behind Rogue, who led the stallion from his gelding. He grinned at Lyrik over the head of the stallion. "Bit of a statement you made there, Rik."

She smiled sweetly at him. "You know I love misogynistic asshats. He was asking for it."

Rogue nodded, eyes innocently wide. "Oh, of course. You didn't enjoy wiping the ground with his face at all."

Lyrik snorted. "Let us hope the rest of the men remember it. It's going to be a long trip back, now we are not flying."

She looked longingly at the sky and Rogue grimaced, following her look. "I can't say I'm complaining about that." He patted his horse. "Nothing wrong with riding. It will weed out the roses from the thorns."

"Pussy," she teased. "Don't pretend you don't like it up there."

"What I like, Lyrik, is not dying. And your Freyja seems to get a sadistic pleasure from terrifying me every time I go near her. If we were meant to fly, we would have been born with wings." Lyrik chuckled, glancing behind her at the sound of horses trotting towards them.

"Speaking of sadistic," Lyrik said wryly as Cecily pulled up beside Rogue. Shadows lips were already drawn back over her teeth as she eyed Rogue's gelding.

Rogue's horse baulked at the black mare, pushing away from her, the whites of his eyes showing as he bumped into the stallion next to him.

Drawing up next to Lyrik, Gryffon chuckled as he watched Rogue struggling with the two horses and cursing under his breath. "Cecily and I will leave you at the crossroads ahead. Are you prepared?"

Lyrik nodded, looking back at the men stretched out behind them. "We are. Gods help them if they are not, but we will soon find out."

Gryffon laughed. "Rayvn seems to hold respect with the men."

"He does," she agreed, urging her mare on as she slowed, watching the stallion warily. "I think of all of them, he has the most promise, even though he is young."

Gryffon eyed her with a raised brow.

"No, I'm not just saying that because of who's brother he is. I like Amylia, but that doesn't mean her brother gets a free pass. He seems genuinely interested in the Sylkies," Lyrik protested.

Gryffon grinned. "That's an easy way to get on your good side then. Smart lad."

She made a rude gesture at him, pulling back to move across to Cecily, exchanging quiet words with her as Rogue's horse gratefully edged further away towards Gryffon.

Rogue grinned at Gryffon. "It's good to be moving again. We will see you in a few days?"

"A week at most," Gryffon answered. "I've promised Amylia time to talk to Drakon, but if we leave within three days, we should catch up to you within the week."

"And... are we expecting two of you... or three?" Rogue's query sounded casual, but his face was sly.

Gryffon laughed again. "That's entirely up to Amylia, though I would prefer not to leave one of our own behind. Not a word to Rayvn. Either of you, okay?" He sighed. "And try to stop Lyrik killing any of them. I'm not sure the trade alliance would stand up to murder."

"Yes m'lord," Rogue saluted. Sarcastically, he added, "We will anxiously await your return."

Chapter 10

Amylia paced in her room. Counting her footsteps as she went, she balled her hands into fists and flexed, mulling over the conversation she wanted to have with Drakon.

Should she tell Mica first? How would he take it? And then he could come with her when she talked to… No, she didn't want to see the look of fear in his eyes like Harriet. Not yet.

She groaned, stopping in front of the large windows, and looked out.

The Wynters had left with the trade party the day prior. She knew they'd only gone back to town, but still… she wasn't sure if she wished they had just left entirely.

Why were they staying on? To make sure she could control this power? Were they worried Drakon would blame them for this?

She pulled her skirts up and glanced at the anklet snug against her ankle. Dropping her skirts with a sigh, she rubbed a tired hand across her face.

Why? Why did this have to happen? She rubbed at her arm absently, feeling the small ridge of the scar and a wave of anger passed through her.

She didn't ask for this. Mica hadn't asked for this.

Last night at dinner, she hadn't been able to look at him and he had avoided her, too, busying himself in conversation with some of the keep guards after rushing through his meal in silence.

He probably thought she was still furious over Shadow. She was; the ache of the horse leaving was a constant grief that she was trying to ignore… for now. And she knew, after the look he gave her when he saw Shadow with Cecily, that he was going to be upset with her again. But she was putting off that conversation.

Amylia fought the wave of guilt that threatened to drown her. He was her betrothed. But he was unaware that she was a Sylvyn... not even just a Sylvyn... a damned Elementyl.

Wearily, she sighed and watched the door. Footsteps in the corridor beyond signalled, no doubt, a maid who would know where Drakon was.

Better get it over with before she lost her nerve entirely.

She swung the door open then jumped back violently. A large guard filled the doorway, his fist raised to knock where the door had been moments before.

His surprise mirrored hers as he eyed her suspiciously, visibly pulling himself together. In a deep voice, he said, "Lord Drakon sent us for you, m'lady."

"Oh!" Amylia said, surprised. "Okay, I'll come now. I was on my way to see him anyway. Where can I find him?"

"I will take you now," the guard replied, taking her elbow.

His grip was like iron, and she shook her arm, trying to dislodge him.

"I can make my way alone. If you just tell me wh —"

A painful squeeze to her elbow stopped her. "Lord's orders, m'lady. I will be accompanying you down."

"Down?" Amylia asked, her brow furrowing in confusion. "He's not in his rooms?"

She got no answer. He hurried her through the servants' doors sunk into the walls and hidden behind hanging tapestries.

These connected to passages and winding staircases through the keep, shortcuts for the staff to flit unseen from one room to the next.

They descended one such staircase to the lower levels: the war chambers, Drakon's personal library, and the keep's treasure vault.

Entering a well-lit chamber, Amylia saw a large wooden table in the middle of the room. At it sat Mica, his face pale as he watched her.

Drakon sat at the head and next to him — her stomach flipped — stood Harriet. Her maid's face was an odd shade of grey. She held a pitcher of wine, pouring it into a cup next to Drakon's elbow with a shaking hand.

Drakon smiled gently at Amylia, gesturing to the seat at his side when she entered. "Sit, my dear... please, we have some things to discuss."

Her guard pushed her towards the seat and, moving forward mechanically, she tried to gather moisture in her suddenly dry mouth as she looked at the men.

Drakon cleared his throat, gesturing to Harriet to fill the empty glass next to Amylia as he did so.

Amylia tried to catch the eye of the maid as she filled it, but Harriet refused to look at her. She looked as if she had been crying, her beautiful soft brown eyes slightly red-rimmed.

"I have been informed you are aware of your bloodline," Drakon said quietly.

Amylia's eyes snapped back to Harriet's face accusingly, searching for an answer, before she slowly met Drakon's gaze.

"Yes," she said. Her voice came out shaky. She took a deep breath and tried again. "Yes… my lord, I was actually on my way to talk to you when I got dragged here by the guards." She scowled over her shoulder at them, and they shifted slightly.

"My apologies, my dear. I didn't mean them to be so… direct. I had only just heard and, as you can imagine, I was worried."

"So, you knew?" Her voice was steady as she met his stare, not giving away the tide of emotions coursing through her.

He didn't flinch. She could feel Mica watching her, and she wanted so desperately to reach out and take his hand. But she didn't know if he would flinch away, repulsed by the revelation of what she was now.

"I knew," Drakon said softly, taking a deep sip of his drink. "I'm the one who bound you and your brother."

She stared at him, her mouth falling open as she struggled to take in what he had just said.

"I only just found out, too," Mica murmured, looking at her with a pained expression. "He did it to help you, jewel… to help both of you."

Starting to stand, a firm hand on her shoulder stopped her and she looked up into the stone face of the guard.

Drakon waved him off. "No, it's okay. It's a shock. Please leave her be."

The guard backed away, his hands crossing behind his back.

Drakon leaned towards her. "Amylia, I didn't know how else to keep you safe. Attica was searching for you… and for Rayvn. Searching for a Wytchling girl, and we wouldn't have held against them. A mortal girl, however, daughter to a mortal lord. They had no reason to think it was the same person, no reason to even come looking without your Gifts calling to them. Some of those Sylvyns can feel your kind."

He sighed and touched her hand gently. She fought the urge to shake him off, but her stomach lurched.

"I was going to tell you when you turned sixteen, and there was never the right time. Then I was going to tell you after your betrothal. But you and Mica were so happy, I preferred not to take that away," he said earnestly.

Mica reached out then, taking her other hand gently. "It's okay, jewel. We can fix this. Keep you safe still. No one has to know."

She stared at them in confusion and shook her head slightly. "What do you mean fix this? You… you knew all this time, my lord. Who my family was and… This is why we never talk about my parents isn't it? You knew I could remember my father's Gifts and you wanted me to forget." She broke off, pulling her hands away and burying her face into them.

"Where is the stone, Amylia?" Drakon's voice was firm, but gentle.

She let her arms drop. "So, you didn't tell them everything then, Harriet?" she snapped, instantly regretting it as her maid's lip trembled.

"I didn't —" Harriet started, but Drakon cut her off.

"Raol told us this morning." He glanced at the girl with disdain on his face. "His wife told him in confidence it seems."

Amylia sighed. "The stone is in an anklet. It's… it's keeping my Gifts bound… to give me time to talk to you." She looked at them. "Lord and Lady Wynter have offered to help me learn how to control them. I wanted to ask you if I could have time to do this, maybe push the wedding back slightly. If you still want me, Mica."

She looked at him pleadingly as he took her hand again, blanching at the dark anger that rippled across Drakon's face before he masked it.

"There will be no need to push the wedding back, nor for the Wynters' help," Drakon snapped. "The fewer people who know about this, the better. You are still at risk from Attica, and we must continue with the way we know works."

Drakon paused. When he spoke, his tone was calmer. "The stone must be put back, Amylia. It's the only way we know you are hidden."

She felt cold as the words sank in. Put it back? Live with this hollow feeling… forever?

"No." She shook her head. "I can control this. I can wear the anklet in public. No one needs to know… but, my lord, I want to know this part of me. This part of my parents."

He stiffened, straightening in his seat. "I'm not debating this, Amylia. I couldn't save your mother from the Sylvyns, but I will not fail in protecting you, too. The stone is going back in to ensure your safety and Rayvn's. Do you want him to die protecting you if Attica learns you have been here all this time?"

Amylia's chest tightened at the thought, horror creeping over her as she shook her head and her eyes filled with tears. "No, but…" She trailed off, staring at her hands.

Drakon turned to Mica. "Go fetch the physician," he murmured.

Mica stood, rounding the table to Amylia, and kissed her gently on the crown of her head before slipping out the door.

"Physician?" Amylia asked in confusion.

"Better now, while it's still new… before these 'Gifts' set in properly." Drakon nodded and handed her a cup of wine.

She took a deep gulp of the ruby liquid. It was strong and the spices swam through her head as she swallowed. The decision settled into her stomach like a lead weight, and it was wrong. It felt so wrong. Placing the cup down firmly, she shook her head.

"No." She looked at him. "No. I'm not putting that stone back. Not yet. I need to see first."

Drakon sighed. "Amylia, I'm sorry, but you have no choice in this. It's what is best." Though his voice was firm, he watched her cautiously, his eyes flicking from her face to the cup and back up.

She blinked, trying to form an answer, but her tongue… her tongue felt strange… almost thick. She paused, pondering this new feeling. Her head felt like it was filled with the night sky, as if it was hard to see through. Looking at the cup she had just been holding, it swam across the table in front of her, swaying slightly as if a reflection in a rippling pool.

"M'lady? Amylia?" a worried voice said near her. She turned, seeking the voice.

The last thing she saw were large brown eyes full of concern and then… nothing.

Chapter 11

A burning, white-hot pain tore through her thigh, ripping her from unconsciousness, and Amylia screamed.

A muttered curse as the source of the pain stopped suddenly. "Apologies, my lady. You were not meant to feel this. Here, let me get the poppy juice."

Scuffling off to her side out of sight had her craning her neck to try to find the source of the voice.

"What are you doing?" She moaned, shaking her head as her eyes adjusted and a wave of nausea washed over her. She sobbed, heaving against the tethers that kept her arms above her.

She lay on a large, flat table tilted up at the head, her weight resting on her bound wrists.

Heart racing as her thigh pulsed in pain, panic vied with the other overwhelming emotions as she craned her neck to look around the stone room.

Bunches of herbs sat in glass bottles along the back of a table on the far side. A leather pouch was rolled out in front with multiple pockets in it, each one holding a wicked little instrument. The sharp point of a tiny hook poked out of one and she shuddered, pulling her attention away, and tried to look down to her thigh.

The tickle and warmth told her blood was running down her leg as she wriggled, trying to loosen the bonds.

"Let me go!" she seethed as the man came back into view.

He was old, greying hair balding at the top, and large bushy eyebrows straggled over his deeply set eyes.

"Nonsense, lady, this won't take but a minute, and then it will be over." He patted her on the shoulder feebly as he held a cup of a sickly-sweet smelling liquid to her mouth.

She turned her head sharply, spilling the contents down her bodice as he tipped the cup towards where her lips had been.

Grunting in annoyance, he tutted and fumbled to right the cup, sloshing more down his hand in the process. "Now, Lady Sylvers, there's no need for that," he scolded.

"Let… me… go!" she snarled at him. The anklet was still around her ankle though, her powers dead, sucked away into the stone nestled in it.

"Now, now. It's Lord Drakon's direct instructions. I'm just doing what he's ordered, and it won't take but a minute if you calm down. It really is a simple process. I've done it before." He wheedled, "Here… drink this, my lady." He held the cup back up to her lips.

She glared at him before taking a large mouthful.

"Ah… there we go." He sighed and relief flooded his craggy face. "That's much better isn't i —"

She spat the mixture as hard as she could into his face. Rage washed over her in waves.

He leaped back with a cry, trying to wipe the sticky liquid out of his eyes, and tripped over the stool, landing heavily on the cobbled floor.

Stone-faced, she stared at him and spat the last traces of the sweet liquid onto the ground, wiping her mouth on her shoulder.

He groaned while slowly trying to drag himself into a sitting position and glared up at her, his arms shaking slightly as he braced himself on the seat and pulled himself up.

"If you want to do it the hard way," he said coldly, "that's fine. I'll be back with the guards shortly."

He turned, favouring his left leg as he braced himself against the wall.

Amylia panted as her heart raced in her chest as she glanced around the room. Nothing was in reach. She contemplated yelling, but who would she call for? Mica?

Gryffon's face flashed across her mind, and she pushed it away crossly, pulling hard against the tethers at her wrist. Her muscles barked in protest, the skin on her wrists raw as she strained against the strong leather, but still the tethers held.

Groaning in frustration, she kicked the table, feeling the sting of the new slice across her outer thigh. It felt deep. A new rush of blood came from the wound as she tensed her leg and groaned, her head going dizzy again. Amylia kicked again as the sensation cleared and felt some movement in the ties on her ankles, loosening enough to move them freely.

She went still. Reaching as far as she could, she wriggled down the table and stretched her leg out, her ribs aching as she stretched her back so far she could barely breathe.

There.

The edge of the table hit painfully against her ankle, and she relaxed, panting. Hissing out a breath, she strained again, stretching for the corner. Her ankle took another hit on the sharp wood, making her give a small cry. Stretching as far as she could, she finally felt the anklet snag on the corner. She yanked her leg back up quickly. Her skin scraped painfully against the corner of the wood. A tug, a snap, and then she felt the rush at the same time a small chink announced the stone had fallen to the floor.

She fell back, breathing slow and steady, pulling all the powerful threads into herself. She curled protectively around those threads as footsteps clunked down the stairs.

Groaning softly, she shut her eyes, trying to control her breathing. Calming herself as her power roiled in her chest, she let anger feed it until it swirled and eddied in a depthless pool inside her.

Amylia welcomed it, this old friend, and she waited, letting it fill… and fill.

"Now, enough of this nonsense." His voice came from close to her side. "Jakob, Viktor, hold her still. This will not take long if she does not move."

Large, hard hands gripped her as his voice came closer.

"Now, here… take some of this. There is no need for you to feel any of this, Lady Sylvers." A dry, weathered hand grabbed her chin and squeezed. The thumb dug painfully into the side of her mouth, trying to pry her jaw open.

She could smell onions on his hands, feel the rough callouses against her skin, and she resisted the urge to gag.

"Lady Sylvers," he snapped. "You do not want me to do this without taking this first… but trust me, I will."

She opened her eyes, feeling the wisps of power pushing at her hold, and met his eyes with a small smile.

The bowl smashed at his feet as she looked straight at him. Her power burning in her as she met his horrified gaze, and with a feeling of detachment, she saw the moment he realised his life was over.

The guard holding her left arm grunted and jolted… but it was too late.

Reaching down, she yanked on her power, letting it rush through her like a storm before unleashing it from every part of her. The room exploded in blue and silver flames, scorching everything it touched to dust in seconds. The men didn't even have time to scream.

The tethers disintegrated from her skin, and she dropped lightly to the ground, not daring to look at what was left of the men.

Stooping, Amylia picked up the anklet, the braided material scorched and warm to the touch, and went to shove it in her pocket, then looked down in surprise, touching only skin. Flames licked over her in little waves of heat, but her clothes had turned to ash, some of it still dusting her skin.

She ran.

She raced up the stone steps; her thigh screamed as she went. The blood ran down her leg as she slipped against the stone floor, bloody footprints leaving a trail behind her.

Throwing open the door to the main floor, she bowled a startled maid clean off her feet as she passed, hearing the shrieks behind her as she left scorched tapestries and drapes in her wake.

Amylia glanced behind her once as she ran, to the door left swinging open from the servants' access down to the horrors below. Black smoke billowed up the staircase. Only the rushing noise of flames came from it.

Throwing herself down the servants' access to the kitchens and the courtyard beyond, she felt the threads reach out to brush against everything she passed, hearing the hiss and steam of destruction as she went.

Blindly reaching, she hauled the threads back in as she sprinted, scared they would touch more than just the keep. The rational part of her knew this wasn't the servants' fault.

Throwing open the final door, she stumbled into sunlight, ignoring the yelling behind her as panic overrode the humiliation of her nudity. She didn't give herself time to catch her breath and lurched forwards, crashing into someone who had stepped from the shadows at the commotion. Lylith stumbled backwards at the impact but kept a grip on Amylia's arm, though it must have burned her hand.

Lylith's horrified gaze travelled up Amylia's body, the flames still curling around her, and she snatched her hand away, fumbling for the clasp at her throat. Without a word, she dragged her cloak off and threw it around Amylia's shoulders, the cloth hissing as it singed against Amylia's flames.

"Go," she croaked, giving Amylia a small shove, and stepping away from her.

Amylia fled, not looking back. Her lungs burned with effort as she raced towards the gates at the far side of the grounds.

A loud male voice yelled behind her, and the gates ahead moved, creaking slowly towards each other.

"No!" she cried hoarsely and threw herself forward faster, willing her legs to push as the cloak wrapped around them, sticking to the blood, and making it impossible.

A commotion rose before the gates. Men shouted commands as hoofbeats thudded wildly, the scream of an angry horse piercing the air. She groaned, skidding to a stop, and looked wildly for somewhere else to get out, somewhere safe, as panic tore through her.

A rider burst through the gates, leading a horse who thrashed and kicked at the guards trying to grab at it.

The massive horse lashed out a huge leg, landing a powerful kick to a guard's neck. Dead instantly, he fell limply to the ground. The whip that had been about to land on the beast dropped to the dirt.

Amylia sobbed as she lurched forward "Shadow." Her cry was ragged as she raced for the black mare, for Gryffon, who had dropped the lead rope. His arm was held out towards the three remaining guards. They backed away from the swirling golden fire circling his hand.

She threw herself onto the mare and wrapped her legs around the huge bare back. Twisting one hand in her mane, she tucked the anklet into an inner pocket of the cloak and pulled the material of the cloak around herself with the other as Shadow launched them out of the gates and away from the keep.

Glancing over her shoulder, she saw Gryffon's Gift explode towards the guards as they attacked. The powerful golden flames dropped them where they stood. He wheeled his chestnut mare and took off after her, the horse stretching to catch up.

They galloped hard towards town, flying across frozen roads and paddocks. Amylia's breath came in gasps as she fought to keep the power inside her down, refusing to let it touch the mare under her.

Shadow slowed when Gryffon's mare fell further back, waiting as Gryffon cantered up next to her, his face tight.

"Are you hurt?" he asked urgently, scanning her, his eyes darkening as he saw the cloak, her bare leg poking out where the edge had fallen back in the mad ride.

"Not badly." She shook her head, subtly adjusting the cloak to cover her raw wrists.

She was shaking now, everywhere. She could feel her legs, tense as she held tight to Shadow, rippling with cramps as the muscles convulsed.

Gryffon grabbed the lead rope to pull Shadow slower and Amylia felt his eyes roving over her. "You're in shock," he said gently, their legs bumping together in time to the horses' gait.

"I need to get you out of here, though. Are you going to be okay? Just for a bit while we get you to safety?"

Amylia nodded, feeling faint. "How did you know I needed help?"

"Your maid… Harriet? She ran for the town, for us when… did Drakon drug you?" He waited for her reply. His eyes flashed when she gave a small nod. "She was hysterical. It took a while to get out of her what was happening. Cecily is with her now."

Gryffon urged the horses faster again. "We will go collect the supplies and Cecily, and then we will leave."

He glanced behind them again. Amylia followed his gaze. The road was clear, but a faint plume of smoke drifted up in the distance. He grimaced. "I think they will be busy for a little while."

Cecily had her mare saddled and loaded when they arrived, looking up and blanching as the horses trotted into the yard.

She ran to Amylia, face pale. "Are you okay, sweetling?" she asked, her gaze focused on her leg under the cloak. She touched it gently and then looked at her fingers, blood shining on them where it had soaked through the fabric.

Cecily's expression turned pained, and she glanced around at Gryffon, who hurried to load extra packs on his mare.

"I'm so sorry you had to go through this. I'll heal you. I'll fix all of it, but right now, I need to get you something to wear, and we need to go. I've packed all of our clothing, but I think there was some women's clothes in the house." She patted Amylia's knee gently as Amylia nodded, dazed.

A small cry from the door made her look up as Harriet ran out, skidding to a stop at the base of the steps when Shadow's ears flattened in a warning.

Amylia slid off carefully, awkwardly holding onto the cloak and Shadow's mane as her leg buckled under her.

The maid babbled, "I'm so sorry, m'lady, I… I didn't mean this to happen. I only told Raol. I didn't mean this to happen." Harriet wrung her hands as Amylia slowly limped to her. She swallowed, going quiet as Amylia drew up face to face.

"Thank you," Amylia said softly, her voice shaking. "For getting them, I mean. I know you didn't mean for any of this." Harriet sobbed and threw her arms around Amylia's neck.

"I'll try to send them in the wrong direction. I'll say you were scared of going to the Dead Forest alone… and… and you went for Credence because you heard there were Sylvyn still there." She squeezed Amylia tight against her.

Amylia nodded against her shoulder, pulling back, and holding her at arm's length. "You're not coming?" she asked.

Harriet shook her head. "I can't leave Raol," she answered, pain in her face. "He's not a bad man, Amylia. He didn't know what they would do. He was worried for Rayvn, that we should call him back home if he has those Gifts, too."

Amylia nodded, giving her a half smile. "I'll miss you. I'll come back when I can. When it's safe." She hesitated and let out a shaky breath. "Can you give Mica a message for me?" Harriet nodded, her eyes anxious as they searched her own. After a steadying but still shaky breath, she said, "Tell Mica… for love to hurt this badly, it was never love at all."

Harriet's eyes filled with tears as she nodded, giving her a last hug before she turned and ran towards the keep.

Amylia watched her friend disappear, jumping slightly as Cecily gently touched her elbow and slipped some clothes into her arms. She glanced down at them; a plain but warm cotton dress and a thick cloak. Hers was now singed and blackened.

She limped into the house, ducking behind the door to slip into the dress that hung loosely on her but covered her well, then made her way gingerly back to Shadow. Gryffon stood beside the mare buckling up the saddle and packs.

Cecily slipped the bridle over the large head, the mare holding her head low so the small woman could reach, and she smiled at Amylia.

"I kept her here with us, just in case you needed her."

Amylia nodded. Resting her hand on the mare's side, she did not trust herself to speak. The emotion crashing over her threatened to escape as tears pricked behind her eyelids. Cecily squeezed her hand before turning to her own horse. Gryffon moved to help her, clasping her hips, and throwing her effortlessly into the saddle.

Amylia climbed painfully onto Shadow, guiding her out behind Gryffon, and relief filled her as they took the road out of town towards the mountain looming in the distance.

She looked back once, towards the keep that had been home for eleven years. Smoke still wafted up in the distance, and she let the feeling of bitter anger surface, distracting her from the effort of keeping the churning power inside her. Her face set in determination as she nudged Shadow onwards to join the two riders ahead, towards Asteryn.

Chapter 12

They rode hard into the evening, stopping only to water the horses when they came across the small mountain streams. Keeping the coast to their left, they headed towards the giant mountain that loomed in front of them. It jutted proudly out from the coast, the Dead Forest curling around its base and across to the mountain range to the far east coast of the country.

Amylia noticed Cecily's worried glances at her leg as she rode; the blood had now seeped through the new dress, a dark stain on the rough material. She had slipped her bare feet from the stirrups, dangling them on Shadow's sides and stretching her legs out to ease the cramping muscles.

She had no idea where her shoes had gone. Probably burnt in that small stone room that was now a dark cavern of charred stone and smoke. She shuddered, thinking of the men left in there, their hands on her just a few hours ago so full of life, and now nothing but ash.

The soles of her feet ached from her frantic run across the courtyard, feeling small cuts break open as she flexed them.

Stretching her stiff back, she took a deep breath. Though still a fair distance away, the saltiness of the coast began to mix with the earthy odour of the forest.

The Dead Forest.

She shuddered again looking at it. Mortals didn't cross the forest. Beyond the Dead Forest were Sylvyn Lands. Asteryn, which the Wynters ruled over, was its capital, while smaller townships dotted over the craggy terrain.

Behind Asteryn were ancient mountains, snow-capped year-round, and home to the Sylkies.

Uninhabitable by humans, or Sylvyns. Gorgeous and wild, set on a peak of land surrounded by sea that crashed against the coast.

Shipkiller Coast, it was called. For good reason: no ship could get near the land there without risking wrecking on the jagged rocks.

The Dead Forest was a haven for vicious beasts, many she had never even seen. Such beasts could easily kill a group of mortals, even with weapons, if such a group survived the treacherous terrain that was especially bad in winter.

The river between the mountain pass was frozen over this time of year, giving travellers the choice of risking an ice crossing, or bypassing it. But that would mean going deep into the forest and skirting around it to the river's source, a huge, depthless lake near the forest's centre.

It would take nearly a week to navigate, following the coast and hugging the base of the mountain where the trees were less dense. The bypass would take weeks.

Amylia turned towards Gryffon, who was watching the sky. "Are we heading for the mountain?"

He looked at her, though he appeared distracted. "Yes, the trade party are barely a day ahead of us. We can catch them by tomorrow night. Lyrik has orders to do the ice crossing and then take the gap between Mount Ithicus," he gestured to the mountain on the coast, "and the Elixus ranges." His hand followed the range of tall mountains that trailed off into the distance.

"It's much safer travelling together, especially deeper in. It's not too bad in this first part," he added. "It's been a while since we risked the forest, especially as there have been so many Sabyre sightings on our side."

"How were you intending the return journey?" she asked, puzzled.

"We told Drakon we were meeting the Sylkies on the far side and flying the rest of the way. In fact, we intended to meet them this side. We wanted to avoid risking an ambush on them. Lyrik was concerned at how much interest Drakon was showing regarding them. And I tend to trust her gut." Gryffon paused, looking at her cautiously, before he added, "They are a weapon that I do not want to commit into his hands."

Cecily pulled up her grey mare next to Amylia, clucking to Shadow as she stamped irritably at the other mare.

"I think we need to rest the horses, Gryff. They have had enough for the day."

Gryffon nodded, eyeing Shadow. "Well… ours have. I'm still deciding if Shadow isn't some Druka crossbreed."

Amylia grinned at him. "I did say she had heart."

He huffed a laugh, holding his hands to his mouth and blowing into them to warm them. The mist from his breath curled out between his fingers as he blew. "There's a patch of trees up ahead next to that stream that I was aiming for, let's use them as cover for the night."

Cecily nodded in agreement, spurring on ahead in a slow lope.

They made camp and set up two tents quickly. Cecily wandered over as Amylia was tying the last bits of the light canvas to the sturdy branches that Gryffon had cleaved off a slender tree with a small, deadly looking axe.

"I packed you some clothes of mine." She smiled as she absently patted Shadow's massive shoulder. "We are roughly the same size. It might be a bit tight in the chest." She chuckled. "But they will be more comfortable than skirts. Those are much too big anyway. There are a few other bits in there, too." She pointed her chin towards a small bag strapped behind the saddle. "We can get you everything you need in Asteryn."

"I don't know how to thank you… either of you." Amylia dropped the bedroll she carried into the open tent and waved her hand at it. "For all of this. I have nothing, I don't even own the clothes on my back. I can't even repay you. Everything I have… everything I was… is back in that keep."

Cecily shrugged a delicate shoulder and shook her head. "That is not everything you are, sweetling. There is far more in this life just waiting for you to discover about yourself. But don't worry about that. Right now, I want to look at that leg."

Amylia glanced down at the stained fabric of her dress, stiff with blood and dirt, and cringed. "I think I'd like to wash first," she said, looking towards the icy stream.

Cecily snorted. "Are we going to add hypothermia to the things I need to fix?"

Amylia glanced at her, a blush creeping up her neck. "I'm filthy," she whispered, embarrassed.

"I'll grab a skin. Let's fill it with water and heat it. We can all use it to freshen up. Don't worry," Cecily soothed, leading the way to her tent.

She leaned into the opening and pulled out a folded leather object, flapping it out to reveal a large, dark, leather container. A slight shine showed it was watertight.

Cecily walked to the busy stream, dipping it into the flow and filling it before hauling it out of the water. Staggering slightly at the weight, she clambered back up the bank.

Gryffon snagged it off her with one hand, giving her a smile as he lifted it effortlessly over her head. Carrying it back to the camp, he chuckled at her mumbled retort to him. He hung the bag under a tripod of poles he had lashed together, putting an arm into the freezing water.

"Warm?" he asked Cecily, who nodded absently as she rummaged in another bag.

Amylia stared in fascination as Gryffon swirled his arm and the water started steaming.

"You're doing that?" She looked into the skin when he pulled his arm out.

He grinned. "I'm pretty sure you could, too. But it's probably best not to try with our only water skin."

"Gryff's an Elementyl," Cecily explained, passing Amylia a cloth. "Some Wytchlings can manipulate an element. Water is common. In Asteryn, we have a lot of Earth Wytchlings who can nurture plant life. Elementyls can harness all the elements, though are usually stronger in one or two."

She threw her own cloth into the bag and watched it sink below the water.

"I don't know how much you have been taught, so please don't take offence if you know this already."

Amylia shook her head. "My parents... They taught me... but I was young. I don't remember most of it and Rayvn will know nothing at all." She looked at Gryffon. "You have all the elements? Which do you prefer?"

He gave her a wicked smile and opened his hand, a small flame dancing on his palm. "Fire." He grinned as a miniature twister sucked the flame, shooting it upwards into a spiral. "And wind."

Snuffing it out, he shrugged nonchalantly. "I've been banned from using them in the castle, though."

Cecily huffed. "I got tired of replacing my bed." She gave him a fiendish grin.

Amylia felt the hot glow of a blush rise up her throat, throwing her own cloth into the skin.

The water felt glorious. Her skin, pink with the heat, rapidly cooled in the cold air as she wiped the blood and grime away. Taking the clean clothes to her tent, she slipped her skirts off, glancing briefly at the gash in her thigh before slipping an oversized shirt over her head that she guessed was intended for sleep.

It smelled like Gryffon, and the blush that had only just begun to fade came back fiercely, as she paused to press her nose to the collar.

Rummaging in the bag Cecily had packed, she found a brush, woman's monthly supplies, a spare breast band, and ties for her hair. Amylia glanced towards the flap of the tent, feeling a rush of appreciation as she dragged the brush through her hair, wincing at the snarls that tugged her scalp.

The shirt came down past her thighs. Still, she grabbed a blanket from the bed and wrapped it around her before she stepped back outside. Cecily, clean and warm in a similar shirt and loose pants, stood by the crackling fire wrapped in her cloak.

Her face glowed in the firelight, the tip of her silver ear glinting and hair pale against the frozen forest behind them. Amylia was struck by how beautiful she was.

She smiled when she noticed Amylia and nodded towards a log next to the fire. "Sit."

Amylia lowered herself, groaning as her thigh pulled. The wound opened and made her feel slightly queasy as the edges rubbed against each other.

Cecily grabbed the corner of the blanket and pushed it away, exposing Amylia's long, muscled leg with the deep, neat cut on her upper outer thigh.

She whistled softly as she looked at it. "I didn't realise how bad this was, or I would have stopped sooner." Scowling, Cecily cupped her hand gently over it and her eyes flared. "I hope he suffers for this."

"He's dead," Amylia said quietly, and Cecily stilled.

"Good," she murmured, forehead creasing as she reached with her free hand for Amylia's and grasped it, her grip warm and firm. "If you want to tell me what happened, I'm here."

Amylia's leg tingled as the skin knitted, drawing together slowly. "I tried… telling them I wanted to manage it myself," she whispered, staring at the hand that clasped hers. It gave hers a gentle squeeze. Her skin was so soft.

"Lord Drakon wouldn't listen to me. He drugged me." She looked at Cecily's face as her eyes filled with tears. "I woke up as that man…that physician was cutting into me. He… he was going to put the stone back in there. Drakon said it's for my own safety… that Attica killed my parents and were looking for me, too, and that binding me was the only way to hide me from them. But I wanted to just use the anklet… and he wouldn't listen… even Mica."

Amylia broke off, her breath catching as the words tumbled out, "I burnt them, Cecily. The two men holding me… and the physician… I killed them. I burnt everything; I was so angry."

She sobbed quietly. Cecily took her into her arms, crooning softly.

"It's okay, sweetling," she soothed. Her hand smoothed the hair away from Amylia's face. "It's over now, and you will be safe in Asteryn."

Amylia pulled away and wiped her eyes with the corner of her blanket, feeling ashamed.

Cecily grunted as she noticed Amylia's wrists and motioned for her to hold her arms out. Amylia studied the twin raw lines wrapping around her wrists where they had been tied. Cecily's face was stony with anger, at such odds with her beautiful, soft features. She turned them over to reveal a particularly deep cut where the buckle had sliced into Amylia's inner wrist.

Amylia heard a soft growl in the darkness behind them and turned as Gryffon stepped into the firelight, wiping a wet towel across the back of his neck.

He glared at her wrists, golden eyes glowing in the firelight. "They will not touch you again," he snarled quietly. "The Gods help them if they come to Asteryn."

They sat around the large fire Gryffon had made in front of the two tents. There were smaller ones around them, and the horses had been hobbled close, in case anything came prowling during the night.

Cecily leaned against Gryffon, warming her feet by the fire and humming softly as Amylia laid back, watching the stars, her head resting on her pack. The warmth of the fire seeped through her clothing. Her skin felt pleasantly hot. The power inside her moved in eddies as she slowly got used to the feeling.

It was a struggle to keep it in. She would have to put the anklet on to sleep, she mused.

"Tell me again what age you were when you were bound?" Gryffon asked, his voice hushed in the dark. She looked at him, surprised

"Uh… eight," she answered.

"So, you are nineteen now?" He raised an eyebrow in question.

Amylia nodded. "I turn twenty in… oh… next month."

Gryffon chuckled. "We will have to remember that. Rogue likes to make birthdays… obnoxiously big."

She grimaced.

Cecily chuckled softly. "Don't even try to stop it, Amylia. Any chance to throw a party with him."

Gryffon snorted. "I guess he is the youngest of us. When you are as old as us, birthdays pass faster."

Amylia eyed them dubiously. "No offence. But you both look barely older than me."

Cecily laughed. "I'll take that as a compliment then." She batted Gryffon's hand away as he tweaked her nose.

"I've seen a hundred and seventy-five years. Not as old as Gryff, though."

Gryffon huffed. "I'm not that old. Lyrik is the old woman."

The earth had stopped moving. Amylia felt lightheaded. The smiles faded on Cecily's and Gryffon's faces.

"Oh," Cecily said quietly, "I'm gathering that's something your parents hadn't told you?"

Amylia shook her head. "No, well... yes, I knew Sylvyns had a long life. I didn't realise quite how long."

Gryffon whistled softly. "Sylvyns have an extended lifespan. Many lifetimes in mortal years... but our children age alongside a mortal lifespan until about their twenty-fourth year."

Cecily chimed in. "For females it's about twenty-four. For males, a bit longer; they will slow at about twenty-seven, thirty. We tell age by our ears."

Gryffon pushed his silver hair back, showing the tips of his ears. They were slightly more pointed than Cecily's. "I'm two hundred and thirty-five," he said quietly, looking for her reaction.

Cecily sat up, moving her hair back to show hers, also tipped with a point.

Amylia stared at Gryffon. Two hundred and thirty-five? He barely looked a day over thirty. She touched her own ears. "Is that why mine are not like yours?"

Cecily nodded. "They will start shaping in a few years once your body settles. Though, Lyrik was telling us Helix nullifies Sylvyn power; those who wear it continually age as a human does. Not that it will affect you now, as it's been removed before you got to settling age."

Chilled by the knowledge, Amylia looked at the small bulge in her pocket where the stone nestled. Her brow furrowed. "But... you can die? My parents were Sylvyn. They died."

Pain flashed across Cecily's face. "Yes, we can die of old age, too. Though it takes a very, very long time. So long that we are considered immortal. We have a few ancient Sylvyns in our territory. We are young compared to them, but we can be killed." Gryffon looked at her, sadness in his eyes.

"Did you know my parents?" Amylia asked, her face pale.

Cecily shook her head. "No. We had heard a group of Sylvyns had taken over Oryx, but we never had a chance to find out who they were, or where they had come from. Lyrik headed a search party to go investigate after we heard of the deaths, but by the time she got there, there were nothing but graves. Mortals controlling the keep didn't know anything useful, so she returned. We... were grieving. Our court suffered some big losses from Attica. So, we stopped venturing past the Dead Forest... and we stopped population control on the Sabyres and Dyre wolves in here as a way of preventing anyone venturing our way." She looked at Amylia. "If we had known one of our own was out there, Amylia, we would have found you."

Amylia nodded slowly, letting it sink in. "Grieving?" she asked. "Did Attica attack you, too?"

Gryffon squeezed Cecily's knee as her face dropped.

"We had another in our court, a woman. She was our Third... the position Rogue holds now," he said, his eyes sad.

"Thirteen years ago, the raids from Attica were at their worst. We didn't know, but we had one of theirs infiltrate our territory. He fooled all of us. He thought the way to take us down was to break us, split us up. He knew Cecily was my weakness, and so he planned to murder her."

Cecily touched his hand. "I was out hunting with him and Callysta, and he shot me with an arrow. He shot Callysta, too, but she managed to kill him. Then her Sylkie got us both home."

Amylia inhaled sharply. Cecily said, "Callysta wouldn't let me heal her, not that I could if I had tried. I was so weak I couldn't heal myself... or the babe I carried and when I woke up... a long time later, I found I had lost them both."

Cecily pulled up her top to reveal a small scar on her abdomen, tracing a finger along it. Amylia looked on in sympathy, hand to her throat.

"Attica hoards healers; if you don't join them, you die. The queen does not want her enemies to be able to heal. There are none left in these lands anymore. Except me," Cecily said sadly. "Otherwise, they may have healed us. They would definitely have saved Callysta... and I wouldn't have been left unable to bear children. If I had the strength to heal myself, I could have repaired this... but natural healing." She looked down at her stomach. "Scars can be hindersome." Pain lanced across her face. "The queen does not take kindly to being denied — of me or the Sylkies that she wants as well."

Gryffon nodded. "We are too strong for them as we are currently, with the Sylkie riders and Rogue's warriors, but we know they are growing their forces faster than ours. Hence why I allied with Lylican." He looked at her. "Not that I'm confident that's on the table anymore." He gave her a lopsided grin. "And not that I regret that now. We will find other ways to stand against Attica."

They woke at dawn. Gryffon was turning a hare over the flames as Amylia emerged from her tent. Across the space, Cecily, too, stepped into the weak sunshine. Amylia hummed appreciatively as the delicious smell wafted to her and looked around for a bowl.

"Did you shoot it?" she asked, taking the juicy leg he handed her, fat gleaming on the sizzling meat.

He shook his head. Reaching into his shirt, he pulled out a lethal-looking little knife and handed it to her.

It was plain, no decoration at all. Its hilt made of dark polished wood, but its blade... Amylia marvelled. It shone in the sun, the razor-sharp edge glinting.

"Gryff prefers knives," Cecily said dryly, taking her breakfast from him and kissing him softly. "I'm the one that prefers the bow." She winked at Amylia who appreciatively eyed the roasting hare still turning over the fire.

Amylia held the knife out to him. "Could I learn?" she asked cautiously.

Gryffon took the knife back carefully. "You can learn anything you want," he answered, smiling. "But first, you need to learn your Gift."

He eyed the anklet she had tied around her leg again "Rogue is the best for that. Lyrik, too, has good knowledge in learning control, but anything else you want to learn... Knowledge is given freely in Asteryn."

They ate quickly and then packed, loading everything onto the horses behind the saddles, and smothered the fire properly, throwing dirt and snow over the charred ground to cover it.

Shadow was disconcertingly well-behaved as they rode in amicable silence, her head near Cecily's leg. The woman reached out now and then to pat her gently.

Gryffon, riding at the rear to look out for anyone trailing them, moved up next to Amylia. He followed her gaze to where Cecily's hand lay on the huge black neck, smoothing the mane, and shook his head.

"I've seen her calm a bull Sylkie with a broken wing that put two of Lyrik's riders in the infirmary moments before... and yet, I still cringe when your beast's teeth are that close to her."

"You just haven't learnt to love her yet." Amylia grinned at him.

"I'll take your word on that one." Gryffon snorted, handing her the waterskin he had just untied from his belt.

The day passed quickly. There had been a fresh layer of snow overnight, so the tracks from the trade group the previous day had been covered.

"They will have passed the river by now but there is only one way through from there skirting the base of Ithicus. Once we reach the river, we should catch them fast," Gryffon said, grunting as he pulled himself back into the saddle from where he had been searching the ground. He looked at the sky. "We have time to cross this afternoon and then we can try to catch up with them before dark. Lyrik will make camp early with lots of people to settle." He looked at Cecily. "What do you think?"

Cecily nodded. "From memory, the river can't be far ahead." She nodded to a tall, spindly tree reaching high above the others. "I remember that as we flew over it."

Gryffon pivoted in his saddle to look back at Amylia. "Are you okay to push on?"

She nodded. "I'm fine. Cecily healed everything last night. I can go as long as you need. Shadow will keep up easily."

"All right, then." He grinned and nudged his horse into a lope as the women fell in behind him.

Chapter 13

The river was far wider than she had thought.

The ice looked strong, but patches to the side of the bank had pooling water after sitting all day in the sun.

They all dismounted, moving up to the edge together. Gryffon passed his reins to Amylia then walked cautiously onto the ice, testing it.

"It's holding. This must be where the others crossed, too," he called, walking back to them, and taking his mare.

Gryffon took the lead, slowly guiding his chestnut mare across the frozen river. His feet slid along the surface, putting weight slowly onto it in a fluid motion, his Gift curled around his free hand as he went, reinforcing the ice with his own while the two women waited on the bank behind him, watching the slow progress.

"Spread out as you come. It's thick here, but it won't hold both horses together," he called back when he had reached the far side. He tied his mare to a large tree further up the bank and walked back to the edge.

Amylia looked at Cecily, who was whispering soothingly into her mare's ear and gave her a nervous smile. She stepped out onto the snow-covered ice. It held, and she let Shadow step cautiously onto it behind her. The whites of her eyes showed, and she huffed loudly at the unfamiliar surface as they both moved together slowly.

Shadow mimicked Amelia's steps, leaving a loop of lead between them as they went. Gryffon smiled encouragingly as they neared, one eye remaining on Cecily as she began her walk.

Amylia reached the bank with a sigh just as Gryffon jolted beside her. He sucked in a breath with a sharp hiss. A loud crack behind her had her whirling back to see Cecily frozen in place. Her anxious horse was too close to her, trying to keep contact with its mistress.

Another loud crack came as the ice gave way too fast even for Gryffon's Gift as he desperately threw it towards Cecily, trying to strengthen the ice under her. Cecily's horse lunged for the bank, hind feet smashing through the ice as it pushed off, sending Cecily plummeting into the dark water below, disappearing in seconds.

Gryffon launched himself towards the spot she had just been. A hoarse cry ripped from his throat as he skidded to the edge and plunged his arm into the water, feeling for her.

Amylia dropped Shadow's reins and raced after him, but Cecily's mare bolted past her, smashing into her shoulder, and sent Amylia sprawling across the ice before disappearing into the trees.

Shadow took off after Cecily's mare as Amylia hauled herself to her feet. Winded from the blow, she slipped and stumbled, running to Gryffon and the hole in the ice. She saw nothing; just black, icy water flowing under the ice.

Together, they ran downstream, desperately searching for any glimpse of her, any movement under the ice.

"Cess!" Gryffon yelled. There were broken things in his voice, his face bone-white as wisps of gold shimmered around his fists.

Amylia dropped to her knees, sweeping the snow off the ice with long strokes of her arm. She moved quickly across the surface as Gryffon started doing the same.

It was clearer here, but thick. She could just see the water running below. And there... a flash of colour!

"Here!" she screamed, panic flowing through her, as cold as the water beneath. "She's here!"

Gryffon lunged for her, eyes glowing bright as he smashed his fist into the ice. Nothing. It was so thick here.

Swearing loudly, he put both palms on the ice and sent a bolt of fiery power through it. Gold shot in a web across the surrounding ice. The whole expanse of ice trembled as it buckled under their feet, cracking around both of his flaming hands and beginning to melt.

This was taking too long. Cecily was running out of air. Amylia ripped the bracelet from her ankle and threw herself to the ice next to Gryffon as the rush started.

Putting her hands to the ice, uncertainty coursing through her, she grasped in panic for the power. She ripped a handful of it through her. Blue flames surged out of her, rippling across her arms as she pushed it towards that wall of ice.

Not enough. It wasn't enough. She reached back down to that burning mass and pulled. A tidal wave came up. She let it follow the flow already moving out towards that ice, towards Cecily.

Gryffon threw himself back when Amylia exploded. Heat erupted from her hands and the ice hissed and melted in a crater. Water ran away from her in rivulets.

"Stop!" Gryffon yelled. "That's enough, Amylia. You'll burn Cess, too."

She fell back. Gryffon threw himself into the crater. Pulling his arm back, he smashed through the now-thin ice to the freezing water beneath.

He plunged into it, water coming up to his chest, and waded across. Smashing the ice as he went, he reached with his other hand under the ice, feeling for Cecily.

Relief flooded his face. "I've got her!" he cried.

Amylia sobbed in relief and crawled to the edge as he hauled Cecily's limp body up into his arms.

White as a ghost, Cecily's lips had a blue tinge. Amylia reached for her. Pulling her out of Gryffon's arms and across the ice, she tugged Cecily to the bank where she collapsed, Cecily's weight on top of her, panting heavily.

A second later, Gryffon was there, dripping and shivering, kneeling in front of them.

"Cess, breathe." He cupped her face in his hands and shook her slightly, searching her face.

Cecily coughed and then wretched. Water bubbled up from her throat before she vomited it onto the ground. Gryffon gently held her wet hair away from her face, Amylia bracing her from behind and rubbing her back.

"Thank the Gods," he said and sighed.

Cecily took a ragged breath, coughing and retching. She started shivering violently as Gryffon murmured soothingly to her, his face set in lines of worry.

Between them, they got her up the bank and into a clump of dry grass under a tree. Gryffon grabbed his cloak off his saddle and threw it around both women.

"I need to get her out of these," he said, stiff fingers shaking with cold as he tried to undo the laces on her jacket.

"Go," Amylia gritted out, struggling to force the tendrils of gift back down. She put her hand on his and looked at him with concern. "You're wet through. Go change. I've got her."

She nudged him to the side, deft hands pulling Cecily's sodden jacket off. The shirt came next, dripping and freezing over her head. Cecily was barely responsive, stiffly trying to move her body to help but fumbling helplessly at the buttons and ties. The pants came off last, stubbornly clinging to her frozen legs.

Amylia yanked them off and quickly covered Cecily's naked body against the cold. She pulled her own jacket off and slipped in behind her. Gathering Cecily against her on her lap, she wrapped her arms around her, using her body heat to warm the frozen woman.

Cecily's wet hair soaked into the front of her shirt as she tucked the cloak tightly round them and started to shiver herself. Amylia could feel Cecily's breath on her neck where her cold cheek rested against her collarbone and her breaths were reassuringly steady, but her skin… her skin was as cold as ice.

She clenched her fists, letting a tendril of her gift curl into them, nestling like a small animal, alive in her palm. Focusing hard, terrified of losing control of it, she concentrated as a subtle heat started to fill the enclosed space.

Amylia glanced up when Gryffon came back. He had changed his pants and was pulling a dry shirt over his head as he dropped to his knees in front of them.

Eyes full of pain, he pulled the cloak back from Cecily's face and held a hand to her mouth.

He sagged in relief after a moment and reached up, brushing a hand against Amylia's cheek. "Thank you. You were incredible. Are you warm enough, too?"

Amylia nodded, tears welling in her eyes as she looked down at Cecily.

"Have you got control? Do you need your anklet?" he asked.

"I'm okay," she whispered. "I'm concentrating, and anyway, the anklet's on the ice, and no one is going back on there to get it."

He nodded, squeezing her shoulder gently. "I'm going to go put the tent up. We need to get her warm again. We can't move her like this."

Standing, he scanned the trees. Amylia followed his gaze but saw no sign of either Shadow or the grey mare who had carried the second set of tents and bedrolls.

While Gryffon worked, Amylia dozed lightly against Cecily. He set up the tent from his packs, lining it with the bedroll and blanket that had been on his mare, waiting patiently by the tree.

He roused her with a soft touch to the shoulder when he was done, unwrapping the cloak for her to crawl out before he lifted Cecily into his arms.

"Come," he said. "I've made a bed, and you need to get those clothes off, too. You're wet through the front of them."

Amylia looked down, cold prickling where Cecily's body had been moments before as the breeze chilled the wet fabric. Nodding mutely, she stood and stumbled after Gryffon as he disappeared into the tent.

She didn't have the energy to feel shy as she stood with her back to them pulling her top off. The wet fabric stuck to her skin. She turned slightly, holding an arm over her breasts, and dropped it by the entrance. Gryffon had turned his back to her, tucking Cecily into the bedroll.

Amylia grimaced as she unlaced her pants. The fabric was almost as hard to remove as Cecily's. She peeled them off and dropped them on top of the shirt before stepping over Cecily's huddled form. Lifting the blanket, she slipped in next to her, shivering hard. She curled her body around the woman and pulled her in close, her chest to Cecily's back and arm around her ribs. Cecily still felt too cold, and the underside of her breasts grazed Amelia's arm, frozen against the warmth of her skin. She listened to the sounds of Gryffon collecting wood for a fire and sighed as warmth slowly seeped in between them in their nest of blankets, letting herself drift into the darkness, her arms tightly wrapped around Cecily and her power locked firmly down deep, warming her core as she in turn warmed the cold woman.

The fire was crackling merrily outside when she opened her eyes again. It was dark, but she was warm... really warm. She stretched carefully, pulling back as her foot slipped from under the cover and into cool air.

Rolling slightly, she felt soft skin next to her, soft... warm skin under her arm, still draped over Cecily. She breathed a sigh of relief as the other woman stirred, too.

Her skin had regained its colour, though her lips were still pale and the silver tattoos across her cheekbones stood out starkly, glinting in the low light. Cecily lay on her back, face turned towards her as a lock of ashen hair fell over her face. As pale as she was, she looked ethereal, and Amylia fought the urge to brush the hair away from her face.

Steady breathing came from the far side of the tent. Amylia raised her head to see Gryffon asleep on the other side of Cecily. His arm lay over his face as he dozed. She rolled onto her back gingerly, careful not to wake either of them, and stretched her lower back, stiff from the hard ground, groaning slightly as her muscles protested.

Golden eyes cracked open, falling first on Cecily's face before flicking to Amylia. The worry in his eyes had gone, and he ran a hand over his face, looking at her apologetically. "It's snowing outside. I hope you don't mind?"

Amylia shook her head slightly, careful not to bump Cecily.

"Of course not," she whispered, smiling shyly at him. "Just don't get up and take the blanket with you."

He chuckled softly. "Deal. Go back to sleep. It's a long time until morning."

"Mmm," she murmured in agreement, then rolled over and nestled her back into Cecily.

Hoofbeats woke them a couple of hours later. Gryffon sat up with a start, earning a cry of protest from both Amylia and Cecily when the blanket wafted cold air down them. A whicker sounded in the darkness.

"Shadow." Amylia sighed in relief, sitting up carefully. Holding the blanket to her chest, she looked around for something to put on.

"I'll go," Gryffon said softly. "I'm already dressed. Yours are still drying." He disentangled himself from Cecily and crawled out of the tent. A blast of cold air billowed through the open flap as he went out, and she heard him suck in his breath at the temperature.

She listened to him padding towards his horse in the darkness, in the direction the hooves had come from, and murmuring to the horses as he did.

An irritable grunt from Shadow told her he had caught her, and he muttered a warning to the horse.

Cecily stretched next to her, and she stiffened, very aware of how naked she was. "I think it's a bit late for that," Cecily said hoarsely, amusement in her voice.

Heat flooded her face and Cecily's soft laughter turned into a wracking cough.

"How are you feeling?" Amylia asked, trying to pick out her outline in the shadows.

"Warm, tired, and my throat hurts," Cecily rasped back. "I feel like I threw up half the river, but I'm starting to heal. It's just slow because I'm weak. You're not wearing your stone?"

Amylia shook her head, then, realising Cecily couldn't see her, said, "No... I'm okay, I think. It's gone anyway."

She shifted slightly, trying to get her hip into a better position against the hard ground.

"It feels better without it. I don't feel empty."

An arm snaked across her stomach as Cecily turned her body towards her, leaning in to kiss her cheek lightly before resting her forehead on Amylia's shoulder. "Thank you, sweetling. I think you saved my life."

Amylia felt the blush roaring through her, and she swallowed hard as she clutched at the strands that threatened to escape again, stamping them into submission.

After a thump and the crackle of sparks as a log was thrown on the fire outside, Gryffon emerged back into the tent, rubbing his hands against the cold. The rush of air blew his scent into the tent with him, and it curled around the enclosed space, mixing with woodsmoke.

Gryffon's eyes softened when Cecily's turned toward him, his eyes glowing softly in the dark. "Please don't ever do that again," he said to her.

She snorted, nudging his knee with her foot.

He looked at Amylia. "Shadow's fine. She was herding Cecily's mare back here judging from the bite marks on the wretched beast's rump. I've tied them up under shelter together, and I've thrown the spare tent over the branches above them. They will be warm enough, and the fire will keep anything away from them."

Amylia sighed with relief, not realising how worried she had been about the mare. "Thank you," she murmured, adjusting the blanket across Cecily to give him some.

"I grabbed some clothes for you girls from your packs, too." She could hear his amusement as he threw some clothes over to her. "Not that I'm complaining about two gorgeous women naked in my tent."

She heard Cecily thump him gently, and the "Oof," as it connected with his stomach. "That's for calling it your tent." She laughed hoarsely. "You know it's mine."

The deep chuckle that rumbled through the enclosed space made warmth pool in Amylia's stomach. She was glad for the darkness, feeling heat creeping even further over her as she hurriedly pulled on the fresh top.

Chapter 14

Sleeping on the ground was far from ideal and Amylia groaned as she rolled over.

The sun shone into the tent through the open entrance, the smell of woodsmoke trailing in with it, and her stomach grumbled loudly. She heard a sleepy laugh coming from the mound of blankets next to her, and Cecily turned over, yawning, and stretching.

"I'm starving, too." She sat up slowly, kneading her knuckles into her lower back as she did, and peered out the entrance.

Gryffon's amused voice came from outside. "Are you ladies going to sleep all day, or are you going to come join me for breakfast?"

Amylia threw off the covers, startling Cecily with a whoop as she tripped out of the tent. She gasped when her bare feet hit the icy ground, snagging her socks hanging over a branch above the tent as sniggers at her hasty departure came from inside.

Gryffon held out a cup to her, grinning as she took it. He poured the steaming tea, and she curled her hands around it as the warmth radiated through the cup.

She sat and pulled on the socks and then draped her cloak around her shoulders while he hooked a pot from where it hung over the firepit and poured the contents into a bowl.

Rabbit stew. It smelled delicious, and she hummed in appreciation when he handed it to her. Balancing it on her lap, she pulled the small knife they had given her out of her belt and took turns spearing chunks of rabbit with it and sipping the broth.

Gryffon looked on with an expression of approval. "It's a novelty having another morning person around," he teased.

Cecily emerged from the tent, hair tousled. She eyed him sardonically and blinked in the morning light. "I think nearly dying excuses me from being chipper this morning, Gryff," she grumbled.

"And every other morning, my love?" He asked innocently.

The trees had stopped the snow from accumulating, so dry leaves crunched underfoot as Cecily walked over and picked up her boots by the fire, now dry. She yanked them on, glaring at him darkly.

Settling next to Amylia, she took the food, yawning widely.

Gryffon studied her. "Are you going to be okay to travel today?" he murmured, reaching out to rub her arm.

Nodding sleepily, Cecily took a deep sip of her tea and sighed.

"I'm just a bit tired from healing." She looked towards the river and shuddered. "It would be nice to get away from here, though."

Gryffon packed camp as the women finished their breakfast. Amylia rose to check Shadow and the other horses as she finished her tea. Shadow nuzzled the cup in her hand, huffing at the smell of peppermint and Amylia tipped the dregs into her palm, smiling as the mare licked it off with a rough tongue.

"I'm glad you didn't leave me, beastie," she whispered as a velvet nose bumped against her cheek.

Gryffon walked up, arms full of the rolled tent, and eyed Cecily's mare. "Shit," he swore, dumping the armload on the ground and bending to pick up her hoof.

Amylia peered over as he untied the mare and led her forward a few steps. The animal's lower leg was swollen. She heard him swear again. The horse moved freely but favoured her swollen leg.

"It looks like a sprain. She will be okay to carry the packs." He sighed. "But I'd prefer not to put a rider on her and Cecily is too weak to heal anything just yet."

He glanced at his mare. "We need to keep up the pace or Lyrik will get too far ahead, and we are getting into dangerous territory, but that mare isn't strong enough for my weight and Cess's in this terrain."

Gryffon cringed. "Would Shadow take a second rider? Both of you are probably lighter than one of me as it is."

Amylia nodded and patted Shadow's huge cheek. "She will be fine. We haven't done it before, but I'm sure she will manage."

Gryffon looked up at Amylia where she sat atop Shadow. "Ready?" he asked, looking concerned, and Cecily snorted.

"Stop being dramatic, Gryff. Shadow will be fine."

He eyed the back of Cecily's head darkly then gripped her by the waist and hoisted her up behind Amylia.

Shadow shifted her weight to her other foot, flicking one ear back in a delicate movement as Gryffon froze, arms slightly raised as if ready to catch them if the irritable mare exploded.

"See," Cecily laughed, patting the muscled rump. "She's a good girl."

Amylia echoed her laugh, seeing the doubt on his face as he mounted his own mare and grabbed the reins of the grey.

"At least go ahead," he grumbled, "so I can watch first-hand if she dumps you both."

Amylia nudged her forward, shaking her head and laughing as Cecily stuck her tongue out at him.

The air was brisk as they rode. The morning birds set up a chorus for them, several beautiful songs mingling with one another. Amylia looked up into the canopy of trees above, seeing small flashes of colour here and there.

Cecily's hands rested on Amylia's hips. The smooth bounce of Shadow's long gait made her bump gently into her as they rode. The feeling of the woman, pressed so close, stirred things inside Amylia, her mind sliding to memories of soft skin against hers in the darkness of the tent.

"There," Cecily murmured in her ear, reaching her arm around her to point at a low-hanging branch. An unassuming brown bird sat there, watching them suspiciously.

The only pretty thing about it was its long tail that curled out behind it. Then it opened its beak and a beautiful trilling song warbled out of it, echoed deeper in the forest by another.

"What is it?" Amylia asked, entranced.

"A lyrebird," Cecily whispered back. Her breath tickled Amylia's neck, and she shivered. "Are you cold?" Cecily asked, concern in her voice.

"Oh, just a little." Amylia flushed, glad the other woman couldn't see her face, and hoped her neck wasn't giving her away.

Cecily tugged at her cloak, wrapping the thick material around one side of her and crossing over the other side. Her arms snaked around Amylia's stomach and locked in front, holding the ends closed.

"Can you still use the reins?" she asked, peering over Amylia's shoulder.

"Mm-hmm," Amylia nodded, not trusting her voice as Cecily's breasts pushed against her back.

A soft chuckle sounded in her ear. "Did you know, you have a pulse, right here under your ear?" Cecily slid an arm out and traced a delicate finger down the side of Amylia's neck. "It's going rather fast," she teased, slipping the arm back around her.

Gryffon reined up next to them as the track widened slightly, raising a brow at Amylia's burning face that she could feel was fast spreading down her neck.

Amusement lacing his voice, he asked, "You girls okay?"

"Oh, yes." Cecily laughed, her voice filled with wicked mirth as Shadow lunged for him, ears flat to her skull.

Gryffon swore, flailing. He grabbed for the grey mare who had baulked backwards, almost yanking him out of the saddle.

"That was elegant." Cecily snorted as he sidled up next to them again, careful to keep out of Shadow's range.

"Shadow's not a massive fan of men." Amylia grimaced apologetically at him.

"You don't say," he muttered, face deadpan.

As the day passed, Cecily got stronger, dozing for intervals against Amylia's back. Amylia glanced at her over her shoulder, noticing her eyes had finally regained their unearthly shine.

Cecily returned the look. "They are beautiful," she murmured. "I've never seen anything like them. Even Gryffon's eyes are not as unique as yours."

The blush returned and Amylia looked away quickly.

"Does that mean there's something wrong with me?" she asked and felt Cecily shake her head.

"There is absolutely nothing wrong with you, sweetling. Though I think the faster you learn your Gift, the easier it's going to be for you. How are you coping with it at the moment?"

Amylia paused to consider before responding. "It's okay. It feels better without the stone. Not so hollow, but it's as if I'm always holding a cup of water that I'm trying not to spill."

"Gryffon had a hard time controlling his Gifts, too, especially in the early days of our relationship. It was a long time ago now, but he got there in the end. You have time and Asteryn is a safe place to do it." She laughed. "We are excellent at putting out fires now."

Amylia gave her a half-smile over her shoulder. "How long have you been together?"

Cecily sucked in a breath, looking up as she pondered. Finally, she said, "One hundred and thirty-two years this spring." She laughed softly as Amylia's jaw fell open. "It's not that long. We have an old couple in our town, they teach young Sylvyns the old ways. They have been together two hundred and seventy-seven years, and I do not dare ask how old they are." She smiled softly. "I only hope to be as happy that long. They still look at each other as if they have just met."

"How did you meet Gryffon?" Amylia asked.

Cecily sighed wistfully. "It was not long after he took over the rule of Asteryn, about thirty years before the Great War. He came to my parents' territory, Nymaria, which is south of Attica, looking for allies as the unrest in Labrynth toward the Attican rule was growing."

Warmth filled her voice. "I knew I wanted him as soon as I saw him, except my parents didn't approve." She snorted. "Lyrik and my older sister, Estelle, managed to get into a disagreement."

Gryffon laughed and interjected, "That's an understatement. Estelle and Lyrik beat each other senseless. We were lucky Nymaria was still full of healers."

Amylia stared at them. "What about?"

"I think it was because she said something along the lines of Wynters being not worth the dirt Castarions walked on," Gryffon replied, laughing darkly.

Cecily sighed. "You can imagine how well that went down. Lyrik ended up knocking out my sister… and my brother Wylder when he tried to join in, and neither of them are easy targets."

"Remind me not to piss off Lyrik." Amylia grimaced. She turned to look at Cecily. "So how did you end up marrying him, then?"

"Oh, I stole her." Gryffon laughed. "Consensually, I might add. Nymaria still hasn't forgiven me."

"My family come from a long line of healers," Cecily explained sadly. "My mother, Celeste, I miss, and my siblings. My father, however… he isn't a pleasant person. He allied with Attica many years ago for the Great War, after I had left. He was furious that I had chosen Gryff and Asteryn over Nymaria and evidently lost land because of it." Cecily's voice hardened slightly. "I was unaware that Father had promised me to a lord in the south of Nymaria, who was unhappy at the union being unfulfilled."

Amylia noticed the look of anger that passed over Gryffon's face, but it was gone as fast as it came, her attention dragging back to Cecily as the woman continued.

"My mother and sister, being healers, are highly prized by Queen Imogen," Cecily continued. "I haven't seen them in seventy-nine years, not since they visited Asteryn and asked me to leave Gryffon and go to Attica with them, it was then they found out Gryffon was my mate and Mother gave me her blessing."

The words held a note of finality to them, the grief still evident and Amylia bit back the questions that she was aching to ask. Mate. It was a term she had heard before. Not husband. Mate.

They paused next to the river, allowing the horses to drink and graze, as the sun hit its peak.

Gryffon disappeared to hunt some fresh meat and Cecily looked at her mare's leg.

"Are you strong enough to heal it?" Amylia asked, worried, as Cecily soothed the mare, wrapping small hands around its fetlock.

"I haven't got much, but I've got enough for this," she replied, face serious as she concentrated on the mare. "Our Gifts have a limit. It's different for each person and some have near depthless power. My mother, for instance, she has far more healing capability than I do. However, mine has steadily grown over the years and I may end up close to hers." She frowned and paused as she changed her grip slightly on the mare.

"How do you know your limit?" Amylia asked, watching in fascination as the swelling in the mare's leg went down before her eyes.

"Oh, our bodies tell us." Cecily smiled, looking up at her briefly. "Gryffon is forever upset at me for ignoring it until I've spent too much. And then I usually need to eat and rest while it renews. All Wytchlings are the same. They will drain and have to renew again and how long that takes depends on how much Gift you have and how much you have used."

She held her hands up, one above the other. "Imagine this is a container you are filling with water, and you need to fill it this much." She widened the gap. "Now imagine you need to fill it this much. It would take longer, yes?"

Amylia nodded, her brows creasing. "How do I know how much I have?"

"Your body won't let you give more than what it can. It will stop you before it starts taking from your life force. You will simply... pass out. Or your Gifts will just flicker out," Cecily said, standing up and patting the mare on the shoulder. "Unless you are a healer and can sacrifice."

"Can what?" Amylia looked alarmed.

"Sacrifice," Cecily said, her face slightly tighter. "Healers can choose to push past that limit... I have felt it a few times and it's terrifying to feel that wall there. But we can, if we choose, push through it... to that life force, and use it. It can make even the slightest of healers incredibly powerful. I've seen it done once." Her face was sad as her eyes unfocused in memory.

"A healer I knew from my homeland chose to save her mate who was beginning to pass over from his injuries. He couldn't be saved. Not even with numerous healers treating him… so she sacrificed. She gave her life force to him and passed on instead."

She looked at Amylia, still smiling sadly.

"I would have sacrificed for my babe had I been given the chance."

They sat, enjoying the sun warm against their skin, and listening to the steady ripping of grass as the horses found the new shoots that pushed through the melting snow.

Gryffon returned to camp, face tight. "I've found Lyrik's and Rogue's tracks. They are following a path just inland, and it looks like they're moving okay."

"Why do you look so worried, then?" Cecily asked, frowning.

Gryffon rummaged urgently in his pack, pulling out more of the lethal little knives and pushing them into his belt. "Because, they have a Sabyre tracking them."

They mounted up fast. Amylia, her hands shaking slightly, boosted Cecily onto her now-healed grey mare and then mounted Shadow.

Striding to Cecily, Gryffon handed her a long, curved bow which had been strapped behind her saddle and a small quiver of arrows. She slung the weapons over her shoulder. He then passed Amylia a wicked-looking blade, its black leather sheath plain, but an emerald sunk into its hilt glinted in the sunlight.

Taking it back, he strapped it to her calf. The hilt rested just under her knee.

"Stay close," he said, voice firm. "Do not stray off the path. Keep Shadow moving and keep an eye behind you. The Sabyre will hear us coming before we see it, but the horses will smell it. So, watch for what Shadow is looking at."

She nodded nervously and he squeezed her knee gently. "I won't let anything hurt you two, but don't forget, you have your Gifts. Try to warn us if you feel your control on them slipping so I can get Cess out the way."

He vaulted onto his mare, wheeling her into the trees. Cecily pushed after him, glancing back to make sure Amylia followed.

They located the path quickly, the tracks of the larger group easy to follow as they kept up an urgent pace, eyes tracking every movement around them.

The tracks grew fresher a couple hours later. All three horses' ears flicked wildly, their attention focused ahead. Suddenly, Cecily's mare threw her head up, letting out a piercing whinny. Cecily tried to hush her.

A whistle rang out across the trees and Gryffon heaved a sigh of relief, answering with the same whistle.

Heliacle Rising

They spurred up, remaining silent as the faint hooves of a lone rider came towards them in the distance. Shadow danced, eyes rolling as Rogue's bay gelding skidded to a halt in their group, and he grinned at them, bowing to Amylia from the saddle.

"I'm glad to see you with us, m'lady." He glanced at Gryffon. "And you two, of course."

Gryffon looked behind him up the road. "Are the rest of you okay?" he asked urgently.

Rogue nodded as his horse danced away from Shadow. "Lyrik's in a foul mood. Knocked a couple of heads on the first day, but they're all okay now."

He grinned at Amylia. "Your brother is a fine lad. I don't think I have ever seen Lyrik warm to anyone as fast."

She breathed a sigh of relief and smiled back at him.

Gryffon glanced around the trees behind them. "Let's get to the group. You have a Sabyre tracking you. We have followed its tracks on you for a few miles and if it's not caught up already, it's skirting us."

The grin vanished from Rogue's face, and he whistled through his teeth. "Well... it can join the line. We have a pack of Dyre wolves moving with us as well. We heard them last night, and they have been following us since. A couple of men at the rear have spotted them during the day and it's unsettled the horses badly."

Amylia caught Cecily's eye as they moved off. "I have to tell Rayvn about..." She waved her hand at herself. "And the men. They are Drakon's... I'm not sure how they will take it."

Cecily nodded, watching the group ahead as they approached. "It will be a shock, but it will be okay," she murmured, reaching over, and squeezing Amylia's hand.

The look of shock on Rayvn's face made her stomach flip as he saw her ride in with the Wynters. The murmuring of the men worsened it, but she avoided looking at them as she slid off Shadow, keeping her face to the mare.

Lyrik strolled up to her, her face set in a slight frown. "I'm glad to see you," she said softly. "Are you okay?"

She nodded, throwing a nervous glance in Rayvn's direction where he talked with Gryffon in a low voice. Lyrik followed her gaze.

"He's a good kid," she said quietly. "I haven't said anything, but it will be fine, I promise." Her gaze hardened as a man walked past sporting a black eye. "Some of these men, however, are debatable."

Rayvn looked at her, his face pale, but then he nodded to Gryffon, murmuring something before he turned and walked to her.

Amylia took a deep breath as Lyrik patted her shoulder in reassurance before heading back to Gryffon. "Don't go where we can't see you," she warned over her shoulder.

Rayvn approached her slowly, his eyes searching hers as his face paled even more.

"Milly?" he asked softly, a slight shake in his voice as he stopped an arm's length away from her. Her heart ached to see the confusion, disbelief… and fear on his face as he studied her. "Lord Wynter said you came with them after something happened at the castle. Are Mica and Lord Drakon okay?"

Her heart dropped and she looked at the floor.

"Yes, the last time I saw them they were fine," she said, her voice strained. "Rayvn… they are not who we thought they were. We need to talk."

Together they moved away to the edge of the clearing. In a low voice she told him everything that had happened, aware the surrounding men were throwing cautious looks at them.

Rayvn's face darkened as she told him about the physician, but he didn't say a word, letting her finish. Though his hands balled into fists.

After she had finished, she whispered, "Say something." The silence stretched between them, but he didn't look up. His eyes remained fixed firmly on Shadow's hooves.

"So… I… I'm one of them, too?" He rubbed a hand over his arm, where she knew a tiny scar puckered the skin in the crook of his elbow. She nodded slowly, watching him.

"Gryffon can take it out, like he did mine." She held her palm up, shielding it from the men with her body, then let a thread go. Rayvn's expression grew fascinated as the tiny blue flame curled there, illuminating his face.

Shadow shifted uncomfortably next to her, and she pulled it back quickly, the flame winking out.

"Oh, my Gods," Rayvn sighed. He dragged a hand through his hair and mussed his inky curls. Raising his eyes to her, he looked horrified for a moment then lurched forward, pulling her into a hug. "I'm so sorry that I left you to go through that alone," he said against her ear. His young, barely-there stubble scratched against her cheek.

"I will never let them hurt you again," he gritted out. She felt the muscles in his jaw tense.

Over his shoulder, her eyes met Cecily's. The other woman gave her a warm smile. Amylia snorted, pulling back as Shadow baulked, fidgeting against the reins. Absently, she put a soothing hand on the mare's shoulder.

"I'm older. I'm the one who's meant to be looking after you." She chuckled and Rayvn laughed, emotions roiling over his face as he met her eyes again.

"Mother and Father." He shook his head. "I wish I had known them."

Shadow pawed the ground, ears back as she flicked her head at the reins irritably, bumping into Amylia.

"Stop," she scolded as the mare backed up, dragging against her arm and unbalancing her. Amylia clucked irritably at her. "You are going to have to get used to my Gifts girl."

Rayvn stilled, looking back towards the camp, and watching Lyrik, who had unsheathed her sword and stood, an unearthly stillness to her. She was eyeing the string of horses tied to some trees who were fidgeting and pawing the ground as their ears flicked, searching the surrounding trees.

The stallion, tied slightly separate from the group, let out a high-pitched, challenging scream and pulled against his tether.

"Milly," Rayvn said, putting a hand on her arm. "Move back to th —"

"Amylia, Rayvn! Run!" Gryffon roared.

They spun around, towards the trees. A huge tawny shape leaped for them, and Amylia glimpsed wickedly curved fangs as the beast hurtled towards them, a snarl ripping from it. Shadow lunged, ears flat and teeth out, knocking Amylia back as she crashed past her, and horse and Sabyre collided in a snarl of claws and teeth. Rayvn grabbed Amylia around the waist and hauled her back.

"No!" Amylia screamed, struggling against Rayvn.

The gigantic cat fell back, hissing at Shadow. The mare screamed at it. Spinning, she lashed out with two powerful back legs and clipped the cat in the shoulder. It staggered back, then lunged. Its claws raked down the mare's flank, making Shadow grunt as flesh tore, blood spraying.

Chaos erupted behind them as the horses exploded in panic.

Rayvn glanced back over his shoulder, desperately clinging to his struggling sister. Three giant wolves prowled out of the trees on the far side, the noise and blood finally enticing them closer.

The men shouted as Rogue snarled at them to get together while Lyrik sprinted to the head of the chain of horses to face the massive Alpha stalking in. Grizzled grey, the beast had scars down his face which stretched as he snarled at the tiny woman.

A wrenching scream from Amylia made Rayvn look back to see Shadow, reared up as she lashed at the Sabyre desperately with her front legs.

The cat had sunk its teeth into her neck. Its front legs viciously clawed her shoulder, ripping deep slashes where they landed. Shadow fell heavily on her side with a heart-wrenching squeal, unbalanced by the weight.

Flames erupted from Amylia and Rayvn let her go with a curse. She lunged away from him towards her horse with a cry of rage, knife drawn.

The blade sank deep into the cat's neck, evoking a furious scream from the animal.

Amylia pulled out the knife and drove it in again. Flames rippled across her body and the cat's hair singed. The smell of it was harsh in the air, its skin blistering under her touch, but its fangs were still deep in Shadow's neck.

Gryffon wrenched Amylia away, throwing her behind him as he blasted the cat with an explosion of golden fire and wind. It finally let go, falling back with a snarl. Gryffon drew the long dagger from his back and crouched over Shadow, hefting the blade between his hands.

Lunging, Gryffon snarled as he slashed at the cat.

Hissing, the Sabyre backed away from Gryffon's golden flames licking the ground in front of it. With another hiss, it turned and ran, skirting the edge of the clearing and aiming for the direction it had come from.

A young Dyre wolf, considerably smaller than the rest and with an unusual white coat, was startled by the Sabyre. It jumped back from where it had been crouched in the long grass and staunchly held its ground, snarling as the cat prowled towards it.

They both attacked at the same time. The cat, already angry, grabbed the smaller beast's neck between its teeth as it shook the wolf like a rag doll.

There was a brief struggle, the Sabyre's claws raking the wolf before throwing it off to the side, the small body crashed against a tree before falling to the ground and going still. Blood bloomed from its side.

Gryffon lunged for Shadow, who still lay on the ground. Her sides heaved and blood ran from the ragged punctures in her neck.

"Amylia!" he said urgently, ripping his shirt off and wadding it into a ball.

She dropped next to him as he pushed the fabric against the mare's wounds.

"Hold this hard against the wound."

She did, sobbing. He grabbed his blade and ran after Rayvn who had drawn his weapon and headed for the wolf Lyrik struggled with.

Heliacle Rising

Cecily stood with her back to a large tree, bow drawn, and faced down a smaller female Dyre wolf that circled at the edge of the camp, eyeing the horses.

It turned its head towards Amylia and Shadow and began to move toward them, just as Cecily's arrow took it in the neck and dropped it. Her next arrow took down a small male leaping over the body of the first one. Straight through its gleaming eye.

Rogue's blade took down a third that had leaped for Cecily from the side.

She spun, arrow nocked. One eye stayed on Amylia, defenceless as she knelt over her mare. Gryffon landed a killing blow on a huge black female that had three men backed against a tree.

The wolves fell back.

Cecily flexed her shoulders, an arrow pulled back to her cheek as it followed the snarling Alpha that eyed Lyrik and Rayvn. It looked for an opening, head low.

Movement from the corner of her eye showed Lyrik, moving slightly to put herself in front of Rayvn just as the muscles in the huge wolf tensed to spring. She waited, letting it come closer, her focus fixed on the hulking animal. She wouldn't have time for a second shot. It sprang and she let the arrow fly, watching with satisfaction as the deadly tip lodged deep in its skull. Seconds later, Lyrik's blade found its heart, the remaining wolves scattering as the Alpha fell.

Sighing in relief, Lyrik ran to check the horses. Rogue followed her as the men gathered themselves.

"Is anyone hurt?" Cecily yelled across the camp, scanning the white faces as she dove into what was left of her Gift, helplessness clutching at her as she felt what little she had left.

Calls back confirmed no injuries and she sprinted the last distance to Amylia, skidding into the dirt next to her as she looked at the woman's shaking and blood-covered hands.

Shadow breathed shallowly, blood foaming from her nose, and she groaned softly with every exhale. Amylia sobbed quietly as blood pulsed slowly over her fingers.

"She saved me."

"Amylia, are you hurt?" Cecily asked urgently, her hand hovering over Shadow, and Amylia shook her head, staring at Shadow's neck.

Cecily glanced quickly over the other wounds, deep scratches, but not fatal. She pushed Amylia's hand aside, hissing at the spurt of blood and covering it quickly with her own hands, rallying herself. She poured everything she had left into the horse, feeling the torn artery knit together, the rush of blood under her hand slow and, finally, stop. Muscle knitted together, a chipped bone fused, and skin just started touching as she used the last of her Gift. She swayed dizzily, a slight ringing in her ears, and panted slightly as she looked at the horse.

Shadow was still in bad shape, but she would live.

She turned to Amylia and rested her forehead against her shoulder. Both of them leaning against the horse, listening to the mare's breathing, steady now, as she collected herself.

"Thank you," Amylia whispered, muffled against her hair. Her tears dripped onto Cecily's hand where it still lay against Shadow's neck.

Chapter 15

The group was subdued as they made camp. Lyrik and Gryffon decided Shadow and Cecily were still too weak to move.

Shadow had gotten to her feet but stood with her head hanging low as Rogue carefully smeared a poultice over the deep wounds in her flank and chest.

Weak from only just recovering herself, Cecily had pushed too far and fell into a deep sleep against a tree, Gryffon moving her to bed as soon as the tent was up. Amylia glanced at the tent, worrying for the woman.

"She is okay, just exhausted. She's done this before. She will be okay tomorrow after sleep and food." Gryffon smiled reassuringly.

Amylia nodded mutely, relief flooding her.

The men kept to themselves and collected a considerable pile of firewood. Though, Silas helped Rayvn and Lyrik pull the dead wolves away from the camp and skin them, hanging the five massive pelts to dry on a tree to be cured later.

The pelts were beautiful to look at, ranging from the black of the Alpha's mate, to the grizzled grey of the Alpha himself. Afterwards, the men stared into the flames as meat from the supplies roasted slowly.

Gryffon vanished into his tent with a plate of food for Cecily and didn't reappear. Low murmurs came from within as he roused her to eat, her soft objections met with his firm encouragement.

Amylia kept an eye on Shadow, who slept close to the fire. Her breathing was steady, though the occasional ripple of pain went across her skin followed by a low groan.

"Bravest horse I've ever seen," Rogue murmured approvingly. "Not much will take on a Sabyre."

"Mmmmm." Lyrik hummed in agreement and nudged Amylia with her shoulder. "She will be okay; Cess will heal her when she has the strength."

Amylia nodded, looking at her hands, and the emotion from the last few hours, the last few days, overcame her.

"Rogue, can you teach me how to..." She raised her hands in helplessness, searching for the words. "Be useful with this?"

He looked at her over his cup. "Of course I can... but I don't think you're useless. I think it's more I can teach you to harness what you have and focus it."

Amylia nodded, looking at Shadow again. "I want to be able to stop anything from hurting anyone I care about."

Rayvn padded over, putting a hand on Amylia's shoulder. "I've chucked my stuff in your tent. I don't want you to be alone tonight."

She looked up, giving her brother an affectionate smile. "Thanks, Rayvn. I would be fine, though."

He shook his head. "Not with Dyre wolves still around. Even with those pelts hanging, they still might come back."

She nodded sleepily, looked longingly at the tent and then back to Shadow. Her mare's velvet nose rested on the ground as she lay with her legs tucked up against her belly.

"Go to bed, Amylia," Rogue soothed. "Lyrik and I will be on watch through the night. We will keep an eye on her."

Amylia shot him a grateful look and took Rayvn's hand as he helped her up. She stumbled towards the tent as exhaustion washed over her.

Inside, they lay head-to-head as they had as children, talking quietly. She filled him in on all the missing parts of the last few days and felt sleep drifting quietly towards her.

"I'm sorry I let Drakon distance us," Amylia said quietly. "I've felt it for the last couple of years. I should have done something about it." She felt Rayvn shake his head.

"I did, too," he admitted quietly. "I felt like he didn't want us being close. He would almost get irritated when I wanted to spend time with you."

"I wish I knew why he did all of this," Amylia said. "I'm still so confused. You should have seen him, Ray, he was horrible."

Rayvn reached up, taking her hand. "I think he was trying to do the right thing, but in the wrong way," he said sadly.

They lay in silence, lost in their own thoughts.

"I'm almost scared to take the Helix out and see what I am," she heard Rayvn say softly into the darkness as she drifted away.

She woke before it was light, turning her head to see Rayvn still fast asleep.

Her bladder ached urgently, and she rolled carefully away from him, crawling slowly out of the tent so as not to wake him.

Lyrik dozed by the fire, wrapped in Rogue's cloak, head resting on his leg as he propped himself against a tree scanning the woods. He nodded to Amylia sleepily as she came towards the fire, warming her hands.

"Is it safe to, uh... nip behind a bush?" she asked quietly.

"I'll come, too," Cecily said softly, rustling out of her own tent and staggering slightly. Amylia crossed the space between them and grabbed her arm, steadying her, and Cecily gave her a grateful look. "I'm still a bit lightheaded."

"Just go behind that first bush," Rogue warned. "I'll keep an eye."

They made their way over to the edge of the camp. Amylia glanced nervously around while Cecily disappeared. Then she took her turn. She was just tying the drawstrings of her pants when she heard a faint whine carry across to her. She froze.

"Cecily," she whispered.

"I heard it, too," Cecily called back in a low voice, hurrying over to her.

Amylia steadied her with a hand as Cecily paused, blinking while her eyes focused.

A moment later, Lyrik was there, sword drawn, blinking sleepily and frowning.

"What is it?" she asked, voice gravelly from sleep.

"I heard a whine from over there," Amylia pointed to a small clump of trees. Lyrik edged forward, sword out towards the trees, then she sighed, relaxing slightly.

"It's a young one, looks like it was wounded badly. It must have been by the Sabyre."

"A white one?" Amylia asked. "I think I saw it take it on after it attacked Shadow. I thought it had gotten away afterwards."

They crept up to the animal which lay on its side, so small compared to the huge wolves they had skinned earlier. It whined softly, raising its leg, and trying to rise as it sensed them standing over it.

Lyrik raised her blade, tutting sadly. "Shall I end its suffering?" she asked, face impassive.

"Wait," Cecily answered, kneeling stiffly on the ground next to it.

"Careful," Lyrik warned, keeping her blade aimed at its heart even as Cecily reached out, ruffling the soft fur. It was no bigger than a large dog.

"Brave wee thing," she crooned sadly, running her hands over the animal's body. "Nothing is broken, but she has some puncture wounds on her neck, she's lost blood… and has a lot of ripped muscles," she said, patting her gently. "She's barely past a pup. Look." Cecily raised the wolf's lip, exposing sharp teeth. "Those are milk teeth." She sat back on her heels, eyeing the pup, and looked up at Lyrik. "She's just a baby… and she took on a Sabyre."

Lyrik ran her hand over her face, groaning and sheathed her sword. She looked resignedly at Amylia and sighed.

"That's Cess speak for she wants to save it." She whistled a two-tone note towards the fire. A moment later, Rogue made his way over, brows rising when he saw the prone animal.

"Can you carry it over to the fire?" Lyrik asked, taking Cecily's arm to help her back.

"Uh… What?" he asked, sounding incredulous. Lyrik flapped her hand in Cecily's direction.

"Lady Wynter has spoken."

Rogue snorted, looking down at the pup with raised brows. "Well… we have a fire-breathing horse, and you have a hoard of man-eating pigeons." He dodged as Lyrik aimed a kick at his ankle. "Why not add a deadly doggo to the mix?"

Cecily laughed weakly, leaning heavily on Lyrik.

Rogue eyed Amylia. "Want to grab the sharp end or the fluffy end?"

"Does it have a fluffy end?" she asked dubiously.

"Well… fluffier end." He pointed to the long tail.

It was deceptively heavy and protested as they tried to lift it in their arms. They abandoned that idea and shuffled it onto Amylia's cloak, lifting it like a stretcher. Trying not to jostle it too much, they carried it back to the camp. Its low whines of pain made Amylia's heart ache, and they laid it on the far side of the fire, away from Shadow, who flattened her ears at it across the flames.

"Glad you're feeling better, beastie." Cecily laughed, patting her gently as she inspected the gashes with approval. "Rogue patched you up pretty well."

Gryffon pushed the flaps of the tent aside, pausing when he saw the white wolf almost directly in front of his tent. He turned an accusing eye on Cecily. "Your doing?" he asked ironically. "You know, they tried to eat us, like… yesterday." He looked at Lyrik. "And I suppose you let her do this?"

Lyrik huffed. "I'll take it as a compliment that you think I have any chance of stopping her when her mind is made up."

Looking at the animal, Gryffon groaned and ran his hand over his face. "Cecily you're too weak to heal it yet. You need rest and it looks like it won't last the day."

She sighed, crossing to him. "Have faith, Gryff. She's strong. If she can hold on a bit longer, I can pull her through."

Amylia folded the edges of the cloak over the animal, wiping her hands on her pants as she joined them.

"What was it doing with a hunting party if it's a pup?" She looked at it skeptically. "If it really is a pup. That's bigger than my father's old hunting hounds already."

"The young ones usually get looked after in the dens by an older sibling," Lyrik answered, squatting back down by the fire, and holding her hands to the flames. "But it looked like that was the whole pack. We may have disturbed them as they were changing territories. Usually pups will hide, but that one was probably startled and got in the way."

"No," Gryff said, eyeing the pup with respect. "I saw her. She took on that Sabyre squarely. I didn't realise how small she was, though, until now, up close." He looked at Cecily tucked under his arm and laughed softly at her expression. "Okay, fine. But you have to promise me you won't try to heal it until you are strong enough... if it makes it."

Cecily nodded, resting her head against his shoulder.

The men were not impressed, protesting loudly at the wolf's presence as soon as they noticed it.

"You have to be fucking kidding me," a tall, dark-haired man yelled, glowering at Cecily.

Lyrik snarled, a hand on her sword. "Watch your tongue, the wolf's under Lady Wynter's protection."

He stared at her in disbelief. "And who's going to protect us when that thing gets up in the middle of the night and eats us?"

"Scared of a puppy, Jacob?" Rayvn chuckled, jabbing the man in the ribs.

Jacob shut his mouth with a snap and glared at the ground. "No, my lord. It's just absurd, taking one of those monsters in after what they did."

Silas grinned. "Ohhhhh, I think it's adorable!" He crouched, not getting too close to the wolf who watched him through a slitted, sapphire eye.

It snarled weakly and Silas fell backwards. A couple of the men laughed as he scrabbled away from it.

Amylia noticed Lyrik turning away to hide the smile on her face and grinned as Rayvn held an arm out to Silas and hauled him out of the dirt.

"How are we going to carry it?" she asked, watching the men pack the camp onto the horses.

"I'll strap it across my horse," Cecily said, brows furrowing as she looked at the prone animal. "She's the only one quiet enough to risk it." She nodded towards Shadow. "And she's too weak for a rider, so she will need to be led, too. We can both take one of the trade mares and lead them. I'll be strong enough tonight to try the rest of Shadow's neck and get those scratches started, at least the muscle."

Amylia nodded. "Thank you for helping her."

"Of course. If I had not used so much on myself, I'd have been able to fix her already," Cecily replied, looking fondly at the mare.

Travel was slow. The sun was out in full force, warming them as they neared the base of Mount Ithicus. The group was remarkably silent most of the day. Only a few of them chatted in low voices, nervously watching the forest for signs of anything sneaking up on them.

Lyrik led the group and the Lylican men filed behind her. Rogue was in the middle, leading the stallion, and Rayvn led the spare mare.

Cecily and Amylia moved slowly, the two big mares they rode amicable enough as they led the wounded animals next to them. Gryffon brought up the rear of the entire party.

Shadow plodded next to Amylia, her head low as they navigated the rough terrain. Her gait slowed towards the end of the day. Gryffon ambled up next to Amylia and once again they fell back, matching Shadow's pace. He looked at the mare, sympathy plain on his face.

"I'll call for Lyrik to stop for the night," he murmured. Amylia shot him a grateful smile and moved aside for him to push past.

Cecily circled her mare back. "Is she done for the day?"

Amylia nodded, patting Shadow on the neck. "She's struggling, Cess."

Cecily hid her smile at the nickname as Gryffon cantered back to them.

"The river bends around just ahead and there is a clearing. We will make camp there for the night. Good grazing for the horses, too."

Camp set up quickly, the men in a routine now as they erected the small tents and created a semicircle of fires surrounding them to protect the rear of the tents from predators.

Amylia let Shadow go to graze, but the mare ignored the lush grass to lie down instead, letting out a huge sigh and resting her head against the ground.

Cecily hurriedly got the wolf unstrapped and gave Rogue instructions where to put her before she rushed over to Shadow.

"It's the scratches on her flank," she said, forehead creasing. "I think they're starting an infection. Sabyre claws are brutal."

Cecily rested her hand over the deep wounds and shut her eyes, concentrating. Slowly, very slowly, the muscles underneath knitted, healer and horse sitting together a long while after Cecily's gift was once again, spent. Amylia helped her up as Shadow, immediately livelier, got to her feet and started grazing.

"Isn't this bad for you? Stretching yourself this far constantly?" she asked, concerned as she felt the woman shaking.

Cecily snorted. "You sound like Gryffon," she teased as they headed back to the tents.

As they approached, the wolf opened its eyes. The beautiful deep blue eyes had a startling human quality to them.

It didn't snarl when Cecily lowered herself next to it. Crooning softly, she stroked its head and picked up a cup of water, drizzling the contents into its mouth.

The first bit splashed onto the ground, but soon the white wolf let its thirst get the better of it, its pink tongue lapping out to catch the water as she poured.

The group around the fire that night chatted late, and Amylia stared into the flames as the warmth heated her face. Her stomach was comfortably full as she listened to the men tell stories from their training in Lylican.

Silas, it seemed, had a gift for storytelling, having the men — and Lyrik, she noticed with amusement — roaring with laughter. He regaled them with the many unfortunate incidents that had befallen him during this time.

Over the fire she caught sight of Gryffon leaning against a tree on the far side, a soft smile on his face as he watched her.

Her stomach flipped and heat rose up her neck as his smile turned wicked, watching her blush furiously. He was beautiful in the firelight. The golden light made his eyes dance as the flames flickered. She bit the inside of her lip, grateful for the distraction when Rayvn passed her a mug of tea and sat next to her.

Cecily sat with the wolf's huge head resting on her lap, feeding it small bits of meat ripped from her dinner. It took the pieces from her gently, eyes watching everything around it.

It rumbled a warning growl when Shadow, still loose, wandered up to sniff it.

She waved her hand at the mare, chuckling. "Away, beastie, you already have enough war wounds."

Rogue shook his head from where he sat on the far side of Cecily, the wolf's body between them. "Do you think it can go back once it's healed?" He reached out a hand to pat the thick fur, stopping when the wolf's lip curled back in a silent snarl. He held up the hand in surrender.

Cecily grinned down at the wolf, affection for it rising. "We can see. I'm not sure if it's too far from the pack now… but I won't stop her if she wants to."

He nodded. "Rayvn was asking me about Helix today," he murmured, and she turned her face to him, the fire warming her face as she waited for him to continue.

"How is he coping with it?" she asked, after the silence stretched.

Rogue shrugged. "He has a good head on his shoulders. I think he and Amylia have talked about what it's been like for her, and he wants to avoid looking weak in front of the men if he can't control whatever the Helix is binding. He was asking about ways to manage it."

She hummed approvingly, looking across to the young lord sitting next to his sister.

"They are both full of surprises," she breathed, noticing with amusement the blush creeping up Amylia's neck, and raising her brow in the direction of the cause of that blush, and giving him a wink.

Gryffon noticed her wink and grinned wolfishly back at her, his look telling her that sleep was not the first thing on his mind for the night.

Chapter 16

Amylia woke as first light crept through the sky. She crawled out of her tent to muffled curses as she accidentally kneed Rayvn in the stomach, giggling softly as he pinched her calf in outrage. She scurried out the rest of the way, stretching as she scanned around for Shadow, left free to roam the camp, unlike the rest of the horses, and faltered.

Shadow stood close to the Wynters' tent, the white wolf curled asleep between her front legs as she watched over it. She yawned widely, shaking her mane, as Amylia approached cautiously and the wolf cracked open a sapphire blue eye at her.

It was still very weak, unable to lift itself to an upright position, but clearly more in control of itself.

"Made a friend, have we?" Amylia murmured in amusement to the mare, who flicked an ear in her direction. "Figures that you pick an animal with the same fierce soul as your own." She snorted and patted the velvet nose as it huffed against her shoulder, keeping an eye on the wolf so close to her ankles.

"She's been standing over it all night. I've led her away a few times, and she just comes right back," Rogue said dryly as he emerged from the trees behind the tents.

Amylia shook her head at the mare, rolling her eyes as Lyrik appeared at her elbow.

"I'm headed to the river to wash if you want to come? Cess is still asleep so I will leave her be," she murmured, throwing a towel to her.

Rayvn looked up as Lyrik and his sister returned, their hair still damp from the river. He and Cecily were seated next to the fire and Gryffon heated his blade with a small golden flame that curled in his palm.

"We were waiting for you," he said, taut with anxiety. "I want to get this done while the men are asleep."

Amylia sat next to him, and he felt her concern when she put an arm around his shoulders. "It's going to be fine, Ray. If I can do this, you definitely can."

Gryffon approached them, waving the knife to cool it, and squatted in front of Rayvn. "We can wait longer, if you're not ready," he said gently. "We didn't know what it was with your sister, but we're more prepared for you."

Rayvn shook his head. "No, just get it out. I need to know what I am."

Gryffon nodded, giving him a small smile, and took his arm. Cecily ran her finger over the scar, grimacing then pointing towards the edge of it.

Amylia grabbed Rayvn's free hand and squeezed it as Gryffon placed the tip of the blade against where Cecily had pointed, pausing to wait for Rayvn's nod.

He cut quickly into the small scar, and metal grated on stone as the blade met the Helix, making Rayvn's stomach clench as he hissed out a breath.

Gryffon flipped the blade over, quickly flicking it back through the cut, dislodging the small stone. It fell to the dirt by Rayvn's feet and rolled slightly, ignored as they all stared at him.

Rayvn closed his eyes, his head spinning slightly as Cecily's warm hand took his wrist. Then the pain of the cut dissipated suddenly, and he heard a small intake of breath from her. He felt the rushing Amylia had described and braced, waiting for the burning heat. It wasn't heat that enveloped him, but instead a cool wave washed through him, creeping though his veins. It curled around his senses, as if a cool towel had been placed over feverish skin, and relief flooded him. This was okay. He relaxed slightly, feeling Amylia's hand crushing his, and opened his eyes, smiling at her in relief.

Her gaze burned into him, searching, and he watched from the reflection of her eyes as his own started to glow in that eerily backlit way.

"How are you feeling?" Cecily asked.

"It's okay," Rayvn breathed. "It's not hot. It's cooling. It feels okay." He looked at Cecily, and she smiled at him, relief sweeping over her features.

"That's good," Gryffon said. He carefully picked up the stone on the end of the knife, balancing it, holding it for Rayvn to look at. It was slightly oval and about half the size Amylia's had been.

"That's it?" Rayvn snorted. "That tiny thing changed me completely?"

Gryffon wrapped it in a bit of cloth and handed it to him. "Lyrik can make a bracelet with it if you need one, but it looks like you have control fine," he said cautiously.

Rayvn relaxed. "I can't describe it. It feels like I've just had a vital part of me returned, that I didn't even know was missing. I feel... whole." He smiled widely. "Thank you!" he breathed.

He turned to Amylia. "It's okay. Really. I can feel it, but it's not overwhelming."

She grinned at him. "Can you pull it up? Like I explained?"

Rayvn held a palm out, reaching down and pulling on a thread like Amylia had described. It was gentle, almost sleepy, as he coaxed it out into his palm. He looked in wonder as a delicate latticework of frost coated his palm, cooling the skin there. He raised his eyes to hers and grinned.

"Well... it makes sense that with fire comes ice." Cecily smiled. "But," she held up his unblemished arm, the cut healed now without a trace, "I didn't heal that, Rayvn. You have healers in your line it seems."

Amylia's mouth fell open as she looked at her brother. "You're a healer?" she gasped. "Like Cecily?"

Gryffon chuckled. "With the company we keep, I think the Gods have finally decided to sympathise with me and sent me another healer to help keep you lot alive." He patted Rayvn on the shoulder. Rayvn felt a wide smile cross his face and exhilaration curled in his stomach.

"How did you end up with a mare like that?" Gryffon chuckled to Amylia as they came out of Mount Ithicus's shadow five days later, they had passed through the mountain valley, the Elixus ranges now stretching out to their right as they moved into easier ground.

Cecily had healed the animals as her strength had allowed, leaving the lighter scratches that criss-crossed the mare's chest, as they had already scabbed over. The mare had returned to her normal self and had started harassing Amylia's substitute mount, angrily nipping at her rump from where she was being led. Amylia, resigned, had started to ride her again, bareback so as not to irritate any lingering tender patches, which had seemed to mollify the cantankerous beast.

Gryffon had been subtly watching Amylia all day, admiring how her long, lean legs curved around the considerable back of the mare as the party rode in amicable silence, beginning to tire after days of travel.

She had the hood of her cloak thrown back and the cool air had turned her cheeks rosy. Skin tanning subtly from the days of being out in the sun, her long hair slightly curled around her face as it escaped from its loose braid.

She grinned back at him. "Shadow was my secret. I used to go down to the stables in my spare time, which in truth, was a lot. One day, there she was. A spindly-legged black foal, all anger and fuzz."

Gryffon snorted, eyeing the huge black mare in disbelief.

"Her mother had died and there was no foster mare available, so I bottle-fed her… and then she grew." Amylia laughed. "And didn't stop growing for a long time. She had a temper on her, right from the beginning. The grooms were happy for me to deal with her… and it just got worse from there." She grinned, patting Shadow's sturdy neck.

"The stable terror. Once she reached three, one of them tried breaking her to saddle, and she broke his leg. She gave the next one concussion, and the third." She grimaced. "He quit the same day."

Gryffon laughed quietly. "So… who ended up breaking her?"

"I did," she said quietly. "Though it was less breaking, and more learning to accept each other."

Gryffon glanced at her again in surprise, admiration growing, and saw her eyes soften as the mare's ears flicked backwards to her voice. Amylia looked at him and laughed. "I'm not any outstanding horse trainer. I couldn't do it with any other, but Shadow trusted me. One day I got on her back and off we went. That is, off we went very, very fast."

She giggled as he doubled over in laughter, imagining a dark-haired young Amylia clinging to the back of a bolting Shadow.

"How old is she now?" Cecily asked, moving in next to Amylia. Gryffon saw her eyes scanned the trees as they rode, concern for the wolf who had vanished after breakfast playing across her face. The wolf had gained strength with her healing and good food and was no longer content to be strapped to the mare. It followed the group at a distance, slinking into camp as they settled for the night, seeking out Cecily's tent and sleeping in the entrance.

"Almost six," Amylia replied. "We share the same birthday… so, it's easy to remember."

They crested the last small hill on the far side of Mount Ithicus as the sun began its descent, giving them an unhindered view across the beautiful landscape. In the far distance, other mountains jutted up, just visible against the darkening sky. Below them, the forest thinned, leading to craggy countryside with the coast stretching off to their left.

Lyrik nudged her mount up next to Amylia. "That's the Eclypse mountains you can see in the distance." She pointed in front of them. "Home of the Sylkies. Asteryn sits at its base, on the coast." She swept her hand across the expanse in front of them. "Everything from the Dead Forest onwards is the territory of Asteryn."

"How long does it take to get across this part?" Amylia asked, judging the distance in front of her.

"It's deceptive," Lyrik answered. The men pooled around them as they crested the hill. She motioned for Rogue to lead the way. "About four days ride. Five, possibly. But we have been making good time."

"Welcome home, Amylia," Gryffon murmured, coming up on her other side. "It's yours as long as you want it."

She stared ahead at the beautiful landscape ahead, a lump in her throat as she felt the tension of the last few days slip away. *Home... could this become home? A real home?*

The camp that night was festive. A few men, relieved at getting away from the dangers of the forest, hauled in fresh fish for their dinner and roasted them over the fire, the skins gloriously crispy over the tender white meat.

Cecily breathed a sigh of relief as a white speck detached itself from the edge of the forest at dusk and made its way towards them. She slipped a bit of fish into a bowl, pushing it aside.

Gryffon's eyes softened as he rubbed her neck, fingers playing with the fine hairs there. Cecily moaned when his fingers dug into her stiff muscles. The sound sent shivers down Amylia's spine, and she couldn't help but glance over, meeting Cecily's eyes.

"Looking forward to a bath?" Cecily asked, grinning.

Lyrik groaned and dropped next to Amylia on the log where she sat. "Gods, I am." She glared in disgust at her leathers. "These are not made for long travel. I tell myself this every time."

Rogue hummed in agreement from where he sat feeding small sticks into the flames. "Yep, we hear it every time, too."

Gryffon laughed as Lyrik threw Rogue a filthy look. "I've heard your share of whining recently, too, Rogue," she quipped.

Rogue ignored her and turned to Amylia. "Have they told you about the pools yet?" he asked.

He shot Cecily a look of mock outrage when Amylia shook her head.

"The castle sits on thermal land. It keeps it at a good temperature inside, but the real treasure is below." He grinned. "There are a few caverns down there that have hot pools flowing through them. A lot of my men visit them after training. It helps to loosen muscle," he said, whispering loudly behind his hand.

"I should warn you… he tries to get all the women down there to impress them," Lyrik said dryly, grinning at Rogue. "Though I'm not convinced it works well for him. Does it?"

Amylia looked at the tall man. He was staggeringly handsome, with the firelight flickering off his strong jaw, and the muscles in his shoulders flexing as he moved.

He met Lyrik's eyes, not looking the least bit ashamed and shrugged. "Well… I need some sort of edge, otherwise, I'd never have a chance with you around, Lyrik," he teased. "Especially as you tell them all that your sword is bigger."

Gryffon roared with laughter as Lyrik pulled a rude gesture at him, laughing herself. The men off to the far side of the fire, who had been chatting amicably, threw curious glances their way.

Amylia felt herself going red and glanced at Rayvn, to see her brother grinning along with them. Cecily quietly detached herself from Gryffon and got up, picking up the bowl of fish and moving towards the shadows on the outskirts. Two sapphire eyes glowed in the firelight, watching her approach. Cecily murmured quietly to the beast before dragging a blanket out of her tent and laying it by the entrance. Amylia watched her walk back, empty bowl in hand, the firelight kissing her face and her eyes glowing softly in the light. It took her breath away. She wrenched her eyes away, aware she was staring, and realised Gryffon had been watching her. She felt her face heat with embarrassment when he gave her a knowing smile.

Four days later they arrived on the outskirts of Asteryn, a bustling hive of activity.

Beautiful stone cottages peppered rambling streets lined with evergreen trees.

Winter was milder this far up the country and children played in the streets, gathering, and waving as their procession passed. Cecily smiled and waved at them. A few children called out welcome to her as she passed, then shrank back when they noticed the wolf stalking close to Shadow's feet, between Amylia and Cecily.

Gryffon sidled up next to Amylia, blocking the children from getting too close to Shadow.

Heliacle Rising

Amylia watched him subtly. He smiled fiendishly at a young boy who trotted up to him. He bent low in the saddle, reached down, and grabbed the boy by the scruff of the shirt, hauling him into the saddle in front of him.

"Does your grandfather know where you are, young rascal?" he teased, handing his reins to him.

The boy nodded fiercely, and his red curls flopped around his head.

"Mamma said I could play with my friends until dinner and then come home, but I came down on Chunky and he ran back home while I was playing," he protested.

Gryffon snorted. "Well, lucky for you, we are passing through and you can get a lift. Chunky will be back at the stables eating his oats by now. It's getting a tad late, Olly."

The boy grinned happily and leaned his head back against Gryffon's chest, sticking his thumb in his mouth and eyeing Amylia with huge green eyes.

He pulled his thumb out with a 'pop'. "Who's you?" he asked bluntly.

Gryffon laughed softly, nudging the boy. "Manners, boy. This is Lady Amylia Sylvers, a friend of mine and Lady Wynter's."

The boy nodded, sticking his hand out to her, his wet thumb glistening in the sunlight. "I'm Olly," he said. "Pleased to make your qu'waintance."

Amylia laughed, leaning over to take his hand. He kissed it with a resounding 'smack' as Gryffon chuckled again. "Much better," he said approvingly, patting the boy on his curls.

They skirted around the main part of the city, taking the short, coastal edge of it, and made their way up the final stretch to the castle. Amylia stared at it as they rode in the gates. The full magnificence of it was made greater by the dusk light rosily tinting the rock walls.

Cecily sighed as she pulled up next to Amylia and dismounted.

"It's good to be home," she murmured, reaching up to take the boy who had been sleepily dozing the last stretch of the ride on Gryffon's lap. Setting him on his feet, she patted his backside. "Straight to mama," she called as he scurried off. "I'll check, mind."

A tall, older Sylvyn with dark auburn hair hurried out to meet them, a group of younger men following him. The man skidded to a halt, throwing an arm out to stop the man nearest to him, a look of awe coming across his face.

"Sweet mother of a god, she's the most beautiful thing I've ever seen!" he cried gazing in Amylia's direction as she dismounted. Amylia froze, horrified.

Cecily nudged her gently with an elbow. "He means Shadow." She sniggered and put a soothing hand on the head of the wolf, who had shrunk against her and growled at the noise.

The man strode over. "Oh, princess, look at you. You glorious creature!"

Shadow flattened her ears at him, stamping her foot in irritation at the attention.

"Oh, and she's spicy!" he exclaimed, throwing his hands in the air. "Oh… I'm in love. And look at the ass on her!" He clutched at his heart.

Gryffon laughed softly as he dismounted, winking at Amylia.

Cecily laughed openly now and smiled warmly at the man.

"It's good to see you, Grymes. I have just sent your grandson back to his mother. We found him on our way in."

Grymes touched his heart, bowing to her. "You're too kind m'lady. The wee imp turns up all over the show, never stays where I put hi — Oh! Oh, sweet mother above!" He interrupted himself, his hands flying to his mouth. "What are those?"

Gryffon strolled to him and put an arm around his shoulder, watching the small band of men who were just entering the courtyard.

Rogue led the trade stallion who pranced next to him, excited at all the noise, his neck arched proudly.

Rayvn came up behind on his war-horse, leading two of the mares who were putting on their own show.

"Those," Gryffon grinned, "are the new breeding herd that are part of our new alliance. Except the black mare. She belongs to Lady Sylvers."

Grymes fanned himself with his hand, tears in his eyes as he flitted to each horse, welcoming them individually.

"Grymes really loves his horses," Cecily whispered to Amylia, looking at the man fondly. "The only reason Gryff took the horses was because he knew how happy it would make him."

Amylia looked at Gryffon, his eyes soft as he watched the man and felt her heart melt a little bit, which rapidly changed to alarm when Grymes charged back towards her.

"Lady Sylvers." He bowed to her. "It would be my honour to look after your wee darlin', here."

Hearing Rogue and Lyrik snort in unison as they reined up, she shot them both a dark look before turning back to the man and smiling at him.

"Shadow is a tad difficult," she explained hesitantly.

"Oh, that is no issue!" he cried, taking her reins. "Nothing a good feed of oats and some apples won't fix. Come on, wee darlin'. Let's go find you a nice cosy stall and lots of hay."

She watched in alarm as Shadow trailed after him, ears flat and eyeing up his arm. His voice trailed off into the distance as he animatedly told the horse about her new home, the feeding regimen, and making her all kinds of promises. The rest of the stable staff followed behind, leading away the other trade horses.

Cecily chuckled, watching Amylia's face. "Welcome to Asteryn. Come, Rogue will get the men and Rayvn settled. I'll show you to your rooms."

Amylia picked up her bag, throwing a last look towards the stables before she sighed. With a small smile, she followed Cecily towards the entrance as the wolf trailed behind.

The castle was stunningly beautiful. Sitting nestled on the edge of the coast, with the Eclipse mountains at its back, it looked out to sea. The coast was shaped so that it gave the castle its own private cove. The simple gardens ended in steps down to the white sand beach.

As they entered the castle, Amylia looked up to see crystal chandeliers hung in the entrance and winding stairs lined both sides of the entrance hall, branching off to separate wings.

Tapestries in the Asteryn colours of forest green and silver hung from the walls and massive fireplaces had been constructed in each room. Cecily gave her a quick tour, pointing down to the lower-level kitchen and staff quarters before taking one of the staircases.

"There's a guest wing to the left side, but we don't tend to use it. The best views are this side." She smiled. "I'll put you on Lyrik's and Rogue's level. Gryffon and I are the last level just above. But one of the perks of this side is that it has direct access down to the pools."

She pushed open a solid wooden door and poked her head into the room. "Here you are."

Stepping aside, she let Amylia walk in first. She paused in astonishment at the sight of the lavish room. A huge, four poster bed sat against the far left wall, covered in thick quilts that begged her to lie on them. A beautiful antique desk, ornate carvings decorating it, sat in an alcove to her right. A chest and armoire stretched along the wall either side of it.

In front of her, though, louvred windows stretched floor to ceiling and opened up a large section of the wall to the sea views beyond. A huge, deep bath, big enough for two, squatted in front of it.

Her jaw dropped as she looked around. "It's beautiful," she murmured.

Cecily grinned. "I'm glad you like it," she said. "I'll ask some maids to bring up some clothes for you. And anything else you need, please, just ask."

She turned to go, but Amylia stopped her with a hand on her arm.

"Cecily… I'll repay you for this as soon as I can."

Cecily shook her head. "Nonsense. Please, just enjoy it, that's all I ask."

She paused in the doorway and Amylia noticed for the first time how tired she looked. "We always eat together here, dinner at least. We try for breakfast, too. I know it's not… usual, but we enjoy doing it. I'll get Lyrik to pop her head in and let you know when she's headed down?"

Amylia nodded her thanks as Cecily took her leave.

Chapter 17

Amylia looked out on the beautiful sunset over the Asteryn coast. Standing in front of the tall windows, she watched the sun recede below the horizon.

Hearing Lyrik's soft knock at the door, she padded over to it, enjoying the feel of the new white shirt and loosely fitted pants that hung at her hips, comfortable and soft against her skin. She opened the door to Lyrik wearing similar attire, looking clean and relaxed. Still-damp hair fell in waves around her shoulders.

"Hungry?" she asked, looking over Amylia with an approving eye.

"Famished." Amylia said enthusiastically as she followed the woman out into the hall.

They wandered down past the doors, pausing only for Lyrik to pound brutally on Rogue's door, yelling at him to bring Rayvn. Her words were met with a muffled expletive from inside which she answered with another wood shuddering thump.

She found the dining hall elegantly furnished. Comfortable chairs were placed around an impressive fireplace. A thick rug stretched between them and along the far wall stood a solid dining table, already filling with food.

Cecily dozed in front of the fire, stretched out on one of the long, padded benches, her pale hair splayed over Gryffon's lap as he read, a book casually balanced in one hand as his other ran a finger idly up the bridge of her nose, as if soothing a child.

The white wolf lay on the ground under her seat, its head resting on Gryffon's foot.

Cecily wore a loose, cream dress, the deep slits up the sides allowing her legs to show as they curled underneath it and Amylia's eyes drifted to them, admiring the lean lengths of them.

Gryffon glanced up, catching Amylia's eye and he smiled softly at her as Rayvn and Rogue emerged in the hall laughing quietly between themselves.

He shook Cecily gently, and she hummed at him, sitting up and stretching.

She smiled at the wolf, ruffling the white fur on her head as she got up, padding to the table barefoot to pick up a small, cooked bird and hand it to the animal who took it gingerly and slunk off into the shadows of a corner to eat.

Rogue eyed the beast. "Have you got a name for the wolf? Or do we just call it 'murder fluff' for the rest of its life?"

Cecily smiled at the shadows where wet crunching sounds could be heard. "I've called her Athyna."

Rogue chuckled. "Such a pretty name for such a deadly creature," he said, ducking as Cecily swatted him good naturedly as she passed.

Everyone sat, in no particular order, helping themselves to the steaming dishes in front of them in amicable silence, the hall filling with the sounds of clinking cutlery on plates and bowls.

It was incredible food. Amylia marvelled over the delicately spiced fish, stuffed quails, roasted root vegetables, and an abundance of leafy greens.

"How do you get these to grow this time of year?" she asked, picking up a lush green leaf and waving it gently.

"Our people figured out how to harness the natural thermal vents into glass houses. It keeps the air warm all year round and our produce grows in abundance," Rogue said, offering her a bowl of steamed broccoli dripping with garlic and butter.

This was the first proper meal they had had in weeks, and Amylia ate until her sides ached. Rogue and Rayvn fell into conversation about the men, Lyrik chiming in occasionally.

"I have a few of my generals setting them up in the soldier's barracks," Rogue explained. "They will be most comfortable there and can get to the roosts easily. I would bunk them with Lyrik's troops... however, most of them are female." He chuckled as Rayvn looked surprised.

"Not all of them," Lyrik interjected. "It just happens that way. But the male Sylkie riders tend to go to the warrior barracks and the female warriors tend to come to the Sylkie keep. Unless they are mated. Then they get couples' lodgings. Or move into town."

"I'll go check on the men at breakfast," Rayvn said, eyes bright. He looked excited to get into it the following day. "When do you want us to be ready?"

Lyrik laughed. "We start early. Sylkies like to sleep in the heat of the afternoon, so we train early, clean the roosts after, and then you are free for the day. Unless you want to join Rogue's trainings, which are held in the afternoon. We do it this way as some of our people are both Sylkie rider and warrior. We feed the Sylkies in the evening before our own dinner and check the new cubs again in the lower roosts."

Rayvn nodded. "I'll do both," he said quickly. "So will Silas, if none of you mind. The rest of the men can make their own decisions."

Lyrik nodded approvingly. "All right then. I'll knock on your door first light. I go off early to check cubs before we start training."

Cecily yawned widely, covering her mouth with the back of her hand. Gryffon smiled softly at her and stroked her hair.

"Come, my love," he murmured. "Let's get you to bed."

Nodding, Cecily threw an apologetic look at the rest of them. "I'm sorry, healing took it out of me. I'm still catching up to myself."

"Don't apologise, Cess," Lyrik said. "You deserve a rest. Have a good sleep."

Cecily smiled at her fondly as she got up — the wolf appearing at her side in moments —and looked at Amylia and Rayvn.

"You have everything you need?" she asked. They both nodded, murmuring their thanks. "I'll ask the servants to introduce themselves tomorrow… but you will see we are fairly relaxed around here."

She smiled, exhaustion showing through it, and moved away as Gryffon swept his arm around her.

The rest of them melted away to their rooms not long after. Rayvn walked with Amylia back to her door and then headed to his room on the level below.

Back in her room, Amylia stretched in the luxurious bed after pulling the windows open. The soft sheets enveloped her in warmth and a feeling of calm washed over her as she listened to the crashing of the waves against the coast. The salt air drifted through the open windows, fresh and crisp.

Safe. This place felt safe, as if she had come home somehow.

Rayvn was awake and dressed when the tap on his door came the next morning. Immediately opening the door to Lyrik's surprised face. She grinned.

"I think we are going to get on well." She laughed. "Want to come meet some Sylkies, then?"

He returned the grin and took the oat-loaf slice she handed him, pulling the door closed behind him. The woman barely came up to his chin, but he had to rush to keep up with her as she strode through the halls to a small wooden door that opened to the soft dawn light outside.

A track led to the side of the castle, winding around it to the rocks jutting up behind, the start of the massive barren mountains the castle nestled against. She pointed to narrow steps cut into the face of the mountain, stopping at a wooden door that led into the mountain.

"That's one way to the roosts," she said. "That door leads to tunnels through the mountain that come out in the various roosts we have." She whistled, loud and piercing. "But it's far too early to be climbing those."

A faint shriek pierced the air a moment after. Rayvn looked up at a huge, wheeling creature circling above them. Tucking its wings, it suddenly dove towards them.

Rayvn sucked in his breath at its breakneck speed. It threw massive wings out at the last second with a whoosh that took his breath away.

With a few powerful downward flaps, the creature landed gently in front of Lyrik.

Rayvn's jaw dropped, and a tide of emotion ran through him that he wasn't ready for. "She's beautiful," he gasped, his voice cracking.

Lyrik looked at the Sylkie, her eyes dancing as she reached a hand towards her. "She is, isn't she? Rayvn, meet Freyja."

Freyja was slightly bigger than Rayvn's war-horse. Her powerful hindquarters resembled a giant, lightly dappled feline. Her long tail swished the ground, tipped with a small black bristle of coarse hair.

Her front quarters were claws, dark grey scales tipped with lethal black talons. Her wings and upper half were covered in raven-like, midnight-black feathers that gleamed in the sunlight. Long feathered ears were set high over intelligent tawny yellow eyes and a wicked beak that looked like it could rip apart a human in seconds.

Her wings, huge, beautiful wings, with tips so long they kissed the ground. Each one capped with a deadly looking spike at the joint.

Freyja clicked her beak, blinked at Lyrik, and rumbled softly. With a sound similar to purring, it pushed its face into the tiny woman, lifting her half off her feet.

"I missed you, too, Frey," she crooned, tugging gently at the beast's long ears and scratching under the feathers on the side of her head.

The beast closed her eyes in bliss, the feathers of her head puffing out comically as Lyrik's fingers scratched tender new feathers that looked to be breaking through the protective sheaths.

Lyrik jumped onto her back, snugly hooking her knees under the wings, and held a hand out to Rayvn. Freyja eyed him with a huge yellow eye.

He stared at Lyrik dumbly. "You want me to get on... now?"

Lyrik laughed. "Unless you want to walk those steps... by which point I'll already be finished... yes."

He gulped, then stepped forward to Freyja's side and reached a trembling hand towards her.

"Not the wings," Lyrik cautioned. "They are very protective over those. Even Frey doesn't like me touching hers. Anywhere else is fine."

He stepped under the wing, careful not to bump it, and put his hand on her massive shoulder, right where the silken fur met plumage, the tiny black feathers peppering through the dappled hide. Muscle rippled underneath, and Freyja angled her head slightly to keep him in sight as he looked at Lyrik in awe.

"Come on." She laughed, took his hand, and hauled him up behind her.

Settling, he wrapped his legs around the wide sides.

"Hold on tight," Lyrik said over her shoulder. She clicked once, and he felt Freyja crouch, muscles bunching, before they launched skyward.

Slipping backward fast, he grabbed for Lyrik with a whoop, holding onto her with a death grip as she laughed.

The Sylkie's powerful wings cut through the air and the ground rapidly fell away. Rayvn squeezed his eyes shut, every muscle in his body tense, until he felt them level out.

Risking a glance, he sucked a breath in. They were slowly wheeling over the sea far below. It glistened in the morning sun and the wind whipped around them. The currents up here felt almost warm.

When they banked to the right, his muscles tensed again. Freyja turned, following the coast around the mountain.

Waves crashed harshly against jagged rocks. It looked completely impossible to gain access to the mountainside from the sea.

"Shipkiller Coast," Lyrik yelled at him over the wind, pointing with her chin below.

They were on the coastal edge of the mountain now, and Rayvn spotted a wide ledge jutting out from the side. Deep scratches lay all around it. Behind was a cavern opening where another Sylkie with slightly different colouring lay, sunning itself.

Freyja landed gently on the ledge, a good distance away from the huge Sylkie. Rayvn slid off, knees wobbling. He paused, composing himself, and braced his hand against her warm hide.

Lyrik clapped him on the back when she jumped down next to him.

"Not bad for your first flight." She grinned. "Better than Rogue did."

He glanced queasily at her. "He told me you tried to kill him on his first flight."

She snorted. "He wouldn't stop screaming, so Freyja dumped him in the ocean. Took him forever to swim to shore."

Rayvn gawked at her. "You could've said that before I got on!"

She chuckled, patting Freyja on her rump, sending her flying off the cliff and turned, staying a respectful distance from the other Sylkie.

"That's Skaruk." Lyrik waved her hand at the beast. "He's the sire of most the pups here at the moment. He's a cantankerous old bull, but fine if you don't bother him."

Rayvn eyed the bull as he slipped past; while the beast appeared relaxed, it watched his every movement like a hawk. He shivered slightly.

Going through the entrance, Rayvn found himself in a wide cavern, the floor dry and smooth. Hollows had been scratched out of the ground in seemingly random places.

At the far back sat a smaller Sylkie. Another hovered over her with a goat carcass at its feet, and on the other side, a group of three Sylkies sat resting together.

Lyrik walked slowly towards the couple, her hands out in front of her, and the two Sylkies eyed her but made no move towards her. Eventually, she drew level with the one standing and petted it gently.

"Hey, there, pretty girl. I see you have been hunting."

The Sylkie clicked its beak. One foot on the carcass, it reached down and ripped off a strip of meat.

Rayvn tried not to think about how easily it tore through the tough hide as the Sylkie stretched it's neck out towards the belly of the sitting Sylkie.

Lyrik gently pushed on the stomach of the sitting Sylkie and it half-stood, moving instead to crouch over its cubs.

Two fuzzy little heads looked up sleepily from where they had been tucked in the hollow underneath the mother. Light grey fuzz on their heads melded to tawny coats on their hindquarters.

The Sylkie pushed her beak-full of meat towards them, croaking gently at them. The one nearest her opened its beak and peeped back.

"Oh, you have done well, my girl," Lyrik crooned. She stood up to pat the mother's beak gently.

Reaching into a sack that she had picked up close to the entrance, she pulled out a large fish and held it out to the mother who downed it in one gulp. Another offered to the other vanished just as fast.

"Sylkies raise their cubs together," Lyrik said over her shoulder. "The mother, and another female, sometimes even two, will help. In this case they are sisters and always help each other raise their litters." She eyed the pair fondly and then spoke more to them than to Rayvn. "And always do a magnificent job, don't you, my darlings?"

Lyrik stepped back and the Sylkie settled back down, the other ripping off more hunks of meat to push under the mother.

"Do you take them off the parents to train them?" Rayvn asked, enthralled as he watched them.

"No, we never take cubs from their mothers." Lyrik walked over to the other group. "We start working with the cubs when they are slightly older. This one here is nearly the right age. But the parents stay with us. They teach the babies manners, how to hunt… how to be a Sylkie, and we teach them what we need them to know. Our whistles, how to behave around riders. What they are not to touch… and eventually, when the mothers wean them, we move them to the training roosts, and they start to learn how to fly with us. Eventually, they get taught how to hold a rider, how not to throw us off and not leave us on the ground during take-off."

She grinned at him. "Cess comes in handy during that time. And now we have two of you; even better."

Rayvn grimaced at the mention of his healing Gift, stopping short as they approached the trio of Sylkies. A larger cub nestled between the other two, standing to prowl towards Lyrik as she neared with the sack.

She pushed it off her and pulled the fish out, handing them to the three females, who took them gently.

The cub snapped at the bag, and the Sylkie closest to Lyrik nipped it hard on the leg.

It yelped and clicked its beak as it ran back between the two sitting Sylkies. Lyrik snorted in amusement as it hid its head under one of their wings, angry, muffled clucks coming from it. She pulled a smaller fish out and threw it to the floor by the cub. One of the adults put a foot over it, tearing it in half easily before offering it to the sulking cub.

"It's usually only the females in here," Lyrik told Rayvn. She gave the group one last look before heading back to the entrance.

"Occasionally, a young male will come hide out if he's sulking after a fight. Or one that has just been weaned will come back to see a parent but it's mainly just the female nesting groups. Then a dominant bull will guard one or two of the roosts. Skaruk is a mean old bull and guards this one well, but only this one. I have another bull that guards the other two at the moment. He's younger, but I trained him myself, so he has a good temperament."

Rayvn stared around in awe as she whistled for Freyja, the Sylkie landing a moment later.

Flying to the other two nest roosts, they followed the same procedure at each until Lyrik was satisfied all the cubs were doing well and they headed to the lofts, the open space dug into the side of the mountain where the riders trained.

Though training was brutal, all the Lylican men held up relatively well.

Focusing on the core muscle needed to hold themselves in the saddle, they worked for hours, Lyrik showing them through the movements again and again.

Then they tackled the stairs to the roosts. The men gasped for air as they climbed the stairs, following one of Lyrik's captains through the tunnels.

The roosts for the trained Sylkies were very similar to the nesting roosts, though larger and opening up high in the mountain side to look down over Asteryn.

For the men, it was their first time seeing Sylkies and all watched wide-eyed as Lyrik and Freyja landed at the entrance.

She strode in, scattering a pair of squabbling Sylkies with a hard word.

"A big part of being a rider is caring for these beasts. We do it all. If you ride, you feed, and you clean the roosts." She eyed the men, some of whom nodded respectfully to her. "We don't worry about water for this lot. Only sick beasts and the nesting roosts get water. The rest take themselves to the river when they want, we do not lock up or restrain any Sylkie here."

She beckoned some of the women over. "Ingryd and Arya will go through what is needed with you all today, but this roost is yours to look after while you stay here, and as such, the beasts here are under your care. They are all younger Sylkies and shouldn't give you any trouble, but there is a male that pops in here regularly. You will recognise him. Huge, black, and missing an eye. Keep clear of him, though, and he won't bother you."

Some of the men looked around anxiously, fidgeting slightly as they milled around the women, taking orders.

Silas and Rayvn worked together, silently and efficiently checking all the Sylkies as Lyrik showed them what illness to look for. They treated a cut to a young Sylkie's rump and filed a jagged bit of another's beak while the rest of the group cleaned out the roost.

They stayed late. Silas was particularly taken with a young female, her feathers a gorgeous mix of speckled silver and grey fur that blended to dappled black on her lower hindquarters. Her yellow eyes were gentle as she let Silas scratch her.

"I'm in love." He groaned as he stared at the young Sylkie.

Lyrik smiled, coming up to them. "That's Asspyn," she said. "You have good taste, Silas. She's one of my best."

"Oh, pretty Asspyn," he crooned, stroking the length of her neck as she purred at him.

Lyrik raised a brow. "Well, you're welcome to come feed her tonight, too, if you wish. The food is flown in just before dusk, but we have to portion it for them. You can join Ingryd if you wish. She's assigned to this roost this week. I'm sure she would be grateful for the help."

Rayvn nodded excitedly, looking to Silas whose eyes were shining.

Chapter 18

As the sun peeked over the horizon, Amylia stood at the windows in her room, watching the Sylkies wheeling through the sky above the water. She smiled tenderly at the memory of Rayvn, so obsessed with them that Lyrik had struggled to keep him sitting long enough to eat before he was back out, running the steps of the mountain back to the roosts.

Changing quickly into a loose white top and leather training pants, she tucked the top in and secured it with a belt to keep it down when Rogue inevitably threw her across the training yard after breakfast.

She loved the freedom of the pants. She loved the freedom of the choices she had now and hadn't realised how little of it she had at Lylican. The little decisions she now made every day felt like someone had opened the window in a stifling room and let fresh air blow over her.

Rogue had started her training the day before, though to her surprise, he had insisted on building her body before her mind.

So far, it had been less building of her body and more getting her ass handed to her. She enjoyed it, not that she would admit this to him. Not so much the gruellingly punishing fitness regimen, but when he had shown her the basics of blade combat, the feeling of control she got from it soothed some of the anxiety that still riddled her.

Rogue moved her through the different weapons but seemed to be letting her gravitate toward the daggers.

He showed her again and again where to aim between collar and neck. She practised with a wooden dagger until the movement became fluid and her arm was near dead. Sweat poured off her as he grinned at her across the training yard.

He was sadistic, she told herself. He must derive a sick sort of pleasure in slow death by training. She swore silently to herself when her knife yet again skittered off the wooden post she had been trying to jab and he laughed softly behind her.

"That's enough for today. I think you are appropriately exhausted, though..." He stepped back and crossed his arms, brow raised and grinning wickedly. "I must say, your stamina needs working on. It really is slightly pathetic."

Amylia whirled, her face flushed. Full of outrage, she threw the dagger at him... which he dodged easily, laughing.

"Shall we start on your Gifts?" He asked, brow raised. "Or are you too tired, Lady."

Grabbing the ladle off the water barrel in the yard, she sighed, taking several long gulps before pouring the rest over her face.

"You know, I liked you until today," she said sarcastically, passing the ladle to him.

"I get that a lot, don't worry. You will learn to love me again one day." He winked at her, then took a deep drink and poured a second ladleful over himself while Amylia scowled at him.

He had taken his shirt off in the sun, and his chest gleamed with sweat and water as it dripped down tanned skin and rippling muscle.

"Have you been using your Gift at all?" he asked, amusement on his face as he noticed the direction her eyes had gone. She shook her head, looking away quickly.

"Well, let's start small," he said, throwing the ladle back with a splash. "Tiring your body first helps with control at the start. Don't ask me why, but it seems to relax the body and let the mind take over. Let's try little fires first."

She took a breath, holding it as she held her hand out. The flames licked into her palm eagerly and, sensing his focus on her, she glanced up.

"Now what?" she asked nervously.

"Try to manipulate the size. Get used to growing and shrinking it and see if you can move it around you. Hand to hand and such." He gave her an encouraging smile. "It will help you create control and learn what that feels like."

For hours, she followed his directions, pushing threads of fire up to burn in her palm, pulling them back to barely embers, then transferring them hand to hand. She felt them push against that space inside, eager to get out now. She had shown it freedom, and now it was hungry for more.

Rogue strolled over from where he had been sitting quietly, sharpening his blade, and watching her. "Have a break," he said. "You have been doing really well. I need to grab some food before I go to my men's training. I'm sure you could use some, too."

Amylia nodded, realising her stomach grumbled unhappily as she glanced at the sun. "I didn't realise how late it was," she said, surprised.

"Time flies when you have such great company as me," Rogue teased as they headed towards the waiting horses.

Cecily was waiting for them at the stables when they got back and Amylia felt her calm presence before she saw her. Spurring Shadow up to meet her, her brows rose when the mare dipped her head to let Athyna lick her soft nose.

"I wanted to check how Shadow's chest was healing." Cecily smiled and held her palms out for the mare to sniff, pushing the wolf gently away.

Rogue touched his heart to Cecily, in the gesture she had noticed many make towards the woman before, making his excuses that he needed to pick up food quickly and cantering off towards the castle.

Amylia slid off and patted Shadow gently. "They don't bother her, but the hair hasn't grown back yet," she answered, peering at the wounds that crisscrossed the large chest, and pushing the inquisitive nose away as it searched her pocket for treats.

Cecily leaned over to a basket and picked up an apple from its depths, offering it to the mare. Shadow snatched it quickly, flicking it into her mouth, and crunched happily while Cecily unbuckled the bridle and Amylia pulled the saddle off.

"Oh, there's my wee princess!" Grymes exclaimed, walking up with an armful of hay and dropping it into the nearby stall.

Shadow's ears flattened immediately, and she glared at him, swishing her tail in irritation.

"I've got her, m'lady," Grymes said jovially, coming up to take the lead from her and looking up at the mare lovingly. "A nice warm bath for you, isn't it, lass? And then how does a warm bucket of mash sound?" He dodged when Shadow lashed out at him, teeth scraping his arm.

"Now, none of that, ya spicy wee thing," he scolded gently. "We had this discussion yesterday; teeth are to remain to yourself if you want extra apples before bedtime."

Both women laughed as he tipped his grubby cap to them. He led Shadow away, still chatting amicably to the mare.

"Do you think he will win her over?" Cecily laughed as she watched them.

"Not a chance." Amylia sniggered. "I actually feel quite bad for him."

Cecily held up a bag. "I was going to go have lunch on the beach. I have got enough for two if you want to join me?"

They wandered the short distance through the castle gardens to where the steps led down to the white sand of the cove, the wolf trailing behind them. The tide was out, and seabirds ran along the wet sand looking for crustaceans to eat.

"It really is beautiful here." Amylia sighed as they walked barefoot up the beach.

"That it is." Cecily smiled, looking at her.

They picked a spot, nestled against the bank, to sit and relaxed against the warm sand. Above, Sylkies soared slowly, and Amylia watched them in awe.

"Lyrik is quite taken with Rayvn," Cecily murmured, following Amylia's gaze. "She has a soft spot for young people who show passion about her Sylkies."

Amylia looked at her. "He looks up to her," she answered, smiling gently as she thought of her brother. "He always tried so hard to please Drakon." The name made her skin crawl, and she grimaced, but carried on. "He trained so hard, and he wanted to be the best for him. Drakon didn't deserve him."

Cecily looked at her sympathetically. "Drakon didn't deserve either of you," she said softly.

Amylia nodded. "After Mother and Father died, I lost myself a little bit. The world felt dark, as if I was in a hole that I couldn't quite climb out of." She grimaced. "Rayvn was only three. I should have been there more for him, and the guilt of that has killed me since."

Cecily watched her, eyes sad. "No one would have expected you to look after anyone at that age, Amylia, especially with how badly you were grieving."

Amylia shook her head sadly. "I'm still his sister, and he was alone, too. By the time I started coming out of it, he had bonded with Raol and idolized him. He wasn't looking to me for anything." She frowned. "Raol was the one who told Drakon about me."

"That's your maid's... Harriet, was it? Her husband?" Cecily asked gently.

"Yes." Amylia nodded. "He's a lot older than her, but she loved him. He was always so good to Rayvn. I don't know why he did it," she murmured, looking out at the sea.

They ate their lunch, Cecily gently coaxing her to keep talking and telling Amylia about their own history. Amylia watched Cecily surreptitiously as she talked.

"Gryffon wasn't here when his parents passed," Cecily said sadly. "He was away trying to rally alliances from the far Wytchling kingdoms with Lyrik.

She had just been promoted as his father's Second. He got word they had died when they were still over there." She sighed. "Grymes did a lot for him back then… and so did Lyrik. She helped him through the grief and Grymes made sure he kept on getting what he needed."

She smiled and Amylia nodded.

"That's why he has such a soft spot for him. Not that you can help but love him." She giggled. "And then I came to Asteryn, as you already know." She continued, "And a while after, the Great War happened. Attica, for the most part, ignored these lands. We don't hold lands that are of much use to them as a tactical advantage, as far up as we are. Solos and Ataraxya were where the bulk of the war took place."

Cecily paused and sighed.

"We have been worried that Imogen is trying to get more spies in recently, to finish what she sent Kretus in for."

Alarmed, Amylia looked at her. "For what?"

"The Sylkies," Cecily answered. "Because of our remoteness, they never knew we had the Sylkies until Lyrik headed the flights into battle. It took them by surprise and turned the war in our favour. It was horrific, though. The Sylkies fought so bravely, but we lost so many of them. Freyja's mother and Skaruk were some of the only Sylkies to fly away from that battlefield. I never want to see Lyrik that heartbroken again. It should have been their extinction, and they wouldn't be here today if Lyrik hadn't hidden a good line of breeding females in the mountains."

She grimaced. "Kretus was Imogen's attempt at spying on us, to make sure that if she couldn't have the Sylkies, they were at least dying out and to see how many healers we had. We were lucky he never got back to Attica and told her our true numbers. She wants to know exactly what she's up against. If she knew how fast we've grown she would come for us before we're ready."

Amylia shuddered, feeling cold even though the sun warmed her skin.

Rayvn and Silas finished hauling extra bedding up for the roost as Ingryd stood to the side with an expression of approval. Most of the young Sylkies had flown at first light for the mountains, coming in only now at dusk to be fed.

The other men had already been and gone, doing their chores efficiently before disappearing to join Rogue's training groups.

Asspyn had come back early, looking for Silas who had paid her special attention, sneaking in extra fish. Ingryd looked away, smiling, pretending not to notice as he spoiled the beast.

A piercing screech in the sky beyond the entrance announced an incoming Sylkie, and they looked up as the considerable bulk of a dominant bull landed heavily on the ledge.

Ingryd swore softly, backing up. "Let him pass," she called to Rayvn, who stared in utter awe as the Sylkie prowled to the back of the cave.

Rayvn stepped back, giving the beast space, and noticed a slice down the length of the underside of his wing oozing blood. The obsidian feathers were stiff with it and the Sylkie held his wing at an awkward angle, trying not to bend it.

"Ingryd, he's injured!" he called to the woman and stepped in closer to look at the animal. She grabbed his shoulder when he neared the beast and hauled him away.

"That's Falkyn. Don't go near him. How bad is it?" She peered at the underside of the wing and swore again, wiping her hands on her pants. "That's going to need Cecily's healing, and Lyrik will want to check him, too."

She looked at Silas. "Can you go for Lyrik? She'll be in the upper roosts at this time. Just take the tunnel to the left and up the stairs; it's the next door you come to. I'll go for Cecily."

She turned to Rayvn as Silas ran out of the roost. "Stay here and keep an eye which direction he goes if he takes off again."

Rayvn nodded and watched as she strode to the ledge, whistling to call her Sylkie. Moments later, the both of them disappeared in the drop over the ledge.

Rayvn turned in the direction the beast had gone. He loomed at the back of the cave, yellow eye glowing out of the darkness as he watched him.

He picked up a couple of fish out of the nearby sack and slowly, very slowly walked towards him. The beast watched him, his intelligent eye lazily looking him up and down as he approached. It reclined on its side, back leg stretched out. Its massive body was tipped slightly, and its wing was held away from it. A steady drip... drip... drip echoed in the silence. Rayvn dropped his gaze to the small pool of blood seeping into the dusty floor.

"You're okay," he murmured. Holding the fish up in one hand, he held his other palm towards Falkyn. "That looks like it's sore."

The beast was even larger up close, larger than Freyja, his great muscled body tense, coiled like a spring as he neared. Rayvn carefully held the fish out to the beast, who let out a low rumble but made no move to take it.

Falkyn's single eye held his, sending a shiver down his spine. One burned gold and the other was a dark, scarred mass from an old injury and on a level with Rayvn's now in his prone position. It felt like the beast was looking through him and into his soul. He didn't look away and curiosity flared through him as they stood weighing each other up in the utter silence of the cave.

Rayvn felt something nagging at him, flowing from the beast in dull waves, almost palpable as he got closer. It was stronger here, he realised, surprised at how close he was now.

His head went silent. He saw no fear, just mutual fascination. The dull waves sharpened into a steady, burning pain that spiked when the bull shifted, easing the awkward angle of the wing he held out.

Pausing, Rayvn stood close enough to reach out and touch the huge, viciously curved beak that was level with his throat.

He slowly bent and placed the fish between Falkyn's feet, straightening as he felt the waves of pain stronger now, biting at him, and he had to consciously relax the muscles in his shoulders as they bunched under the feeling.

"Can I look?" he murmured to the beast, reaching a hesitant hand towards the wing.

Falkyn didn't move, his low, deep breaths tickling Rayvn's face.

Rayvn held his breath as he inched forward until his fingertips touched the huge wing. He could feel it intensely now, the sharp, hot pain. It made his fingers ache as he gently brushed his hand along the inside curve of the huge limb. He jumped slightly when Falkyn moved, extending the wing, making it easier for him to get to the wound. The huge head came around, following his movements.

Rayvn gently placed his hands on the start of the wound, the ache of it burning across his palm. In fascination, he felt that cool power he had felt in the forest flow into the beast. The skin slowly knitted together as he followed the slice along, fingers rippling over the smooth, silken feathers.

More movement and he glanced over his shoulder to see Falkyn pick one of the fish up, flipping it in the air before catching and swallowing it whole. The second followed suit rapidly, and he grinned.

"I knew you wouldn't be able to resist those. Fresh today, even," he said dryly, relaxing slightly.

He turned back as the last of the wound closed, the deepest part of muscle and tendon knitting back together. The line of fresh skin underneath was pink against the black of the feathers, but it was totally healed. Stepping back, he stared at it. Falkyn stretched the wing wide, flaring it. Then he tucked it neatly back into his side, shuffling the two wings until they sat comfortably.

Rayvn reached his hand out, tracing gently over the wickedly curved beak, running his hand up the side of it to the soft feathers.

Falkyn watched him for a minute, before lowering his head slightly and puffing up the feathers around his head. Rayvn recognised it as permission to scratch him. They stood like that, the huge beast's eye closed in ecstasy, and as he gently scratched behind the enormous ears, a faint purr rumbled up through the solid chest.

Wings beat the air and Rayvn turned, feeling slightly ashamed. Lyrik stood in the doorway of the tunnels looking shocked as Ingryd's Sylkie landed on the ledge. Cecily slipped off its back from where she had been holding on to Ingryd.

"I-I'm sorry," Rayvn stammered, moving away from the Sylkie. "I know you told me to stay away from him. I just wanted to give him fish... but I could feel it... I could feel his wing."

Lyrik's eyes darted from him to Falkyn and back again as Cecily approached.

"Ingryd said Falkyn had an injury?" Cecily asked, her face worried as she peered over towards the Sylkie.

"He did have an injury," Lyrik answered. "But I just watched Rayvn heal him... and then scratch him." Her voice was incredulous as she stared at him.

Cecily startled, looking at Rayvn. "Falkyn let you touch him?"

"Falkyn let him touch his wings..." Lyrik answered, her face still a mask of shock.

Both women looked at him with amazement, then Cecily slipped by him to approach the bull, murmuring to him as she looked at the healed line of pink skin running along his wing. She was careful not to touch him, only getting close enough to see clearly before backing away.

Lyrik let her breath out with a whoosh, and patted Rayvn on the shoulder.

"I should be mad, but no one has been able to touch Falkyn since his rider passed thirteen years ago. Thank you, Rayvn, for healing him. I think even Cess would have had trouble."

Cecily walked back to them, her eyes appraising him. "That's beautiful work, Rayvn. I think it's time you and I started training. If I can steal you off Lyrik for a bit each day." She smiled softly. "And thank you. Falkyn has a special place in my heart. He belonged to a person who meant a lot to me."

Rayvn felt his cheeks heat as he gaped. "I... It was nothing... really."

Cecily grinned, touching Lyrik's arm. "Do you need me for anything else? I've left Amylia on the beach… and she hadn't seen a Sylkie up close until Ingryd almost landed in our lunch."

Lyrik snorted. "No, thank you, Cess."

Cecily nodded, smiling again at Rayvn. "Come see me after you have done evening feeds, before dinner tomorrow, and we can make a start."

He nodded as she jumped back up behind Ingryd. Ingryd laughed low at her request to not terrorise his sister on the return journey, and they dropped over the ledge and out of sight.

Chapter 19

Amylia watched the Sylkie descend through the air, wheeling slowly rather than the rapid plummet to the ground it had made the first time she had seen it, the two riders coming into view as it neared. She tried not to obviously stare at Cecily. The woman's hair was windswept around her face as she sat, arm thrown casually around the gorgeous woman in front of her, laughing as the woman twisted to talk to her. Her eyes glowed, her face achingly beautiful as she threw it upwards to laugh, the sound sending ripples through Amylia's stomach.

The massive beast settled on the wet sand with a huge swoosh of its wings, sand blowing up in a cloud around it as it did, and she waited until Cecily walked towards her before she breathed again.

"There was no time before for you to properly meet Ingryd and her Sylkie." She grinned, holding out a hand to help Amylia up. "Ingryd, meet Lady Amylia Sylvers of Oryx."

She stepped aside for the woman following her, who touched her forehead and then chest in the Sylvyn way of greeting, a small smile on her lips.

"And Amylia, this is Ingryd Galyspie, Lyrik's Captain, and her Sylkie, Calypso."

Amylia inclined her head in return, touching her forehead and chest, while wondering if it was right. "Pleased to meet you," she said to the woman, unable to stop her eyes flicking over the woman to the huge beast waiting patiently behind them.

Ingryd smiled warmly. She asked, "Would you like to meet her?"

Amylia's breath whooshed out of her. "Oh, yes!" Heart pounding, she asked, "She won't mind?"

Ingryd shook her head. "Calypso is one of the more social of the Sylkies." She chuckled. "My problem is keeping her away from people and her mind on what she is meant to be doing."

She led her to Calypso, showing her where to scratch and how to approach a Sylkie. Calypso purred softly under Amylia's hand, and she looked over at Cecily with shining eyes.

"I can see why Rayvn is so enthralled by them." She laughed, then jumped slightly when the Sylkie pushed its huge beak into her chest, begging for more attention.

Ingryd laughed, shoving her off. "Enough of that," she scolded, her tone holding none of the reprimand the words implied. "We should be getting on now, anyway. I'm sorry to have disturbed you, Cecily." She touched her heart, nodding to the women before she mounted back up onto the Sylkie.

"Not at all, Ingryd. I'm glad he was okay." Cecily smiled up at her.

Amylia and Cecily backed away, giving the Sylkie space to spread its large wings and launch itself into the sky, watching until they gracefully arced back towards the mountains.

"Your brother has been making friends," Cecily murmured to her as they watched them into the distance.

"Oh?" Amylia asked, turning to walk back to the now sand-covered blanket. She picked it up, flapping it off, and spread it back out. Sitting on one half, she watched Cecily sit on the other and fold back the flap of the bag to pull out two meat pasties wrapped in a cloth.

Handing one to Amylia with a smile, Cecily said, "Ingryd was just filling me in. Lyrik is very impressed with him. And so, it seems, is one of the more cantankerous of our Sylkies."

Amylia groaned as she bit her pasty. Swallowing it quickly, she asked, "What has he done now?"

Cecily laughed, swallowing her mouthful as she shook her head. "Nothing bad at all. In fact, he healed a wound on it with remarkable precision considering how new he is to his Gifts, but Falkyn hasn't let anyone near him... since Callysta died."

A small crease appeared between her eyebrows and Amylia had to stop herself reaching out to smooth it away. "You mentioned Callysta in the Dead Forest." She asked curiously, "Is Falkyn the one that flew you back when you were injured?"

Cecily nodded. "He was. He's a beautiful creature. The only thing Callysta loved as much as him... was me." She gave Amylia a sad smile. "I swore over her grave that I'd look out for him, but he was so broken by losing her that he lashed out at anyone who came near him. We just make sure he's fed and let him roost where he wants, but he seems to have opened up to Rayvn." She smiled again. "And that makes my heart happy."

They were silent for a while as they ate, sharing a canteen of beautifully sweet cider between them.

"You... and Callysta?" Amylia hesitated, wishing she hadn't started the question, but burning to know. "That was thirteen years ago?"

Cecily nodded, wadding up the cloth and pushing it back into the bag. "Callysta joined us from Calibyre, our biggest trade partner across the seas to the North during Gryffon's rallying for allies for the Great War. But that's not your question, is it?" She grinned at her wickedly, and Amylia blushed again.

"Callysta was my lover," Cecily offered

Amylia's neck heated and she knew the colour was rising up. Cecily's smile turned amused, and she put her arms around her knees.

Resting her chin on her arm, she raised an eyebrow at Amylia. "From the colour you're turning... I'm guessing that's not common in Lylican?"

Amylia shook her head with a breathy laugh. "Oh, no, it's not that... I mean yes, it isn't... wasn't, I mean." Realizing she was stammering, she paused to take a breath. "But... you were with Gryffon, too?"

"Yes," Cecily laughed, her eyes twinkling. "Gryffon is my mate, I guess similar to what humans call a husband, but it's more than that." She glanced at Amylia's confused look and laughed. "Mates are part of each other. Their souls are connected in a way that is only separated by death... and even then, they take a bit of each other with them until they are reunited in the land of the Gods. From what I've seen, humans can marry and not love each other. With mates that's impossible. Those feelings do not fade or die out. It is why my mother gave her blessing when she sensed it between Gryff and I. There is no stronger bond between souls, denying it would be to rip out someones heart."

"So... you had two mates?" Amylia asked, watching as Cecily shook her head.

"No... I loved Callysta dearly, but we were not mates. And Gryffon and Callysta were good friends, but they were not lovers. It does happen, though, that one will be lucky enough to find two mates." Cecily smiled at her. "We have a few in Asteryn, and it's common in Calibyre and Nymaria. My brother has two mates."

"They don't get jealous?" Amylia asked.

"Why would they?" Cecily said. "You can love more than one person without it diminishing the love for either. You love more than one friend, don't you? A mother can love all her children the same, it is no different. The love I have for Gryff is one thing, but it does not make me incapable of loving another. Gryff knows that, and he would never be jealous about it." She huffed softly. "The same as if he found another mate or took a lover. I would be happy that he had another person loving him, too."

Amylia took a breath, letting it out gently, and laughed softly. "I'm not even sure I know what love is anymore. I thought I did… and it turns out I was very wrong. Or maybe I'm just difficult to love."

"I think you would be very easy to love," Cecily murmured softly, reaching out and squeezing her hand. "Don't give up on it so soon."

Days melted away fast here. Amylia felt herself relaxing into the easy way of life in Asteryn. Everyone had their part, it seemed, all working in sync to create an intricate moving structure that ran meticulously.

She loved the mornings the most, the beautiful sunrises up over the cove. Its warm light glowed into her room through the huge windows. She rose early every day, slipping out to visit Shadow before coming back for breakfast. Lyrik and Rayvn were usually absent at these, busy up in the roosts until later in the day.

Amylia trained with Rogue every day and felt her body get stronger as the repetition of the drills worked her core. Her Gifts, too, rose in her as her body strengthened, as if waking sleepily from their long rest, and she practised control, rolling the little fires across her palms, and snuffing them out.

She grinned at Rogue as she made a small bird out of the flames, letting it flap gently in her hand before she sent it skittering towards him in the air, dancing between them until it snuffed out with a hiss of smoke in front of him.

He whistled, impressed. "Not bad, Lady Sylvers. Where did you learn that?"

"My father." She laughed. "Father used to make them for me when I was a child."

Amylia felt someone approaching in the distance and looked up just before the hoofbeats sounded. Rogue, noticing her gaze, stood and shielded his eyes against the sun as the horse approached.

Gryffon loped slowly into the training ring, riding one of the trade mares, looking with appreciation at the small flaming fox now running up Amylia's arm. She twirled her finger over it, and it morphed into a dragonfly that flitted over and circled him twice before dissolving into smoke.

"You're doing well," he said, eyes dancing as he smiled at her. He turned to Rogue. "The ship is coming in now from Calibyre. I'm on my way down to the dock to check it over. Can you organise some men to see that the shipment gets brought in, and the supplies get to where they need to be? Lyrik has just left to do a sweep over the Dead Forest again."

Rogue nodded. "Of course." Turning to Amylia, he asked, "Are you going to be okay to head back to the castle alone?"

"Actually, I was going to ask if you wanted to join me?" Gryffon interrupted. "Cess has taken Rayvn with her to one of the rural villages. Lyrik won't be back until later tonight, and I've realised no one has shown you around the city yet. We could go in after I've checked the shipment?"

Amylia nodded eagerly and smiled. "I'd like that." She brushed her pants off and clipped her training knives into the sheaths at her thighs as she whistled for Shadow.

As they rode slowly into the town, Gryffon pointed to the ship moving slowly in around the coast in the distance, staying well clear of the rocks that peppered the coastline.

"How far has it come?" Amylia asked, straining her eyes towards the white sails. A Sylkie soared lazily overhead, watching the progress of the ship.

"Calibyre is a fair way away. Almost three weeks in good weather," he answered. "Most of our trade comes from there. Our farms provide a large portion of their crop foods." Gryffon grinned at her. "That, and our blacksmiths are some of the best there are."

She looked over the rolling city as they crested a small hill. "It really is the most gorgeous place." She sighed.

"It is." He laughed. "But this is only half of it. We came up the short edge of the coast. The lands to the east are expansive, with a lot of smaller farming towns that trade through the city. That's where most of my people reside."

He pointed into the distance at the mountain range.

"The Elixus Ranges shield anyone coming across into our lands without coming through the Dead Forest... which is close enough that Lyrik's riders pick off anything moving. It's why the attacks on them have been so troubling. The only way they got past the Sylkies was to come directly over the mountains. And the only way to do that is through the skies."

She threw him a glance. "You think it's come from Attica?"

"I do," he said simply, "though why now, I'm not sure."

"Is that why Lyrik is sweeping the forest at the moment?" Amylia asked, glancing into the skies to see if she could see the riders in the distance.

Gryffon didn't answer immediately. "No," he finally said cautiously. "Well, routine surveillance, yes, but it's one of the reasons I wanted to talk to you today. No… it's not bad, don't worry," he soothed, responding to the alarm in her eyes.

"Your brother," he began carefully, "came to me a couple nights after we got here and told me of a plan Drakon had that involved Rayvn destroying my copy of the contract… the only copy that proves I have not agreed to hand Sylkies over to Lylican as part of this trade agreement." He looked at Amylia and snorted as he saw her face. She could feel the heat of the anger that washed through her. "I guess that answers my next question." He chuckled.

"And what was that?" Amylia said, pushing down the hot fire that roiled in her stomach, outraged that Drakon would implicate her brother in something like that.

"I wanted to know if you knew anything about it. And I also wanted to know where you stand if I have to break ties with this new alliance?"

Amylia looked at him, cold replacing the heat suddenly. "I-I don't know. I can understand if you don't want me here…"

"That's not at all what I meant," Gryffon hastily interrupted. "I'm sorry. I didn't mean you to take it that way." His eyes were soft as they looked at her. "I meant it when I told you that Asteryn is your home as long as you want it, and so is my protection. What I meant is… before I can look at how I take this information, I need to know if you want to return to Mica. It will influence how I go abou—"

"No!" Amylia blurted. Then she took a breath. "No," she said, quieter. "I don't want to go back there."

Gryffon nodded. "I'm relieved to hear it." He gave her a half-smile. "I think, however, Drakon is going to object to that, and I just needed to know what you wanted before it came to it." He reined his horse up, turning to look at her directly. "I'd like to formally invite you to join our court, Amylia. And Rayvn, too. If you are officially Asterynian, Drakon has no power over either of you, and to try to make you do anything you do not wish would be an act of war. You are Sylvyn, true blooded Sylvyn and with Asteryn being the only Sylvyn held territory in Labrynth, even with the fact that you were under his care for eleven years, we can claim you if you do not object."

Emotions rolled over her, and she swallowed. "What about everyone else? Do they want us, too? You all have a place here… a purpose. Even Rayvn has found a way to be useful… I'm just… me. I'm useless."

Gryffon edged his horse closer and looked into her eyes, the golden depths of them warm. "You are anything but useless, Amylia."

She huffed a laugh. "I was Drakon's ward. A child of his court. That was one thing. I'm a grown woman now, and I do not want to be a burden on you."

Gryffon studied her, his expression gentle. "I think I can speak for everyone when I say we all want you to stay with us, to join us, and I speak for myself… and Cess, when I say we feel you were meant to be here, that we were meant to meet you. And I speak for Asteryn when I say that with whatever is coming from Attica, another Gifted Elementyl and healer to protect the people and our lands is more valuable than gold. But it is ultimately your choice, and I will help you regardless of what you decide."

Amylia blinked away the tears that threatened. "I'd be honoured to join Asteryn and protect these lands alongside the rest of you. Lylican was a refuge for us, but Asteryn… Asteryn feels like the home I should have had. Like what Oryx would have been if my parents had lived."

Gryffon bowed in his saddle and Amylia laughed, sniffed, and wiped her eyes on her sleeve.

"Well, then, Lady Sylvers, let me introduce you to your new home properly." He smiled and clucked at his horse to move on.

Chapter 20

Gryffon was true to his word and showed her everything, starting at the docks, having checked over the ship on its arrival. A second, bigger ship, he explained, was still on its way from Calibyre and would take a bit longer. This was their smaller vessel, still impressive, and the faster of the two.

They rode through the city, stopping at an eatery to buy food for lunch before he showed her through the bustling streets. It was beautifully laid out; cobblestone streets with tall cherry blossom trees growing along either side of them, most of the buildings closer into the city having living accommodation above them, while towards the outskirts stood little stone houses, quaint and well-built.

Gryffon pointed out the school, full of happy-looking children who waved as they passed, a library, a hospital where minor ailments were seen to until Cecily could get to them, and the community gardens towards the outskirts.

"None of our people go hungry here," he explained. "Everyone takes turns tending the food gardens, especially our young. It is part of their lessons, and anyone who is in need comes and takes from it." He waved at a group of women bent over, industriously planting seedlings. "We have a lot of Wytchlings with earth Gifts, especially out in the villages, who make our crops thrive. The thermal heat helps, but without them we wouldn't be able to supply as many other lands as we do."

Amylia looked around in appreciation. Everyone seemed so happy here.

"We don't have much sickness here either," Gryffon said, waving at a young Sylvyn who passed by. "Cecily will see anyone who comes for healing, and she travels out to the surrounding districts on Sylkie to make sure no one is missed. I must say, if Rayvn wants to use his Gifts in that way, it would take a huge pressure off her."

They stopped along a street full of colourful shops. "If you need or want anything, please just get it, and tell them to put it on the castle's account," Gryffon said as she eyed the rows of leather-bound books in a bookstore window.

Amylia shook her head. "No. Thank you. I already owe you so much." She turned to him. "Rayvn inherits Oryx when he comes of age, if we can't get it back sooner, and my fortune is tied into it. We will repay you everything when we get our lands back."

"Amylia," Gryffon soothed, "I do not expect anything to be repaid. If we had known of you when Oryx was attacked, you would have joined our court then. It's just taken longer is all. Oryx will have no debt to us when Rayvn takes his title." He eyed her, his gaze curious. "Can I ask why it is Rayvn who is to inherit Oryx?"

Amylia looked at him, confused. "Because he is the heir?"

"And you are full siblings?" he questioned.

"Yes, of course." Her tone was cautious as she watched his expression.

Gryffon appeared to mull it over for a moment as if choosing his words carefully. "The Sylvyn way is for the firstborn to inherit, whether male or female. I understand this is not so with the humans, though," he added. "By rights, as Oryx is Sylvyn inheritance, it should go to you."

"Oh," she said, lost for words. After a moment she said, "I couldn't though. I couldn't take Oryx away from him. He has trained his whole life to be capable of taking over as lord. I wouldn't even know where to begin."

Gryffon smiled gently. "And that's entirely your right as well. I'm just letting you know you have more options than you realise. I want you to choose to be here because you want to be here, not because it is your only option."

Amylia looked around the town, watching the people, round-cheeked children playing in the streets as the smells of the baker wafted across to her. Then she looked at Gryffon. His brow creased in an expression which could almost pass as anxiety. "I want to be here." She smiled softly.

Gryffon cringed every time a child got too close to Shadow's massive form as they walked through the streets, leading the horses. Finally, Amylia laughed at Gryffon's tension. "She's good with children," she soothed. "It's only adults she doesn't like."

Gryffon snorted. "Tell that to the chicken I saw her belt across the yard the other day." He held his palms up at her horrified expression. "It's okay. It lived." He laughed as she glared at the mare in outrage.

"Really, Shadow?" she scolded.

"I don't know what it is with the people in my court." He shook his head. "My mate brings home a Dyre wolf, which insists on eating every pair of shoes I own. You have—" he waved his arm at Shadow, "—that… which I'm not even sure is really a horse. Your brother has fallen in love with Falkyn, of all creatures… a Sylkie that truly terrifies me, and Lyrik—" he shook his head, "—in truth, she's the most lethal of the lot." He snorted. "I honestly think Rogue is the sanest one of you all, and that is really scraping the bottom of the barrel."

Amylia eyed him darkly. "You're the one who invited me to join you," she said sardonically, and Gryffon chuckled.

"I didn't say I was the sane one, did I?" He laughed and dodged as she swatted him. Hauling himself into the saddle, he waited for her to do the same. "I'm glad I got you to agree to join us before you found out what that entails."

Amylia's face dropped. "What?" she squeaked, alarmed.

"Oh, the process is simple enough. We swear you in over the Asteryn Crest… but then we get to throw an obscenely large party in your honour, and no doubt Rogue will take it and run with it." He grinned and it turned fiendish, his eyes on her face "I thought you would like that one." He urged his horse forward out of town. "And," he called over his shoulder, "I seem to recall it's your birthday soon, too?"

Amylia groaned, dragging her hand over her face as she watched him canter away.

They ran the horses hard. She let Shadow work off her attitude as Gryffon took her over the rolling countryside, pointing out several of the nearer villages in the distance. They met some of the farmers, too, who all paused their work to touch their foreheads and chests in honour to Gryffon as he passed. Gryffon returned the gesture every time, but also paused sometimes for brief conversations with his people.

"What does it mean?" Amylia asked as they moved on. "The greeting they use?" She touched her forehead and chest as she had seen them doing.

"It means you greet someone with an open mind and heart," Gryffon answered. "That there is no bad feeling towards them. A touch to the head—" he demonstrated the gesture, "—is if you greet someone you know nothing of, more like 'I'm open to knowing you'. Touching the heart as well means 'I see you, and I am here'."

"Oh," she breathed and thought of Ingryd, now touched at the gesture. "What does just touching the heart mean?" she asked; she'd seen the gesture used a lot towards Cecily.

"It means greetings with respect and love, if I were to simplify it," he answered.

They paused at a stream, letting the horses drink and graze for a while, sitting on the springy grass as they watched the water bubbling by.

"How are you doing with learning your Gifts?" Gryffon asked, his deep voice rumbling through the still air. "You seem to be picking them up fast."

Amylia sighed, reaching into herself. Pulling up a few threads, she let the fire dance on her palm. The blue flames flickered gently before she sent them out as a bird swooping across the river.

"They feel stronger every day," she said, watching the bird's progress as it neared her again. She sent it back away with another flick of her finger. "And they scare me sometimes. I feel like they're screaming to get out at times, but Rogue wants me to practice control before I let more go."

Gryffon nodded, holding a hand to the water and drawing it towards him, moulding it until it became an otter, crystal against the water as it chased the bird across the bubbling surface.

Amylia smiled, watching them.

"Rogue has struggled with his own Gift before," Gryffon said. "Trust him, even if it seems strange. He is good at what he does."

Amylia looked at him, her brows raised. "I didn't know he had any Gift. He hasn't shown it at all."

Gryffon shook his head. "He won't use it if he can help it, he thinks it gives him an unfair advantage in training, but don't let his personality fool you. He is one of the strongest people I know, and his skill with the blade is unparalleled… except, of course, by Lyrik." He grimaced. "That woman is death walking even without touching her own… abilities. She learnt a long time ago how to mute them and refuses to touch them."

Amylia grinned at him. "Oh, I remember her handing your ass to you in Lylican."

His smile was positively lupine, his eyes burning golden as he looked into hers.

Amylia felt her blood heat and couldn't look away as he purred softly to her, "Oh… don't underestimate my own Gifts, Lady Sylvers. I just don't get them out very often."

Her face heated as she looked away, watching the otter slice through the water, agile and swift as the bird teased and danced in front of it. It leaped, catching the bird deftly and pulling it into the water with a hiss as Gryffon's soft laugh rolled over her, sending butterflies through her stomach.

Rogue's training picked up slightly and Amylia pushed herself to learn. Slowly... very slowly, muscle built. Her movements became fluid as she followed the routines he showed her, over, and over again until they became second nature. Her confidence grew as the knife she wielded became an extension of her arm.

"Good," he encouraged when she blocked his advances again and again. "You are far better with the knife than you are with the sword."

Amylia panted, sweat running down her chest as she used her body to block his arm from coming down, sweeping her knife around to come up under his chin. His arm caught the movement, the tip stopping as it brushed the stubble there. She grinned at him and then yelped when his leg came around, taking her legs out neatly. He flipped her over his arm, catching her by the back of the shirt before she hit the ground.

"Damn," she muttered, taking his hand as he hauled her up. She stamped out the small fires on the ground where they had sparked out of her as she fell.

"You're doing well." He laughed. "It's not been long, and you already have the basics of self-defence down, though I think we don't bother with the sword anymore and stick to knives. You are fast and we need to focus on that, being how little you are." When she scowled at him, he laughed. "I can teach you to use someone's weight against them. I've seen Lyrik throw a man three times her weight because she knows how to unbalance someone."

Amylia nodded, still catching her breath. "Can I not just burn them if they get that close?"

"You can," he said. "But discipline is a two-sided coin: the mind and the body. I can teach you your Gifts, which is discipline of the mind, but without the body as well, they are not nearly as strong."

"I'm pretty sure you just get a kick out of making me suffer," she teased, holding a stitch in her side, and leaning into it when Rogue stared at her in mock outrage.

"I've been going easy on you!" he cried.

Amylia glared at him darkly. "Is that so?"

"Well... I preferred not to break you before we got to the good stuff." He grinned. "Though, I have to admit, you haven't had to resort to the pools yet, so I think I've maybe been too easy on you."

She snorted. "Though the pools sound lovely, I can handle whatever you throw at me Rogue."

He crossed his arms, raising a brow at her. "Ohhhh, you've done it now." He grinned. "Challenge accepted." She had the good sense to feel slightly nervous when he poked her in the stomach. "Time to work on that core muscle, Amylia."

Chapter 21

Everything ached. Amylia rolled over in bed, kicking at the blankets wrapped around her legs with an irritated sigh, wincing as her muscles barked in protest.

"Gods damn Rogue," she grumbled, reaching her arms out in the air, and flexing them, trying to stretch them gently against the tug of healing muscle.

She scowled into the darkness, imagining Rogue's face again as he struggled to hold back his laughter when she had rasped and wheezed her way up the rocky terrain behind the castle. Rogue had jogged on the spot each time he waited for her to catch up.

She cringed at the memory, ripped the covers back, gingerly hauled herself out of bed, then padded naked to the open window.

The soft breeze from the night sky cooled her skin, curling along her arms, and the flat of her stomach as she stood, eyes closed and taking deep breaths. The wind whispering in the trees surrounding the huge fortress carried with it the faint scent of gardenias. She put her hands to the small of her back, stretched, and felt the tug of abused muscles pull across her stomach. She groaned.

The luxurious expanse of soft towel hanging to her left caught her eye. Reaching out, she hooked it neatly with a deep sigh of defeat.

Briefly rummaging through the drawers, she looked for anything she could wear into the pools but came up fruitless. She paused, biting her lip, and pondered if any of the servants would still be awake. No, it was late. They wouldn't want to be disturbed at this hour anyway.

Shrugging on a dark silk robe she found hanging on the door of the armoire, she blew out the candle that lit the room before cracking the bedroom door open to peek out.

The hallway was dark. Lyrik's door was shut, but she could feel her and another. Their soft voices came from inside, and she raised a brow, smiling slightly.

No light shone out from under Rogue's door at the end, but she felt his presence there. She made a rude gesture in the darkness towards him. Her pride had taken enough ruin today. She would not let him gloat at winning this bet.

Clicking the door softly closed behind her, she used the moonlight streaming in the large windows to find her way down the stone stairs that Cecily had told her led to the pools. Running her hand along the rough rock wall as she went, down and down she descended, legs screaming as they took her weight from step to step. The rock started to warm against her hand the lower she got. The air felt thicker down here; heavy, and warm.

Glow worms peppered the ceiling, illuminating the way, and the sound of gurgling water reached her. She sighed when, finally, she stepped into the steam-filled cavern. Amylia glanced around. Soft, bluish light from the glowing bugs above filled the small cavern. The pool itself was big enough to swim in. Boulders jutted up from the water in places. Several other stones were submerged and formed natural seats and ledges. A crack in the far back wall fed the pool; on the other side, it disappeared between two large boulders.

Piles of soft cushions in shades of forest green and silver sat round the edges against the wall. Off to the far side, a heavy wooden trunk overflowed with towels.

Puffs of steam wafted invitingly up from the dark water. She untied her robe, the soft silk sliding across her skin, and she dropped it on a large boulder by the doorway, laying her towel on one of the plush cushions at the water's edge.

Stepping slowly into the water, she moaned; heat caressed her skin and soaked through her body, soothing her aching muscles. She waded into the hot water a little at a time until her hair floated around her shoulders. Pausing there for a minute, she acclimated before lowering herself and kicking off from the edge. The water lifted her gently and she floated lazily towards the far side and came to rest on a large, flat boulder that sat low enough to sit on comfortably..

Leaning back against the side of the pool, head resting on the ground, she ran her hand through her hair, pulling it back from her face.

This was blissful.

Sighing, she silently kicked herself at her stubbornness for not exploring this before. Already, she could feel her tight muscles relaxing and the tension leaving her body. Steam from the water pooled around her, leaving droplets on the tops of her breasts, which just rose above the surface of the pool.

Closing her eyes, Amylia drifted in and out of a relaxed sleep, the water holding her gently. It touched her skin in small waves of heat and cool as new water passed by her on its way to an unknown destination. She absently mulled it over, imagining the warm water flowing down through the earth, heating the rock and the fortress above. Idly, she wondered where it ended up. Abruptly, something interrupted her thoughts. A presence… no, two people. The familiarity of them nudged at her. She strained her ears as the sound of faint footsteps gradually became more audible. A low male voice rumbled something and was answered by a soft female one, laughing at whatever he had said.

With a splash, Amylia sat up and glanced around quickly. Her robe was by the entrance. Too far to get to before these people arrived in the cavern. Glancing back over her shoulder, she looked at the trunk and the towels inside, judging the distance as the two voices emerged into the cavern.

Nothing moved in a moment's silence as she was sure they now noticed her. Then Gryffon's amused chuckle floated across to her.

"Ohhhhhhh, he's going to be insufferable tomorrow. Rough training today, was it?"

Heat seeped up Amylia's face, letting her know just how red she must be going. She pulled her knees up to her chest and wrapped her arms around them.

"Not that I'm going to admit it to him. But yes, I feel like Shadow dumped me off a cliff," she admitted. "I… I was just getting out. I couldn't find anything to wear in here." Her flush deepened.

"The water ruins anything we wear in there. It's the minerals, we tend not to bother," Cecily said softly. Stepping out from behind Gryffon, she carefully picked her way around the side of the pool to select two towels from the trunk, handing one to Gryffon who had followed behind her.

"Please, don't get out. Unless it makes you uncomfortable?" Her voice was casual, as if careful not to sound as if she was hoping for either.

Amylia shook her head and gave them a small smile. Cecily grinned, throwing her towel at Gryffon, who deftly caught it. Then she reached to untie her robe and let it drop to the ground in a billow of white fabric.

Amylia averted her eyes quickly, but not before catching a glimpse of long, beautifully shaped legs and a slightly rounded hip leading to the curve of a buttock. Keeping her eyes on the water lapping at her fingers, she listened to the sounds of them both slowly entering the water, the deep groan from

Gryffon and the answering breathy sigh from Cecily as the water enveloped them.

"Oh, that's better," Gryffon sighed from off to her right. Carefully, she glanced over to where he sat submerged to his chest in the dark water on another rock, the only other underwater seat.

Cecily did a slow lap before coming to rest on the large rock where Amylia sat. She shuffled over, giving her space, and Cecily glided backwards until her back rested against the ledge, too.

Amylia's eyes were drawn to her back; silver tattoos, done with the same ink as those across her face and ears covered her entire back in an intricate, delicate design.

"That is… beautiful," she blurted.

Cecily's eyes met hers, seeing where she had been looking and smiled, resting against the rock next to her. She sighed deeply, reaching to flick her long, pale hair up onto the ledge behind before resting her head back and gazing up at the twinkling roof.

"Thank you," she murmured, holding a dripping hand out of the water to study the designs across her fingers. "I forget they're there most the time."

"I haven't seen any other Sylvyn with them." Amylia looked to the silver tip of Cecily's ear which peeked out from under her hair.

Cecily chuckled softly. "No, it is a tradition upheld by the Wytchlings of Nymaria. Healers in my home land get our first tattoos as we age into our Gifts. Our ears are tipped." She smiled softly, tracing the delicate shell of her ear that glinted silver in the soft light and glanced at Amylia. "They get added to as we age, and our Gift grows." She turned her back slightly to Amylia, giving her an unobstructed view of it. "This was the last one I received before I left; my grandmother gave it to me."

"It must have taken so long," Amylia traced a finger along the lacework of silver between Cecily's shoulder blades. It covered nearly her entire back, the design complementing the slender curves and dips.

"It did, but I enjoyed it." Cecily's nose crinkled as she grinned at Amylia over her shoulder. She reclined back against the rocks again, closing her eyes as she asked, "How was your training today?"

"Rogue is a sadist," Amylia muttered.

Gryffon chuckled quietly. "What did you say to get the full Rogue treatment?"

Amylia sighed. "He informed me that he had been going easy on me, which I took offense to and did not keep my mouth shut."

Gryffon laughed outright. "And how is that working for you now?"

"Astounding, can you not tell?" Amylia said darkly, wincing as she slowly extended her legs again, carefully sinking further into the water as she did so.

The scent of them carried across the water to her; it was intoxicating. She had never noticed how good a person could smell before, but these two… both of them sent her senses reeling whenever they got close to her.

Amylia steadied her breathing and tried to shift her attention onto the glowing bugs above. She failed, dismally.

Gryffon's head rested back against the ledge, silver hair drawn up in a bun behind his head. His eyes were closed and face relaxed. He looked… utterly beautiful.

Amylia studied his face a moment longer before her gaze dropped to a bead of water which trickled down his neck, pooling at the base of it for a second before running over his broad, muscled chest and down to where the water lapped around his navel. She wrenched her eyes away from him, guilt washing over her as she felt Cecily's gaze on her.

Cheeks flaming, Amylia ran her hands through her hair and pulled it away from where it stuck to her neck, using the movement to look surreptitiously at Cecily.

Amusement played across the woman's beautiful features as she gazed at the ceiling and idly drew lines with her fingers across the tops of her breasts.

"Can I fix your aches?" she asked softly, rolling her head to look at Amylia.

"It's… it's just aches," Amylia stammered. "The water has helped so much. You have already healed me so many times."

Cecily silenced her, lifting her hand from the water. "It's nothing. Honestly, I barely notice the drain with something so minor." She smiled. "I do it for the others all the time, when they have not irritated me." She lifted a brow and nodded in Gryffon's direction, a smirk playing across her lips. "Getting back up those steps won't be any fun if you stay as you are. Where is the worst of it? Let's start there," she suggested.

Amylia swallowed and looked at the black staircase, then sighed in surrender. "My lower back and my legs are the worst, I think."

The water moved around her as Cecily shifted, and then a slender hand grazed her back, settling at the base of it, right where the deep ache was coming from. Her other hand touched Amylia's shoulder.

"Lie back, put your head against the ledge," she murmured.

Amylia did, unable to stop the small groan that escaped her as the last of the ache from her back slipped away. Cecily's gift drawing it out, soothing it.

The other hand moved from her shoulder to whisper across her stomach, the touch so light it felt like a ripple of water passing, except for the tingle it left in its wake.

Cecily pulled away and around, coming up in front of her. Her hips brushed Amylia's knees. A touch to her elbow guided her upright, her shoulders and breasts coming out the water as she did. She felt her stomach flip as Cecily's eyes dipped to them, so briefly she nearly missed it.

The woman leaned forward, reaching out to place a hand gently on either side of Amylia's neck. The stiffness in the muscles there disappeared entirely as the warm touch began to glide down, whisper-soft but taking every bit of Amylia's focus.

Her heart thundered in her ears when thumbs brushed the sides of her breasts. There was a slight pause before they carried on down her forearms to her fingers and closed around the smallest finger on Amylia's right hand where Rogue had accidentally pinched it while disarming her that day. The sharp pain that had nagged at her disappeared into the water.

Hooking her hip into Amylia's knees, Cecily nudged them apart before turning slightly, fitting her body between them, her eyes fixed on the side of Amylia's neck, right where she had pointed out the pulse during their ride through the dead forest.

Cecily's eyes were glowing in that eerie way they did while using her Gift as she ran both hands up her ankle, kneading her calf, her knee. Amylia couldn't look away from the depthless blue of them as those hands rose dangerously high, feeling her pulse begin to hammer as Cecily's thumbs pressed into the aching muscle of her thigh.

The other leg got the same treatment and Amylia's head was whirling when Cecily finally gently let go of her, water moving as she backed away.

"Better?" she asked huskily.

Amylia could only nod dazedly, searching for words that had retreated into the dark recesses of her mind.

"Thank you," she said, her voice barely a whisper, taking a deep breath and letting it out slowly. She stretched carefully, feeling no tug of muscle anywhere.

"Anytime, sweetling." Cecily smiled and pushed off, swimming lazily to Gryffon who dozed, head resting back against the rock, golden eyes closed.

When she settled against him, his arm came down from resting behind his head to cradle her. She rested her head on his shoulder, his thumb rubbing the curve of her shoulder in long, lazy strokes. He opened his eyes to smile down at her, kissing her softly on her forehead.

They reclined for a while, silence filling the cavern, broken only by the bubbling of the water. Gryffon's hand moved from Cecily's shoulder to her neck, thumb kneading softly into the back of it, a low, quiet moan escaping from her.

Amylia pulled her gaze from them, trying to ignore the weak feeling that moan caused — her mind immediately dragging up ways she could hear that moan again — and swam to the rock steps. "I'd better go to bed. I'm pretty sure Rogue's got more torture planned for tomorrow." She grimaced.

Gryffon grinned, averting his eyes to allow Amylia to get out of the water. "If you think he's bad," he teased, amusement in his voice, "wait until Lyrik gets hold of you. She's been dying to see how you handle her Sylkies ever since your Shadow got a taste of her."

Amylia laughed softly, wrapping her towel around herself. Her tone grim, she said, "I don't know if even Cecily would be able to piece me back together after that."

They both made a sound of amusement.

"Enjoy your night, my lord… my lady," she said, needing the formality to give her some distance, though she gave them a shy smile.

"And you, Amylia," Gryffon rumbled, his eyes glowing as they looked at her through the dim light.

She flushed again, turned, and hurried out of the cavern, bracing herself with her hand against the rock as she started the climb back up. Her head swirled with foreign emotions, and she tried to get her traitorous body back under control.

A cool breeze touched her skin and she reached to pull her robe closed, pausing when she touched bare skin. She looked down and realised she had left with just her towel wrapped tightly around her. Hesitating on the stairs, she contemplated carrying on and collecting the damn thing tomorrow, but a second gust brushed passed her and raised the hairs on her arms, sending a shiver down her back. Sighing, she turned back and descended quickly on silent feet.

Water lapped quietly as she reached the cavern. Peering around the entrance, she spotted her robe crumpled on top of the rock where she had left it. She glanced towards the pool and tried to slip in without being noticed, then froze.

Cecily straddled Gryffon's lap, their sides to Amylia, his hands on her hips as she kissed him deeply. Water lapped around them to their movement, her breasts crushed against his chest and arms around his neck. They moved together, rocking slowly as Cecily moaned softly against his mouth.

Amylia's breath caught, heat flooding to her core as she watched, unable to drag her gaze away from them.

Cecily's head fell back as Gryffon moved his mouth to her neck, biting softly, his hand cupping her breast, engulfing it entirely. Amylia could see his fingers sinking into the soft flesh there as the edges of his teeth traced a line down the long column of Cecily's throat. The tips of her long pale hair brushed the water as his other arm snaked around her hips, muscles flexing as he pulled her harder onto him, his growl of pleasure echoing around the cavern as Cecily let out a gasp.

Amylia lurched forward, grabbing the robe, and fled. She ran, feet flying back up the dark staircase, air growing cooler the further she went until she reached her floor again, chest heaving as she leaned against the huge wooden door of her room. She stayed there, ears straining for any sound as she caught her breath before cracking her door open on its silent hinges and slipping inside.

Her room was dark and warm. Hanging the towel up, she slipped back into the silk robe and sank onto the soft bed, taking long, even breaths as she waited for her hammering heart to slow. Her mind betrayed her and swam with the images from the cavern as her core turned molten. She gave into it, running her hand idly over her stomach as she let the image of Cecily, neck arched as she melted in Gryffon's arms, run rampant through her memories.

Amylia let her mind wander in the dark, her fingertips tracing over her skin as Cecily's had done, feeling goosebumps raise as her fingers trailed past. She felt restless, unable to relax her body as her mind raced away from her, a low ache building in her that made her fidget irritably against the sheets. Groaning, she shook her head, looking to the ceiling. This was ridiculous.

She stood up brusquely, picked up her brush as she went, and paced, trying to ignore the odd pulsing in her body as she dragged the brush through her hair.

Amylia paced and brushed until her hair gleamed and her body had regained some sort of normalcy again, dragging the locks over her shoulder and braiding it into a long plait.

Pausing in front of the huge windows, she looked out across the inky night sky beyond. The glass fogged in front of her from her breath and she reached up, tracing her finger through it — the same designs that were inked across

Cecily's skin. She sighed, leaned forward, and rested her forehead against the cool glass, closing her eyes and breathing deep, slow breaths.

A soft knock sounded on the door. She startled, staring at it for a long moment before padding over to it. She hesitated a moment, her hand on it, before tugging it towards her, the presence behind the door drawing her like an undeniable force.

Blue eyes met hers. Cecily stepped towards her on silent feet, her silk robe tied loosely around her.

Amylia stopped breathing as Cecily came closer and the air around them heated slightly, her Gifts singing as her heart began to hammer again.

Cecily's hand traced across her hip and stilled her. She heard the silent, gentle question and her body answered on its own volition. She leaned towards her.

The world fell away as soft lips met hers. Her lips parted as Cecily ran her tongue over them gently.

She was fire and ice, her body humming, as the kiss deepened. Reaching out, her fingers twined into the silk of Cecily's robe, pulling her closer.

She couldn't tell where she ended, and Cecily began. Desire washed over her and through her, and something deeper, something stronger, pulled them together.

The kiss broke when Cecily pulled back. Her face swam into view again and she smiled wickedly at Amylia.

"Goodnight, sweetling," she murmured, her thumb caressing across Amylia's swollen and sensitive bottom lip. With a whisper of her robe, she vanished into the dark corridor.

Chapter 22

Cecily and Gryffon were not at breakfast the next morning. Amylia couldn't tell if she felt relief or disappointment as she stabbed her knife into a hot roll and flicked it onto her plate. It smelled incredible. Cracking it open, she spread a layer of butter and drizzled honey on it. She watched it melt slowly, and blearily stirred her steaming cup of tea.

Lyrik sprawled on a large chair at the end of the table, legs propped on its arm. Her deep hood was pulled up and over her head, covering her face. A cup of cold tea sat in front of her, clearly forgotten as its owner dozed.

"Who died?" Rogue laughed as he strolled in.

Lyrik lifted the edge of her hood and eyed him from the shadows of it. He pinched her toe as he walked past, earning him a snarl.

"You, in a minute," she muttered. She pulled her hood back, running a hand through her long hair which for once was unbound, and flowed over her shoulders to her waist, her face puffy with exhaustion.

"Oooooohhhh." Rogue grinned. "Too much ale last night?"

"Too much everything last night," she retorted, sitting up and grimacing before tenderly rubbing the side of her temple. "You would think at my age I'd know better."

"The blonde?" Rogue asked. Chuckling, he filled his plate with food and pulled a chair out next to Amylia.

Lyrik sighed, waving away the roll he offered her. "Anika. The redhead," she amended as Rogue looked at her quizzically.

Amylia stared at them, confused. "The redhead what?" she asked.

Rogue snorted again. "Woman. In Lyrik's bed… with a lot of ale and not much sleep, by the looks of her."

Amylia opened her mouth to reply and snapped it shut again, feeling, with irritation, her face begin to burn as Lyrik eyed her sardonically.

"I like both. I prefer women. In answer to the question that's stuck in your throat." Lyrik grinned and leaned forward to steal Rogue's now buttered roll. Eyeing it dubiously, she ignored Rogue's grunt of outrage. Her eyes flicked back up to Amylia's. A sly grin on her face, she asked, "My question is, which do you prefer?"

Amylia choked on her tea, spluttering as Rogue thumped her on the back helpfully. Eyes watering, she rasped, "What do you mean?"

"I've seen how you look at Cecily," Lyrik teased, biting into the roll, and groaning quietly, closing her eyes in brief bliss. She opened them, still grinning slyly, her voice slightly muffled as she continued. "And I know what that look means."

"Especially as you seem immune to my charms." Rogue chuckled, leaning against the back of his chair, and waggling an eyebrow at her. "I mean, come on." He gestured to the length of his body.

"You know, you're attractive until you open your mouth, Rogue," Lyrik said snidely, grimacing as she washed her mouthful down with the cold tea.

Rogue turned his amber eyes to Lyrik, his expression bemused, giving Amylia a moment to compose herself. "Hey, you know I'm open to being gagg—" A roll hit him dead between the eyes, crumbs exploding across the table. He laughed, wiping melted butter from his face. "Got it, hard pass."

Lyrik turned back to Amylia, eyebrow raised in question.

"I... I'm not sure," she mumbled, face flaming as Cecily's expression last night flashed through her mind.

Lyrik nodded, eyeing her with consideration and leaned back in her seat. "Just so you know... it's different here." Her voice softened. "We don't care who you decide to love, as long as it does no harm."

Rogue nodded. "Humans tend to have a stick up their ass when it comes to rules about who can be with whom. It's ridiculous, really."

"So... You like men, too?" Amylia asked, irritated at how red she knew she was turning.

Rogue chuckled. "No. I only like women. But the point is, here, we have the choice, though we're not all greedy like Lyrik." He flung an arm up as Lyrik picked up the butter knife but paused as voices sounded from the hall.

Rayvn and Silas entered, joking between themselves. Cutting the conversation short, they pulled out chairs and greeted everyone cheerfully.

Heliacle Rising

"Do you want me to do the cubs for you this morning?" Rayvn asked Lyrik, taking in the butterknife she was grudgingly placing on the table again. "I went out early and got some fish for Falkyn."

Silas nodded, his mouth full of food. Swallowing quickly and eyes watering as he nearly choked, he said, "I got some for Asspyn, too. And we have spare for Freyja."

Lyrik gave them a warm smile. "That would be great. Thank you, I'm sure Freyja would appreciate the attention if she's around. Though, Cess was looking for you before, Rayvn. She said she's going into the city later today to see if anyone needs healing and wanted you to go along with her."

Rayvn nodded. "I'll leave word for her that I will be back before lunch."

Amylia's heart melted at the look of excitement on her brother's face, his eyes glowing with the emotion. Hiding her smile in her cup, she watched them wolf down their breakfast, stuffing extra rolls in their pockets and chugging their drinks before leaving again, making hasty farewells. She watched Lyrik eyeing the fleeing boys, noticing the affection on her face as Rogue laughed softly.

"Well, they sure know how to impress you. Clever lads..."

Lyrik turned to give him a withering look. "They have put their hearts into training. I respect them for it. And they're good with the Sylkies. Rayvn especially. I've never seen Falkyn take to anyone... since Callysta passed."

Amylia swallowed, her brow creasing as she stared at the cup in her hand. "Thank you, Lyrik," she murmured, offering the woman a warm smile. "For giving my brother a chance. It means a lot to him."

Lyrik returned the smile. "He's a good kid."

Rogue grabbed Lyrik's hand and squeezed it. Amylia had noticed the strain on her face at the mention of Callysta and the look that passed between the two of them. Rogue tipped another buttered roll onto Lyrik's plate, then turned to Amylia with a grin. "Right, then. Ready to get your ass handed to you again?"

Amylia groaned, sagging in her chair, and he laughed. Standing up, he offered her a hand. "No running, I promise. Knives. And then we are going to go see how hot I can get you."

He laughed as she shot him a sharp look, winked at Lyrik and strode out. Amylia trailed after him.

Lyrik saluted her with the bread roll. "Good luck!" She laughed.

They worked late into the morning. Her muscles screamed as she lifted her blade to counter Rogue's as he drove it down towards her head in a long arc.

"Good."

He grinned, disengaging to come up with a fast blow aimed at her ribs. She blocked the slash, his blade reverberating up hers and into her aching fingers, but still she held fast, sweat beading on her brow. He swung a quick combination of fast strokes, left, block, right, block, and… there. There was the opening she noticed too late, her side exposed. He flicked his blade in and around, the flat of his blade headed for her side, aiming to bruise, not cut.

Amylia flinched away, inadvertently letting the iron hold on her Gifts go.

A wall of fierce wind blasted out at him, sending him reeling back. She leaped at the opening bringing her blade up in a quick arc, throwing herself into the blow. Fire licked up her blade and she yelped, dropping it.

Rogue barked a laugh and stopped, eyeing her to make sure she had it back in hand and whistled.

"You're learning faster than I thought you would."

She grinned, her chest heaving as she caught her breath. "Thank you," she gasped. "But that wasn't intentional."

He snorted. "Maybe not. But it was effective… until you threw it. Maybe don't throw it next time. Grab a drink and then let's head out. A change of scenery is always good. I think it's time to start really delving into those Gifts of yours since they are intent on showing themselves."

Amylia nodded, apprehension gnawing at her.

"What are you worried about?" he asked.

She grimaced, looking around. "The last time I let them go, I… hurt people."

"Well, I'm taking you out there." He pointed to the mountains jutting up behind the castle. "Not much to hurt out there except trees and the odd goat. Worst case scenario, we will have crispy goat for dinner. And we have Cess to sort any burns."

Amylia nodded, taking a deep swallow of her flask, and pushed Cecily's face firmly out of her mind.

"Go tack up the dragon," he said, uncorking his flask. "I'm sure she could use a good run. I heard she was terrorising old Grymes yesterday. We can leave the horses by the river and walk up, so they aren't in range. Can you ask him to ready my gelding as well? I'll grab us some lunch to take with us."

Amylia groaned. "I keep telling him to leave her to me. He swears he will get her to come around to him."

Rogue laughed. "Well, if he's set his mind to it, the dragon has met her match. The man's as stubborn as a Sylkie, especially when he takes it personally."

Entering the stone stables, Amylia smiled to herself, hearing Grymes amicably chatting to the horses in the pens.

"Now, now, it's just a wee brush," he crooned. "No… no, we don't do that now, darlin'. We keep our teeth to ourselves here."

Amylia hid her smile before she turned the corner. Shadow, ears flat and eyes flashing, eyed Grymes who stood at arm's length, trying to pick a snarl out of her long tail. The horse whickered and flicked her ears forward when she saw Amylia. Giving Grymes a warm smile, she crossed to the mare and ran her hand over her neck in welcome. He eyed the mare bitterly.

"She's a stubborn wee lass this one, isn't she?"

Amylia huffed a laugh, nodding. "She needs a good run."

She ran a hand over the healed scratches, brows bunching as she noticed the hairs that had just started growing out of them were pure white. She leaned closer, squinting at them.

"Oh, don't worry about those," he said. "It's normal for wounds to grow back with white hair. Nothin' to worry about." He patted Shadow on the flank, watching unbothered as she whipped her head around, teeth snapping. "She will have some pretty war wounds is all. Shows how brave she is, doesn't it, princess?"

Amylia cringed, hauling Shadow's head back around and cupping her hand over the velvet nose.

"She's all right." He laughed. "Some of the spirited ones just take a while." His face was soft as he looked at the mare. "Fine wee lass she is, too. I'll grab your tack for you now."

Amylia grinned. It was impossible not to like him. "Thank you. Are you able to get Rogue's mount ready, too? I will sort Shadow out."

He nodded, dropping the brush into a wooden bucket. "I can indeed, m'lady."

They readied the animals fast. Amylia was swinging into the saddle when Rogue arrived. He carried a bag over his shoulder, tying it to the saddle and murmuring his thanks to Grymes as he took the horse.

The sun warmed Amylia's skin as they rode, enjoying the peace in amicable silence. The horses, content, stretched out in an easy loping walk, snatching the odd mouthful of grass as they went.

They followed the small, snaking mountain stream up the valley towards the mountains. Letting the horses have their heads when they hit the open plains, they raced each other to the end, Shadow winning by a mile.

Amylia waited for Rogue, grinning as his horse pulled up, its sides heaving.

He looked at Shadow with appreciation. "I'm still waiting for you and Lyrik to have that race." He laughed. "Though I think Shadow could even beat Freyja in flight, and I cannot wait to see Lyrik's face when she does."

They left the horses picking grass at the edge of the plain and walked towards the base of the mountain, stopping a while later in a small glade.

Rogue handed her the flask as he looked back towards Asteryn. The castle jutted up in the distance, beautiful against the glistening sea in the background.

"Ready?" he asked.

"Nope," she answered with a grimace.

"I want to see your worst," he said, face serious. "So we know what we're dealing with. You are doing remarkably well in your restraint. Too well, in my opinion, and I'm not really sure what's hiding in there."

Amylia nodded, apprehension filling her as she looked at her hands. "What if I lose control?"

He squeezed her shoulder. "If you feel yourself slipping, just tell me. I'll bring you back."

Amylia nodded, clenching her hands. "Okay... what do I do?"

He stepped behind her, large hands on her shoulders, and gently turned her until she faced the general direction of the mountain.

"Close your eyes," he murmured. She did. "I want you to draw your power towards your hands, focus it. Start with fire. We know you have that. Call its heat towards your palms."

Amylia reached down, searching for the hot threads that surged inside her and grasped them, feeling them eagerly flow through her. The rippling flames burned along her arms, and she felt Rogue's grip on her shoulders release as he stepped back. Opening her palms in front of her, holding her hands out, she looked at the blue flames burning brightly in her palms.

"Good," Rogue encouraged. "Keep it there but reach again. Bring more up, as if you are feeding wool into a spinning wheel. Control it but feed it."

Amylia reached again, feeling the threads happily move towards the flame, sucking into it as the flames danced around her hands. She kept the size the same but let the heat increase. The centre of the flames above her hands got white-hot quickly.

"You're doing great." Rogue's calm voice sounded from behind her. "Do you feel like you can hold that for a bit?"

"I can do more," she murmured, concentrating on the flames. The power inside her felt barely touched, and it pushed against her, like a cat brushing against her legs, asking to follow.

She let it, bringing more up as the flames glowed hotter and hotter in front of her, the blue merging with silver. The surrounding air shimmered with the heat, and she felt Rogue take another step back.

"Don't take too much, Amylia," he warned. "You don't want to burn yourself out."

Amylia gritted her teeth. "There's more," she hissed as, again, she opened up more, allowing the power to flow freely into her hands.

It blazed as twin infernos in her palms, and she looked at them with wonder, losing herself in the dancing flames. Pouring more and more into them, she felt relief as the power, locked down for so long, flowed out, singing to her as she unleashed it.

She let everything fade as she delved into herself, opening that channel, and feeling it flood out. The air around her crackled and sparked as the flames crept over her, dancing across her skin in patterns.

Vaguely, she could still feel Rogue's presence behind her. He had moved away to the corner of the clearing. Behind him she sensed someone else. Another person was coming towards them. The feeling of them was familiar but laced with concern.

Amylia let the thoughts drift away and sighed. Her breath came out as smoke, curling in the air in front of her. She watched it join the inferno in her hands. Beautiful designs of fire snaked up her arms, a molten lacework that rippled over her skin, the fabric on the sleeves of her shirt falling away to ash.

"*Amylia!*" She heard the name faintly, a sense of irritation washing over her at the interruption. "*Amylia!*" The name buzzed around her again and she cocked her head, the familiarity of it itching at her as she turned her head, her peripheral vision picking up movement behind her.

"AMYLIA! Pull it back *now!*"

She snapped back to herself, jolting, and turning back to look at her hands.

Rogue skirted the glade, keeping back from the wall of heat around her that made the air shimmer until he came level with her side.

"Pull it back, Amylia. Take a deep breath and shut it down. Close the channel off."

She sucked in a breath and glanced around, the heat from the flames making the air dance around her.

Why, it was such a relief to let this... this pressure go.

"Don't panic. You're okay. Just breathe and pull it back."

She frowned slightly. She couldn't. It was flowing too fast out of her. Bottomless power in her happily fed the flames. She closed her fists, trying to pull back, trying to cut the tether.

Nothing. Still the fire raged around her. The grass at her feet withered and caught fire, her clothing flickered in flame. She groaned, suddenly feeling anxious, and gritted her teeth, grasping for it again, pulling it back to her.

She couldn't break it. Sweat beaded on her forehead as everything slowed.

Cold panic curled into her stomach and Amylia grabbed her Gift tightly, as if strangling it. It fought her, a wild animal in her mental grasp, and she struggled with the connection, trying to break it as it roared. Desperate, she threw it away from her, forcing the connection to snap.

Fire blasted out from her and the trees in the clearing exploded, splintering from the wall of heat that erupted around them, grass turning to dust underfoot. She whirled, shock and fear surging through her, a scream caught in her throat as she reached, reached to stop the flames from engulfing the lives behind her. Rogue fell to his knees, an arm thrown over his head. Around him, a cocoon of swirling air protected him.

The grass he knelt in was still green. Off to the right, a second, larger cocoon wrapped around another person. Cecily knelt within, her arms wrapped protectively around the white wolf.

The shields snuffed out as both the crouched figures rose. Rogue, his face white, took in the clearing as Cecily lurched forward, running to him across grass that crumbled underfoot as she scanned him for injuries.

When he shook his head, Cecily changed course, cautiously approaching Amylia, who stood in stony silence, staring at her shaking hands. She tore her gaze away and looked at Cecily blankly. "What are you doing here?"

Cecily shook her head, taking her cloak off and throwing it around Amylia. Her clothes had disappeared in a wisp of ash.

"I was hunting, and I heard Rog—"

"What are you doing here? I could have burned you!" Amylia interrupted, terrified as she surveyed the clearing. "I could have burned both of you!" Her body had started to tremble all over.

Cecily looked at Rogue, who joined them. His face was deathly white as he touched Amylia's shoulder carefully.

"Amylia, I'm sorry. I didn't know. I didn't know what you were holding back. This is my fault."

Amylia moaned, her breath coming rapidly as her eyes swung wildly around, her hands waving them back. Cecily caught them, holding them gently between her own, turning her so her back was to Rogue as the cloak parted with her movements.

"It's okay, sweetling, you didn't hurt us. That wasn't us putting those shields up. That was you." She turned to look at Rogue. "Did you teach her that?"

He shook his head, running a hand over his face. "I didn't know. I would have if I'd have known. How was she holding that in? And how did she know you were there, too? I didn't see you walk up."

"I felt her," Amylia whispered. "I felt both of you, can you not feel each other? You feel… different from each other."

Rogue looked at Cecily. "Lymbical Gifts?" His face was a tide of stunned emotion.

Amylia looked at him, confused. "Lymbical?" Cecily squeezed her hands, so she turned her attention back to her.

"It's the power to feel others, feel their life force. Sometimes it can go as far as feeling their emotions, or even influencing them. They are ancient and powerful gifts." She swallowed. "They are Heliacle Gifts, Amylia."

Amylia stared at her. "What are you saying?"

"It means… the reason you survived the Helix… and now… I think the reason Attica was searching for you. It's because you're not an Elementyl, sweetling… you are a Heliacle."

She pulled her hands away, confusion coursing through her. "You told me there were no Heliacles left."

Rogue took a choking breath.

"There weren't…"

They left the burnt glade, walking slowly back to the horses. Cecily's grey mare, two rabbits hanging from the saddle, grazed with them. Cecily eyed Amylia who had been silent, walking next to her and holding the cloak tightly around herself, and turned to Rogue.

"You go on ahead. Amylia and I will ride a bit longer, give her a moment to think."

Rogue nodded, casting a worried glance at Amylia as he mounted his gelding.

The women mounted, after Amylia had slipped into the spare hunting clothes Cecily had in her pack, and paused to wait as Rogue mounted and nodded his goodbye.

"Come." Cecily smiled at her. "I want to show you something."

They rode for an hour, in silence, following the base of the mountain, meeting a small stream that curled through the valley. They followed it upstream, the horses deftly picking their way over rocks and thick trees until they came to a small clearing. The stream had opened up to a beautiful blue pool with a waterfall burbling into it at the far side. Boulders peppered the edge with tall trees interspersed with birds flitting around between them.

Cecily grinned at her. "This is mine and Gryffon's secret. We come here in summer to swim, and when the noise of everything just gets a bit much for us… and now… it's your secret too."

"It's beautiful," Amylia said, eyes wide as she looked around the clearing.

Spring wildflowers poked up in the grass around the pool. An old, gnarled tree off to the side provided shade next to it. They dismounted, tying the horses to a sturdy tree on the edge of the clearing.

Cecily untied a small bag from her saddle and wandered over to the tree, choosing a soft patch of grass to sit in. Amylia followed and lowered herself next to her.

"It's a lot to take in," Cecily murmured. "But you have our full support, and you will get control of it."

Amylia let her head fall into her hands, resting her elbows on her knees, and watched a dragonfly flitting across the surface of the blue water. "It felt good, so good to let it go. I didn't realise how hard it had been to hold on to it until I didn't have to anymore." She met Cecily's piercing blue eyes. "I don't want to hurt anyone. I could have hurt you, Cess, and that scares me."

Cecily smiled, reaching out to brush her cheek. "But you didn't. Rogue can help. I think you took us all by surprise." She huffed a laugh. "It's not every day Rogue is lost for words."

Amylia glowered at her. "Thanks."

Cecily chuckled. "Any time." She picked up the bag next to her and pulled out a couple of apples, handing one to Amylia. "Give yourself time. You have gone through so much in such a short time. No one expects you to have everything under control immediately."

The small glade worked its serene magic as they sat in silence, and Amylia felt the tension of the last few hours slip away slowly, her body relaxing in the silence as they ate the apples.

"You weren't at breakfast this morning," she murmured, the question hanging in the air as she wasn't sure how to continue. Cecily threw her core into the trees, turning to look at Amylia, a wicked smile on her face.

"I didn't know how you would react if I came. I wanted to see you alone first. That, and I hadn't gone hunting in a while. Gryff had meetings to attend in town, so he left at first light anyway."

Amylia flushed, opening her mouth to speak, and shutting it again, throwing her core after Cecily's.

"Do you wish I hadn't kissed you?" Cecily's eyes danced as Amylia slid her gaze to her.

She took a shaky breath, considering for a while before shaking her head. "Is it terrible of me that I want you to do it again?"

Cecily's smile changed as she looked into Amylia's eyes. She leaned forward and cupped her cheek, whispering against her lips, "I'll kiss you as much as you like, sweetling."

She tasted faintly of apples. Cecily's tongue explored Amylia's mouth, flicking along the edges of her lip and teeth in a gentle question. When the kiss deepened, Amylia moaned softly. Cecily bit her lip, and desire curled in her stomach, the familiar burning sensation kindling.

Just as the world disappeared in a soft haze, Cecily pulled away, laughing huskily at the small sound of protest Amylia made.

"You are very addictive," Cecily whispered to her. "But we really should be getting back."

Chapter 23

Amylia kept an iron fist on her powers, anxiety at the risk of losing the slightest control snapping at her, even though the strain of them abated slightly after the drain of the day.

She noticed Rogue watching her subtly through dinner and felt her cheeks flame, the look on his face after she had exploded the clearing burnt into her mind. Cecily also threw anxious glances her way during dinner, making her emotions flare; lust, guilt, anxiety, they all battled for dominance in her head as she listened to Gryffon's deep voice murmuring to Cecily, laughing at something she had said.

Half-heartedly, she listened to Rayvn and Silas animatedly chatting to Lyrik. The woman wore a small, bemused smile as she watched the boys.

Amylia poured herself a glass of rich wine and moved to the fire. Athyna lay next to it and sat up as she neared. The giant animal's head came to her waist as she looked up with startling sapphire eyes. Absently, she ran her fingers through the smooth fur on Athyna's wide head and twirled a lock of it around her finger as she stared into the flames. The heat touched her face and curled around her neck and limbs, both bare to the flames.

The intoxicating aroma of her wine filled her senses and took away some of the stress of the day as Rogue moved up next to her, jug in hand, and quietly refilled her glass.

"Are you doing okay?"

Amylia grimaced, taking an appreciative swig of the wine before answering. "I should be asking you that, you're the one who was nearly charcoal."

He nudged her shoulder gently with his and she turned her face up to look at him. "You're being too hard on yourself," he murmured, his eyes soft as he looked down at her. "You have remarkable control considering what you are holding on to. I've known people with less Gift, and less control, than you already have."

Amylia looked back at her glass, forehead creasing, and drained it again, welcoming the warm numbness spreading through her, and held her glass back out to him. He hesitated before refilling it again.

"Have you told anyone yet?" he asked quietly. "Rayvn?"

Amylia shook her head, glancing at the boy, who was smiling widely at Lyrik. "No, he's happy. I prefer not to stress him with anything else at the moment." She flicked her eyes to Gryffon who was sitting at the dining table. Cecily had perched on his lap as he rested his forehead against her collar. Her shoulders shaking as she laughed at something he had said.

"I feel like I need to tell Gryff what is living in his home, though."

Rogue frowned. "You are living in his home, Amylia. Still the same person. This hasn't changed who you are."

"Hasn't it?" The question came out sharply, her eyes searching his, and she fought to keep her emotions in check. "Because it feels like I'm discovering this whole other person that I don't recognise."

Rogue nodded. "I understand that. Keep it to yourself as long as you need but know that we're all here to help you with it when you're ready."

Amylia huffed. "I don't even know what I'm keeping to myself yet... fire... lymbics? I don't even know what that is. I can't feel you now like I felt you in the clearing."

He held his hand palm up, towards her. "Then try."

She looked at him flatly. "I can just push you into the fireplace if you have a death wish. It would probably be safer."

He chuckled, hand still out. "Let the fire sleep. Let's see what else you have." He wiggled his fingers at her. "May as well get all the shocks out at once, Lady Sylvers."

She hesitated, hand hovering over his. He watched her before sighing and placing hers into his large palm.

"Now what?" she said, feeling ridiculous. She looked at their clasped hands and raised a brow at him, feeling Cecily's and Gryffon's attention turn to them.

"Close your eyes, smart ass," Rogue said dryly.

Amylia sighed deeply, taking a swig of her wine, and closed them.

"Don't reach into your powers. Lymbical Gifts are not a source you draw from. It's part of you, your soul listening to mine," Rogue murmured, stepping slightly nearer her.

She reached out to him, feeling her fire try snaking out with it, and stopped, stamping it firmly down again. "I can't," she whispered. "It all comes with it."

"Then follow our connection. Don't reach... just move through it."

She cracked an eye at him, brow raised, met his stern gaze, and shut it quickly, shifting on her feet.

Focusing on their grip, she moved towards it and felt... felt that fingerprint of him behind it. She recognised it, as if seeing a familiar face in a crowd, flowing into him as if stepping into a pool of warm water, sensing his surprise and delight as he felt her presence.

She floated lazily, looking back at herself. She felt his worry for her, noticing how he looked at the slight line of strain on her brow as she held herself in check and realised with a snap of exhilaration that she was looking through Rogue's eyes.

Amylia felt his slight nervousness as he stood next to the Dyre wolf, her large head dangerously close to a part he held very dear to himself. She felt the deep respect he had for Gryffon, his protectiveness over Cecily... and then, when he looked at Lyrik, she felt his warm flash of desire.

Quickly pulling away, she felt as if she was peeping in a window she wasn't meant to. She glanced back at herself again, noticing with sudden shock that blue flames rippled across her hand as she touched his. She noticed the faint sting in his palm where his hand twined with hers.

She ripped herself away from him with a cry, the flames sighing out as she grabbed them again, ripping them back angrily, just as the glass in her hand exploded from the flames in her other hand. The quick bite of pain from the glass shard digging into her palm was enough to firmly root her back in her own body.

"I'm sorry," she breathed as she pushed past him, running for the door.

Cecily half-stood as Amylia rushed out, pausing as Gryffon placed a hand on her back. He kissed her gently behind the ear as she sat back down, breathing in her scent and felt her lean back against him.

"Just give her a minute. I'll go after her." He nodded towards Rogue. "Maybe go check his hand, my love."

She nestled her ass into his thigh, making him clench his jaw as he eyed her and she smiled softly, kissing him on the nose as he patted her behind.

"She's had a rough day already, Gryff," Cecily said softly, watching the others who had looked up at Amylia's departure, too. "See if you can make her go easier on herself; she's just scared."

Gryffon nodded, nuzzling her neck briefly before she stood and walked to Rogue, murmuring softly to him as she took his large hand in hers. He grabbed his glass, tipping his head back to drain it, reached out to pick up the full decanter, and then headed in the direction Amylia had disappeared.

Amylia ran barefoot across the castle garden, feeling the sand start peppering through the grass as she reached the shore. The white beach was illuminated in the moonlight as the waves whispered against it, gentle caresses as if the sea were holding its breath, letting the people around it sleep.

Taking a deep breath of the salty air, the panic in her eased the further away she got from anyone she could hurt. She sank to the sand — the lingering warmth from the day's sun still seeped from it — and looked out at the vast sea in front of her. A gentle breeze kissed her face and strands of her hair tangled around her shoulders, pulled free from her bun. Amylia reached up, tugging the bun free, and shook it out. Feeling her black tresses cascade around her back, she ran her hands through them and sighed.

She felt Gryffon before she heard him, stiffening as his footsteps crunched behind her.

"Mind if I join you?" he asked quietly, holding the wine out to her.

She shook her head, reaching out and grasping the decanter, and he lowered himself next to her. Taking a deep swig, she held it on her tongue for a moment, letting the rich aroma steal through her senses before swallowing.

His shoulder felt warm as it touched hers and his bulk was comforting and solid next to her.

Amylia shot him a look under her lashes. He stared out at the water. She took another swig before handing it back to him.

"No one expects you to have control of this right away," he said softly, still looking out to sea, and she startled, surprised at his directness. His golden eyes glowed softly as he looked down at her and grinned. "We did tell you that I burned a lot of stuff while I was learning, didn't we?"

She sighed unhappily. "Yes, but you didn't burn people."

Gryffon hissed through his teeth. "I did, actually… and it still haunts me to this day. My mother. I was mad at something else, and she was in the way. She never held it against me, but still, I hurt her, and it took a long time to forgive myself afterwards and she always bore the scar on her arm. The men you burned deserved it, Amylia. They would have done a terrible thing to you."

"I wasn't meaning them." Grimly she said, "Did Cecily not tell you about today?"

Gryffon shook his head, reaching out to take her hand and uncurl her fingers from the cut on her palm slowly leaking blood. "Just that you had had a rough day. And were being harsh on yourself."

Amylia huffed. "She was being kind."

Gryffon pulled a handkerchief from his pocket, gently winding the white fabric around the small wound, tying it with a small knot.

She told him in a quiet voice about the glade, about losing control and the explosion, the shields, and the revelation of her Lymbical Gifts. He didn't look surprised at her Heliacle status, sitting quietly until she was done, and sharing the wine amicably.

"What are you afraid of, Amylia?" he asked her softly when she fell silent.

Tears burned her eyes. She looked at him, holding her hand out to him, a pool of blue fire flickering in her palm. "I'm afraid I'll get to that point again. It was so easy to let it go. I'm afraid I'll hurt someone I don't want to… and that I won't be able to take it back."

Gryffon held his palm up next to hers. His flames merged with hers, blue and gold twining around each other, then he hooked his finger around hers, pulling her hand closer. With a feline grin, he blew into them.

Ice crusted delicately over their palms. The flames winked out as the ice continued up her arm. Swirls of it appeared as lacework up her forearm as she watched, and it cooled her blood.

"I'm not afraid of you, little firebug. And neither is anyone else." He chuckled softly. "The only thing I ask is that you trust us; the rest will sort itself out."

Amylia stared at the ice, mouth open slightly as it finished ascending her arm and began to melt from the warmth of her skin.

Gryffon picked up a handful of sand, drizzling it into her palm, before he cupped it with his own. Flames licked through their joint hands, little gusts of wind coaxing them into an inferno. The sand disappeared in a white-hot, molten centre.

Transfixed, Amylia stared as the wind manipulated the flames, whipping them until they danced around like a living thing. Then he blew delicately again, cooling air, dulling the flames, and leaving a red-hot glowing object in her hand.

The red faded, going white and then clear. Its features became visible, and she gasped. It was Shadow. The tiny glass figurine was a perfect replica, rearing in her palm.

"Our Gifts can be a thing of beauty, but they are wild and powerful. It will be hard learning as you are now, but Amylia, if anyone can do it... as strong as you are, it's you."

She gulped, her emotions threatening to take over as she cradled the tiny figurine in her palms and a tear slipped down her cheek.

"I don't deserve such kindness," she whispered, looking at him. "I'm staying in your home, and I..." She trailed off, looking at him with pleading eyes. "You and Cess... I can't..."

"We are not just talking about the Gifts here, are we?" he interrupted mildly.

Amylia shook her head miserably, then looked up in disbelief as he laughed softly.

"I've been with my mate for over a hundred years," he said, smiling as he looked out at the sea again. "You don't think I know who she is? It's been a very long time since I've seen her look at anyone other than me like that, and it warms my heart to see her letting herself open up again after being so broken." He grinned at Amylia. "And I'm not going to pretend I'm not drawn to you as well, or that you aren't to me. I saw you, down in the pools."

She felt her cheeks heat in the dark and took a deep drink of the wine, cradling the sculpture to her breast with one hand. The laugh that rumbled from his chest made her toes curl as she fumbled for what to say, passing him back the wine.

"I... didn't mean to," she said, almost inaudible, and traced a finger over the tiny glass head.

"Cecily has a habit of sneaking under your skin when you least expect it." He chuckled, giving her a knowing look.

"You both do. To use Cecily's words, you are addictive," she murmured.

They sat quietly, listening to the waves crash as they finished the last of the wine.

Gryffon held the decanter upside down after a while, raising an eyebrow at her.

"I think it's best we get back. They'll be starting to worry." He stood gracefully, offering her a hand, which she took, staggering slightly as her head swam. Gryffon snorted, dipping to sweep her off her feet, holding her easily cradled in his arms as he began to walk up the beach.

"So, are you not going to remember your grand declarations in the morning with all that wine in you?" His tone was teasing, and Amylia looked up at him, admiring the strong cut of his jaw.

"I'll remember." She put out a hand towards his chest, hesitating, and looked up at him in question. He stopped walking, looking at her for a minute, his eyes glowing softly in the dim light, and he nodded.

Amylia placed her hand on him, closing her eyes as she did, and stepped into him. His fingerprint was so different from Rogue's, yet similar in an odd way. The feelings wrapping around her had the same undertones: loyalty, and compassion.

Cecily was strong in his mind, the bond between the two, their minds melded in a way completely impossible to separate. It burnt with such passion and love that it made Amylia's breath come short.

She watched her face out of his eyes as her neck flushed in the cool night air and let the feelings swirl around her. Burning desire as he looked at her, desire mixed with something else. Protectiveness, possessiveness? All of them swirled through him in a confusing mass. She pulled back into herself and opened her eyes to see him watching her. Flames licked over the hand that touched his chest and he looked down, blowing them out with an icy breath.

He hesitated for a long moment before dipping his head to hers and kissing her softly. It took the breath away from her, the taste of him in her mouth, mixing with the wine. Gryffon went to pull away, but she slipped her hand around his neck and pulled him harder against her. His lips were warm as his arms cradled her gently to him.

The beach melted away as he kissed her soundly, exploring her mouth. She felt his heart pick up tempo, a solid beat she could nearly hear in the still of the night until he pulled away, a sheepish grin on his face.

"You're drunk and I've just taken advantage of that," he said regretfully and began to walk again.

Amylia shook her head, resting it against his collarbone as they walked. "Then kiss me again when I'm sober." She sighed and his laugh rumbled next to her ear as they walked up the steps to the castle gardens.

Amylia woke the next morning to light streaming through the windows. Vaguely, she could remember Gryffon placing her into bed and pulling the covers around her. Feeling something hard in her hand, she looked down and smiled at the tiny glass figurine nestled in her palm. Running a thumb across the delicately arched head, she marvelled at the detail.

She sat up and groaned when the full effects of the wine slammed into her as she reached to place the ornament on the bedside table. A soft knock came at the door and Cecily pushed it open a crack.

She asked softly, "Okay if I come in?"

Amylia winced as a bolt of pain shot through her head and groaned, grabbing it in both her hands. But she nodded gingerly at Cecily, who whistled in sympathy, then chuckled softly and nudged the door open. She carried a cup of hot tea cradled in her hands.

The mattress dipped as she sat beside Amylia.

"I'm pretty sure I'm dying, Cess," she whispered as a wave of nausea washed over her.

Cecily snorted. "I think you will live. Normally, I don't heal hangovers," she teased and reached out and touched the side of Amylia's temple. The pain melted away and Amylia's body went loose with the relief. "But I think in this case I'll make an exception." Cecily chuckled, handing her the cup.

It was chamomile and honey. The sweet steam wafted up to greet Amylia as she raised it to her lips and took a sip. She groaned as the hot liquid burned deliciously down to her stomach.

"Gryff said you might be feeling the worst for it this morning." Cecily said dryly.

"Thank you," Amylia breathed.

"Anytime, sweetling." Cecily stood, clicking her tongue at Athyna who was exploring the room. Turning to go, she called over her shoulder, "I put some food aside for you, too, when you're ready."

CHAPTER 24

Lost in thoughts of both Gryffon and Cecily swimming through her mind, Amylia barely noticed anyone else all day. Her training with Rogue passed in a blur.

She tried to focus through dinner as Rayvn gushed about Falkyn, her brother's excitement making him trip over his words. She was keenly aware of both Cecily and Gryffon watching her and the amusement that came from Lyrik when she briefly sat next to her.

Amylia kept her distance from them, knowing where to look now for the emotions, the feelings that emanated from the people around her, knowing what she would feel if she got too close, and not trusting herself.

Dark amusement, tinged with a hint of jealousy wafted to her and she turned her head towards Rogue.

"Lymbics chafing a bit there, Amylia?" he teased, his eyes filled with humour.

"It's a bit overwhelming," she breathed, and he chuckled.

"I can tell." He threw a pointed look towards Cecily and back to her, and she eyed him sardonically.

"Do you really want to get into that conversation?" Her eyes flicked to Lyrik and back to him. He actually flushed before holding out his hand to her.

"May I suggest a truce?" He grinned sheepishly.

Amylia took his hand, laughing softly. "It's okay. I'm sorry. I feel like I'm intruding on everyone. Is there a way of turning it off?"

Rogue sighed. "To be honest, I don't know. As we said, Heliacles have been gone for a while. I wouldn't even know where to start with Lymbical Gifts. I'm sorry, we don't even know the extent of yours, they seem to be growing by the day."

Amylia groaned softly, putting her head in her hands. He leaned in, patting her gently on the back. "I'll try to keep my feelings to myself." He chuckled.

She dropped her hands to look at him and snorted. "That would be very much appreciated."

Amylia fled to her room soon after, the dimly lit peace of it soothing her mind as she tried to calm her body as well.

The rush of need that had flooded across her when she attempted to sit next to Gryffon had completely derailed her, and she had quickly made her excuses and left.

Pacing through her room, she pulled off her restrictive clothing, stubbing her toe on a chair and swearing softly as she hopped on one foot, rubbing the offending appendage. Her whole being itched and hummed softly as she threw the windows open in an attempt to cool herself and braced her arms on the sill, letting the breeze whisper over her skin as she closed her eyes.

In her mind's eye, golden eyes looked back at her from the dark, and she cursed again, sighing as she closed the windows. This was unbearable. She needed to talk to them, find some way of managing this before it burned her from the inside out.

"Enough." She grabbed her robe, throwing it on and tying it around herself firmly before yanking her door open. The hallway was dark, except for the dim lights glowing out from under Lyrik's and Rogue's doors.

Running silently to the stone staircase that led to the level above, Amylia climbed it swiftly, her stomach knotting with doubt as she went.

There was only one room on the upper level. A huge wooden door split to open in the middle was lit dimly by windows in the hallway. The moonlight cast its soft glow across the gnarled wood.

Amylia took a breath, feeling them as she neared. Her heart pounding, she reached out and knocked. She detected no movement from within. Her breath left her with a whoosh; she hadn't realised she had been holding it. They must be asleep.

Maybe that's for the b—

Her thoughts flatlined when the door swung inwards on silent hinges. Gryffon stood there in loose-fitted white cotton pants tied at the waist... and nothing else.

She made herself look at his face. Her breath caught when she saw his eyes glowing softly in the candlelight of the room.

"I don't know what I'm doing here." Doubt and embarrassment surged through her.

Gryffon smiled tenderly. "I think you do. And can I make a suggestion?"

She nodded mutely as he stepped towards her. He reached out, pushing her hair behind her ear. His other hand slid across her hip, then he was kissing her.

Her mind exploded and went silent at the same time. Her focus stayed entirely on where their lips met, no wine dulling her senses this time.

Her Gifts roiled inside her, threatening to break free. She shoved them down deep, slamming the door firmly on them, the fire of them licking their way around the edges of that door.

His hands ran across the small of her back and down. Cupping her ass in his large palms, he lifted her effortlessly until she straddled him, her robe hitched high up her thighs. His hands held her secure against him, one arm curling around her back and pulling her closer.

He turned lazily, still exploring her mouth with his own and she heard him kick the door shut with a thump. With her in his arms, he crossed the dim room, her legs wrapped around the warm, bare skin of his waist. His muscles were hard under her arms where they rested against his shoulders, her hands hooked behind his neck.

Breaking the kiss, Gryffon halted and the look of hunger in his eyes washed over her in waves and started a burn in her stomach, slow and smouldering. He lowered her to the ground, letting her slide against his chest as she did until her toes hit the floor.

He turned her gently and her eyes met Cecily's blue ones, burning softly in the dim light of the room.

"Hello, sweetling," she murmured. She was close enough for Amylia to see the flecks of turquoise in her eyes. Cecily reached out, not breaking eye contact, and tugged on the tie holding Amylia's robe closed, the silk whispering across her skin as it parted.

Amylia's breath hitched as Gryffon's finger traced up her spine to her collar, sliding his hands along either side of it, pulling it from her and dropping it to the side with a hiss of silk. She leaned into Cecily, who stopped a hair's breadth from her lips, teasing her playfully. Through her Gifts, Amylia felt the emotions pouring out of the woman, rushing over and around her until Cecily's hands slid across the curve of Amylia's naked hip and pulled her into a kiss.

Cecily was a soft and sweet contrast to Gryffon's burning steel and Amylia's heart raced as the room faded away. Everything except her connection with these two people. Cecily pulled back, taking a deep breath, and cupped Amylia's face as she looked into her eyes again.

Heliacle Rising

"Are you certain?" she whispered. Amylia nodded, moaning softly as Gryffon bit her shoulder gently. "Have you ever…"

Amylia hesitated, a curl of apprehension snaking into her belly, and shook her head.

Cecily's eyes flicked to Gryffon over her shoulder, and his teeth left her skin. He placed a feather light kiss on the spot as his hands ran down her sides, raising goosebumps as they went.

Then Cecily was kissing her again, skimming her tongue against Amylia's lips as she parted them. The kiss deepened as she ran her hand behind Amylia's neck, fingers twisting into her inky curls.

Amylia lost herself in the taste of Cecily, sweet like wine, noticing Gryffon had moved away by the cool breeze against her back that came from the windows, the same as in her own room, open wide to let the sea breezes in.

Cecily pushed the straps of her gown off her shoulders, dragging her attention back, and Amylia heard the swish as it fell to the floor, reaching for her impulsively. She nervously ran a hand over the smooth skin of Cecily's side and traced the curve of a breast with her thumb.

Cecily took her hands and stepped backwards, pulling and turning Amylia until she felt her thighs hit a cushy mattress and Cecily give her a light shove, sending her tumbling onto the soft expanse.

Cecily's skin was warm as she stretched next to her and pressed her soft lips to Amylia's collarbone. Her hair tickled Amylia's stomach where it cascaded over Cecily's shoulder. Down her lips went; the tip of her tongue traced over Amylia's breast. Her hand trailed over Amylia's abdomen and the burn there grew hotter, molten fire aching for the hand to go lower.

Cecily rested her lips on the base of Amylia's neck, kissing the pulse that fluttered frantically there as Amylia lost herself, surrendering entirely, gasping as her hand dipped lower and brushed across her thigh. Fingertips lightly teased across the sensitive skin of her thigh as Cecily claimed her mouth again and Amylia arched her back, moaning into Cecily's mouth as delicate fingers moved to the apex of her thighs, dipping in to tease the small bundle of nerves there, gently stroking it in circles. Amylia fought to keep her Gifts down, small embers of fire flickering over her skin in the dim light.

Cecily smiled against Amylia's mouth and pulled back to watch her face as she kept up the pattern with her hand, gentle circles around and around. She twined one leg with Amylia's, pushing them further apart, her mouth slightly open as she watched Amylia's reaction.

Dimly, Amylia heard the chink of a cup being put down on the chest next to the bed, and then the bed dipped to her other side.

Gryffon's warm hand on her hip pulled her briefly out of the haze of pleasure when he slid it down her thigh. He eased her leg up, bending her knee over his hip. Lifting, he rolled her towards Cecily slightly, his hard chest against her back, his mouth on her neck. His hand moved to her breast, rolling her nipple gently in his fingers. Cecily's hand never stopped its movement.

Amylia was sure she was going to shatter. The sensations reached a crest as she felt him hard against her ass. He pushed his hips against her, and then, just as she thought she couldn't take it anymore, the wave crashed over her.

The sensations intense, Amylia moaned as they washed over her. Cecily's hands stilled to gentle strokes while Gryffon held her against him, kissing her shoulder while she shuddered in his arms.

Panting, Amylia opened her eyes to Cecily's satisfied smile.

"Are you okay?" Cecily whispered, kissing her on the tip of her nose.

Amylia took a shuddering breath, humming her assent as she nodded weakly. She still pulsed with desire, but felt so sated at the same time, her limbs heavy as if they had been filled with lead.

Gryffon moved against her back. There was the faint scrape of a cup he picked up. She heard him take a sip then he passed it to Cecily. She took it with a wicked grin at him and tipped the cup slightly, letting a few drops drip onto Amylia's breast then dipped her head to lick them off.

Gryffon's finger touched Amylia's chin, turning her to him. Then his lips were on hers, rich wine flowing into her mouth. The kiss was deep and stole what breath she had left. A trickle of wine escaped down her chin to pool in the hollow of her neck.

He pushed his hips against her ass and Amylia moaned. The feeling of him hard against her made her heart skip and nerves skittered in her chest.

Cecily's hand was back then, her touch feather-light against sensitive skin. Gryffon moved her up slightly, breaking their kiss to bring his mouth to her neck and then her shoulder again.

The wave was rising again, and the burning deepened. She was slick against Cecily's hands, slight shockwaves still going through her, and Gryffon's cock nudged against her entrance.

Stiffening, Amylia's hand flew back to grab his arm. He stilled, his hand caressing her hip.

"Just breathe," Cecily murmured against her mouth. "We've got you, sweetling. It will only hurt for a moment."

Heliacle Rising

They stayed like that while Amylia calmed, Cecily's hand working its torturous circles. Gryffon kissed her gently, his tongue sliding into her mouth, tasting of the sweet wine, and the low growl in his chest rumbled against her spine with the effort of holding himself still.

She arched her back as Cecily's hand teased her towards the edge again, the ache building, becoming too much. She needed something, anything, to help ease it. Running her hand up Gryffon's arm and across to his hip, she pulled him to her, needing him closer.

He gripped her hip as he thrust and she cried out as a quick flash of pain seared through her, but it was gone immediately as Cecily put her hand on Amylia's abdomen. The warm feeling of her healing flared and then receded.

Amylia gasped at the sensation of him inside her, stretching her, while Cecily resumed her slow strokes, driving her to the brink and back again mercilessly.

Gryffon slowly moved inside her. Her nails dug into his hip and her breaths got shorter. His hands on her waist pulled her hard against him, and there were slight twinges of pain as he pushed deep inside her.

A second wave hit and ripped through her, and he tensed as her internal muscles spasmed around him. He stilled entirely as she moaned into the pillow, letting her shudder through her release without adding more sensation. She was boneless when he withdrew gently, and he kissed her shoulder. His arm went around her, gathering her to him.

"I didn't hurt you too badly?" he murmured.

Amylia sighed, a deep sigh of contentment, and rested her head back in the crook of his arm. "No," she breathed, stroking the arm across her hips.

Cecily propped herself on an elbow, still lazily drawing patterns with a fingertip on Amylia's stomach. Amylia caught her hand, twined their fingers together, and looked at their joined hands.

"I've wanted to touch you like this for so long now. I just didn't know how."

Cecily smiled gently, her eyes burning softly. "I've wanted you since the second I walked into that hall at Lylican," she murmured back, kissing Amylia's fingers. Her eyes flicked to Gryffon, and she grinned. "He did, too. Though he didn't admit it until later."

Gryffon rumbled a chuckle as she relaxed against him. "It was about the moment I saw you leap naked onto that dragon of a horse bareback — sparking with fire and fury, the both of you — and charge out of there."

Amylia turned to look at him. His beautiful golden eyes stared back at her as she smiled at him. "I'll never forget you came for me that day."

"We will always come for you," Cecily whispered, squeezing her hand. "We have known for a while what you meant to us. We just wanted to give you space to see if you wanted us, too."

They slept, twined around each other, the blankets strewn across the bed. Amylia woke as the dawn light cast a rosy, dim glow across them, taking a moment to marvel at the beauty of them.

Gryffon woke next and smiled sleepily at her, rousing Cecily with a teasing hand until she was writhing between them. He took Cecily hard, as if releasing the tension of holding himself back as Amylia kissed her deeply, feeling her own deliciously slow ache build when Cecily moaned into her neck, her hand guiding Amylia's down, showing her where to touch.

Gryffon lay panting after, his gaze fixed on them as Cecily returned the favour. Amylia's cries were breathy as Cecily coaxed her again and again into ecstasy with an expert tongue.

Amylia lay utterly exhausted some time later, her head on Cecily's thigh as Gryffon poured them both a cup of water. He walked naked to the window and looked out and Cecily sat up with a groan, her hair falling forward to tickle Amylia's face.

"You ruined me, Gryff," she teased, stretching slightly. "I think a soak in the pools before breakfast might be needed."

Amylia nodded enthusiastically and Gryffon snorted, hooking the two silk robes up with a hand and throwing them.

"You may want to put these on, then." He laughed. "I'm pretty sure the others will be moving soon, too."

They didn't see anyone as they slipped down the stone steps to the pools.

The water heavenly as it soothed abused skin, Amylia unashamedly watched them both as they floated lazily in the water.

Cecily pulled herself out of the water after a while and collapsed onto her stomach on a pile of soft pillows on the ledge, her skin flushed from the heat. Gryffon prowled towards Amylia, grabbing her ankles where she sat on the underwater ledge.

He yanked her towards him roughly, her squeal turning to a gasp as he pulled her to him. Her legs automatically wrapped around his hips to save herself from dipping under the water.

He stood, water streaming off them, and turned to settle her ass on the stone ledge and kiss her. Clouds rolled across her vision. She scratched her nails across his back, making him groan softly, his hardness pressing against her thigh.

"Do you need me to be gentle?" he growled against her neck, and she shook her head, biting the tip of his pointed ear. "Good."

Grabbing her thighs, he pulled her to him, sheathing himself hard, a low groan rumbling through his chest as she cried out, her fingers running up his neck and into his hair.

She pulled his head down to her, kissing him again, slowly, teasing his lip between her teeth.

Gently he pushed her flat, one hand grasping her waist, the other dipping lower. His thumb gently caressed her in that exquisitely sensitive spot as he took her against the rocks until they both climaxed together, her heart skipping as his deep groan echoed softly around the small cavern.

He gathered her up to him after they had both caught their breath. Her arms slid around his neck as he pulled her off the shelf and back into the water. She rested her head on his shoulder, boneless as they floated gently. Gryffon moved them across the pool, and she opened her eyes as she felt Cecily's finger trace down her shoulder. The other woman wore a lazy smile and her blue eyes smouldered in the dim light.

"Let's go find some breakfast." She stretched like a cat. "I'm famished."

Chapter 25

Breakfast was horrific.

Amusement pulsed off both Lyrik and Rogue as the three of them entered together.

"'Bout time," Lyrik teased as Amylia sat next to her. "We were almost getting singed from the sexual tension over here."

"That is quite enough of that," Cecily quipped, eyeing Lyrik, and wincing slightly as she sat down next to Rogue, opposite Amylia and made space for Gryffon on her other side.

"Forget to heal yourself up there, Cess?" Lyrik said dryly.

Rogue snorted loudly but wisely kept his eyes on his plate, seeming to suddenly find his bread fascinating as he concentrated on spreading honey over it. Gryffon said nothing, but Amylia could feel amusement seeping out of him.

"Are you not usually with the cubs this time of the morning?" Amylia sighed, reaching for the pot of tea.

Lyrik snorted. "And miss this? Absolutely not. Rayvn's checking them for me." She grinned slyly, leaning back in her chair. "Plus, I thought that sparing him from —" she waved her hand in their general direction, "— this… was the right thing to do."

Rogue made a strangled noise which turned into a cough, and he pounded himself on the chest.

"I won't save you," Cecily said. "You can just go ahead and choke." She poured her tea and ignored the hiccupping noises from Rogue as he tried, and failed, to keep his amusement to himself. For a while, silence reigned as everyone concentrated on their food, broken by a small clink when Rogue flicked a gold coin at Lyrik. She caught it deftly and pocketed it with a wink at Amylia, though she avoided looking at Cecily, who glared at her over her mug.

Gryffon's lips twitched as his eyes met Amylia's, his amusement palpable as his arm moved under the table, reaching towards Cecily. "I have some other news that you might be interested to know, since you are both so invested in Amylia's escapades," he offered.

Rogue looked up at him suspiciously. "Should we be worried?"

"No." Gryffon laughed. "The opposite. Amylia has decided to stay." He raised a brow at Rogue over Cecily's head. "She will be sworn in tomorrow. Know anyone who wants to organise a celebration?"

"Wow, Cess, you *must* be good." Lyrik waggled her eyebrows at Cecily.

"Lyrik," Gryffon warned. His hand moved to Cecily's shoulder, holding her in her seat as though he expected her to launch herself across the table.

Amylia interrupted quickly, feeling the rush of irritation spike out from Cecily, and turned to Lyrik, allowing a wicked smile to creep across her features. "Oh, she was."

Rogue choked again, clearing his throat, and taking an exceptionally long swig of his tea, his eyes darting around the table, watching the three women in turn.

"And so was Gryff," she continued. Willing the blush in her cheeks to stay away, she met Lyrik's gaze without flinching. She sat back in her chair and let a tendril of her power go, blowing a breath towards Lyrik. Smoke curled through the air and brushed Lyrik's cheek. "I'm still cooling down."

Tea exploded from Rogue's nose as he lost it entirely and Gryffon chuckled with him.

Lyrik took a moment to compose herself, clearly struggling to decide between surprise and amusement, then laughed loudly and touched her heart, inclining her head to Amylia.

"You and I are going to be great friends, Lady Sylvers." She smirked.

"I think you boys are ready to start training with them," Ingryd said, as Rayvn and Silas fed the last of their fish to the waiting Sylkies. Falkyn sat away from the others, at the back of the roost, his cold eye watching Asspyn rub her shoulder affectionately against Silas and bowl him over.

Rayvn faltered, staring at her, a half-smile creeping across his face as the thrill of anticipation and slight nervousness raced through him.

"Really?" he breathed.

Ingryd snorted. "If Falkyn will let you, that is. I have no doubt about Asspyn."

Rayvn glanced at his friend. Asspyn pushed Silas across the floor with her beak, purring loudly while he batted her away and struggled to get up.

"She's smitten," Ingryd carried on, "but it's been weeks now. You have shown skill with them. If Falkyn won't accept you, we can find another that will suit you for your training."

Rayvn shook his head. "No," he said softly, gazing at Falkyn, "if he's not ready, I'll wait for him."

"Well, then," she said, "shall we see?"

Both boys looked at her in shock. "Now?" they chorused in unison.

Ingryd nodded. "Down in the training field, though. The drop from here is too much until you get used to it. And then we will see if they come to you."

Racing at breakneck speed through the dark corridors and down the steep stairs, Rayvn paused to catch his breath, resting his hands on his knees as Silas puffed heavily next to him. The sprawling field was heavily scarred with deep scratches, evidence of massive claws digging into the earth when Sylkies pushed off to rocket into the sky. Ingryd stood next to Calypso, gently scratching under the soft feathers behind her eye.

"That was fast." She smirked at them and then turned to greet Lyrik in the Sylvyn way as she approached from the castle. Lyrik returned the gesture, including both boys in it, as she grinned at Rayvn.

"You sure you don't want Amylia here for this?" she teased, shielding her eyes against the sun, and looking up towards the roost entrance high above.

"I think I'd prefer Lady Wynter here," Silas muttered, his face alight with excitement and deathly pale at the same time.

Lyrik snorted. "You will only fall off once. After that, you learn to hold on better."

Ingryd gave Calypso a resounding slap on her haunches and pushed her affectionately to the side before she walked to the boys.

"You have been using your calls with them?" she asked. Both boys nodded. "Then call them. Let's see if they accept you as their riders."

Rayvn looked at Silas. His knees felt weak under him, but he straightened and nodded once at his friend. Tilting his head up, he let out a piercing two-toned whistle. Silas whistled a short, sharp, high note, and the sounds echoed off the cliff face in front of them.

Everyone watched above. Rayvn's heart pounded in his chest, and he glanced quickly at Lyrik, wondering if she could hear it. She had her face turned up and squinted slightly. He shifted on his feet, trying to calm himself.

Silas sighed next to him. Rayvn looked back up to see a large shape plummet from the clifftop. Lithe wings snapped out, and Asspyn's freefall ended in a graceful arc. She swooped around and past them, circling tight before, with a whoosh of wind, she back flapped and landed softly in front of Silas, purring deep in her chest. She clacked her beak gently at him as he stroked her, murmuring softly to her.

Lyrik strode to him. "Get up on her now. She came to you. Time to seal the bond." A gentle smile on her face, she pushed him forward with a hand on his back. "Lock your knees up under her wings. Push up against them with your legs. It will hold you down into your seat. No, don't grasp her feathers." She moved his hands and placed them gently on the muscles that rippled over Asspyn's back. "Hold the base of her wings there as you take off. Once you're up, you can move them, but she won't like it if you rip out feathers as she jumps." She punched him gently on the shoulder. "And don't puke on her."

Lyrik slapped Asspyn on the rump and stepped back. The huge animal crouched and then leaped, her wings wide and powerful as she launched herself from the ground, Silas's shriek quickly melting in the air as they soared straight up.

"Lean forward!" Ingryd yelled belatedly.

Lyrik smiled widely at the rapidly receding figure, and they all turned to watch as Silas and Asspyn began circling over the bay. Rayvn felt Lyrik's hand on his shoulder as his stomach knotted.

"It's hard for Sylkies who have lost a rider to accept another. He may need more time, Rayvn. Don't let it discourage you."

He nodded. "I know. I'll wait as long as he needs." He avoided her gaze as he watched his friend.

Ingryd mounted Calypso next to them. "I'll go check Silas is okay."

Lyrik nodded at her, and then stilled, her eyes flitting upwards. She squeezed Rayvn's shoulder, turning him gently back to the cliff face.

"I'll be damned," Lyrik said, her voice filled with awe. Calypso fidgeted under Ingryd, shrinking away to the far side of the field, and grumbling softly.

Rayvn looked up in time to see Falkyn's massive wings snap out. The gust of wind that rushed towards them took his breath away as the beast landed in front of him, his claws cutting deep into the earth. Falkyn's deep rattle rumbled up his chest, vibrating through the ground as he tucked his wings neatly back in, the beautiful obsidian feathers glinting blue in the light.

He was huge, so much bigger out in the open than Rayvn had realised. Calypso looked small next to him.

Rayvn couldn't unravel the emotions washing over him as he stepped up to the beast and looked into his golden eye. He touched his forehead, and then his heart, and reached out to place that hand on the beast's beak.

"I see you, Falkyn," he murmured to him.

"Up," Lyrik whispered, her voice thick with emotion. Rayvn mounted. She checked his seat and nodded in approval before she stepped back. "I'll see you up there." She smiled and he felt Falkyn's powerful, wide back tense, the muscles rippling beneath him.

He looked to the skies as Falkyn dropped low. And then he was flying. They were flying.

Rayvn held his breath as they rocketed into the sky. The world blurred around him, his ears full of the booming of Falkyn's wings and the air rushing past them.

They levelled out high above the sea, and he sucked in a breath. His heart pounding in his ears, he looked down at the waves so very far below. Falkyn was warm under his legs, muscles bunching with every beat of his wings as he soared out over the bay in a wide arc.

Rayvn looked around in wonder, gently running his hands under the soft feathers of Falkyn's neck. He felt an answering rumble under his hands as Falkyn tilted his head, looking back at him.

Below him he heard a whoop and peered over Falkyn's shoulder to see Lyrik and Freyja rising rapidly to his side.

Freyja, only slightly smaller than Falkyn, caught them fast. The two Sylkies' powerful wings beat close enough that they whispered past each other.

Lyrik's eyes danced as she watched Rayvn and Falkyn together. Her grin widened when Silas and Asspyn flanked the other side, Ingryd and Calypso in their wake. Asspyn screeched a loud call, answered by Falkyn's booming one as all four Sylkies tucked their wings and simultaneously plummeted towards the sea.

Rayvn's heart sang as the water roared up to them, the exhilaration, the power of these beasts making his blood burn in his veins. He could see the reflection of Falkyn's golden eye in the crystal blue water under them as all four Sylkies threw their wings out in unison. The speed of their descent sent them flying across the surface of the waves. The mist of the water peppered his skin and only the tip of Calypso's huge claw grazed the water, leaving a slipstream of bubbles in their wake.

Then they flew high over the mountains, letting the beasts go where they would, over the Elixus ranges, the Dead Forest, and the sparkling waters of the sea.

With every flap of Falkyn's wings, the bond that wrapped around Rayvn's heart grew stronger. His heart sang, feeling the soul of the Sylkie beneath him curl around his, forming an unbreakable alliance unlike anything he had felt before.

It was utter freedom, and Rayvn knew his life would never be the same again.

Staring at her armoire, Amylia sighed loudly and ran her hand through her hair.

Lyrik's laugh sounded. "That doesn't sound good." The woman stood in Amylia's doorway wrapped in a towel that came down to her knees. Her long hair was damp, and hung tousled around her shoulders, a fresh, pink tint to her skin from the hot water of the pools.

Amylia looked at her, her hand over her mouth as she contemplated the clothes that she had arrayed around her.

"Rogue said the party was formal." Amylia sighed again, waving her hand at the surrounding clothes. "I don't know what to pick." She groaned as she looked around. "Back at… back at Lylican, I had Harry. She loved this kind of thing… but me?" She sat heavily on her bed. "Not so much."

Lyrik snorted and walked into the room. "Well, the answer is none of these." She laughed, eyeing the clothes. "Not that anything is wrong with them," she amended quickly, holding her hands up at Amylia's glower. "But it is your and Rayvn's ratification celebration!" She snorted again as Amylia looked at her helplessly. "It's a big thing!" She laughed. "I think this calls for a visit to the seamstress. It's a bit tight with it being tonight, but she has some beautiful gowns already made; we can see if there is anything that suits."

Amylia nodded, feeling defeated, and put the strewn clothes back into the armoire.

"That's the spirit," Lyrik chuckled. "I'll get dressed. You go ask Grymes to ready the horses."

Shadow, for once, was in a good mood and Amylia watched in silent surprise as Grymes passed Lyrik the reins to a sturdy gelding and walked Shadow to her, patting the mare's neck.

Shadow's ears flicked back slightly as she side-eyed him but didn't snap her teeth.

"Tha's my pretty wee lass. You're ginna go for a nice wee stretch," he said to her. "And then by the time you're home, I'll have your oats ready for you, my princess."

Amylia smiled warmly at him as he passed over the reins. "Thank you, Grymes." She swung into the saddle.

"Oh, my pleasure, m'lady." He grinned broadly, grabbing Olly by the shirt as the small boy darted dangerously close to the mare's legs. "Git away with ye, ye wee heathen," he scolded gently. "You be spookin' my wee darlin' here and I'll tan ye." He gave the boy a gentle tap on the rear with his boot, sending the boy hurtling back the way he had come. Then he patted Shadow again.

"Enjoy your ride, ladies." He bobbed his head at them.

Amylia and Lyrik rode fast, letting Shadow stretch out in a gallop even though the gelding struggled to keep pace. Amylia finally pulled the mare up as they reached the outskirts so Lyrik could guide the way through the streets to the seamstress. She took in the beautifully thatched cottages and stone-walled gardens that peppered the quaint cobbled roads.

The seamstress was a tall, gentle-voiced woman, her slender-tipped ears only just starting to show the Sylvyn point. She worked swiftly, taking Amylia's measurements while Lyrik browsed the garments on racks along the walls.

"I have a bit of free time today, so it was a good day to come." The woman, Rayne, stepped back and looked thoughtfully at Amylia's figure. "You have a beautiful figure, my girl, and with that dark hair, I think we can have you looking like a real jewel tonight."

Amylia blanched slightly at the term. "I'm no jewel," she said, avoiding Lyrik's eye when her head snapped up at her tone. She turned to look at the gowns Rayne laid out. She ran her hand over the beautiful material, finally picking up a dark green one for Lyrik to look at.

"What about this?" she asked.

Lyrik studied and dismissed it in a single glance, going back to the rack. Amylia groaned internally, looking back at the gowns again and picking up a deep maroon one. "What about this one?"

Lyrik snorted. "You're right. You are bad at this." She laughed, holding up a dress from the rack. "I think… this one," she said, walking over with the gown draped over her arms.

"That's one of my favourite's." Rayne smiled. "You have good taste, Lady Damaris."

Amylia stared at the dress in horror. "You want me to wear that?" She gasped.

The gown was beautiful. Its bodice was made from a sheer black material, with a deeply cut neckline, golden thread work laced in an intricate design over the breast and down the bodice. The skirts had slits cut up the side. The front and back panels overlapped slightly so when still, the dress closed modestly. But when the wearer moved, it would part, allowing view of the legs all the way up to the hips. The fabric shimmered slightly with gold highlights as Lyrik moved it backwards and forwards in front of her.

Smiling wickedly, Lyrik held it out to her. "Go, try it on." She pushed Amylia towards a dark alcove off the side wall and pulled the curtain closed behind her.

Amylia sighed heavily but stripped quickly and slipped on the dress. It fit like a glove. She stared at her reflection into the murky, full-length mirror.

On the other side of the curtain, she could hear Lyrik impatiently tapping her foot. Dryly, she asked, "Are you stuck?"

Amylia opened the curtain, and Lyrik stepped back, but her face remained blank.

Abruptly, Lyrik gave a low whistle. "Woah. That's definitely the one."

Rayne strode over, nodding. "Oh, yes, that looks like it was meant for you, Lady Sylvers. You look like an ember glittering in a fireplace."

The gown hugged her torso, sitting like a second skin. The gold threading covered enough to keep her modesty but allowed the curve of her breasts to barely show through.

The shimmering skirts floated around her, just kissing the floor, and parted as she walked, showing off her long, sculpted legs and slender hips.

"We will take it," Lyrik said quickly before Amylia could protest. "And I'll pick up mine while we are here, too. Saves you a trip later." She smiled at Rayne and held the curtain open for Amylia to duck back in.

Lyrik threw a small parcel to Amylia, who caught it, bewildered, as she came out of the changing room.

"What is this?" she asked, peeking inside.

"Something that matches the dress." Lyrik sniggered as they waited for Rayne to bundle up the two dresses. Taking the bag Rayne offered her with a nod of thanks, Lyrik swung it over her shoulder and walked out.

Amylia thanked Rayne and followed Lyrik out, blinking at the sun. Carefully, she pulled one of the delicate bits of fabric out of the parcel.

"What is this f — *Lyrik!*" She gasped, crumpling the sheer underwear into her palm, and stuffing it quickly back in the bag.

Lyrik howled with laughter and leaped up onto her horse. "Trust me. It really makes the outfit." She winked. Amylia, mortified, felt her face heat.

"I can't wear those!" Amylia hissed.

Lyrik snickered. "I'm sure Cess and Gryff would enjoy them," she teased. "Oh, wow." She laughed again. "I didn't think you could go any redder... but there you go!"

Amylia grumbled as she mounted Shadow. "You are worse than Rogue," she muttered.

They moved off, taking the short path out of town and into the country beyond.

"You still need to tell me how exactly that hap—"

Amylia sent a gust of wind howling over the rump of Lyrik's gelding, a trick she had been practicing. The startled gelding leaped forward into a gallop. Lyrik yelped in surprise. But it turned quickly into gales of laughter as she sped away from Amylia.

Amylia shook her head and watched the woman's departing form before laughing softly and urging Shadow after her.

Chapter 26

It was afternoon when Gryffon knocked on her door and interrupted Lyrik who was helping Amylia with her hair.

"Can I steal you away for a bit?" he asked, eyes soft as he looked at her.

Amylia nodded, suddenly feeling shy in front of him. Together they walked down the flights of stone stairs towards the throne room.

"I haven't had a chance to speak to you," he said gently. "Are you okay from the other night?"

Amylia blushed, looking up at him from under her lashes. She let herself sway towards him and felt the reassuring wave of tenderness and protectiveness that washed over her and nodded.

He stopped her, putting his hand on her arm. "I don't make it a habit of sleeping with people within my court. With you, it's different." His eyes burned softly. "You are different, Amylia. Both Cess and I can feel it."

Amylia looked up at him, her heart feeling warm. "I just don't want you to feel like I expect anything more from you. From either of you."

"And what if we want to give you more?" he asked, moving closer. "What if I want more from you?"

She felt the heat of the blush spreading. "You want me to come back to your bed?"

He rumbled a low laugh. "I don't just want you in my bed, little firebug." He grinned like a wolf. "Though I can think of many, many things I'd like to do to you in that bed."

He gripped her hip with one hand and pulled her close. Tipping her face up, she let him kiss her and let the heady feelings wash over her. Her body melted against his.

He growled low in his throat and pulled away. "As much as I want to continue this, bug, the priestess doesn't take well to waiting." He kissed the tip of her nose. "But later..." Trailing off, his eyes glowed slightly brighter. Her stomach clenched, and a slow burn started.

In the throne room, Rayvn and Cecily stood alongside a stunningly beautiful Sylvyn woman, her long copper hair braided into an intricate design. Cecily's eyes followed Amylia's approach intently as if searching for any hint of anxiety as the priestess smiled at the two Sylvers.

In a low, rich voice, the priestess asked, "I understand that you, Lady Amylia Sylvers, and you Lord Rayvn Sylvers of Oryx, would like to join the court of Asteryn until Rayvn is of age to take over your home territory?"

They both nodded solemnly. The priestess smiled again and bowed her head over the altar they stood around, a book bearing the Asteryn crest emblazoned on its cover resting on it.

"As a high priestess for the Gods, it is within my power to grant this and will place you both under the protection of Lord and Lady Wynter." She turned to Gryffon. "Do you accept these two Sylvyns into your territory, Lord Wynter?"

He answered solemnly, "I accept them gladly, into my territory, and my home."

The priestess turned to Cecily. "And do you, Lady Wynter, accept them as well?"

Cecily smiled broadly. "I accept them gladly, into my territory, my home... and my family," she said softly.

The priestess hummed in acknowledgment, drawing a small knife from her belt, and gesturing to Gryffon and Cecily to hold out their wrists. She made two small cuts, one on each of their wrists, and caught the drops of blood in a small golden bowl. She swirled them together before dipping a finger in it. Turning to Cecily, she ran the bloody finger down her forehead from her hairline to the tip of her nose. "It is our custom for oaths to be made in blood," the priestess murmured for the benefit of Rayvn and Amylia. "Our oaths are binding, rooted into our souls." She made the same mark on Gryffon's forehead, before dipping a quill into the remainder of the blood and writing their names into the book. "This is Asteryn's oath to you both: that it will forever have a place for you, a home for you, as long as you want it. Even after you take your place in Oryx, it will be as the sister of Asteryn, and as such, will protect it as if one of its own."

Rayvn looked emotional as he bowed his head to them.

"It is an honour," the young man, really no more than a boy, said quietly, "to be accepted into your territory." He glanced at Amylia. "And as the future Lord of Oryx I would like to make my own oath."

He held out his hand to the priestess, who glanced at Gryffon, waiting for his approval.

Gryffon nodded, looking surprised, and she made a small cut in Rayvn's wrist, catching the drips into a new cup and then waiting for him as he drew a breath and took Amylia's hand. "It is our oath that Oryx will recognise Asteryn as its sister territory, and under my rule will provide protection and support in whatever capacity it can when needed."

The priestess made the same mark down Rayvn and Amylia's brows, her eyes warm as she smiled at them both. "Welcome, Amylia and Rayvn of Asteryn, future heir of Oryx." She waved her hand over the golden bowls and the contents burst into flames. "Your oaths are sealed."

Cecily saw Amylia grimace as she walked into the dining hall to cheers from the waiting people already milling around. They had slipped back to their rooms after the ceremony to dress and her mouth still tingled from where Gryffon had pushed her against the wall of their room, kissing her soundly and murmuring promises and growled threats for later that night.

"I warned you he made a big deal of parties," Cecily whispered conspiratorially as she sauntered up and passed her a glass of wine. "And he knows it's your birthday tomorrow."

Her gaze lingered on Amylia's figure; the dress sparkling in the firelight looked like a night sky as she walked, twinkling softly. The deep slits up the side showed long, beautifully shaped legs to a near indecent length and her fingers ached to reach over and pull Amylia against her and nip her way from earlobe to the breasts that peeked through the sheer fabric. "Just drink, it makes it easier," she murmured, eyes coming back up to Amylia's face, her voice husky.

Cecily's outfit was beautiful, soft cream trousers, tight at her slim hips and flaring out at the legs to look like a flowing skirt as she stilled, but allowing easy, comfortable movement. She ran a hand idly over the delicate gold chain that rested around her waist, noticing as Amylia's eyes followed the movement. They lingered on her top, the same colour as her trousers and crossed over her breasts, tying at the back, and leaving her midriff bare, the small scar on her abdomen just peeking out over the waistband of her pants.

"Just be glad he stopped throwing people into the sea on their 'special day'." Lyrik grinned, walking up from a group of riders. She wore a deep wine-red dress, cut down to her navel; it hugged her slender figure with panels of fabric that overlapped in the skirts, parting as she moved to show flashes of leg peeking alluringly from under them. "Ten consecutive years in a row, he got me in. And Cess… and Gryff, too, didn't he, Cess?" She laughed.

Cecily wrinkled her nose, remembering the wrestling match in the sand before Rogue had slung her over a shoulder and charged into the waves, thoroughly unconcerned at her hissed threats. "I think we have you to thank for that ending, don't we?" She chuckled

"Actually, you have Freyja to thank for that." Lyrik's smile was lupine. "Getting hung by his ankles over the Eclipse mountains changed that little tradition pretty rapidly." She raised a brow at Amylia, pausing to take in her dress properly and whistled. "Oh, I'm good," she breathed. "You look stunning."

"Thank you." Amylia laughed, cheeks pinkening, and took a gulp of her wine. She glanced across the room, and Cecily noticed her brother chatting to Silas and a group of the young riders by the fireplace. No doubt the dominant subject was everything Sylkie.

Musicians started in the corner of the hall, their skilled fingers flitting over the strings in perfect harmony with each other, the music filling every corner of the considerable space.

Amylia ran her hand through her hair, casting her eyes over the full room. "He didn't have to go to this much effort, honestly." She sighed.

"It makes him happy." Cecily chuckled as she reached to refill her glass. "Just go with it. Trust me, you can laugh at us when it's our turn."

They danced, and drank, and danced some more.

Amylia reluctantly admitted to Rogue she was enjoying herself as he spun her in an elegant dance across the floor, leading her effortlessly.

He grinned at her. "Oh, you are quite welcome, Lady Sylvers." His eyes followed Gryffon's and Cecily's dance across the floor behind them, their bodies close as Gryffon leaned in to murmur in Cecily's ear. "So how did that —"

"No, Rogue," she interrupted. "We are not going to have a conversation about that."

He rolled his eyes. "Oh, come on!" he teased. "That's the first time I've seen Lyrik surprised in decades."

Amylia smiled at him. "And you can all stay that way."

A tap on her shoulder had them pausing and Lyrik stepped between them deftly.

"You have hogged her long enough," she teased Rogue. "Time for someone to show her how to really dance."

Amylia giggled at Rogue's face as Lyrik took her hand, her slender, muscled arm slipping around her back as she led her off into a graceful spin across the floor. She really knew how to dance. She led Amylia through two fast-paced songs, their bodies close and complementing each other as she dipped Amylia expertly, raising her to spin her in a beautiful pirouette before catching her gently again. Amylia marvelled at the strength she could feel that rippled from the woman, yet her movements were as graceful as a swan.

Amylia saw flashes of the faces around her as a few cheered them on, and Cecily and Gryffon paused on the edge of the floor to catch their breath, watching. The next song was slower, and they moved gently with it, other dancers melting onto the floor to join them as Amylia caught her breath.

"You dance well." Lyrik grinned, her hand light on Amylia's hip as they whirled.

Amylia snorted softly. "The future lady of Lylican was expected to be adept in all things, from dancing to needlework, and popping out little heirs." A shadow passed over Lyrik's face, and Amylia grimaced. "Sorry, bad joke," she mumbled.

"I'm just glad that's not your life," Lyrik said gently, "but for too many, it is all they can be in the world and I detest it."

Amylia nodded. "Me, too. Maybe one day we can help change that."

"Maybe we can." Lyrik smiled.

Amylia felt a wave of heat... tenderness and... lust?... wash over her from Lyrik. When she looked up, following Lyrik's gaze, she saw Rogue dancing with a young rider.

"Ohhhh," she said and laughed quietly as Lyrik's eyes snapped back to hers, the feeling disappearing as if a blade had come down, cutting it off abruptly.

"Shit," Lyrik grumbled. "I forget we have a Lymbic in the court. I forgot how annoying it is."

"I won't say anything." Amylia chuckled. "But just for my own curiosity, why don't you tell him?"

Lyrik laughed humourlessly. "Oh, he knows, unfortunately… I told you, I lean more towards women." Her smile was feline. "Rogue and I have been there before. Rogue is…" She glanced towards him. "Skilled."

Amylia's mouth fell open as she gaped at Lyrik. "What!" she choked, half-laughing as she felt the blush rise furiously up her neck. Lyrik chuckled.

"Well, he was!" she protested. "We have all been together a very long time. Sometimes it happens." She looked pointedly at Amylia, who shut her mouth quickly, refusing to look at Cecily and Gryffon. "I care deeply for him, and maybe in another life we would have been something incredible. But we thought of the positions we both held, our oaths to this court, and made the decision to stop it before it started," Lyrik said, swirling to a stop as the song ended.

They walked to the throng of people gathered around the table which held the pitchers of wine and cider and Lyrik poured them each a glass.

"That must be hard?" Amylia asked her carefully after taking a mouthful of the sweet liquid.

"Oh, I have my distractions," Lyrik said, her eyes following a gorgeous woman who walked towards them. Nodding to Amylia, she stepped away and met the woman. Her eyes were soft, and they murmured to each other, soon walking back towards the dance floor.

Amylia watched them go, sipping her wine and laughing to herself, her stomach grumbling slightly. Turning towards the dining table, still full of a mouth-watering array of dishes, she headed to it and sat on the far side of it in the shadows. Resting her aching feet on the chair next to her, she nibbled on a pasty, the juices filling her mouth with rich flavour as she watched the dancers. Lyrik and the woman swirled round the dance floor, Lyrik caressing the small of the woman's back as they gazed at each other with looks that made Amylia blush.

She felt breath on her neck and jumped, spinning to meet sapphire eyes watching her.

"*Athyna!*" she gasped, letting out a breathy laugh. "Are you hungry, girl?"

Reaching over, she grasped a thick hunk of sliced beef, the meat tender and dripping with juices, and gingerly held it out to the wolf. Athyna sniffed it delicately, her lips pulling back from viciously pointed teeth. She took the meat gingerly before backing away into the shadows.

"She knew who the soft touch was." Cecily laughed. Coming up on Amylia's other side, she sat with a sigh and rubbed a hand up her calf. Her scent was intoxicating, and Amylia's stomach fluttered at the proximity. "She's growing so fast. I can't get enough food into her half the time." Cecily's gaze followed the wolf's retreating form.

"She's grown so much already." Amylia laughed.

"From the size of her paws, she's going to keep doing that for a while," Cecily agreed, groaning as she kneaded her thumbs into her calves. The sound made Amylia's stomach clench and a shiver go down her spine. "I think she was younger than I thought when we found her," Cecily mused.

Amylia grimaced, remembering the massive Alpha, and took a deep drink of her wine. As she felt Cecily's gaze she turned and met her eyes.

"Have you had fun tonight?" Cecily's gaze scanned her face.

Amylia nodded. "I have. I'm not one for parties, but this was lovely."

Cecily smiled, her face lighting up. "Good."

Feelings drifted to her across the space between them from the woman and her breath caught. She found herself watching Cecily's mouth and the slow, heart-stopping smile that spread over them. Memories flowed through her, and her blood started to heat. She yearned to lean forward, to taste her lips again but took a breath, picking up her wine as Cecily scanned the table in front of them. The music launched into an enchanting song as more people took to the floor, and Amylia felt the wine taking effect.

"Could you pass the grapes, sweetling?" Cecily asked, her voice low.

Glancing across the food, Amylia located the bowl of plump red fruits and nodded. She put her glass down and stood, reaching across the table. Hooking a bunch of the fruit with a finger, her eyes half-followed the whirling dancers as her concentration honed in on the woman next to her.

Cecily's hand whispered across her rear as she stretched over the table, then hooked her hip and tugged.

Letting the woman pull her across, she stepped back carefully and sat on Cecily's lap, her legs between the woman's knees.

"Cess, I'll crush your legs," she whispered, holding the fruit out to her, and tensing to rise.

Cecily's hand snaked around her hip, holding her lightly. The other slid across her knee and her eyes danced with humour.

"I appear to have my hands full," she purred, voice like liquid honey. Her eyes glided down to Amylia's mouth and then down to the fruit between them.

Amylia's blood went molten at the wave of desire that flowed out of the woman holding her. Swallowing heavily, she took a deep breath and pulled one of the small fruits off the bunch, holding it out to Cecily with a soft smile.

"I can help with that," she murmured, watching Cecily dip her head and take it, biting the tip of her finger gently when she did.

Cecily's hand roved down her leg slowly, bunching the sheer fabric in her hand until she got to the long split up the side of the material. She paused, taking a second fruit from Amylia, glowing eyes never breaking contact.

Amylia's pulse started to hammer as the hand glided up her bare skin to her thigh, resting there gently for a moment.

"It's been two days, and you haven't come back to my bed… our bed," Cecily murmured, then she kissed the curve of Amylia's shoulder gently. Eyes flicking back up to meet Amylia's, her hand inched ever so slightly upwards, fingers stroking gently.

Amylia's mouth went dry as she popped another fruit into Cecily's mouth. "I wanted to. But I didn't want to… intrude on your space with Gryffon, and I didn't know if you wanted me to come back," she whispered, fighting the urge to lean into the woman as the lust, and something else, something deeper, flowed from Cecily and woke a fire in her that she was struggling to keep down.

The hand moved higher under the table and Amylia glanced up at the dancers in alarm, seeing Gryffon had whisked Lyrik into an intricate dance. The two of them flowed together like a beautiful storm, fierce and devastating. All eyes were on them, some people applauding and whistling as they dominated the floor. All eyes, except the burning blue ones that met hers again as she looked back, the humour gone. Hunger now shone from them as the tip of a finger traced the edge of Amylia's thin undergarment. Amylia parted her legs slightly — her body moving of its own volition — her eyes unable to look away from Cecily, aching to close the gap between them and kiss the soft lips just inches from her own.

"You are not intruding," Cecily said. "I want you in my bed every night. So does Gryff, but only if you want to be there, too."

Amylia held her breath. The finger hooked the fabric across, and she let out a breathy sigh as Cecily lightly stroked the delicate skin beneath. Her mind filled with clouds. The only thing keeping her from floating away were those eyes, intent on her.

"I do," she finally murmured, the fruit forgotten in her hand as it clutched them. Her heart pounded as her mind locked on that finger, its slow progression.

"Are you sure?" Cecily purred.

Her finger had reached its destination under the fabric, dipping into slick, sensitive skin, and Amylia swallowed a gasp, stomach fluttering as she saw the look of hunger on Cecily's face at how wet she was.

"I haven't been able to stop thinking about you both since it happened." Amylia's voice strained as she tried to keep it under control.

"Well, that makes the three of us," Cecily answered huskily. Her finger began slow, torturous movements. Amylia groaned quietly and Cecily's free hand tightened against her hip.

"Hush, sweetling," she whispered against her neck, kissing her softly under her ear. "I want you in our bed and I want you at our side." Her finger circled gently. "I want you to be there when I go to sleep, and when I wake up." Her foot nudged Amylia's legs wider apart and the finger pushed inside her smoothly, her thumb replacing where it had been, continuing its slow, gentle circles.

Amylia gasped, throwing her arm around Cecily's shoulder.

Cecily whispered into her ear, "But what I really want right now, is to lay you back on this table, with your thighs around my neck, and make you moan loud enough that Attica will hear. But this will have to do… for now."

Biting her shoulder, Cecily continued her slow torture, her fingers stroking until Amylia shattered around her hand, her face pressed into Cecily's neck. They stayed like that for a moment until Cecily shifted slightly and withdrew her hand, resting it against Amylia's knee.

Taking a shaky breath, Amylia moved back enough for Cecily's lips to take hers in a fierce kiss that stole the last of the breath she had left.

A wicked smile played on Cecily's features as she took the crushed fruit from Amylia's hand and threw it onto the table. The juice had run down Amylia's wrist and Cecily grasped it, tracing her tongue up the line of juice to her palm, following it to suck each finger gently until they were clean.

Her gaze held Amylia's when she paused, sucking her own finger, still wet from Amylia's climax, her eyes glinting with mischief.

"I think it's getting late, and it's time for bed." She patted Amylia's rear. "Also, I think Gryff is having some mild difficulty concentrating."

Amylia looked up, searching for him. She found him leaning against the fireplace talking to a group of riders. His eyes flicked up to meet hers, and the look in them melted whatever was left inside her. She smiled at him, slow and sensual, then turned back to Cecily, kissing her gently, her hand sliding up and into her hair. "Bed sounds good," she whispered against her mouth as she pulled away. "But I hope you're not tired because it's my turn."

Chapter 27

"Happy birthday, sweetling," Cecily whispered, running a finger up Amylia's spine.

She rolled, smiling sleepily at Cecily, who lay on a pillow next to her, hair tousled across her naked breasts. The blankets had been thrown hastily back onto the bed and were rucked around her hips. Amylia glanced around.

"He's gone to get us all breakfast." Cecily grinned. "I, for one, don't want to have to move just yet."

"That was an excellent idea on his behalf." Amylia sighed, running a fingertip down Cecily's side, tracing over her hip to the small scar. She circled it gently, her brow creasing, and Cecily reached up to smooth it away. "Such a small scar, and yet it did so much damage," Amylia said, leaning to kiss it gently.

"It wasn't the damage to me I cared about," Cecily said quietly, "but what it took from me, and Gryff, was unbearable."

"I can't even imagine," Amylia replied feelingly. "I'm so sorry."

"I won't pretend to understand why things happen, but everything has a reason." Cecily sighed, catching Amylia's fingers, and twining them through her own. She stilled. "Oh, that's something I should have thought about." Glancing at Amylia, she asked, "Do you want me to make you a contraceptive brew?"

Amylia looked at her blankly, then processed the question. "Oh… yes, I… I didn't even think."

Cecily laughed softly at her shocked face and kissed her gently. "Don't panic, sweetling, I can make it for you today. It's just a brew you drink that will prevent any pregnancy from taking."

"I… yes… I mean… it's not that I would mind… it's just…"

Cecily put a finger over Amylia's lips, silencing her. "You do not need to explain anything. It's your body and your choice. I only asked so you know you have protection. And if you decide not to, it's okay, too." She smiled, kissing her gently.

Amylia blinked. "But how can you not mind?"

"Any child is a blessing." Cecily snuggled into her, resting her head in the crook of Amylia's shoulder. "And one that came from the two people I care for deeply would be loved like my own. But I would like to be a bit selfish and have you to ourselves for a while first." She smiled up at her. "If you are okay with that?" Amylia nodded, watching their entwined fingers.

Gryffon nudged the door open, balancing a tray on one arm and a large jug in the other. Cecily snorted at the amount of food piled on it.

"Are you planning on holing up in here for the next week?" she teased.

"Is that an option?" He chuckled. "Rogue is having a field day down there. Oh, and I've been told to tell the birthday girl that we need to share, as they have gifts."

Amylia groaned, pulling the blanket over her head.

"I did warn you." Gryffon laughed.

"I know," she replied, her voice muffled by the blanket. She flapped them back down again, hair billowing over her face. Quickly, she pulled them back up to her chin when she caught Gryffon's look. Her face heated.

"We do need to leave here at some point," Cecily teased.

Gryffon nodded solemnly, biting into an apple. "Well, we need to tonight anyway. Rogue has promised the eastern villages that we will all attend the spring Equinox bonfire tonight."

Both women groaned in unison.

What Gryffon had failed to mention to her, was how they were getting to the Equinox.

Amylia buried her face against Lyrik's shoulder, ignoring Lyrik's teasing and holding her breath as they had taken off, but once they were up, she was mesmerised. They flew as a group, various riders taking those who were not, the tight formation practiced and elegant as they flew high, making use of the currents that rolled along the mountain range, boosting them faster.

Pride bursting in her chest, Amylia watched Rayvn as his magnificent Sylkie soared through the air next to them, Cecily riding with him.

Falkyn was impressive, his great wings easily slicing through the air, attuned with the rider on his back who guided him gently. She noticed the small touches Rayvn made, asking him to pull back, or push forward, and the speed at which the beast obeyed him. She wished her parents could have lived to see it. They would be so proud of him, she thought, a lump rising in her throat.

She felt Freyja slow slightly and glanced down as a small village came into view below.

"This is Antykla," Lyrik yelled over her shoulder. "Kayve is further east, by the coast, and Grytt is south of here at the base of the Elixus ranges. There are other, smaller villages dotted over the territory, but these are the biggest. Most of the people from the closer villages will be here tonight."

Amylia pulled her hair back as it whipped around her, the picturesque village coming into focus as they lowered. Orchards surrounded the village, sectioned into neat rows of trees, and vines laden with fruit.

They touched down in a bare space in front of the village. Children ran out, shrieking with delight at the Sylkies. Some, barely toddlers, got dragged by older children.

Calypso purred and rumbled as Ingryd and Rogue slid off her, barely waiting for permission before she scooted forward. Her head low to the ground, she scuttled towards the children, letting them grab great handfuls of feathers and pat her adoringly.

Ingryd shook her head in mock disgust at her Sylkie.

"She's broken, I swear." She groaned, as Rogue sniggered.

Rayvn helped Cecily down before patting Falkyn, giving him permission to leave quietly. The massive beast, eyeing the children disdainfully, had landed farther away than the rest.

"See, Falkyn has dignity." Ingryd snorted. "And I get… her." She waved at Calypso, now prostrate on the ground, her wings held up high so the children who now lay on her back couldn't touch them.

"Oh, she's just a sweetheart," Gryffon said affectionately. "Leave her be. We don't have enough beasts like her." He pointedly looked at Amylia, who flipped him off, but grinned.

The villagers welcomed them eagerly. A great bonfire had been piled up behind the village in a flat paddock and tables were fast filling with a feast of different foods.

"Some of our villages specialize in a certain produce, and the city either buys or trades off them. Any surplus, which has been more each year, gets sold on to Calibyre," Gryffon explained as they wandered through the gorgeous village.

Its houses, with whitewashed walls and thatched roofs, each with small private gardens, were meticulously maintained.

"Antykla, as you can see, thrives on its orchards, and has a spring festival every year to mark the start of the harvest season. Kayve is a fishing village. A lot of our winter meat is supplied through them, and they hold the only gap in the Elixus ranges this side of Asteryn that gives them access to the coast. Grytt is probably one of our larger villages; their village has the autumn grains."

"It's incredible." Amylia smiled at Cecily as she joined them. "I knew Asteryn ran differently than Lylican, but your people, they're all so happy. None of them want for anything."

"Your people now, too, sweetling," Cecily said, slipping her arm through Amylia's as they walked back towards the gathering crowd.

As dusk fell, the bonfire was lit. Gryffon sent an impressive wave of fire across the base of it, forming a spiral of golden flames. Amylia, at urging from Rayvn, sent a menagerie of blue flaming animals through the fire. The children's gasps delighted her as deer ran around the outside of the bonfire, leaping into the middle of the flames and vanishing, only to appear on the other side as great winged eagles, spiralling, burning into the sky as the embers from the fire crackled around them.

The sailors from Kayve struck up bawdy songs and others joined in with rough instruments. The music filled the air and people leaped up to dance. Rogue dragged Ingryd up, whirling her around the throng of people. She laughed, keeping up with him easily, and Rayvn and Arya spun past them.

Gryffon and Cecily dropped, panting, to each side of Amylia after their dance. Cecily's bare feet were stained dark with soot, and she had a streak of it across one cheek. Giggling, Amylia wiped it away with the cuff of her sleeve.

Rogue threw his arm into the air as a song ended, sending a bolt of lightning crackling high into the sky as he did, and gathering the attention of everyone.

Amylia's mouth dropped open. "That's what his Gift is?" she hissed at Gryffon, who grinned at her, running an arm behind her shoulders for her to rest against, his thumb rubbing Cecily's neck. "I did tell you he thought his Gift gave him an unfair advantage," he laughed. "That's why."

"I have... an announcement!" Rogue yelled dramatically, and Amylia's stomach dropped.

Cecily laughed quietly, putting a hand on her knee.

"Don't try to run," she whispered, "it's a long way home."

"I think it's worth the run," Amylia said tightly, "if this is what I think it is."

Cecily shook next to her with silent laughter and Rogue raised his glass to Amylia.

"Shit," she swore quietly, glaring at him.

"It is one of our court's birthday today!" he continued, giving her a charming smile. "So, can you all join me in a salute? To the beautiful Lady Sylvers!"

Amylia felt herself blushing crimson as the crowd erupted in cheers and most raised glasses to her. A few men approached, coaxing her to dance with them, and after much enticing, she grudgingly agreed, shooting Rogue a filthy look as one spun her past him. He touched his heart to her and winked. He saved her after a fourth man begged a dance, cutting in smoothly, and Amylia glared at him.

"Retaliation will be swift and painful, Rogue," she promised, as he whirled her slowly.

"Oh, I'm counting on it." He chuckled, coming to a stop in front of Gryffon. "Here, this might help with that retaliation." He chucked a cloth-wrapped parcel to her. "Happy birthday, Amylia." He turned to grab Lyrik off Rayvn and whirled her onto the dance floor.

Amylia stared after him before dipping her eyes to the parcel. Plain white cloth had been carefully tied with leather strips. Untying it, her mouth dropped open when she saw a beautifully engraved knife roll out of it.

The black leather sheath had the Asteryn crest pressed into it. The polished black wood of the hilt was curved and somehow fit her hand perfectly. There was a glittering blue sapphire at the top, the same colour as her flames.

When she unsheathed it, the wicked-sharp blade glinted in the firelight. To her annoyance, tears blurred her vision. Looking back up, she searched for Rogue in the crowd, catching sight of him. He winked at her, and she smiled warmly back at him, holding the blade to her chest.

"Well, since Rogue has already started the gifts, here is ours, little firebug," Gryffon murmured in her ear. His arms came about her, a delicate chain between his hands. He gently placed it around her neck, holding the ends with one hand, and swept her hair aside with the other.

Clipping it deftly, he kissed her softly on the back of the neck and made her shiver.

She turned, looking up at him as he picked up the pendant that hung to her breasts. "Cess had it made," he explained.

The delicate lacework of silver was stunning in itself. But the crystal it held took her breath away. The top glinted silvery blue in the firelight, deep turquoise in the middle, and at the base, golden tones flickered through it.

Amylia felt Cecily's hand on the small of her back and she turned, still holding the crystal in her hand.

"*It's us!*" she breathed.

Cecily nodded. "It is." She smiled, holding out her hand to lead her onto the dance floor.

The flight back was magical, the Sylkies silent as they flew their tired riders back through the twinkling night sky. It felt as if they soared through the stars, Amylia thought, as she leaned against Lyrik's back, stealing warmth from the woman.

"I can see why you love it so much up here," she murmured to Lyrik, her voice barely audible over the wind, but Lyrik cast a smile at her over her shoulder.

"There isn't much that beats it," she answered, patting Freyja absently.

Freyja deposited them on the edge of the castle gardens, rumbling quietly as Lyrik murmured to her before sending her off to the roosts

Amylia crossed the castle gardens, her feet aching from dancing. The waves crashed against the rocks next to the castle and she looked up at the huge building.

The last couple of months had healed her in ways she had not thought possible, and this place felt like the home she hadn't realised she had been longing for. Peace was what thrived in Asteryn, she realised, watching Lyrik, with Rogue's arm around her, wearily make her way up the steps. She cuffed him gently on the arm at some remark he had made to Rayvn who walked in front of them with Silas. These people, they could be family… They were family, she realised with shock, as her heart sang.

Hands caught her around the waist, and she jumped slightly, until Gryffon laughed, kissing her below the ear.

"Join us for a quick swim in the sea?" he asked. "Cecily is covered in soot."

She gasped. "It will be freezing!"

"No, it won't." He chuckled, walking backwards, and beckoned her with two burning hands. "Come get wet with us, Amylia." He winked at her fiendishly.

Slipping into her room some time later to get some spare clothes, Amylia brushed her hair quickly, towelling the rest of the seawater from it. A package on her bed caught her eye. Approaching it cautiously, she put her knife down on the chest next to the figurine of Shadow, pushed the lid off the box, and then laughed to herself, pulling out a thin, lacy nightgown in a deep wine red. The note read: *Thank me later. Happy Birthday. Lyrik xx*

Amylia snorted, hesitated, and then slipped it over her head, cringing at the indecent length of it. She grabbed the clothes she had gathered before padding quickly up the steps to the next level. When she entered, the room was quiet and bathed in a warm glow from the fireplace. Athyna stretched out in front of the window, the gleam of an eye just visible as she cracked it open.

Dropping the clothes for the morning onto a chair, she padded to the bed, smiling at Cecily's curled form, the woman already deeply asleep. She crossed to the other side, so as not to disturb her. Gryffon's eyes, full of amusement and hunger, followed her as she walked. He raised an arm as she neared, holding open the bedcovers for her, and she slipped under them, nestling into the cocoon of warmth against him.

"If that's a present from Lyrik, remind me to apologise to her tomorrow," he growled, his voice rumbling where her head rested by his chest.

"Apologise?" Amylia asked, craning her neck to peer up at him.

"Because I'm going to enjoy tearing it off you in the morning," he replied, shifting to slip his arm under her and draw her towards him.

She curled her body around him, resting a leg over his and reached across him to brush a strand of hair from Cecily's face, feeling Gryffon sigh contentedly as Amylia rested her hand over Cecily's and let herself be drawn into sleep.

Chapter 28

Amylia grinned as she blocked Rogue's blade. He spun, twisting under her arm, blade pointed at her neck, but she ducked, swinging her leg to take out his from under him. Rogue leaped nimbly over it, catching her arm, and twisting it behind her deftly. Amylia sent flames rippling up her spine, smelling the cloth singe and forcing him to let go.

"Oooooooh, want to play dirty, do you?" He grinned. "Come on, then."

She smirked and circled him. They both dropped their weapons into the dirt. Rogue attacked first, throwing a bolt of electricity aimed at her middle. She dodged and launched herself at him, getting her arm around his neck. He faltered at the change of tactic and tried to get purchase on her waist. But he had to let go quickly with a hiss when her flames circled his arm.

Amylia dropped her leg back between Rogue's muscled thighs and twisted. His body rolled over her leg, and he yelped in surprise, hitting the ground heavily. He lay looking up at her and she whooped in triumph, jumping on the spot.

"Yes!" she cried. Her victory was cut short when he suddenly swung his leg up and around, catching her feet and taking them out from underneath her. She hit the ground next to him, winded and gasping. Rogue chuckled.

"Lesson number two hundred and forty-seven," he said. "Never celebrate too early."

"Yup, I can see why," she rasped, reaching up to pat his face. "Thanks."

Rogue snorted. "No worries. You had me, though. Well done." He rolled to his feet, giving her a hand up, then grinned. "Lyrik showed you that little trick, didn't she?"

"Yes." Amylia rubbed her hip. "That's going to bruise." She laughed and cringed as she prodded the tender spot.

They walked back up to the castle together. Slightly limping, Amylia leaned on Rogue's arm. Rogue, clothes smoking in a few places, held his shirt out, studying a ragged burn hole, and sighed. "There goes another one."

Cecily looked up as they entered the dining hall, smiling, then doing a doubletake as her eyes fell on the scorch marks on Rogue and Amylia's limp.

"What did you do? Try to kill each other?" She strode up and grabbed Amylia's arm, peering into the scorched fabric, looking for burns

"Oh, no, I deserved that one." Rogue chuckled. "I thought I grabbed her shoulder when I had her in a hold… turns out it wasn't her shoulder." He gestured in front of his chest and waggled his eyebrows. "Higher than I anticipated."

Amylia swung her free arm behind her, aiming to smack him in the stomach and misjudged, cringing as she connected with the course fabric of his pants in a solid blow.

Groaning, Rogue dropped like a stone to the floor, cradling his balls and puffing like a winded horse.

Cecily looked down at him with narrowed eyes. "I see." She snorted. Turning to Amylia, she ran a hand over her hip, leaning in to kiss the tip of her nose as the pain melted away.

Rayvn walked into the hall and paused with a brow raised at Rogue's prone form.

"Perfect timing, Rayvn," Cecily muttered. "Rogue, here, finds himself in need of a healer."

"You are a dark woman, Cess." Rogue gasped, still clutching himself. "Entirely worth it, though." He grinned at Amylia, who rolled her eyes and watched as Rayvn knelt and gestured for Rogue to surrender his arm to him.

"You're getting good at that, Ray," she said, watching as pink skin rapidly covered the mild burn.

"Thanks." He beamed, turning back to Rogue with a disconcerted look. "You, uh… don't need the other things healed, too, do you?"

"No," Rogue muttered, sitting up with a wince.

Amylia frowned suddenly, turning to the door just before the shouting began to be audible down the hall, the wave of emotion that rushed from it grating at her.

"Because I do not *trust* them," Lyrik's voice snarled through the hallway. A moment later, Lyrik arrived in the hall followed by Gryffon. They both paused when they saw the people already there and Lyrik stiffened, turning back to

Gryffon. "I mean it, Gryff, they need to go," she hissed, before turning and storming off.

Gryffon took a breath, looking to the ceiling as if asking the Gods for patience, then carried on into the hall, pouring a drink from the table.

"Who's upset Lyrik?" Cecily asked, her forehead knotting.

"The trade alliance men." Gryffon sighed. "Not, Silas," he added to Rayvn, who had looked up. "She has banned them from the roosts. Apparently, they have been getting increasingly agitated over Amylia being here." He sighed. "They had been told Amylia was here for training in her Gifts, which Rogue's training satisfied, but somehow, it's gotten out that Amylia and Rayvn have joined with Asteryn, which we were trying to avoid for now, until we decided what to do with them."

Rayvn nodded. "I agree with Lyrik. I think it's time to send them back." They all turned to look at him. "She's right not to trust them." He grimaced. "From what I hear, they're waiting for the trade ship to return anyway. It might be worth doing it before then."

Gryffon nodded, sighing. "It was inevitable that they return, and report Amylia is here. I'm actually surprised Drakon hasn't sent people to try to bring her back yet or see if Rayvn had his binding removed." He turned to her. "Are you ready for this, bug?"

Amylia grimaced. "No, but I don't think I ever will be. We are not going back, and I guess it needs to be addressed sooner rather than later." She sighed. "What if I write a letter to send with them? Explaining that I'm learning how to control my Gifts here."

"It could be worth a try," Cecily said, glancing at Gryffon. "Not that I think Drakon will accept that easily."

"Ok." Gryffon sounded hesitant, but he straightened his shoulders and turned to Rogue. "Can you let the men know that we will prepare to return them in two days? Riders can drop them on the far side of the Dead Forest, and they can go from there."

Two days later, with a knot of anxiety in her belly, Amylia watched the Sylkies and their riders disappearing into the distance. She startled as arms came around her waist, then she leaned back into Cecily's warmth, smiling when the woman kissed her shoulder.

"It will be okay, sweetling." She reached to tuck a lock of hair behind Amylia's ear. "Surely Drakon and Mica know where you went. They should have followed or sent word by now, if they intended on trying to get you back."

Amylia nodded, her eyes fixed on the horizon. "I know. I just know what Drakon is like… and Mica. Neither of them like to lose." She turned to face Cecily, reaching to drape her arms around the woman's neck and searched her eyes, her face solemn. "Drakon will not like the fact that he's losing Oryx, with Rayvn breaking with Lylican and swearing to Asteryn. It means Oryx and Lylican will no longer have ties once Rayvn comes of age. In fact, it should be Asteryn that manages it until that time anyway."

"Let's see what happens with that letter first, sweetling. There is hope. The first trade ship is due in just over three weeks. The men would have returned to Lylican before it departs which means return word will be sent with the ship." Cecily smiled encouragingly. "If Drakon and Mica respect your wishes, there is no reason the alliance cannot continue. It may be strained, but we can manage that, and no reason he cannot continue to oversee Oryx for Rayvn. It would show good faith on our side and would make an alliance easier to forge between Oryx and Lylican for Rayvn later."

Amylia nodded, glancing over her shoulder. The Sylkies were out of sight now and the knot of anxiety was tightening.

"What else is wrong, sweetling?" Cecily drew her attention back to her. She moved away, pouring herself a glass of the heady, spiced wine, and a glass of the sweeter cider for Amylia and came back, passing it to her. "You have been quiet all day. Is something else nagging at you?" she asked gently.

Amylia took the cider, sinking onto the bed as Cecily sat next to her, curling her legs under herself. "I'm meant to be the Lymbic here," Amylia said, the side of her mouth tugged up in a half-smile as she glanced up at Cecily.

"It's not hard to tell." Cecily chuckled. "You get a tiny little crease, right here, when you worry." She reached out, smoothing a fingertip between Amylia's brows. "Anything you want to talk about?"

"Me being here is causing you and Gryff issues," Amylia said flatly. "You didn't ask for this, and… it's not just that." She looked down into the golden liquid in her cup. "I feel like I've just stepped into your and Gryff's relationship. I don't know where I fit, or… I know how I feel, but Gryff is yours, and you are Gryff's, and maybe it would be easier if I wasn't here —"

Cecily's mouth on hers cut her off, the sweet, spicy taste of the wine on her tongue and Amylia's racing thoughts stilling for a moment.

"I thought you knew, or I would have clarified this weeks ago." She smiled softly. "I'm not going to talk for Gryff. That's for him to do in his own time, but for me… Amylia, I'm yours. There is no hill I will not climb to see you safe and here with us where you belong. I love you."

Amylia's heart took flight as she looked at the woman in front of her, and then reached out, grabbing the front of Cecily's shirt, and pulling her roughly against her into a deep kiss.

"I love you, too," she whispered against Cecily's lips.

Chapter 29

The bell from the dock announced the sails appearing around the coast and Gryffon looked out the window, his brow creasing. Amylia padded up to him, ducking under his arm and looking out as he wrapped an arm around her waist.

"Well, here we go," he said kissing the back of her head gently as he leaned against her, pushing her against the stone sill. Worry radiated from him.

"It's only been what, two weeks?" she asked, trying to keep her voice steady.

"Thirteen days," he replied flatly. "They must have left only a few days after the men returned."

Amylia leaned her head against his chest as he ran his large hand up her body and cupped her breast. Arching her back against him with a small sigh, she felt and heard his chuckle when he reached down to grab her ass and squeezed it gently.

"Don't make me start what I don't have time to finish," he growled in her ear. Cecily moved up next to them, ducking under Gryffon's other arm and looking out to the ship, too, the concern on her face mirroring Gryffon's.

He wrapped an arm around each of them, holding them to him as they each rested their heads against his chest. All three watched the slow process of the ship in the distance. Cecily had a wicked smile on her face as she took Amylia's hand and gently bit the tip of her finger, swirling her tongue around it.

"Oh, don't start that," Amylia mocked, throwing a sly smile up at Gryffon. "Someone told me there's not enough time."

Cecily raised an eyebrow at him, mock outrage on her face. Gryffon snorted, placing a large hand over Cecily's face, covering it entirely.

"You girls are going to kill me at this rate," he teased, yelping, and pulling his hand away as Cecily bit the fleshy bit at the base of his thumb.

"Struggling to keep up, old man?" Cecily giggled, pulling his hand back to kiss the spot.

Amylia pulled herself up to sit on the wide stone sill, eyes level with Gryffon's, facing them both. "If you're too tired, Gryff… you can always just watch," she said devilishly, biting her lower lip. She put a slender foot against his chest and pushed him slightly.

Gryffon eyed them both sardonically. "You know, you are both terrible for the ego." His eyes glazed slightly as Cecily pushed the straps of her dress off her shoulders, letting it fall to the ground.

The breeze making her nipples harden as she moved to Amylia, pushing her knees apart and sliding between them. She kissed her deeply, running her hands up her dress, dragging her nails slowly back down the skin and making Amylia shudder.

Amylia's flames smouldered around her fingers as she gripped the sides of the window to stop herself from falling back. Hooking her foot around Gryffon's thigh, she pulled him towards them.

Gryffon growled and grabbed Cecily in one arm, her bare ass against his skin. He threw Amylia over his shoulder, and she whooped with laughter as he bit her gently on the thigh.

"I'm sure Lylican can wait for a couple of hours." He chuckled and turned to kiss Cecily, walking towards the massive bed.

There was a knock on the door a few hours later and Cecily answered it, wrapped in one of the sheets from the bed. Rogue promptly shut his eyes as he sidled into the room.

"As much as I hate to interrupt," he grinned, "especially with how fast Lyrik and Rayvn hightailed it out of here, Lylican has sent word ahead that they want a meeting." He crossed his arms, waiting patiently, though his eyes stayed firmly shut.

Gryffon snorted from where he stood pulling a shirt on. "I bet they do. Do you know who has come on behalf?"

Rogue turned his face in the direction of Gryffon's voice. "I do not, but from the description the boy gave, I think it may be Drakon himself."

Hands stilling on his laces, Gryffon stopped. "That's unexpected." He looked at Amylia who had sat bolt upright on the bed at the mention of the Lylican lord's name. Covers pulled up to her chin, she stared at Rogue, feeling the blood drain from her face.

"Thank you, Rogue. We will be down shortly. Can you send word to the servants to ready the throne room please?" Cecily said quietly.

"I'll send for Lyrik, too. I think they were headed to the roosts," Rogue said. With a nod, he turned, eyes still shut, and paused, seeming to lose his bearings.

Cecily chuckled, catching his elbow, and guiding him out the door. "It's not anything you haven't seen before," she teased.

He bowed low to her. "Children never want to see their parents naked, m'lady."

Cecily sighed, slamming the door on his face. A muffled curse came from behind it as Gryffon roared with laughter.

They got to the throne room just as the announcement came that Drakon had arrived at the castle gates.

Rogue was leaning nonchalantly against the entrance, picking his teeth with his dagger. "They are armed and pissy, just so you know. Should I get my men to let them in or keep them waiting a bit longer?"

Gryffon shook his head, scowling. "Let them in. We want to try and keep this as civil as possible."

"The weapons?" Rogue asked, sheathing his dagger, and cocking a brow at Gryffon.

"Let them keep them," Gryffon growled. "They will feel less threatened if they are armed, useless as they may be against us."

Rogue nodded, huffing a laugh, and strode out the doors.

Gryffon turned back to the women and gave Amylia a gentle kiss. "This is our territory, and you are one of us, Bug. He has no power here and even less over you."

Amylia nodded nervously. Cecily moved to her other side and took her hand. Athyna prowled over and planted herself in front of them. They all stood on the dais at the far end of the entrance, the floor of which was now covered in the huge Dyre wolf pelts.

Amylia's emotions roiled inside her and Cecily squeezed her hand. "Just breathe, sweetling. Don't let him see that he affects you."

Amylia took a breath, taking in Cecily's scent as it hung around her, letting the woman's calm energy flow into her, soothing her nerves. She returned the squeeze just as the throne room's doors slammed open.

Drakon stormed in, his face grim. He was followed by Mica, half a dozen guards, and the six trade alliance men, all armed to the teeth. Some of Rogue's men filtered in behind them on silent feet and melted into the shadows, keeping a watchful eye on the newcomers.

Gryffon stepped in front of the women, his face stony as Athyna rumbled a growl deep in her chest, her lips drawn back over sharp canines. "You have nerve, Drakon, after what you did, coming into my home with weapons," Gryffon snarled, his tone icy as he glared at the men.

Mica sneered. "After what we did? Says the man who kidnapped my betrothed. Our men have filled us in on everything that has happened here since you left." He glared at Amylia. "A letter, Amylia? You just slip off after burning half our keep down and do not even tell us where you run off to?" he hissed. "We wasted weeks searching through Umber's territory and then down through Credence and Eilysh, after your bitch maid told us you had gone there. She even went as far as poisoning the guards that saw you taking her, Lord Wynter." His tone was mocking as he turned his attention to Gryffon.

Fear for Harriet curled in Amylia's stomach as she stared Mica down. "Is Harry okay?" she asked coldly.

"The maid is alive, if that's what you mean," Mica replied stonily.

Drakon hushed him with a wave of his hand. "I've come for my ward," he said, voice low. "I'm willing to overlook the act of treason on your part if she comes back without a fuss."

"Act of treason! You old fool! You strapped her to a table, cut her open, and then try to tell me I acted without honour?" Gryffon scoffed as Drakon's expression turned thunderous.

"That was for her own safety... and for the safety of others. She has no idea how to manage those Gifts."

"And whose fault was that?" Amylia spat, striding up next to Gryffon. "You robbed me of who I am, acted like it was an affliction, not a Gift. And when I asked to be able to learn how to manage it, you drugged me and had your physician slice me open." She let her Gift go as her anger flared and a flaming blue Sabyre appeared next to her, its lips curled back in a silent snarl. To her satisfaction, they both stepped back suddenly. "It seems to me that I'm learning my Gifts just fine, Drakon," she snarled.

Gryffon rested a hand on her shoulder, giving it a gentle squeeze. Amylia noticed in a bemused way how Mica's eyes flared as he watched that hand, colour rising up his neck.

"*Get your hand off her!*" He strode forward, stopping abruptly when Gryffon raised a hand, his golden flames swirling around his arm.

"Not a step closer," Gryffon snarled at the younger man.

A small door to the left banged open and Lyrik strode in with Rogue on her heels. He casually took up a place to their left and Lyrik stalked to the front of the dais, drawing her sword gracefully as she did so.

"I see I missed half the fun," she crooned, casually placing the tip of the deadly sword on the ground and leaning on it. To her credit, she didn't look twice at the flaming Sabyre that stood next to her.

"Rayvn?" Amylia asked, glancing nervously to the door. Lyrik looked back at her and winked.

"Falkyn has him safe."

Amylia relaxed slightly, letting out a breath in relief as Drakon eyed the woman with distaste.

"Who is Falkyn?"

Lyrik grinned at him sweetly. "Someone I should really introduce you to at some point, my lord," she answered, voice dripping with sarcasm.

Cecily ran her hand down Amylia's back in silent support, stepping up next to her, one hand on the Dyre wolf's head.

"Lyrik will have sent him to the mountain roosts," she murmured to Amylia. "He's safe, sweetling."

"Enough of this," Drakon snapped. "Amylia, you and Rayvn will come home immediately."

"I am home," she answered venomously. The Sabyre shook its head beside her and prowled closer to the men. "Take your son and leave. I reject his marriage proposal. It ended the day I left, and Rayvn is not setting foot back in those lands either. We are with Asteryn, Oryx is with Asteryn, and we recognise this court as our own until Rayvn takes his lands. We will continue to let you oversee Oryx until that time if you do the smart thing and leave."

Flames licked up her arms as her anger took hold. Neither Cecily nor Gryffon moved away, her flames reaching around them and over their skin, but not burning them. She turned to Mica. "You once told me you loved me. That was not love, Mica, I know that now. You wanted to own me, and I will not be owned. I give myself and my heart freely to those who are worthy of my love. That is not, and will never be, you."

His lip curled in anger as he looked at Gryffon and then Cecily. "What is this?" he hissed, his fists balling at his sides. "What have you done to her?"

Amylia looked him dead in the eye. "Nothing I did not *ask* them to, Mica."

Mica launched himself at Gryffon and the Sabyre crouched to leap, but Lyrik was faster, intercepting him with a hard blow to his nose from the hilt of her sword. Bone crunched as she landed it and he staggered back, nose gushing blood. Gryffon's power surged forward, swirling between Lyrik and Mica, his flames forming a wall.

"I suggest you leave," he said coldly. "Before you no longer have legs to walk out on."

"You will not touch us," Drakon sneered, ignoring Mica, who held a sleeve to his streaming nose and groaned.

"Fuck the alliance," Gryffon hissed. "I'll happily kill you where you stand if you try to lay claim to this woman. I was willing to maintain the alliance between our territories, but not at the cost of Amylia's happiness."

"You won't lay a finger on us… because of this." Drakon waved an envelope in his hand and sneered.

"Not even the contract will hold after what you did, and I know what you tried to pull with my copy," Gryffon said coldly, not even glancing at the paper as Drakon grinned maliciously.

"This is not the contract." He looked at Amylia, "This, my dear… this is a letter from your mother."

The world fell out from under Amylia's feet as her knees buckled. The Sabyre disappeared in a hiss of smoke, and she vaguely felt Cecily's arm bracing her, her ears ringing.

"What?" Her voice sounded distant as if someone else were speaking. Drakon held the letter out, waving it as if calling a dog with a piece of meat.

"This letter has everything in it, my dear. Your mother is alive… and in my care. As she has been for eleven years now. And just so you are aware," he looked pointedly at Gryffon. "If we do not return with Amylia when we are expected to — unharmed — they will deliver her here… piece by piece."

Gryffon blanched, seemingly lost for words. Drakon turned back to Amylia, a triumphant look on his face.

"I'll say it one last time, Amylia," Drakon hissed. "You will be coming home."

"How?" she stared at him. "Where is she?"

He eyed her as if deciding what he wanted to tell her before shrugging his shoulder nonchalantly. "This world is not made for humans, Amylia. We are defenceless against your kind." His face flashed with disgust as he scanned the collection of people in front of him. "I tried to unite with your mother, to make my line strong, so our lands would be safe in our family for generations to come when Attica returns to claim these lands. If we had mixed our line with a strong Sylvyn line, we would have been safe with a Sylvyn claim to the lands there and in Oryx. But she laughed in my face, as if she were too good for me." He laughed softly. "And then you were born and my little bird in Oryx later informed me you were emerging as a Heliacle... just like your mother," he hissed.

"Two Heliacle Wytchlings in Oryx. Lylican didn't stand a chance. In fact, none of the territories did; it was my job to save us. So, I sent word to my little bird to start putting Helix dust in their food. Just a small amount, so it was unnoticeable as they got weaker and weaker."

Cecily gasped, looking in horror at the monster in front of her.

"Your parents never suspected a thing," Drakon continued. "They thought they had some kind of illness and your father searched high and low for a cure... until I took the keep."

Drakon smiled, and it was a cruel, twisted smile, a hint of madness showing through. "He was easy to kill," he went on, "with no Gift left to wield against me, and your mother... well, once I put a stone in her, she was no trouble at all. I'll admit, it was harder than you two. We nearly lost her to infection afterwards; the damn woman kept trying to dig it out."

His face was devoid of all emotion as he looked her up and down. "That just left you two. Young as you were, I obviously couldn't take you as a bride. Not that the idea didn't cross my mind once you were of age."

Gryffon snarled, his fists clenching as if he wanted to drive them into Drakon's face.

"But no," Drakon went on, walking to the edge of the flames. "I raised you to be my son's wife. With your children, our line will go on, strong, with Heliacle heirs linked to strong Sylvyn lines to ensure it."

"You raised her to be a damned broodmare," Lyrik seethed and raised her blade, the tip of it inches from Drakon's neck.

"Ah, ah, ah," he tutted, hands raised as he waggled the letter in the air. "I raised her as a guarantee that our lands were safe, and then the Asterynians came and it was another tie that I thought would make us stronger, another connection to ensure we could hold against Attica. It is why I sent Rayvn with you. I knew you would see what a charming boy he is and want to join with Oryx. The three of us together, with your connections, would be unstoppable. And then you took away everything I had worked for."

"She is *not* your property," Lyrik snarled. Her temper was slipping through the tight hold she usually had on it, and it bit at Amylia, the intensity of it terrifying.

"Wait," Amylia said in a strangled voice. "I want to see it."

Drakon reached out over the flames and held the letter out to her, stepping away from Lyrik. "Well, then, my dear, come."

Cecily snarled as Amylia started forward, forcing her legs to move as if through water, her veins icy. Out the corner of her eye, she saw Gryffon catch hold of Cecily's arm. She had lurched forward, reaching for Amylia. Gryffon's face was anguished as he watched her walk away and she turned, meeting Cecily's eyes. Her heart tore from the pain in those eyes as she silently pleaded with Amylia not to go.

Amylia took a shuddering breath, then turned back to the waiting men. The smirk on Drakon's face fuelled the rage kindling in her stomach.

Lyrik fell into step next to her, sheathing her sword as she did so, and Amylia gave her a grateful look as the woman leaned into her, lending her strength, as if knowing Amylia's legs barely supported her.

They paused in front of the wall of Gryffon's flames, Amylia looking back at him, and he sighed, dropping the barrier so they could step across the blackened ground. As they approached, Mica hissed, "That's far enough, Damaris."

"No, come." Drakon smiled. "I have a favour to ask her anyway." He stepped towards them, holding the letter out.

Lyrik took it from him as they got within reach, her face a mask of cold hatred as she observed the seal. Nodding, she passed it to Amylia, who swayed at the disgusting mix of hatred and disdain that flowed from the two men in front of her. This close, the dark cloud of it reached out and its cold tendrils wrapped around Amylia, making her skin crawl. How had she not been able to feel this from them before?

"It's not been tampered with," Lyrik murmured, her glare returning to the men.

Amylia ripped open the letter. Breath shallow, she rapidly scanned the words in front of her, then she sobbed, sinking to her knees. It was her mother's writing, the familiar scrawl she remembered from notes left to her as a child.

I'm so sorry my Milly. Please know I love you both, always. Stay away and live, show the world how strong you are. I will always be with you. Mama.

Commotion sounded behind her as Gryffon lurched away from Cecily, but was stopped abruptly by a hand to his chest from Rogue. The man murmured a warning low into his ear.

"Well?" Drakon asked, face impassive as he idly watched Gryffon.

Lyrik crouched with her hand on Amylia's shoulder comfortingly. "Does he speak the truth?" she asked gently.

Amylia nodded, wiping at her face. "It's her hand," she said, her voice barely a whisper. "And it's dated twelve days ago. It's Mother."

Lyrik swore softly, standing to look Drakon in the eye. "Take me instead," she said coldly. "In exchange for Amylia." Rogue growled from behind them, which she ignored. "I'm not a Wytchling, or a Heliacle, but something else just as powerful. I will take her place."

"No!" Amylia clambered to her feet, her mind reeling. "I'm not having anyone sacrifice themselves for me." She looked at Drakon. "I'll come back. I'll come, and I will not try to escape. But you are to leave Rayvn here… and Mother. Let her go so she can come here to Rayvn."

Cecily sobbed quietly behind her.

Drakon studied her, stroking his chin. "I have plans for Rayvn," he mused.

"Then change them," Amylia snapped. She knew her eyes flashed with the effort to rein in her power, to not burn him where he stood. "You have my word I will obey, but if you try to take him or try to keep my mother, I swear I will not rest until you are both in the ground and your line that you are so obsessed with will die with you."

Drakon stiffened. "Your mother stays in my care until you provide Mica an heir. Once that is done, I'll release her. Unharmed."

Amylia shuddered, nodding her agreement, not able to utter the words as Mica straightened, turning to his father.

"Let's be done with this place." He sneered at Amylia. "And take Amylia back where she belongs."

Drakon nodded once, curtly. "I accept your bargain."

He turned to Lyrik. "And now for that favour, Damaris." He sneered, then looked at Amylia. "And a test as to the strength of your word." He pulled a small, sharp knife from his belt.

Lyrik moved slightly, putting herself between Drakon and Amylia. Drakon snorted. "As if I would try to kill her." He scoffed, holding the knife out to Lyrik. His other hand fumbled with a bag at his hip. He produced a small stone, rolling it around in his palm, slightly larger than the last one. Lyrik blanched in horror at the knife.

"No," she hissed. Stepping back, she stared in horror at Drakon, who smiled maliciously.

"In her leg if you, please, Miss Damaris, and deep. I'm not having her cut this one out."

Lyrik looked at Amylia, her face white. "Amylia, no. I can't do th —"

Amylia stopped her with a hand on her arm, shaking slightly as she looked at her friend, tears rolling silently down her cheeks. "Do it, Lyrik… please. I'd rather it was you."

Gryffon roared, breaking away from Rogue and storming off the dais towards them. Mica threw up a hand, his other still holding a sleeve to his nose.

"Touch us, Wynter, and her mother dies. Slowly."

Gryffon paused, glaring at the men. Amylia turned and walked slowly to him. He met her halfway, taking her into his arms as she buried her face in his neck.

"We can find another way," he murmured, and she shook her head.

"I'm sorry," she whispered, her face wet against his skin, feeling his fury and despair. "I'll always love you and Cecily. You are both my heart. But I can't let her die. I can't let them kill her, and he will, if I make them leave here without me. He will hurt her until I go back." She reached out with her Gifts, letting them whisper across the room to caress Cecily's cheek in a warm embrace as she took a deep breath, remembering the smell of him before stepping away. His arms dropped to his sides as she turned and walked back to Lyrik, ignoring the icy glare from Mica.

"Do it," Amylia said, voice steady as she ripped the side of her pants open and braced herself.

Lyrik neared, face anguished. She palmed the blade and reached out, pulling Amylia down against her tightly, her face next to her ear. A white-hot pain shot through Amylia's leg, making her legs buckle and her head swim. She gasped against the pain while Lyrik held her tightly, whispering into her ear, so quietly she could barely hear her.

"We will come for you when it's safe for your mother. I swear to the Gods I will come." Lyrik braced her, then moved back, her hands on Amylia's waist, holding eye contact.

Drakon passed Lyrik the stone and she took it, never looking away from Amylia. Her face hardened. Amylia's Gift whispered over the woman, flickering and flaring as the pain in her leg seared. She felt the fear and disgust in Lyrik as the stone in her hand sucked greedily at her.

"Look at me, and breathe," she said softly as she reached down next to the wound and paused, waiting.

Amylia nodded, bracing herself as Lyrik deftly pushed the small stone into the wound. Moaning, Amylia swayed slightly as Lyrik's grip on her waist tightened, holding her up.

"Excellent," Drakon breathed. Amylia felt it take over her, her Gift pulling back into herself, away from Lyrik, cutting her off as effectively as if any of her other senses had been taken away, her breath coming shallowly.

"You." Drakon pointed at Cecily. "You heal, yes? Come and heal it now."

Cecily launched herself forward, wrenching out of Rogue's grip and ran to where Lyrik held Amylia. Tears flowing down her face as she reached her, she pulled Amylia into her arms.

"I love you," she whispered. Resting her forehead against Amylia's, she put her hand over the wound, taking the searing pain away instantly.

Amylia sighed as the pain receded. "Look after them, Cess," she murmured. "Look after all of them." Eyes filled with tears, she saw Cecily give a slight nod.

They stayed there. The three women held each other long after the wound had closed, Lyrik and Cecily lending Amylia every ounce of strength they could.

Drakon shifted and hissed, "Enough." He stooped to pick up the knife. Cecily stiffened when he moved. She kissed Amylia softly on the cheek before looking down at the blood on Amylia's leg, the skin healed perfectly under it.

She swiped a finger through it, then turned to face the men, her face contorted in feral rage. Stalking to them, she stopped inches from the taller man, making him take an awkward half-step back. Cecily moved with him, a cat stalking its prey. Amylia's head swam as she watched Cecily draw the bloody finger down her forehead to the tip of her elegant nose. "I bind myself in a blood oath," she snarled, her voice edged in a steel that Amylia had never heard from her before. "I will see you dead, you will take your last breath with my blade in your heart, and I will stand before you as I do now and watch the life drain from your eyes."

Drakon paled slightly as Mica stepped towards them.

"And you." She rounded on him. "You hurt her in any way, and I will hunt you down; there is no place that I will not find you."

Mica scowled at her, though looked slightly paler. "Go back to your husband, Lady Wynter, and leave me to my bride. She is none of your concern anymore."

Cecily snarled at him as she backed away, throwing a last anguished glance to Amylia before Gryffon enfolded her in his arms and pulled her away.

Drakon's guards shoved Lyrik aside, shrinking away slightly when she bared her teeth at them, a growl low in her chest as they seized Amylia by the wrists, twisting them up behind her.

"Do not have us followed, or you know what will happen," Drakon snapped as he waved a hand for his men to leave.

Chapter 30

Drakon's men rode hard to the boat, Amylia behind Mica and hating every inch of contact as she clung to his tunic in an effort to stay mounted. No one followed as they raced through the street. Shocked faces of the Asterynian's turned to them, children snatched out of the way of the flying hooves as the men thundered past.

They dismounted in a flurry, leaving the horses with the dock stable-hands and boarded the waiting ship. Drakon roared orders to cast off as soon as his feet hit the deck.

Amylia stood in shock as the men ran around her, bumping into her in their haste to follow orders. The hollowness inside her threatened to swallow her; the stone's drain left her noticeably weak. A small crowd of people gathered on the dock, whispering among themselves as they stared at her. A young man she recognised from the castle stables stepped forward, concern on his face. He started to walk towards her, but she shook her head at him.

He stopped, confusion etched into his features, but stepped back, bowing slightly to her as he did.

The boards under her feet shuddered as the ship moved away, swaying slightly. Coldness crept up her skin. She took a deep, shaky breath as she looked at the castle one last time, towards Gryffon, Cecily… her family, before she felt Mica's hand on her back, his voice in her ear.

"Let's get you below," he murmured.

Her skin crawled as she reluctantly turned away from the edge, following Mica below. Mica pushed her into a cabin, kicking the door closed behind them. She didn't have the strength to do anything other than turn and meet his stare. The stone sucked at her, taking not just her Gift but her strength too.

"We are to be wed immediately. I'm not having anything else stopping this. Get yourself cleaned up and knock when you're ready." He shoved her towards the bucket of water on the far side of the cabin. "There are clothes in there." He pointed with his chin to the chest next to it then abruptly spun on his heel and left, slamming the door behind him.

Amylia took a deep, steadying breath, looking around the small room. A double-berth cot hugged the wall to her left; to the right, a small porthole looked over the waves, and on the wall in front stood a desk with a chair and the chest. The bucket sloshed gently with the movement of the ship as is rocked in the waves. A kerosene lantern hung from the ceiling above her, unlit. Daylight streamed through the porthole and provided enough light to bathe the room dimly.

She walked to the bucket and dropped to her knees, cupping her hands, and splashing the cold water onto her face. She gasped as the cold water ran down her chest and braced her hands on the sides of the bucket, looking at her reflection on the rippling surface. She looked the same as she had this morning, except her eyes. They looked so flat now, the absence of her Gift mixed with the despair that was growing with every minute as reality set in.

She had never set foot on a ship before, the rolling motion left her feeling queasy and lightheaded. The smell of this cabin didn't help, the kerosene from the lamp was pungent and mixed nastily with the mustiness of the room.

Amylia grimaced as the wet fabric on the front of her shirt clung to her skin, and reached out for the towel hanging on the chair to dry her face.

Moving to sit on the edge of the bed, she allowed her grief to take over. Only here, only while he couldn't see her.

Just breathe, sweetling. Don't let him see that he affects you.'

Amylia wept into a pillow, its harsh fabric scratched at her face as she fell apart. It was too much, her mother alive and captive all this time. Amylia's mind screamed as she thought of what her mother must have endured for eleven years, alone, having lost her children and her mate. And now, to be ripped away from everything she had grown to love, after only now feeling what true love and acceptance felt like… She sucked in huge gulps of air and tried to calm herself.

Just breathe, sweetling. Don't let him see that he affects you.'

She dragged them to the front of her mind and held them there, trying to imagine them standing either side of her. Her peace.

Dragging her fingers through her hair to tame it, she wiped her face and knocked on the door.

It swung open immediately. A guard she didn't know stood back, gesturing for her to walk out. He raised a brow at her clothes — the fitted pants and loose white shirt she preferred — but didn't say anything, and pointed sullenly up the hall, indicating the direction to go. Momentarily gripping the necklace she wore, she glanced down at it, the gold and turquoise glinting up at her, and took a steadying breath.

'Just breathe, sweetling.'

She walked, head up, onto the deck. Refusing to let them see her fear as she looked at the small collection of people. Mica stood among them, next to his father, his face grim as he stared at her.

Personal guards stood to either side of them. Witnesses, she thought with disgust.

At the head, an old man stood dressed in dark robes. A belt at his waist held a sheathed knife. Amylia walked towards them hesitantly and halted in front of Mica. He grabbed her hand in a firm grip, his eyes travelling down her with disgust.

"I told you there were clothes in there," he said in a low, cold voice.

"I'm already wearing clothes," Amylia retorted, thankful her voice didn't waver.

Mica's face hardened, but he just looked at the old man and nodded. "Get on with it then." He scowled.

Nausea washing over her in waves, Amylia's body went hot and then cold in turns, and her palms broke out in a cold sweat. Mica's lip twitched in disgust as his eyes flicked down to their joined hands. He slightly adjusted his grip.

The old man nodded, his grey beard bobbing as he did. In a bored voice, he intoned, "Do you, Lord Mica Drakon, take Lady Amylia Sylvers to be your wife?"

"Yes," Mica said coldly, his eyes staring straight ahead, ignoring Amylia at his side.

The man turned to her. "And do you, Lady Amylia Sylvers, take Lord Mica Drakon as your husband?"

Mutely, she nodded.

The old man's expression sharpened. "I need an answer, girl."

Mica squeezed her hand viciously.

"I do," she blurted, tugging at her hand, but it was locked in Mica's vise-like grip.

"Do you both promise to love and respect each oth—"

"Stop waffling and get to the point." Mica's face was cold. "She has already disrespected me. I expect it will continue, and she admitted not to love me. Just make it legal, old man."

The man stuttered, trying to regain composure. "With the power endowed upon me by the almighty Gods, I pronounce you husband and wife, from this day until you shall be separated only by death." Finished, he smiled near-sightedly at them. "My best wishes for your… uh… happy marriage. You may kiss to seal the union."

Mica pulled her in, kissing her viciously on the mouth, though she put her hand against his chest, weakly trying to push him away. He let her go and another wave of nausea washed over her, rising fast. She pivoted and threw herself to the side of the boat, vomiting over the side.

Mica made sounds of disgust as she leaned limply against the railing, wiping her mouth with her hand. The dark waves that pounded the side of the ship looked inviting as she hung there. It would only take a small push and she could slip into them, she mused.

'Just breathe, sweetling.'

Amylia fought the urge to look to her side, hearing the words as if Cecily were next to her. The mist from the sea touched her face and she took a deep breath of the salty air, settling her stomach slightly. With considerable regret, she heaved herself back up, turning to face the men and her husband, who glowered at her with no sympathy. Drakon's face was a near mirror image.

"Welcome to the family, Lady Drakon," he sneered. "I trust this will be the end of your mutiny?"

She didn't bother answering him. Her energy was gone. She just wanted to close her eyes and rest. There was a buzzing in her ears as she pushed away from the side, taking a wobbly step forward and then the world spun, the deck rising to meet her.

When she came to, the porthole was filled with black, telling her night had crept over them. Her heart ached with the growing distance from Gryffon and Cecily, a constant tug pulling at her soul.

Sitting up, she pulled the covers off and noticed her clothes had been changed. She wore a light nightdress instead. Nausea overtook her again, though she was unsure whether it was from the unknown hands that had changed her, or from this infernal floating plank that bobbed and rolled over the waves.

She retched, throwing herself across the room to the now empty bucket just in time. As she heaved the contents of her stomach into it, misery overtook her. She heaved until there was nothing left. Bile burned her throat as she looked around for water. Anything to wash the taste out of her mouth. There was nothing anywhere. *Probably worried I'll drown myself in it,* she thought sarcastically. She pulled herself up on the desk, wrinkling her nose at the contents of the bucket, and staggered to the door.

Her body felt so heavy, lifting her arm was an effort as she thumped on the door. Leaning against the frame, she waited until a guard pushed his head in, looking at her stonily.

"Water," she murmured. "I need to drink something, and…" She waved her hand feebly at the bucket behind her. "That needs emptying. Sorry."

He nodded, striding into the room to retrieve the bucket, and hastily leaving, shutting the door with a click.

She sighed in relief, staggered back to the bed, and collapsed onto it, her clammy skin making the sheer nightdress stick to it uncomfortably. Grimacing, she pulled it away from her chest, noticing that the damp fabric showed the outline of the slightly darker skin of her nipples. Amylia looked up as the door opened again, expecting to see the guard with water, and her face fell.

"Are you feeling any better?" Mica's face didn't reflect the caring of the question, and she took the steaming cup he offered her, keeping her eyes on it and not on him.

An awkward silence fell. He shifted irritably. Voice softening a touch, he said, "It's ginger tea. It will help with the sea sickness. Drink it."

Amylia sniffed it and the spicy scent drowned the harsh taste in her mouth slightly. Hesitantly, she took a sip of the scalding liquid. Ginger and honey. The sweet, spicy liquid ran down her throat, washing away the vileness left over, and pooled in her stomach reassuringly. It did help slightly, the overwhelming waves of nausea receded as she downed the liquid a sip at a time.

Mica paced slowly, watching her until it was gone. Then he took the cup silently and disappeared for a few minutes. He returned with a water jug, which he left on the table. After handing her another cup, he hovered, but remained silent.

"What do you want, Mica?" she asked wearily, meeting his eyes for the first time.

"I…" His face tinted in a light blush. She couldn't tell if it was from anger or embarrassment. "I wanted to know why you just ran away. Why you just left me… as if I meant nothing to you?"

Incredulous, she looked at him. "Why would I stay?"

Anger, it was definitely anger. The tips of his ears turned red. "Because we were to be married, Amylia. I loved you — I *love* you," he blurted. "And you walked away from me. You went to those filthy Sylvyns and did the Gods know what… I *saw* how Wynter was looking at you, like a piece of meat. Did you whore yourself to him? What, is he bored with his own wife, and now he wants mine?" He sprang back up and paced, hands opening and clenching into fists as he went.

Amylia didn't answer, glaring at him as rage kindled in her belly.

"*Well?*" he yelled, a vein popping out the side of his neck. "What happened there, Amylia?"

She flung the water over him, watching in satisfaction as it dripped from his shocked face. Annoyed at the weakness in her limbs, she stood slowly, her face inches from his.

"Your father killed my father," she said through clenched teeth. "I have lived *eleven* years thinking my mother dead while he watched me grieve for her. *Dead,* Mica. And then you let him tie me to a table be sliced open, after I said I wanted to learn my gift — and you have the nerve to come in here and ask me why I left you?" She pushed him, barely moving him from where he stood. "I left because you should have been on *my* side. You were meant to love me, and you let that monster bind me again, but you were betraying me long before I saw it for myself weren't you, Mica? Let me be abundantly clear, I'm not here for you. I'm here for my mother and for Rayvn because I will not let your family harm one more person from mine, but do not ever expect me to love you again. I *endure* you, Mica, because I have no other choice. And that is all."

He slapped her. Her body spun with the blow which sent her sprawling half on the bed behind, her knees barking painfully against the wooden floor. He moved up behind her and she forced her thoughts to focus again.

The ringing in her ears was back and her cheek burned with pain. She cried out when he twisted his hand into her hair.

Pulling her head back, he hissed into her ear, "It's our family now, Amylia. You are my wife. Do not forget that."

His other hand fumbled with the hem of her nightdress, pushing the front of it up roughly. He gripped a breast savagely, making her whimper as he bruised the tender skin. "And I'm well aware that this marriage is not completed yet, but I'm not touching you until you have been washed of that Sylvyn's taint completely. You disgust me."

"Love doesn't hurt, Mica," she whispered. He stiffened, the taunt of her message from months back no doubt replaying in his mind. He dug his nails in briefly, making her moan in pain, then let her go, shoving himself backwards and glared at her from the middle of the cabin.

"And you think Wynter loved you?" he sneered.

She pulled herself up and sat shakily on the edge of the bed. Her gaze was anything but weak as she glared back at him, raising her chin in defiance.

"Yes, *they* do," she said in a low voice, "and I love them."

He stared at her, confusion plastered across his face. "Them? What do you mean the —" Realisation flashed across his face. Raising his fist, he took a step towards her. She shrank back from the rage in his eyes.

He stared at her for what felt like an eternity, his fist clenched. Then he whirled and stormed out of the cabin, the door slamming behind him so hard it made the timber rattle.

Amylia let out a shaky breath, leaned her head against the wall, and stared at the swinging lamp.

Gods help her.

Chapter 31

Cecily was on her knees, her breathing a ragged rasp as Athyna's nose nudged her cheek, the wolf whining low in her throat.

Gryffon was frozen to the spot; despair, anger, grief all raged through him as he stared at the doors Amylia had just been pulled through. His heart felt like it had just been ripped from his chest and he couldn't stop the groan that escaped. A similar sound from behind him had him whirling back to Cecily. He put his arms around her, urging her up.

Her eyes were unfocused. the grief in them tore at him but he tried to reassure her. "We will get her back." He held her gaze, willing her to calm, wishing he could take her pain on himself too. "Sweetheart, just breath, we will get her back."

Cecily blinked at him. "Why didn't I realise this sooner?" she breathed. "I knew I love her, but Gryff… she's…"

"I know she is." He pulled her against his chest. "I know, my love. And we will get her back. We just have to be smart about how."

Dimly, he heard Lyrik shouting orders to her riders to let the ship leave unobstructed, the tightness in her voice betraying the calm authority she portrayed. Gryffon swept Cecily into his arms as he felt her buckle again, his face stony.

"Rogue, call a meeting to the solar room. I want your generals there, and Lyrik's. Send Ingryd for Rayvn and Silas. I will have them involved in this." He whirled, the wolf on his heels, and Cecily curled against his chest. "Send Rayvn to me first." He called over his shoulder, "I will break this to him myself."

Gryffon set Cecily down on a chaise lounge under the huge windows in the large meeting room. Two maids came in behind him and quickly pulled the white sheets off the surrounding furniture. Athyna sat by her mistress, sapphire eyes intent on her, and Cecily's fingers twined into the thick fur at the wolf's neck.

The room was large, bookshelves lining the walls, except for the wall that consisted of floor-to-ceiling windows that looked across the valley towards the Dead Forest.

A huge round table made from the cross-section of a gigantic, gnarled tree, polished and smooth from centuries of use, sat in the centre of the room, rimmed by ornate chairs.

The behemoth of a table was so large that the room could only have been built around it. Gryffon stood, hands braced on it as he hung his head, breathing deeply. The air smelled of the old books that filled the walls, musty from decades of disuse.

"Shit." He growled and his fingers pressed into the smooth wood. This was the one thing he hadn't prepared for, the one thing he didn't see coming. Cold, almost calm anger coursed through him, distracting him from the feeling of utter loss that pierced his heart.

Gryffon straightened at the sound of running feet in the hall. Closing his eyes, he took a deep, steadying breath.

Rayvn burst through the door, face white and panic in his voice. "Where is she, where is my sister?"

Silas, his cheeks flushed, was on his heels. Gryffon moved towards them, taking Rayvn's shoulders.

"Rayvn, I need you to sit. There is a lot I need to tell you." He guided the boy to a chair, nodding for Silas to sit next to him. "Drakon has taken Amylia back to Lylican," he began.

Leaping back up from his seat, his fists clenched, Rayvn yelled, *"And you let them?"*

Gryffon looked down at his hands, shame coursing through him. "I did. I had no choice."

"*Liar!*" Rayvn spat at him. "Of course you had a choice. You swore she had your protection."

"He *didn't* have a choice, Rayvn," Cecily said, taking a shaky breath and coming to sit in the chair on Rayvn's other side. She took his hand. He didn't pull away from her, but he stiffened, looking out the window.

"Look at me," she said softly. Slowly he turned to meet her red-rimmed eyes. "Amylia chose to leave, to protect you an —"

"I do not need protecting!" Rayvn choked, pulling his hand away and stepping back. "I'm meant to protect her... I'm her *brother!*"

"Rayvn... Drakon has your mother," Gryffon said in a low, steel voice. "There was proof. Amylia left to stop Drakon from harming your mother and made a bargain with him that she would not attempt escape in exchange for you not going as well... and that he will... eventually release your mother to us."

A small sound in the doorway announced Lyrik's arrival. She crossed the room on silent feet, her face tight. Gently, she placed a hand on Rayvn's shoulder as the boy stared at Gryffon in horror.

"Sit, Rayvn." Lyrik guided him to the seat again and he sat heavily, looking at Cecily.

"Mother?" he whispered, his expression a mix of anguish and disbelief. Cecily nodded, taking his hand again.

"I saw the letter, Rayvn. Amylia verified the hand, and it is your mother," Lyrik said stonily.

"I swear, we will get them back. We will get them both back," Gryffon growled.

Lyrik and Cecily filled both Rayvn and Silas in on everything that had taken place in the throne room. Rayvn's face went white and red in turns.

"I'll kill him," he hissed, when Lyrik told him of the Helix, though she left out much detail and Gryffon was grateful. Rayvn didn't need to hurt more than he already was.

"You can have what's left when I've finished with him," Cecily said quietly, her voice cold as ice.

Rogue arrived with three of his generals. One was a huge man with dark hair, and eyes as black as the night sky, who towered over everyone. Another had skin the colour of burnt wood and piercing blue eyes, and the third was a younger man with copper hair and brown eyes. His unremarkable appearance may have made him seem unnoticeable, but a closer look showed sharp intelligence burned behind his eyes.

"This is Dawsyn, Felyx and Edryk," Rogue said, gesturing to the men to sit.

"Most of you know Ingryd," Lyrik said, taking her own place next to Cecily. "And two of my other captains, Arya and Diyanna." She nodded to the other women as they sat quietly.

Gryffon nodded to the solemn faces around him. "I appreciate your swift response." He straightened. "One of our own has been taken. Her mother — who is also Rayvn's mother — is being held hostage."

He took Cecily's hand.

"It has been a long time since we have needed to use our forces. However, this is an act of war which we will answer. We will protect what is ours, and what is Oryx's."

"I can take a flight of Sylkies to retrieve her," Diyanna said, her green eyes flashing in anger.

"It's not as simple as that," Cecily murmured. "If it was, they would not have left our territory breathing."

"Mother… Lady Addelyn Sylvers's life," Rayvn said in clipped tones, "is being held against my sister's commitment to returning to Lylican. And to provide that piece of shit heirs because of our bloodline."

The women around the table hissed, and the men's faces darkened.

"How many men do we have trained and able to fight if needed, Rogue?" Gryffon asked.

Rogue leaned back in his chair, considering. "Seven and a half thousand, that will be including the younger warriors, however. Minus them, five thousand eight hundred."

Gryffon nodded, turning to Lyrik.

"One thousand three hundred mounted riders in the city," she said. "Four thousand four hundred in the Eerie we can call down." Rayvn turned to her, his mouth open, and she gave him a quick smile. "I couldn't risk the men from Lylican knowing our true numbers. Most of our flighted forces reside in the Eclypse mountains, in the Eerie. It is only accessible by Sylkie," she explained. "Diyanna is just one of my captains and manages all the flights that live there."

Silas let out a breath. "Drakon has ten thousand men, easily. And that is not including the men at Oryx."

"Drakon doesn't have Sylkies," Diyanna said, eyes flashing.

"That is all true," Dawsyn said. "But our numbers can do nothing if our hands are tied with Lady Addelyn's life on the line."

"We need to secure Lady Addelyn before we can move on Lylican," Lyrik said and held her hand up to Rayvn as he moved to protest. "We cannot risk your mother's life, Rayvn, not after what your sister is doing to protect her."

"I agree," Cecily said in a quiet voice. She looked at Rayvn. "I don't want her there any longer than you do. But if we took her, and it caused your mother's death, she would not forgive us. We need to follow her wishes, as much as it hurts," she said gently.

Rayvn nodded reluctantly. "How do we find Mother?"

"We start at Oryx," Gryffon answered. "Lyrik, can you send a flight over to assess what's there?"

"I'll head them myself. We can't have word of what we're doing getting back to Drakon." Lyrik nodded

"We need eyes in Lylican, too," Rogue said. "Edryk is my best for that. Rayvn, can you give him a layout of the grounds?"

"I'll go with him," Silas interrupted, looking nervously around the table. "I owe Rayvn and his family everything I have. Please, let me do something." He looked at Lyrik. "Please, let me take Asspyn. I'll keep her safe. I can relay information back to you."

Lyrik eyed him. "I trust you with Asspyn, Silas. But what if you are caught? It's dangerous… and you are young."

"I'm well-liked in the army camp," Silas argued. "I know who I can trust. Not everyone is bad there. Please, give me a chance to see if I can find word on Lady Addelyn there. And if it comes to an attack, time to get some of the good men out of the way." Gryffon eyed him thoughtfully as Silas turned to him. "I know some of those men would not lift a sword to you if they knew what is truly going on."

Gryffon sighed. "I will not have innocent men hurt." He nodded at Silas. "But you need to follow Edryk's orders. If he tells you to get out, you need to get out, and we can't move either of you in too close to the keep until we have an idea where he is keeping Addelyn. If he catches you there without her safe, it could be catastrophic."

Silas nodded, his shoulders dropping slightly..

"I want to go too," Rayvn said. "Silas doesn't know the keep's layout like I do."

"I can't have you going there, Rayvn, not until I know Addelyn is secure, and I could go in and get you out if I needed to," Gryffon said, feeling terrible. But he wouldn't put Rayvn at risk, not after the lengths Amylia was putting herself through.

"You can come with me, Rayvn," Lyrik said softly, her eyes meeting and holding Gryffon's. Silently, they stared each other down. "Oryx is Rayvn's territory. It's his right. That, and I need him to have as much time to bond with Falkyn as he can," Lyrik said, her voice unwavering. "If it comes to a fight, Falkyn's skills could be invaluable."

Gryffon ran his hand through his hair and groaned. "Fine, but you do not enter Lylican territory. I need your word, Rayvn."

Rayvn sighed through his nose and then nodded. "You have it."

"What about the foot troops?" Felyx asked, his rich, deep voice rumbling across the table. "We will need to move soon to keep ahead of you."

"Start readying them now," Gryffon answered. "Be ready to leave when I give the order, but we need to know more before we can act. We could only go as far as the edge of the Dead Forest without risk of discovery, and I won't ask our men to camp in there longer than is necessary."

"I will take Edryk and Silas through to Lylican with a small group of riders when needed," Ingryd said. "They can make camp in the Elixus ranges for Silas to report to."

Gryffon nodded. "They will be expecting some sort of retaliation. They would be stupid not to. But we need them to relax, think we are not coming for them."

Lyrik's party flew out at first light, Rayvn, and Silas with them. Cecily watched them from her window as the small group of Sylkies disappeared in the distance, skirting the coastline towards the Dead Forest before cutting across the ocean. She felt hollow, her heart a constant, dull ache in her chest.

Gryffon moved quietly up behind her, and she leaned into him, murmuring, "I feel so helpless, to be standing here while the Gods know what is happening to her."

Gryffon slipped an arm around her waist, resting his chin on her head.

"He will pay, my love. They both will." He turned her gently, looking into her eyes. "What would it take for me to convince you to stay here?"

Cecily stepped out of his grasp, a chill settling in her stomach. "Don't ask me to do that."

"I can't risk losing both of you, Cess." He sighed.

"But you ask me to risk both of you?" Cecily retorted, irritated that her voice started to shake again. "I won't do it, Gryff. I'm coming… you might need me."

Gryffon groaned, reaching to pull her into a hug. "That was what I was afraid of."

Chapter 32

The sea voyage took nine days… Amylia thought… judging by the small porthole in her cabin. Mica didn't come back, not that she noticed… or cared. Sea sickness ravaged her, and she spent the time she wasn't sleeping heaving into the bucket or picking at the food brought in for her, the still full plates taken away when the next meal was brought in.

She wasn't permitted to leave the cabin, not even to relieve herself. Buckets of water were brought in to wash and then empty ones arrived for toileting.

Most of the time she had fitful, restless sleep, only to wake with pounding headaches, her skin clammy, as she raced for the bucket to try to purge her already empty stomach. Her knees had bruised from kneeling on the hard floor. She felt wretched; the Helix constantly pulled against her, and she knew it was taking too much.

It was dark on the ninth day when she felt the rolling of the ship lessen slightly. She stiffly got out of bed and padded to the small window. Lights on the horizon were dim but noticeable against the dark water, and she couldn't help but feel grateful at the sight of land, even while dread clutched at her stomach at what that meant.

She was still standing at the window, watching, when Mica walked in, his face wrinkling, no doubt at the sour smell of sickness that permeated the room. A guard followed behind him carrying a steaming bucket of water. Amylia had looked up as the door opened, seeing his expression, and then turned away coldly, keeping her eyes firmly locked on the softly illuminated township in the distance.

"We are not far from docking," he said quietly. "There is water to wash. Dress warm. The air is brisk out there tonight." She turned to him and nodded curtly, vaguely noticing his horrified expression.

She guessed at how bad she must look. Her hair was limp. The dim reflection in the water bucket earlier had shown how pale she looked. Her hands shook slightly when she reached for the towel that he held out to her.

Mica rounded on the guard. "You said she had eaten!" he spat.

"Sh-she did, m'lord," the guard stuttered. "Well… some of it… but she been a throwin' it back up."

Mica dragged a hand over his face. "Get out," he ordered. "I'll deal with you later." He turned to Amylia. "I'm… I'm sorry," he muttered. "I was unaware you were still sick."

Amylia shrugged, watching the washcloth sink into the steaming water before she dipped the bar of soap into it and lathered her hands.

When she leaned over the bucket to lift the cloth to her face, the ache of wasting muscles pulled at every movement. She knew it was bad. She could feel her bones too close to the skin as she moved the cloth slowly over her body under her loose clothes. The Helix ripped the weight from her faster than it seemed possible and without keeping the food down, she couldn't do anything to help her body hold its own.

She heard a low intake of breath from behind her.

"It's only been nine days, how have you lost so much weight? What are you doing to yourself? I can see every bump of your spine." Mica strode to the chest, pulling out a blue dress she had worn at the start of the voyage and threw it at her.

"Put this on when you're done." He scowled. "I'll go fetch you a cloak."

Amylia didn't bother answering him as she began on her legs, the now lukewarm water pooling on the floor as it ran in rivulets down her skin.

Amylia sat behind Mica on his stallion as they rode through the quiet town. She detested the closeness, but she was grateful for the warmth he emanated. She always felt so cold lately. Refusing to put an arm around him, she held onto his jacket with one hand and held her cloak tight around her with the other hand.

She looked at the dark houses. Was her mother in one of them? Was she tied? In a cell? Or was she still in Oryx?

Drakon rode slightly ahead of them, surrounded by guards. She glared, wishing she still had her Gifts so she could watch him writhing on the ground. She imagined him falling from his horse to his death in a blazing inferno.

He hadn't said a word to her since the wedding. He had avoided looking at her even when they left the ship, Mica carrying her against his chest as she was too weak to walk steadily across the plank stretching to the dock. She needed him to talk so she could learn something, anything, about her mother. Her stomach clenched as she looked in the direction of the keep. She needed them to think she was accepting this.

They rode past the house the Wynters had leased, or... what had been the house. Amylia's insides went cold when she saw the blackened rubble of what had been a magnificent house. Behind it, she glimpsed the stables, roof hanging by a beam as most of it had fallen into the blackened remains. She wondered what had happened to the owners, hoping they had not been inside when it had gone up in flames, and sent a silent prayer to the Gods for their safety.

Staff rushed out as they filtered into the keep, after what had felt like a very slow ride back. The huge front gates — now fixed — swung back on silent hinges. Mica lifted Amylia into his arms again, silent as they walked through the entrance and Amylia turned her face away from him.

Little sign of her fire remained inside, aside from some slight blackening on some wood trims, high up near the roofline. The servants apparently had scrubbed the soot off the stone. New tapestries and drapes now hung along the path where she had fled.

It hadn't even been that long ago that she had been here, planning a wedding... and now... so much had changed. She glanced up at Mica to find him watching her, his expression tight as he was clearly thinking similar.

Mica strode straight to the west wing. The renovations were now completed and with dawning horror she noted the large bolts that a guard drew back at the main entrance to the wing. It locked... from the outside.

"I'm to be a prisoner then," she muttered to Mica as he swept through the door.

"You are to be kept here until you fulfill your end of this deal," he stated flatly. "Once I have a child... my child, I will release your mother, and she is welcome to come here, or go to that cesspit with your brother. Either way, I will have my heir. I don't think you would be the kind of mother to run away and leave your children behind, so I think we can come to an understanding of more freedom at that point."

Amylia blanched, a cold shiver going down her spine. He glanced down at her and sneered. "You won't support a pregnancy in this state; don't look so horrified. I'm not into Necrophilia." His eyes roved down her. "I don't know how you lost so much weight so fast."

The blue dress, so tight against her breasts at the start of the voyage, had fabric spare now, bunching in the front, and his forehead creased with worry as he looked at it.

Amylia huffed, the idea of not being able to support a pregnancy held a glimmer of hope to her. She could push this out, give herself time to find where her mother was.

"I guess sea travel and I can just agree to dislike each other," she muttered.

He carried her through a large door to a well-lit bedroom. A four-poster bed dominated one side of the room and a large fire crackled merrily on the far side. The whole wing had been decorated in silver and red… Lylican's colours.

Movement next to the fire drew her eye. A servant rose slowly from where she had been sweeping coal dust from the hearth.

Harriet. Amylia's heart lifted a fraction at the sight of her friend.

Mica's voice was cold as he addressed the maid. "Ah, Harriet, please ready some night clothes for your mistress. She has not been well on this trip, so she will need a good meal, and sleep."

Harriet tore her shocked gaze from Amylia's face and bobbed a stiff curtsy to him, rushing through the still open door.

"Don't get any ideas with her," he snapped, catching Amylia's gaze as it clung to the departing maid's back. "Unless you want to see her dead."

Amylia's eyes shot to him, anger rushing through her. "You have made it very clear I'm not to escape, Mica. My mother, my children, and my maid. I get it."

"Good," he said gravely. "It would have caused far less pain if you had learned that months ago."

Harriet came back into the room on silent feet as he deposited Amylia on the bed. He eyed the maid as she pulled a loose, white nightgown from the drawers against the wall and walked towards them hesitantly. Amylia stood, waiting for Mica to leave.

"Well?" he asked nonchalantly, leaning against a large chair. "Take it off."

"Take what off?" Amylia asked, unease starting to ripple through her.

"The dress, wife, take it off." His eyes never left her face. "I want to see how bad it is."

Amylia blanched, looking helplessly at her maid, who looked like she wanted to burst into tears. Harriet stared at the floor, the nightgown loose in her hands, and Amylia's face burned as she looked back at him.

"Mica…"

"Now," he barked. "Unless you want me to take it off for you."

'Just breathe, sweetling.'

Taking a breath, she reached for the laces with shaky fingers and untied them slowly until it hung loose on her shoulders. She glanced at him, hesitating, and he clicked his tongue irritably, reaching out to push the fabric down her arms. The loose gown slipped down her body to the floor, leaving her standing only in the sheer underdress.

"That, too." His face was unreadable. Harriet backed away slightly, as if trying to melt into the shadows behind the bed. "Don't... move... maid," he snapped, each word clipped as his eyes stayed focused on Amylia. Harriet froze, eyes flitting between Amylia and Mica, tears filling them.

"It's not like I haven't seen already, wife. Who do you think dressed you on the boat after our wedding?" He gritted, "I need to see how sick you are compared to then. Now take it off."

Amylia felt nauseous again as she pushed the sheer dress off, crossing her arms protectively over her breasts, her hand curling around the crystal that hung from her neck. It gave her strength, a solid reminder of them.

Mica surveyed her as if assessing cattle at a sale. She knew her hipbones showed clearly, the thin skin taut over them.. Her stomach, usually flat with strong muscle honed from years of riding, was concave and her ribs pushed against the surface, each one outlined clearly.

He walked behind her, running a hand across her lower back, chuckling as she froze. "You used to like it when I touched you," he mocked.

His eyes hardened as he came around in front of her, seeing what she grasped.

"What is that?" he asked coldly. He yanked her hand away from it, distain on his face, and with a quick, vicious tug he pulled it from her neck. The delicate chain broke with a small snap.

Amylia made a small sound and went to snatch it back, but he was too fast, throwing it harshly out the open window. He waved a hand at Harriet.

"Get her dressed. I want her to be eating four meals a day until she regains the weight." He paused. "And a bath, every day." His lip curled as he looked at Amylia. "She needs to wash those filthy Sylvyns off her completely before she shares my bed." He bowed mockingly. "Goodnight, wife. I'm sure you have a lot to talk about with your friend."

A lupine grin spread across his face as he looked at Harriet and a cold finger traced its way down Amylia's spine before he turned on his heel and strode out, leaving her standing naked, her arms still crossed in front of her.

Harriet lurched forward as the door shut, pulling the nightdress over Amylia's head, covering her. Then Amylia was pulled into a bone-crushing hug, and Harriet's little body shuddered as she sobbed.

Amylia hugged her back. The woman had lost weight, too, and she felt her bones easily in her slight shoulders. "I didn't know if I would ever see you again." Amylia clung to the maid. "Are you okay?" Harriet nodded against her, hair tickling her nose. Then she pulled back, looking into her eyes. "Are you certain?" Harriet nodded again, her face taut. "And Raol?" Harriet nodded once, a tear rolling down her face as she looked up at her.

Amylia took a deep, shuddering breath. "He has my mother. She's not dead... He has her locked away. It's why I came back... or he promised that he will kill her. I— I didn't know what else to do."

Harriet stared at her, face white, as she stroked Amylia's arms with her thumbs, shaking her head, her face full of sympathy.

Amylia looked at her, sensing something was wrong. "Harry, what is it?"

The maid shook her head, tears flowing freely now.

"Harry... what's wrong?" A cold twist of fear wrenched her gut as the maid pulled her hands away and looked at the floor.

Amylia grabbed her chin, making her look at her. "Harry!"

With a look of utter misery and defeat, the maid opened her mouth.

Amylia gasped. Hatred, grief, guilt, they all exploded in her at once, and she sobbed, sinking onto the bed behind her. "I'm sorry," she sobbed. "It's all my fault... I'm so, so sorry."

Harriet shook her head, crying with her as her throat bobbed as if trying to move a tongue that was no longer there.

Amylia didn't see Mica for the next week... or the week after.

No one except Harriet was permitted into the wing and as the days slipped past, Amylia's cold reserve slipped. She had begged to see Drakon, to talk to anyone, desperate for news on her mother. The days rolled into weeks, unmarked as she fell into exhaustion, sleeping for long periods and rising only to eat the food Harriet brought in.

The first few days she had barely picked at it until Harriet had returned with her untouched plate, tears tracking down her cheeks and blood running from her nose. Mica would punish Harriet if she didn't eat. He knew it would hurt her more.

Amylia finished the plates that arrived after that, as nauseous as it made her to look at the food, and took the baths Harriet poured without argument.

Her weight didn't improve, but she didn't lose any more either. The sense of utter exhaustion stayed, though, draining her entirely. She could feel the stone sucking at her, her body working overtime to compensate, trying to hold back enough to keep her going. Any spare energy from the food she consumed drained away and any longer than a few hours out of bed and she began to shake. Tremors up her arms and a weakness in her legs that collapsed her into the bed, pulled instantly into fitful sleep.

Amylia woke reluctantly from a dream of Asteryn, her mind fighting to stay in oblivion. She could still feel Gryffon's hand on her hip as he slept and see Cecily's blue eyes, bright, as she smiled at her from across the pillow. She reached a hand across to her, grasping only empty sheets, her stomach dropping as she opened her eyes, reality hitting. Her hand moved to her neck, the empty space where her necklace had hung, feeling her heart crack a little more.

Loss and disappointment washed over her as she blinked at the empty bed, willing herself to go back to sleep, just to be with them again. She sighed, stretched her legs as they cramped painfully with disuse, and froze. The hand on her hip was real.

"Good morning," Mica murmured, voice husky from sleep behind her.

Amylia lurched forward and was brought up short by an iron arm around her waist, pinning her easily to the mattress. "Enough Amylia, I've given you your space... we can't go on like this forever," he snapped. "You are my wife, whether you like it or not... this doesn't have to be this hard."

Amylia panted, brushing the hair out of her face with a shaking hand.

"You say that after all that has been done, as if I'll forget, as if I'm going to welcome you to my bed," she rasped, shocked at how ragged her voice sounded.

She turned to him, her skin crawling at how close he was. Very aware of the thinness of the nightgown she wore, she studied his face. She had loved this face. Now she searched it for any hint of the goodness that had been there.

"What happened to you?" she whispered, watching his pupils contract. He smelled faintly of brandy. It was on his clothes... there. Her eyes flitted to the small stain on his collar. His face had the slightest hint of stubble on his cheeks, auburn in the light of the morning, the deep purple bruising from Lyrik's blow still fading slowly, and his eyes — she met them as he looked at her — his eyes were cold.

"I watched the woman I love... the woman I was meant to marry ... burn part of my keep and then vanish, to the Gods knows where." He seethed. "After I was trying to protect you. For all I knew, Attica had found you, Amylia. And then when I finally find you to bring you home, I find out you have whored yourself to our new ally and done Gods knows what with his wife. It's disgusting, Amylia." His eyes flashed in anger as his face hardened. "You sullied yourself to the first male you came across like some desperate village girl. Of course I'm angry. You are mine, Amylia. You were mine from the day you came to this keep." He kissed her harshly, his beard scratching her face, and she pushed him away weakly.

"Mica, stop," she panted when he released her.

"Why? Because I'm not a Sylvyn?" he spat, running his hand roughly up her nightdress. "Is it him? Or his wife you miss the most?"

She cringed at his touch, and he noticed, his face contorted with rage.

"Am I not good enough for you now Amylia?" His face was inches from hers, and she tried to turn away from the thick fumes of his breath, her stomach threatening to heave.

"Well?" His arm released her, but then iron fingers clamped on her chin, forcing her to face him.

She grasped his hand, digging her fingernails into his skin and wrenched her chin from his grip, glaring at him. "You were no longer good enough the second you stood by and let another person abuse me."

Mica's eyes narrowed, his face darkening in anger and then those iron fingers were at her throat, panic overcoming her as she felt her air cut off abruptly.

She scratched at his hands, feeling the sting as her fingernails scratched at her neck, pressure building in her head as her ears started to ring. He leaned into her, his breath warm against her ear.

"Well don't worry then, my jewel. I won't make you watch."

He flipped her over onto her stomach, and she sucked great breaths of air down as his hand left her throat. Mica gripped her wrists hard, wrenching them easily above her head against the mattress as his other hand ripped the blankets off.

She struggled, bucking against him. The last of her energy sapped away as his hand pushed painfully in the small of her back, holding her still. Tears of anger and frustration pooled on the pillow below her.

"Mica, please," she hissed through clenched teeth. "Not like this."

He scoffed as his weight came down on her, his knees bruising her thighs as they pushed them apart. "It's not like you haven't done this before," he hissed into her ear as he took her roughly.

Just breathe, sweetling.

She couldn't breathe.

No... She could. She was holding her breath. She focused on those words, taking a quick gulp of air, and then another. Amylia forced herself into her memories, following them down into herself.

Breath-in-out-in-out.

She had no idea how much time had passed as a throbbing pain in her wrists and a deep ache in her belly brought her back, realising he had stilled, his weight heavy against her back.

She tasted blood, realising that she had bitten her lip from the sting as she ran her tongue over it.

Mica rolled off, collapsing next to her, and she turned, curling her body into a tight ball away from him, disbelief coursing through her. She hugged herself tightly as he patted her hip roughly, pulling her nightgown down.

They lay in silence. Amylia listened to the sound of her heart thumping, a scuffling at the door as someone tried to open it and found it locked... no doubt Harriet, she thought distantly.

The feeling of the bed moving as he rose had her freezing, her breath catching in her throat.

The bed shuddered as he pushed himself off it, and then his steps padded across the room as he poured himself a drink before coming back. Every step he took towards her filled her with more and more disgust. His robe gaped open as he walked, his lithe muscles bunching under tanned skin as he came into her line of sight. She felt repulsed, dirty, as he neared her and held a cup out to her. She just wanted him gone, so she could call Harriet to pour a bath and scrub him off her. She didn't know how she had kissed him willingly, how she had once looked at him with such adoration.

He banged the cup down on the side table after a moment, the water sloshing over the edge, and scowled at her.

"You need to forget the Wynters," his voice was low and cold. "I'm your husband and you're mine, Amylia. This doesn't need to be as hard as you're making it."

Amylia gazed at his face, watching the irritation build at her lack of response. The silence stretched and he shifted as if uncomfortable under her scrutiny and turned to leave.

"Mica."

He paused, his hand on the heavy bolt of the door.

"Yes?"

"I'm going to burn you to dust and dance on the ashes." Her voice sounded flat. Not a threat, just a statement. "And I will never forget them, no matter what you do to me."

Chapter 33

The coast off Oryx came into view at dusk, Lyrik leading the Sylkies into the mountains bordering the city below to stay out of view until the cover of darkness.

"I never realised how big it was." Rayvn leaned against Falkyn, taking in the beast's warmth, and watching the town light up slowly as darkness took over

"It's grown since I last saw it," Lyrik said, looking surprised. "It was just a small town when I was last here. It has doubled at least and I was here maybe thirty years ago." She looked at him. "Drakon never brought you here?"

"I asked many times to come," Rayvn said ironically, stones crunching under his boots as he shifted from foot to foot, trying to stay warm. "I know how to manage this town's finance, its trade, its people, but I never came back here after the attack."

Falkyn untucked a wing and Rayvn moved under it, resting a hand against the beast's neck in thanks. He looked across the clearing to see Silas in the dim light already firmly tucked under Asspyn's wing, his head resting against her chest as she purred softly.

"Where do we even start?" Silas groaned, his hand snaking out to scratch an itchy spot Asspyn had been nosing at with her beak.

"Taverns," Ingryd snorted, coming up next to them with her arm and cloak around Arya. "People talk when they drink." Her breath misted with the cold as she spoke.

"It's so cold up here. I wasn't prepared!" Arya laughed, tucking herself against Ingryd.

"It's the winds that come off the seas. These mountains would be perfect for Sylkies, actually," Lyrik said quietly, glancing across the small ranges that split Oryx from Lylican, her breath curling around her face.

"This was once a Sylvyn stronghold," a dark-haired woman with hazel eyes growled, coming up to stand beside Lyrik. A second, the image of the first, took up a position on Lyrik's other side. Rayvn hadn't met them before; these twins were from Diyanna's crew.

"It was," Lyrik answered, her eyes never leaving the town below. "The Sylvyns that were here before Rayvn's parents immigrated to Calibyre when the mortals started moving in around them from further south." She looked at the dark-haired woman. "Ataraxya, Solos, Credence, and Eilysh, too, south of here, were all Sylvyn-held until about a hundred and ten years ago. This land was known for its wealth of healers. Powerful ones too." She frowned as she looked out over the coast. "Attica came to claim them. If they did not agree to go, they slaughtered their people in front of them. Those who survived the attacks fled. Some went to Asteryn, but most to Calibyre, not bothering about the land left behind. We eventually heard of the Sylvers' arrival here, but with everything that was going on in Asteryn, I had not yet had a chance to come meet them." She sighed, her eyes flicking briefly to Rayvn and scanning his face.

The last of the sun fell below the horizon and Lyrik waved for them to mount back up.

"Stay close, stay silent." Then Freyja took off, and they aimed for the dark fields behind the city.

Rayvn hissed under his breath as they walked through the dark street, shocked at the state of disrepair on the outskirts of town. This area of the town was poor, the houses cramped and shoddily made.

"There's no need for this," he muttered, rage curling through him. "I never knew these people… my people were living here in squalor." He shook his head. "The books. There is so much money coming through here. Why is none of it going to the people?"

Mongrel dogs slinked in the shadows, looking for scraps, and the odd drunkard stumbled up the cobbled streets. Lyrik wrinkled her nose as a hulking man jeered at her as she walked past. When he made a grab for her, slurring unintelligibly, she neatly tripped him with a sharp clip to the ankle. Ingryd laughed softly and stepped over his prone form. They crept through the quiet streets, towards the keep looming in the distance. The state of the buildings around improved as they went until Lyrik stopped, holding her arm up to them.

"There's a tavern up ahead," she murmured. "Ingryd, you, Arya, Lydia, and Jocelyn take this one. Silas, Rayvn, and I will go further in." Pulling her hood up, she waved towards the inn. "Keep your hoods up, and your hair over your ears. I don't think many Sylvyns come here anymore. We will meet you back here in an hour."

The next tavern was bigger. People laughed and sang inside to the slightly out of tune guitar someone strummed. Lyrik untied her hair, quickly running her fingers through it so it fell in waves around her face and ears before pulling her hood back up. She glanced at the boys and grinned. Putting an arm through Silas's, she ignored his shocked look and tugged him inside the inn.

Lyrik bumped against him as he walked in the doorway, acting as if she were taken with drink as she plopped down heavily at the busy bar. She waved to the barkeep who sauntered over, his face disinterested.

"Barkeep, thank the Gods we have found a decent inn!" She laughed prettily, slurring slightly. "It's my little brother here's birthday today, and I thought we were goin' to have to slum it with the gutter rats in that other tavern." She thumped a fat purse down on the bar and Rayvn, staying a step behind her, as if a diligent guard, watched the barkeep's eyes light up at it. "Ale, for the room!" she slurred again. "And keep it coming!"

The tavern, packed with men in uniform, cheered at the announcement, raising mugs to her. Rayvn watched her, fascinated, as she picked up a jug, sloshing ale over its side, and mussed Silas's hair as she sauntered past him.

"Drink up, laddie!" She grinned at him and turned to eye up a group of men in guard uniforms who sat slightly apart from the rest. Their uniforms were cleaner than the rest, with gold badges pinned on them. She whistled softly, her hips swishing slightly as she walked towards them. "Well, isn't this a good-looking bunch," she purred.

One of them, a tall, well-built man, laughed. "Where are you hailing from, little lady? I ain't seen you round these parts before."

Lyrik sighed, sinking into the chair next to him. She threw her leg over his and leaned back into the cushions, pointedly ignoring Rayvn who leant against the wall next to them.

"Eilysh." She groaned. "We just moved there from a small island off its shores. Horrible place, smells like fish." The men roared with laughter. "Barkeep!" Lyrik yelled, amidst the laughter. "Why is there no ale for my friends here?"

The barkeep scurried over, thunking down two large jugs on the table.

"Doesn't explain what you are doing here, though," the man prompted, his hand resting on her knee. Lyrik gave him a feline smile and stroked the back of his hand with a finger.

"Father has sent my brother to go train with Lord Drakon's army." She sighed. "And I'm meant to marry some filthy fish-merchant back home. Unless I can find some work up these ways… Maybe find myself a better man up here instead," she said, her voice low and sultry. "So, I thought I would come with him and see what Oryx had to offer." She took a swig of her ale and grimaced. "Oh, that's a bit strong," she said, passing it to the man. "Here, would you finish it?"

He took it off her, eyeing her up and down. "What kind of work you lookin' for, then, huh?"

"Oh… as a maid," she said, letting a finger idly trace over the swell of her breast as she talked.

Rayvn almost felt sorry for the man, his eyes greedily following Lyrik's fingers.

"None of that kitchen stuff, though," Lyrik was saying, her eyes fixed on the man as she leaned towards him. "The… looking after the lady of the keep stuff." She sighed, inspecting a nail, and smiled charmingly at him. "I hate getting my hands all roughed up."

"You don't look like no maid," another said, eyeing her pants and loose, low-cut white top.

"I know right?" Lyrik scoffed. "I need to go to the seamstress tomorrow. My horrible mare threw me coming into town and then bolted. Took my bags with her, the silly wench. I had to borrow these off my brother's servant." She looked down, a distasteful look on her face. "I look like a man in these."

"Oh, you definitely do not look like a man," the tall man said huskily, his hand moving slightly higher up her leg and Lyrik grabbed it in her own.

"You're too sweet," she purred, taking his cup. Refilling it, she handed it back to him, carefully holding it to the side so he had to move the offending hand to take it. "So, who's at the keep here? I'll go see them tomorrow and ask if they're looking for a new maid," Lyrik said nonchalantly, as she subtly looked over her shoulder to Rayvn.

"That would be Lord Richard Desmond and his wife, Lady Margo," the man answered. His breath was thick with ale fumes, Rayvn could smell it from him even at a distance, and Lyrik looked as if her stomach threatened to heave. "You want to avoid working for them, though, little miss, no one 'ere likes 'em." He hiccupped, wiping his mouth on his sleeve.

"Oh?" Lyrik pulled her face into a mask of disappointment masterfully. "They can't be that bad. Do you know anyone who works there at the moment I can talk to?"

The man nodded. "All of us 'ere." He laughed "I'm head guard for them."

Lyrik gasped. "Oh, such an important job!" she breathed, leaning into him, and touching his chest lightly. She refilled his mug again, and watched him drain it quickly, before topping it up and moving closer to him on the seat.

Rayvn glanced at Silas, who was now talking to the sweet-faced barmaid who leaned against his table. His friend gave him a subtle cock of a brow and he moved towards them, catching the tail of their conversation as he slipped into the seat next to him, giving the maid a friendly wink.

"Your sister is going to get herself into a world of trouble with those men," the barmaid murmured to Silas as he sat, smiling at her. The girl flicked her eyes up to the men, watching as Lyrik leaned in to whisper something in the tall man's ear. "Jasper is his name. He is a brute. Two of our girls have left because of him."

Rayvn frowned. "Why is he left to treat people like that, then?"

The girl looked at him, surprised. "You been living under a rock, love?" She scoffed. "They are keep guards. Pretty much run this place. You don't say no to keep guards, especially Jasper. He's one of the head guards for them. Just got a promotion a couple of weeks back." She sighed. "It's made him worse than he was. He don't dare mess with me, though. My pa is the owner." She smiled slightly. "Can I be getting you boys anything else?"

Rayvn shook his head. "No, we're good, thank you. We'll be leaving shortly. You're right. We should be getting her away, before she spends all the coin we came with."

He surreptitiously watched the group, Lyrik leaning closer and closer to the man and blocking his attempts to slide his hand up her shirt.

Rayvn's amusement grew as he observed them, noticing her movements were getting more and more irritable as Jasper pawed at her.

Lyrik glanced at him before flicking her gaze across to the door. The message was clear. 'Leave.'

He bit a grin back as he watched the man's hand run up her thigh, her hand clamping over it, and he grabbed Silas, hauling him out of the seat and pushing him towards the door.

"Oh, Si, are you wanting to go already?" Lyrik shouted after them. "I'm just starting to make friends!"

"It's getting late, sister," Silas said sternly. "Father wouldn't be happy at us out so late. Let's go back to the rooms."

"Why don't you go, young man?" Jasper replied. "I'll bring your sister back later."

"I... I really should go with him." Lyrik sighed, pouting. "But he's such a spoilsport." She gave the man a small grin, leaning in to whisper something in his ear. Rayvn saw the man's eyes flit to the back door leading to the outhouse, a grin sliding across his features.

"I need to visit the ladies' room, I will be back shortly," Lyrik called, giggling prettily at Jasper as she stood up and brushed herself down. Jasper slapped her resoundingly on the rear.

Rayvn saw her hand twitch to the knife he knew was hidden at her hip before she turned to him, giggling, and stumbled off, out past the raucous groups of people, to the back door of the inn.

Rayvn hauled Silas out the front door.

"Oh, Gods, she's going to kill him," Rayvn groaned as they got outside, and slunk down the side of the building. The outhouse was a small building just behind the inn, stinking from the men who relieved themselves against it rather than bothering to go inside.

Rayvn saw the shadowy form of Lyrik pause outside the back of the inn and glance over her shoulder at Jasper who had followed her out.

Lyrik backed towards the wall of the tavern, laughing softly as he prowled towards her.

"Oh, you are a pretty little thing, aren't you?" He groaned, reaching for her, and Lyrik let him pull her against him, his hands roaming over her body.

She ran a hand down the length of his body, letting out a noise that sounded more like a groan of disgust than anything else. Jasper suddenly stilled, a small yelp of alarm coming from him.

"Yes, that is a knife," Lyrik said in a low, deadly voice.

"What is this?" Jasper hissed, trying to jerk back and then pulling up short.

"I would advise not moving, Jasper, if you like your testicles attached to... well... Whatever that is," Lyrik drawled. From the angle of her arm, and the way Jasper had gone completely motionless, Rayvn had a fair idea of what she had gripped.

Rayvn stepped out into the space, resting the tip of his dagger under the man's ear. "And if she misses, I won't," he said coolly.

Lyrik's eyes flicked to him over Jasper's shoulder. "Don't be ridiculous, I never miss!" she huffed. "Mind you," she shifted, and Jasper let out a grunt, stiffening even more, and Lyrik raised her brows at Rayvn, "it is a rather small target."

"What do you want? I have no money." Jasper sneered, "You're shit out of luck, thief."

Rayvn almost admired his guts, considering Lyrik had a knife to his nethers and balls in hand.

"The keep. You are head guard, yes? Or was that a lie?" Lyrik asked flatly.

"I am," Jasper retorted. "Why?"

"Is there anyone there under guard?" Lyrik replied, ignoring his question as she pushed the knife a bit closer to him.

Rayvn heard the small 'pop' as the tip of the knife pierced the leather.

"And I would think real carefully about lying to me. I'll know," Lyrik said menacingly.

"Wha...? No, there's only the lord and lady there," he replied, confusion crossing his face.

"No rooms you are meant to guard? No houses in town off limits? Nothing out of the ordinary?" Lyrik pressed.

"No, there's not even many of us guards here. Just the group in there!" he said, sweat rolling down his temple. "That Lord Drakon got the rest of the guards transferred over a couple weeks back. We're running on skeleton staff. We don't even have people to do all our normal shifts."

"What does Drakon need extra guards for?" she asked. "Where did they get sent?"

"I dunno, no one tells me anythin'!" Jasper protested. "I only got the promotion when the old fella left. Lord, woman, take your knife off me balls already."

"Have they gone somewhere in Oryx, or to Lylican?" Lyrik hissed.

Rayvn dug the tip of his own blade in, and Jasper flinched. "It ain't here in Oryx, I can tell you that. They all got pulled out quickly. Made to march over there. Whispers are there's some trouble with the Wytchlings up the coast, and he's pissed them off. I don't want nuffin' to do with that!" he protested. "Not pissin' those Gifted folk off. I heard one of them burned half his keep down. And they expect us to go there? No, thanks!"

Lyrik grinned at him in the darkness. "Smartest thing you have said since I met you." She went to move, but Rayvn stopped her with a brief look.

"The women in this town have a low opinion of you," he growled, digging the tip of his blade a bit deeper into Jasper's neck. "I'll be coming back to check, and if I find you have put your hands on another woman, you will find yourself without hands to use anymore. Do I make myself clear, Jasper?"

Jasper scoffed. "What are you going to do, boy, tell your mother on me?"

Lyrik moved fast, kneeing him in the groin, and he doubled over, the breath exploding from him. A second later her elbow came down sharply on the back of his head, and he collapsed, motionless, to the ground.

"No, I'll tell Lyrik," Rayvn snorted, eyeing him disdainfully.

"Ugh!" Lyrik grimaced, flexing her shoulders, and shaking her arms, as if dislodging ants from her skin. "He smelled so bad."

They met back up with Ingryd's group coming out of the first tavern.

"Nothing," Ingryd said, wrinkling her nose as she wiped a trickle of blood from a split in her lip. "What?" she asked defensively as Lyrik gave her an exasperated look. "He deserved it!"

"Guy was roughing up a barmaid." Jocelyn laughed quietly. "Then was stupid enough to backchat Ingryd when she told him to back off."

"What is it with the men in this town?" Lyrik muttered, striding down the dark street. "I think we can rule out Lady Addelyn being here, though."

They filled in the others on what Jasper had told them as they moved out of town, whistling low to the waiting Sylkies.

"So, it's most likely Lady Addelyn is in Lylican, then? If Drakon has called extra guards in?" Ingryd mused.

"It could be, but it could also be guards on Amylia." Lyrik sighed, leaping onto Freyja. "He wouldn't pull guards from a town where he was keeping Addelyn, though. We need to get people in to Lylican."

Chapter 34

It wasn't Harriet that arrived with breakfast. It was Lylith.

Amylia met her shocked gaze distantly as she sat on the bed, pulling her robe around her. She didn't care that Lylith saw her nakedness, didn't care that horrified green eyes took in her frail body, and the deep purple bruise across the side of her face. Mica's temper had finally snapped at her threat, and she had taken the strike, using it to fuel the fire of hatred that distracted her from the grief of... them.

"Lylith, if you have come to gloat, can it be another day?" Amylia said flatly as she rose and headed to the window to open it, annoyed at the tremor in her arms.

Lylith placed the plate of food she was holding on the counter. "I... I came because I wanted to see you myself..." She trailed off. Amylia braced herself against the stone window, letting the breeze wash across her face, cooling the pulsing heat of the bruise.

"Why?"

Lylith shifted her weight, her beautiful face unsure as she looked around the room. Her usually sharp tone softened as she asked, "Why did you come back?"

Amylia huffed, turning to meet her eyes. "They didn't tell you?"

"Why do you let them keep you in here?" Lylith asked. "I watched you burn half this keep down as you ran out of here, and now you let them keep you locked in this room... what happened in the Sylvyn lands?"

Amylia walked back to the bed slowly, wincing as she sat down, and looked up at her. Ignoring the questions, she asked, "Did you know about my mother, too?"

Confusion flared in Lylith's eyes. "What do you mean?"

"Did you know Drakon had my mother all this time, too?" Amylia's voice was hard as she stared, noting the look of shock that flashed across Lylith's face.

"What are you talking about?"

"My mother is alive, Lylith, and the reason I'm back here — the *only* reason I'm back here — is because otherwise Drakon will kill her, and I will not let that happen. My Gifts? Drakon bound them. They are gone." She glared at Lylith.

Lylith blanched, appearing at an utter loss for words.

"Why are you here?" Amylia angrily swiped at her face as hot tears pricked behind her eyelids. She refused to let them fall.

Lylith took a step forward, hesitating and glancing back towards the door.

"Amylia, I'm not meant to be here. I just needed to see for myself. After everything that happened after you left."

"And what is that?" Amylia snapped.

Lylith looked at her, sympathy in her eyes that unnerved Amylia. She wrung her hands, looking back at the door again. "Amylia, I was there when he… when he did what he did to your maid, to Harry… Harriet. It's not right. It was horrific." Lylith's eyes glazed over as she spoke. "Her husband tried to come to her, and Drakon said he would have her killed if he entered the property. He has been sent out to the barracks… and nobody dared to help her. And I just couldn't stand it. Her screams…" Lylith shuddered. "I couldn't take her screams."

Amylia stared at Lylith as a wave of guilt rushed over her. A lump formed in her throat and she looked down, to where her fingernails pressed into her palms.

"I took her to the cook, and she looked after her," Lylith went on. "He is scaring me. What he has done…" She fidgeted, edging towards the door. "I can't stay. If they find me here… But I'll come back. If you want me to?"

Amylia stared at her mutely, confused, but finally nodded.

Lylith's face relaxed a bit, and she nodded, turning to go, then paused, her hand in her pocket. She turned back, her face unsure, and held out her fist.

"I think this may be yours." Nestled in her palm, Amylia's crystal glinted in the soft light, the chain with its broken clasp curled around it.

Amylia took a breath that caught harshly in her throat, her eyes locked on it. "Where did you find that?"

"I feed the crows here. They bring me gifts," Lylith said, taking a hesitant step towards Amylia. "Harriet saw it on my dresser and wouldn't let it go. It took a while to understand. I don't know the hand signs she's using yet, but I guessed… with how stubborn she was being about it. It's… precious to you?"

Amylia nodded, her fingers curling around it as Lylith dropped it into her palm, and she held it to her chest.

"Thank you."

Lylith didn't say anything further, though Amylia felt her watch her a moment longer until the swish of the woman's skirts told her she had turned to leave.

"Wait!"

Lylith looked back over her shoulder.

"Can you send Harry up if you see her?" Amylia's voice broke. "Can you find her for me? I need her." Lylith nodded, her face tight, slipping from the room on silent feet.

Harriet came into the room soon after and ran to Amylia, pulling her into her arms and rocking her as she let herself shatter, sobbing quietly into her friend's shoulder while Harriet made small crooning noises, patting her gently.

"I need to wash," Amylia hiccupped when she was spent, wiping her face with the sheets.

Harriet nodded, ducking back out of the room briefly to relay the orders. How she did it, Amylia couldn't figure out, but she was back soon enough. Other servants eased soundlessly into the room not long after, carrying great steaming buckets of water to fill the tub.

Amylia soaked until the water went cold, scrubbing her skin until it was pink and raw, yet still, she felt dirty. She let Harriet pull her out once she started shivering, the maid hissing a breath in anger as she saw the bruises on her mistress. "Harry, what Mica did… Lylith told me about it. How they have kept Raol away. I'm so sorry."

The maid shook her head sadly and Amylia caught her hand, pulling her round in front of her. Her arms already shook with fatigue. She had been out of bed too long. "I will get you out of here. I don't know how. But I will."

Harriet's face softened, and she gave her a quick hug, shaking her head.

"I need to go back to bed." Amylia sighed. "It's this stone. It's taking too much. It's so much bigger than the last one."

Harriet helped her back into the bed. The process was slow as she waited for Amylia to crawl into the sheets. She tucked Amylia in gently then turned to clean up.

Amylia caught her arm. "I need you to do something for me." Harriet looked at her, eyebrow raised in question. "I need you to ask the servants, somehow, anyone you trust — there is paper in my top drawer, I could write for you? — if they know where my mother could be. If she's still in Oryx, or if she's somewhere else." Her voice was low and urgent. "One of them might know something." Harriet nodded and patted her hand. Amylia sighed, falling back onto the mattress, her hand slipping under the pillow to grasp the necklace hidden there. "Thank you," she murmured before the tug of oblivion pulled her back down again

Mica came back that night, and the next and then it slipped into a nightmarish routine.

She knew her attitude towards him just provoked him, but she couldn't bring herself to even pretend to warm to his touch, sinking into a deeper hole of depression with every night that passed. She hated him. With every ounce of her being, she hated him. Her skin crawled every time he ran his hand over her.

She had given up fighting him. The bone deep exhaustion from the stone dragged at her resistance more effectively than shackles but she let her hatred burn in her eyes every time she looked at him.

Requests to see her mother were flatly refused, stoking the glimmer of doubt that was curling unwelcomed in her stomach.

She replayed that letter over and over in her head, praying to the Gods it was real and she had not been lured into a trap.

Nausea plagued her constantly during her waking hours, and only the image of Harriet, shaking and bleeding as she returned with the full plate gave her the strength to push past it, eating enough to satisfy Mica.

Lylith started visiting daily, reporting that Mica had requested her to make sure she was in fact eating the food, as her weight had not improved.

Instead, they talked. Mostly, Lylith just sat, lending her presence to Amylia, comfortingly calm as she read in silence. Occasionally, Lylith read passages from the books to Amylia when the silence stretched too long. Grateful for her, Amylia felt the old tension between them fade slightly. Not quite friendship, but both appreciative of the mutual company.

The ache of those she had left behind in Asteryn burned in her heart and tore at her soul. She missed Shadow, too, the friend she had leaned on when life was too hard. She missed all of them, the new family she had carved for herself and Rayvn.

Sitting listlessly on the bed, Amylia listened to Lylith read aloud from the poems she had brought in, watching a bird that was building a nest in the tree outside her window when Harriet's still figure caught her attention.

The maid had been clearing out her armoire, making room for new clothes since the current ones hung on her. She noticed her pale face and rose, wincing at the fresh bruises that mottled up her legs as she did.

"What is it?" she asked, concerned.

Lylith stopped, looking up from her book to follow Amylia's gaze but Harriet didn't look up as she stared at something in the drawer.

Voice sharp, Lylith asked, "What is wrong, Harry?" She rose from her seat and walked over. Harriet picked something up and looked at Amylia, her eyes haunted.

"It's your cloths for your courses?" Lylith asked, confusion on her face as she looked at Amylia. "What's wrong with those?"

Amylia went cold as she stared back at the maid, horror creeping into her as she also realised what the maid had.

"Lylith, how long have I been here?" she whispered, dragging her eyes to the woman's face.

"A month, I think?" Lylith paused, thinking. "No, it must be over five weeks now. I didn't see you for the first two weeks, and it's been a bit over three since then. Why?"

Amylia closed her eyes, fighting down the panic. "My courses should have been here over two weeks ago at least."

"Oh." The book she held dropped to her side as her face went blank. She sat next to Amylia on the bed. "You have lost a lot of weight. My maid lost a lot of weight and hers stopped too for a bit. It could be that?" she offered, taking Amylia's hand gently and Amylia clutched the hand in hers.

"Don't tell him," she said urgently. "Not yet… please."

Lylith blanched, shaking her head gently. "It might make him act kinder to you… leave you be for a while if…"

"No," Amylia bit out, her heart faltering and skipping a beat. "Not yet, please, just… not yet."

Lylith nodded, squeezing Amylia's hand.

Amylia huffed, wiping a hand across her face. "I just need to hang on until… I just need to find out where she is…" Her breath caught. "If I can find where she is… I can get word to them… and then they can come for her. Rayvn will come for her." Tears streaked down her face as she looked at Lylith. "I miss them so much. I feel like my heart has been ripped apart. And now…" She looked at her stomach. "If I am, how could I ever face them now?"

Lylith gingerly reached out a hand and rested it on Amylia's shoulder, shock registering as Amylia felt her hand brush across the bones, too close to the surface there.

"What can I do?" she whispered. "Tell me."

Amylia sighed, letting the tears fall onto her clasped hands. "Find where my mother is?" She laughed wetly. "I'd give anything to be able to talk to her right now."

Lylith arrived at the west wing door just as Mica walked through it. Jumping slightly, she stared up at him.

"How is my wife?" he asked her, looking at the book she held in her hand.

Lylith sighed, sneering slightly. "I don't know why you want me to go sit with her. All she does is cry and whine. Why not pick a woman who actually wants to be the Lady of Lylican... surely it would be more enjoyable."

"That is none of your concern," he grated out. "Did she eat?"

"Yes," Lylith replied, looking out the window as if entirely bored with the conversation. "And if you have finished with me playing nurse maid, I have better things to do," she snapped. Pushing past him, she added, "She's asleep, like she always is these days. You're wasting your time if you were headed that way."

Mica sighed impatiently, turning around, and following her out as she pushed the heavy door open. "Are you sure?" he asked flatly. "She hasn't put on any weight at all. That fucking mute must be hiding the food."

"The maid's giving her all the food," Lylith said. Almost too quickly, she realized, when Mica glanced at her. "I was meaning... it's probably an illness, probably from those Sylvyns. She will probably give it to you if you keep sleeping in her bed."

She made a point of eyeing him with a slightly disgusted look. "Maybe you should give her time to get over whatever this illness is."

It was dark when Lylith slipped out of her rooms and stepped into the eerily quiet hallway. She usually liked the solitude the upper levels had given her all these years, as watching Amylia and Mica grow steadily closer had grated at her.

It wasn't so much Mica. Yes, she had liked him, and he was certainly handsome. But it was the affection she had grown icily jealous of. Amylia had it all. The girl had grown into a stunning beauty. Mica fawned over her. Their subtle touches and looks. Amylia had a maid who had been as close as a sister to her, the two inseparable as they got older, always laughing with their heads together. And she had Rayvn, a brother, who looked at his sister as if she were a queen. Even Drakon had shown more interest in Amylia, letting her sit up at the head of the table with him and Mica at dinners. He left Lylith to languish among the lower nobles.

Lylith ached for someone to hold her like Mica had held Amylia and danced with her at the parties. Drakon did not invite boys her age to his dinners, and no one in the vicinity would dare go near any of Drakon's wards. So, it had just been her; the only warmth she had gotten was from the keeps animals who seemed to seek her out, as if knowing her loneliness, and it had hurt.

Then Amylia had run past her that day, blood flowing down her leg. Lylith had sat in a patch of sun in the courtyard feeding the crows, unseen but stricken by the sight of Amylia burning. Flames swirled around her arms and flickered down her body. Every step she had taken left a charred patch of earth under her feet. The look on her face had chilled Lylith. Utter terror.

That terror is what had made Lylith walk to her, as if her feet had moved of their own volition, and give her the cloak, hiding her from the world, the little protection she could give.

The tall Sylvyn lord had ridden through the gates, leading that wild beast of Amylia's. Relief flooded Amylia's face and she had run to him… had run away from Mica.

Lylith had pulled herself back, into the recesses of the shadows against the castle wall when Drakon exploded from the doors not long after. He snarled for servants to fill buckets of water to put out the rapidly spreading fires inside. The smoke of them wafted up through the open window above her head. She had still been there later when he had snapped at Mica, "Place extra guards on her. With one we have the other anyway." With Amylia's revelation about her mother, the words only now made sense.

In the aftermath, too, Lylith had witness Mica dragging Harriet by her hair across the keep grounds after she had delivered a message from Amylia, had seen him pull his knife out, kneel on the woman's neck, and cut her tongue from her. She had slipped poison into the drink of the two other guards that had been on duty that day, unsure if they had seen anything and worried it would sign the already suffering maid's death warrant.

The memory of the sounds still woke her up at night. Harriet's screams, and the muted gargling of the two guards, clutching their throats as other guards ran for help, help that was too late.

Lylith crept down the hall, the familiar passage cold against her bare feet. Passing the steps that led to the main living areas, she carried on to the end of the passage. She paused at the top of the spiral staircase that would take her down to the lower levels, Drakon's personal levels, and strained her ears for any movement.

The rooms were dark. Lylith glanced at the end of the hall towards Drakon's bedchamber and saw it was closed. No light came from under the crack of the door, and so she stepped into the drawing room.

She knew where the financial ledgers were kept; everything that ran through the keep was in those books. Slipping the most recent massive tome off the shelf, she took it to the window where the full moon lit the pages easily enough to read.

Hours passed as Lylith pored over the pages. Drakon's spidery writings began merging into one another as she squinted at the columns of neat numbers. She saw nothing — guards' salaries, consumables — nothing that pointed to a separate cost for another house or separate guards to those of the keep.

Sighing, she stretched her aching back, then lugged the book back over to the shelf. She looked along the rows of books, finding the one from the year Amylia and Rayvn had arrived at the keep. Groaning as she flexed her neck, she took it down and walked back to the window.

The book was old and not bound well. The pages were loose in the cover. Carefully, she turned the pages, tugging slightly too hard on one as she turned it over. When it came away in her hand, she grimaced and smoothed the old paper to slip it back in. The words on the paper jumped out at her. This was not in rows. This was a letter.

She frowned at the faint writing and held it closer to the window, squinting at the elegant script on the paper.

"What are you doing, Lylith?"

She jumped, her heart leaping, and the book crashing to the floor, and spun, the paper crumpling in her hand.

"Lord Drakon," she gasped. "I... I'm..."

"You were snooping, is what you were doing," he said coldly. "What have you got there?"

She held the paper up, her chin going up slightly. "Why was my mother writing you from Oryx?"

"Ah," he said. He sighed and came into the room, his dark red robe swishing on the floor. Walking to his desk, he pulled his chair out and sat carefully on it before looking at her. "Kestrel was a friend of mine, you know that, Lylith. It is why you came here."

"But why was she informing you of my health?" she asked, a cold feeling growing in the pit of her stomach. "Why was she asking when she could return to you?"

Drakon's lips tightened as he looked at her.

"Because," he said quietly, "I had asked her to keep me informed of your health."

Her usually sharp tone softened as she asked, "Why?" She dropped her eyes to the paper again, scanning the words, her mother's writing so similar to her own.

"Why were you down here, Lylith?" Drakon asked again. "What are you looking for?"

Lylith looked up at him. "It's not right what Mica is doing to Amylia. You must know what he is doing, she is… She is ill, and she's getting worse." She crumpled the paper in her hand and dropped it on the floor. "You have her mother somewhere, don't you? I heard what you said that day in the yard, after Amylia left."

"Ah. You were always a clever girl, Lylith." Drakon smiled, watching her closely. "I'm glad you didn't take after your mother in that regard. You can thank me for those wits, girl."

Lylith stared at him, her mind racing to compute the reality of what he had just said.

"What?" Her voice was weak, and suddenly her legs felt as if she had just run a flight of stairs. "What did you say?" She took a step back, bumping into the window seat, and sat heavily, frowning at him in confusion.

"Come now, I think you know what I'm saying." Drakon chuckled. "As I said, you are a clever girl, daughter."

Lylith felt like the air had been sucked from her lungs, going hot and then cold again. "How?" she gasped.

"You know how, if you think about it. Your mother was a friend of mine. A vapid little creature, but loyal. In fact, I couldn't've done half what I have accomplished without her." His tone was cool as he eyed her.

"Where did I come from when I came here?" she whispered.

"From Oryx, my dear. I couldn't very well bring you here the same time as Amylia and Rayvn, could I?" He chuckled. "And your mother, she didn't know when to just shut up. Shame, really. She was pretty, but I couldn't have her telling people what had gone on in that keep."

"You had her killed?" A lump formed in her throat as she looked at him, horror creeping through her.

"I did." He sighed. "But you were my daughter. I always looked after you, from the moment of your birth. Even if I did not recognise you as my own. I… named you Lylith, after our home. I know your brother will inherit these lands, but it was a small way I could tie you to us, give you something of Lylican," he said. "It's something I do regret, not having you as my acknowledged daughter. I tried to do right by you by at least giving you the status of being my ward after the loss of your mother."

"Do right by me?" she choked. "You killed my mother."

"Trust me, girl, it was no major loss to you. Kestrel was not the best mother. I really don't know how she managed to get herself the nurse position with the Sylvers. But she did, and without her being there, so close to them, I'd never have got the Helix in that nullified their powers." He laughed softly. "Your mother paved the way for us to take over Oryx. It has made us rich, and in turn, you're rich. And with Amylia married to Mica, our line will hold these lands for centuries."

"Mica," Lylith choked. "Mica is my brother?"

"Yes." Drakon sighed. "And that is precisely why you two could not marry. Don't think I didn't see you mooning over him when you were younger."

She felt sick. Mica was her brother. This man, the man who had killed her mother, let Mica treat Amylia as he did, this man was her father.

"I trust you are going to keep this to yourself," he said, eyeing her. "We can tell Mica if you wish, but I will not have this going further. There is too much at stake currently."

Lylith glared at him. "What have you done with Lady Sylvers?" she asked coldly.

"She's safe, has been for years," he said blandly. "I did have her in a safehouse under guard, but with the Sylvyns sniffing around, I moved her."

Lylith swallowed the bile rising up her throat. "And Lord Sylvers?"

"Dead. I killed him myself after Kestrel reported the Helix in his system that she had been slipping into their food had finally nullified his powers. Strong bastard, that one. I almost admire him. Took a lot of Helix to kill his Gifts, and he still nearly had me when I made the mistake of trying to get Addelyn first. I thought she was the strong one." Lylith sat in silence, watching him. "So, as I said, I trust you are going to remain silent on this?" he repeated. "I'm sure Amylia would be upset to learn she has been raised alongside the daughter of the woman who is responsible for her father's death."

"It's… it's a lot to take in," she murmured.

"It is. And it's very late." Drakon groaned as he stood up. "And I'm getting old. Go back to your rooms, Lylith. We will talk again in the morning." He waited for her to walk past him, following her out. Her skin crawled, feeling his gaze on her back. He stopped her with a hand on her arm when they reached the door.

"You have benefited from this as much as Mica has. Remember that, Lylith. You would do well to keep silent on this. Use those brains I gave you and don't be like your mother," he said, his voice stone cold as he glared at her.

She fled.

Chapter 35

"Addelyn is not in Oryx," Lyrik stated firmly, back at the table in Asteryn. "Drakon would not pull guards away from his only leverage in keeping Amylia."

Gryffon nodded, trying to keep his composure. "No, I agree." He sighed, looking out towards the Dead Forest. "If nothing else, he is intelligent. It would be the last thing he would do."

"There were no reports of any guards getting moved to other territories?" Rogue asked.

"No." Ingryd sat next to Lyrik and took a deep swill of her ale, and Gryffon noticed her knuckles were raw. He raised a questioning brow at Lyrik who ignored it, the tiniest of smiles pulling at the corner of her lips.

"We got a fair bit out of them," Ingryd carried on. "Everyone had been called to the same place. Lylican. They were all moaning about being short-staffed everywhere in Oryx. All having to pull double shifts, so the number of men called over must be considerable, even if Drakon was pulling in men in case we come for Amylia, he wouldn't have left anywhere holding his greatest leverage short."

Cecily let out a shaky breath and squeezed Gryffon's knee. "She must be there. He wouldn't hold her in the keep, would he?"

"I doubt it." Edryk shook his head. "It would be too risky. Amylia would have some support in there. If Addelyn was in the keep, it would be too easy for servants to release her."

Rogue nodded. "She will be close, where he can have quick reports on her, but not in the keep. Maybe a safe house nearby?"

"We need to get in there," Gryffon said, looking at Silas. "Are you comfortable doing this? You know the risks. I can't guarantee I could get to you in time if anything happened, but I can swear I would do my best."

Silas nodded without hesitation. "Of course. In two weeks from now is the summer festival in Lylican. It's the biggest event they have all year. And Oryx, Perregrin, even lower territories like Ataraxya and Credence travel in. It would be the best time to slip in unnoticed."

Edryk nodded, humming in approval. "That many new faces would make it harder to pick two people out from the crowd. Though, I want Silas to stay out of the camps. They will know he stayed in Asteryn."

Gryffon raised a hand to silence the argument Silas was about to unleash. "He's right, Silas, we can't risk them seeing you. For not just your safety, but Amylia's and Addelyn's, too." Silas shut his mouth with a snap and nodded solemnly.

"Gryff, that's two weeks before we can begin to get information," Cecily said softly. "If we don't start the army moving until then, it's at least a month until we are even close to getting her back."

Lyrik cringed. "Can we not move into position before then? Hunker down in the Dead Forest?"

Gryffon hated every word as he said, "I don't know if I can ask the men to do that, Lyrik. With a timeline in place, yes, but I can't ask them to stay weeks or even months in there with the Sabyre population what it is now. We got lucky with the low number we spotted on the last pass, and you know how fine that line was. A larger number of people will draw larger numbers in." He flinched inwardly, fighting the urge to give the word that would send the whole of Asteryn after Amylia. But she would never forgive him if he did. He sighed. "If I could, I'd send the entire damn territory there immediately."

"I will get Silas and Edryk set up closer to Lylican, in the mountains, so we can move as soon as the people start arriving," Lyrik said, her voice flat. "I made her a promise I'd come as soon as it was safe. I won't wait a moment longer."

Cecily raised her eyes, clouded with grief, and gratitude flashed across her face as she looked at her friend.

"I promised her they wouldn't hurt her again, too," Gryffon said. Agony ripped at his heart. Not even Cecily's hand on his leg eased it. "And then I had to watch them take her."

After giving the Sylkies time to recover and feed, Silas, Edryk, Ingryd, and Lyrik flew back out the next day at dusk, using the approaching darkness to avoid being sighted as they arrived at the southern tip of the Elixus ranges. Two more riderless Sylkies trailed them, laden with supplies for a stay high in the mountains.

"This is killing me." Cecily sighed as she watched them depart from the meeting room. "I just want to be out there doing something to help."

"I know, sweetheart." Gryffon crossed the room and stood behind her, watching the Sylkies until they drifted from sight. "We are too noticeable. Lylican knows what you and I look like. Even Lyrik isn't going near the township. Only Ingryd and Edryk can go there without risk of being discovered. And even then, anyone who looked close enough would see they are Sylvyn." He cupped her cheek, noticing the dark circles under her eyes. "Have you slept at all, my love?"

Cecily shook her head. "How can I?" She leaned against him, and he wrapped his arms around her. She slipped her hands under his shirt, against the warm skin there. His skin pebbled in gooseflesh beneath her cold hands as she rested her cheek against the fabric of his shirt, her ear directly over his heart. He waited while she listened to it, feeling some of the tension leave her shoulders as her breathing slowed to the beat of it before she tilted her face up to him. "Can we go to the waterfall?"

"Now?" he asked, surprised. "It will be dark within the hour."

"I just want to feel anything other than hopeless for a minute." She sighed, and his heart cracked further at the pain etched so deep in her face.

"I will go get the horses saddled. You get something warmer for later," he murmured, before kissing her again.

Gryffon let Cecily race ahead, sensing her need to let herself loose. Shadow flew through the dusk countryside like a wraith with the white wolf on her heels. The trade mare he had taken to ride, almost as powerful as Shadow, kept a steady pace behind.

He caught up as they got to the clearing and hobbled his mare, leaving Shadow to roam. Turning, he followed Cecily's shadowy form into the dark clearing, the sound of crashing water beckoning him.

The glow from a full moon illuminated the clearing and sparkled off the water, off Cecily who had stripped and stood alongside the water. She stared over the still, dark waters, running a hand over her skin.

He slipped out of his clothes and joined her, taking a moment to watch her in the moonlight, the picture so beautiful and serene compared to the chaos he knew roiled inside her. He ran a hand up her flank and felt her jump slightly as she was pulled from her thoughts, and he gripped her hips, kissing the curve of her shoulder.

She slid from his grasp and dived, slipping into the water seamlessly and he sighed, shaking his head. Anxiety nipped at him. It wasn't often he felt powerless to help her. He dove in after she broke the surface in the middle of the pool, the water cool, but still maintaining a slight warmth from the day as it rippled over his skin. The bubbles from the waterfall felt like hands caressing him as he got closer to it, and he shivered, catching Cecily around the waist as she tread water in front of him.

"Talk to me, Cecily," he urged, turning her to him. He could just reach the bottom here, but she floated, wrapping her legs around his waist to keep herself in one spot.

"I'm going to kill him," she choked out, finally looking at him. "I'm going to make those men bleed, both of them. They took her because they want an heir, Gryff. You know what that means."

His stomach clenched as the thoughts he had tried to keep away hit him, and he nodded, a short stiff movement. "I'm trying not to because I will lose my head if I think about it too closely, and that's not going to get her back to us."

A strangled groan came out of her, and she rested her forehead against his shoulder. The water lapped against them softly as he pushed her damp hair back over her shoulders, rubbing her back gently. Carrying her through the pool, the only sounds were their breathing and the crashing water.

"Kiss me," she said softly, leaning back slightly to look up at him. He did, grateful to let the heaviness on his heart rest for a moment. Letting the feel of her take over, he kissed her as if she were glass under his touch.

She bit his lip, her nails digging into his arms where she clung to him, and he growled, running his hands down her slender back. Cupping her rear, he waded to the far end of the pool, towards the waterfall, and then through it to the far side.

The water lapped around his thighs here, the rock behind the waterfall cool and mossy. He pressed her against it and the moonlight illuminated her face through the water, haunted. He kissed her roughly, trying to chase away that look, trying to steal the pain from her and take the burden for them both.

Her hands plunged into his hair, the tips of her toes catching in the running wall of water behind them and making is splash against his back.

He moved to her neck, his body already hard and aching for her, and grunted as her nails raked his shoulders. Shifting, he lifted her slightly, encircling each thigh with a large hand as he held her against the wall.

She shivered in his grip, and her nipples, hardened against the cold water, brushed across his chest.

"A bit cold, sweetheart?" he murmured, moving to kiss her again, softer this time, but she didn't want soft, not this time.

"Gryff," she moaned against his mouth, a question and plea, and he knew what she wanted. Distraction, even if just for a moment. She bit his lip hard, and he groaned, adjusting her in front of him before taking her roughly, his kiss muffling her cries.

"Harder," she breathed when he let her mouth go and he hissed, his fingers digging into the soft skin of her thighs. Her breath hitched each time he thrust into her, and her legs wrapped around him, pulling him deeper.

"I don't want to hurt you," he gritted, bracing an arm on the rock behind her. Then swore as she turned and bit his forearm, her teeth drawing blood before her Gift whispered out, healing the small hurt instantly. He grasped her shoulder with the other arm and slammed into her in punishing strokes as her cries disappearing into the rushing water behind them. She tensed moments before he did, her back bowing against the rock as they both shattered into each other. They paused there, her forehead resting on his shoulder, panting as his thumbs stroked her shoulders gently. His hands slipped down, back to her thighs, feeling them shake slightly as he braced her. He gathered her to him, rocking back into the stream of water, letting it flow over them in the long, cooling current, and he held her securely as she leaned against his chest, boneless in his arms. She winced slightly when he stepped back into deeper water and slid free of her body.

"I didn't mean to be that rough," he said, running a hand under her knees and cradling her to him. She laughed quietly into his collarbone, and he felt it vibrate up through her body. He hadn't realised how desperate he had been to hear that sound, to know he had eased something in her, even if just in this moment.

"I didn't give you much choice." She peered up. "I'm sorry for snapping at you. I just feel so helpless."

"I know," he said, kissing her forehead. "I feel like biting someone's head off at the moment, too, but I'd rather you snapped at me than anyone else."

They rode back to the castle together on Shadow, the mare for once only briefly flattening her ears to Gryffon as he swung into the saddle. After lifting Cecily in front of him and clucking for the other mare to follow, he pulled the edges of his cloak around her. Her hair was damp against his chest, and he wrapped an arm around her, curling tendrils of his Gifts across his arm to warm her.

Gryffon felt her slowly drift away, her body going limp against him. Adjusting his arm across her breast, he braced her head against his shoulder as Shadow delicately picked her way through the clear, starry night, thanking the Gods for the brief moment of peace sleep had granted her.

Lyrik and Silas finished setting up the camp high on the far edge of the Elixus ranges where it curled around behind Lylican. The keep was just visible in the far distance, its lights peeking through the craggy terrain, and Lyrik couldn't help herself from glancing over at it repeatedly as they worked in silence.

"We will do nightly passes over the keep, to get the lay of the land, and check for any strange movement," she said, peering out into the twilight. "Best to go just after dark, when they can't see us, but there are enough fires and movement to see what is going on down there. It will be too hard to tell once they turn in."

"One of us will need to stay here, just in case someone needs to go to Asteryn," Ingryd said, pulling a warm cloak around her shoulders and dipping into a sack for dried fish for the Sylkies.

"I will go with them tonight," Lyrik agreed, taking a fish from Ingryd, and handing it to Freyja. "But Freyja and I will stay to the outskirts. There's no point taking both in. Asspyn has more chance of getting closer undetected by herself with Silas and Edryk."

They ate a simple dinner of thick bread and cheese and washed it down with crisp apple cider in silence, the heat of the five Sylkies stretching out around them taking the bite from the night air as they watched and waited.

Darkness had washed across the night sky as Lyrik and Freyja glided through the air on the far side of the keep. From here she could see the lights glowing through the windows.

It was unbearable, being this close to Amylia, not knowing what was happening to her and unable to reach her yet.

Her eyes strained as she tried to look into the windows, tried to catch a glimpse of her, just to see she was okay, but there was no movement in any of them. Balling her fist, her nails dug into her palms, that calm, deadly wildness inside her creeping in. She almost welcomed it. She could let it take over, give herself over to it and unleash herself on that keep. It would only take moments and they would all be dead. Her fingers ached to curl around Mica's spine and rip it from his body, but she fought it back, taking the long, slow breaths that were second nature to her now.

She glanced over her shoulder as the faint sounds of wings beat through the sky. Asspyn drew close and then angled off to their camp again, Silas waving an arm to her that they were done.

With one last, anguished look back at the keep, Lyrik urged Freyja to follow them.

Chapter 36

"Harry!" Lylith hissed, grabbing the maid's arm as she passed. The maid stopped, looking startled. "I can't come to Amylia today. I don't want Drakon to think I'm running to her with this. I'm in a precarious position."

Lylith glanced around quickly, dropping her voice low. "I am certain Lady Addelyn is in Lylican. I don't know where exactly yet, but I'm going to find someone to get word to the Sylvyns." She loosened her grip slightly on the maid's arm, realising how hard she held her. "If I go, they will suspect something is wrong. Same with you. I need to find someone they won't notice, but tell her… tell her I'm going to make this right. I owe her that much."

Harriet gripped Lylith's hands, her eyes shining. She nodded frantically, turning to take off, but Lylith grabbed her again

"Don't run, fool," she hissed. Taking a breath, she calmed her voice. "Don't run. Walk. Don't look like anything is different, and for Gods' sake, take that smile off your face!"

Harriet nodded, her face blanked of emotion. Then she darted forward, kissing Lylith's cheek quickly before scurrying away. Stunned, Lylith watched her go, a hand to the spot, holding onto the feeling a moment longer. A curl of warmth filled her stomach and she allowed herself a brief smile, then straightened, wiping her own face clean of any expression, and stalked towards the dining hall.

Harriet pushed the door to Amylia's rooms open, seeing Mica walking around, and paused, waiting just inside the door.

"Come in, Harriet, I'm just leaving anyway," Mica called, pulling a shirt on. Amylia was curled under the blankets in a tight ball, motionless as Mica bent over her, kissing her hair. "See you tonight." He sighed, not bothering to look at the maid as he strolled out.

Harriet waited for him to leave before pushing the door shut with a click. Running to the bed, she ripped the covers back, excitement roaring through her. Gods, she wished she could speak; every moment holding onto this news felt like millennium too long. Her smile faltered slightly when Amylia jumped, fingers clutching at the blankets.

Her skin was horribly pale And Harriet hummed softly, trying not to let the alarm show on her face as she ran a hand over the woman's brow, noticing how clammy the skin felt.

"What?" Amylia asked, taking the cup of water she poured for her.

Harriet ran to the desk, grabbing the small book and pen they had been communicating with when the hand signals they had been using failed, her excitement too much for the patience the signals needed. She threw herself on the bed next to Amylia.

"Gods, Harry, what's going on?" Amylia brushed her hair back. Harriet noticed her hand was shaking badly as she put the cup down. But she leaned in as Harriet scribbled furiously.

Lylith thinks your mother is in Lylican. She's trying to send word to Wynters. Can't come see you at moment.

She thrust the book into Amylia's hands who scanned it, her eyes filling with tears.

"Honestly?" She looked at her.

Harriet nodded, grinning widely.

"She's truly alive?" Amylia dropped the book, covering her face with her hands as her shoulders shook.

Harriet made a small sound of alarm, her voice raspy from disuse. She took the book from Amylia and put it on the side table, taking her hand and stroking it.

"No, I'm okay, I'm sorry." Amylia sniffed, wiping her eyes on her sleeve. "I was beginning to think this was all just a horrific trick, and I'd let them take me for a lie." Amylia smiled through her tears. "She's alive. My mother is alive, and if they can find her…" Amylia grasped Harriet's hands. "Harry, if mother is safe, if they can't get to her anymore." she choked out, "I would just need to get this stone out of me and then I can stop them from ever going after you or Rayvn and mother again… I could go back… to them."

Lylith stared at her plate, lost in her thoughts as Mica strolled in, hair dishevelled from sleep.

"Good morning... sister," he said, his tone strained, and her head snapped up. She stared at him, eyes wide.

"Drakon already told you?" she gasped. Mica nodded, running a hand through his hair and down the back of his neck as he watched her awkwardly.

"Not something I was expecting." He sighed and sat opposite her. "Can we not... can we not mention how you and I kissed... before Amylia and I...?"

"No," she cut him off. "Let's not."

"At least I know why father was so angry now." He huffed and waved for a servant to fill his mug. Leaning forward, he scooped a serving of porridge into a bowl, staring at it blankly as it cooled. They ate in awkward silence for a while, Mica's eyes flitting to her face and down to his bowl before he took a long swig of his drink and sat back, eyeing her.

"Why were you in Father's study last night?"

Lylith jumped at the question, her cup hovering in front of her face. She watched him over the steaming surface, thinking quickly.

"I have a right to know what I'm getting dragged into," she said flatly, frowning slightly. "This is not just a family matter, Mica, this involves multiple territories that could go to war against each other and not only that, Amylia looks terrible. Even you must see that. Do you think the Sylvyns will just forgive and forget if she doesn't get better? Will Rayvn?"

"Of course I see that," he hissed back. "She's doing it to herself, pining over that damn Sylvyn and his wife. Maybe if you and the mute got her to actually eat, she wouldn't be so frail still."

"She is eating. I've seen it myself, and I'm not an idiot. I know you loved each other once, but if you cared about her at all, you would let her leave. She is miserable here!" Lylith snapped, temper rising.

"You know, if I didn't know better, I would be questioning your loyalty, Lylith," Mica drawled. "I know you and Amylia have never gotten on well, or... since she and I got engaged... what is it? Now you know you can't have me, you don't hate her for it anymore?"

Lylith flushed hotly as her temper began to escape her grasp. "I didn't know there were sides to pick, Mica. I just say it as I see it; if you want to save whatever is left of the alliance, let her go back. Maybe then we can work on building the three territories up together, because unlike Amylia and Rayvn, I have nowhere else to go and nobody else that cares about *me.*"

Mica huffed. "So, you being in Father's office was not on her request?"

Lylith gave him what she hoped was a withering look. "It was simply that I am tired of being the last to know everything. I'm tired of being lied to and I'm tired of being a pawn while the men of this keep bring war down on our heads." She pushed her bowl away and glared at him. "But I will say, she's not going to get any better if you keep her locked up, at least let her get some air. Think about it, you utter fool. If anything happens to her, Rayvn will never forgive you and he is the next heir of Oryx!"

Mica's face filled with fury as he stared at Lylith. "You are lucky you are my sister," he seethed, standing to look her dead in the eye. "Or you would be out on your ass for talking to me like that. I am not a servant you can snap at. What I do with my wife is none of your business."

"I'm not sure luck is the right word, brother," she spat back. She turned and stormed out of the room. She heard something shatter in an explosion of pottery and looked back to see his cup in pieces against the wall, its contents staining the rug underneath.

"Leave it," Mica snarled at the maid who hurried to clean it up. She paused, terrified as she looked at him, and then the shards on the floor. "Go get the physician and have them sent to my wife's chambers to check her over," he snapped. "Tell them I'll be in my study when they are done. I expect a thorough examination and a list of foods that will get her healthy." The maid nodded, her face white as she backed from the room.

When a knock came at his study an hour later, Mica stood at the window. This wing looked over the small forest underneath the keep, and the sea sparkled just beyond.

"Come in," he called, turning and taking a seat at his desk. A woman came in, her face solemn. "You're the new physician?" he asked, brow raised.

"I'm the next best thing, my lord," the woman said nervously. "The closest physician to the keep resides in Credence, and after he learned of what happened to the last one, he won't come here." She twisted her hands in her apron. "Apologies, my lord, we tried sending for him after one of the cooks cut a finger clean off a few months back, and… the maid's unfortunate accident." She broke off as his eyes shot to hers.

"What of my wife?" he snapped, glaring at her. "Why is she not improving? Her maid and Lylith both state she has been eating, yet she has been here over two months, and she is not improving. If anything, she has gotten worse!"

The woman bowed her head. "She is very underweight and weak, my lord, though she did eat in front of me when I encouraged her. I believe, however, the reason for her failure to thrive is more because of the child; it seems to be taking from her... far more than the average pregnancy."

The words took a moment to sink in, and he ran them through his head a few times.

"What?" Mica's mouth fell open. "What did you say?"

The woman looked at him, frowning slightly. "You did not know?"

Mica fell back in his chair, breathing heavily. "No," he breathed.

"Your wife did not seem very surprised when I discussed it with her," she said quietly, watching his expression.

"Is the babe okay?" he asked quickly. "She is so thin. She needs to eat more now, surely? The foods... What can I get made for her to help the babe grow strong?" He stood, walked to the woman, and grasped her hands. "I want you to come and check her weekly."

She stepped back a bit, alarmed. "The babe is okay from what I have felt. It's still very early, my lord, and as I have said, she is very frail." She pulled her hands from his and looked at him. "She needs rest, good food, and fresh air."

He nodded, his hand running through his hair as he marvelled at the news.

"And... she needs to refrain from, uh..." she paused, glancing up at him, "bedroom activities, my lord. For the babe's sake."

"Yes, of course," Mica said, thoroughly distracted. "Thank you."

The woman nodded, edging towards the door. "Is that all, my lord?"

Mica nodded, dismissing her with a wave of his hand as he gathered his thoughts for a moment. He strode to the open door as he caught sight of Harriet leaving Amylia's bedroom from just down the hall.

"Harriet," he called, leaning out the door. She paused, half-turning to him, her body stiff and face impassive. "Your mistress is going to have a child!" He grinned and walked out to stand in front of her, he could barely contain the feeling that rose inside him. He noticed the look of distain that crossed so briefly across the maid's face, before she got control of it again, and felt his ire rise. But no, he wouldn't let this girl ruin this news.

He wanted to race to Amylia to pull her into his arms and kiss her. He frowned suddenly as he imagined her going stiff in his arms, her face turning away from his. He glanced up the hallway towards her room, then back to Harriet, waiting patiently. "Go down to the kitchens and tell them I expect her to be getting her meals made separately, fresh produce and newly caught game only. I won't risk her health while my child grows. And I will arrange for her to be taken outside daily to get some sun."

Harriet nodded curtly and headed towards the kitchen. "Wait!" he called, glancing towards where she had come again. "Is she awake? I wanted to congratulate her."

Harriet shook her head, not looking at him. He sighed, the need to shout the news from the rooftop biting at him. "Ah, well, I'll go tell Father and Lylith the good news instead, then." He pushed past her and down the hall to the heavy wooden doors, pausing to hold them open for her as she slipped past him. Feeling magnanimous, he smiled to himself.

Amylia jerked awake when the bed dipped. The pressure of the blankets pressing down against her was uncomfortable, and she shifted, pulling herself away.

"I hear congratulations are in order," a deep voice said softly.

She blinked, trying to focus on the face in front of her. Drakon. If he was shocked at the gaunt look to her, he didn't show it. Only disinterest showed on his face as his eyes trailed over the length of her shape under the blankets, lingering on her middle. She didn't speak, instead pulling herself up against the pillows as another wave of nausea rolled over her. Drakon reached for the glass on the side table, passing it to her.

"You didn't waste any time. Well done, child," he said, smiling slightly.

"I didn't have a choice about it, did I?" she said, though the weakness of her voice took some of the venom away.

He huffed softly. "It didn't have to be this way, you know. I would have been a happy man if you had stayed in love with my son. You could all have been so happy here." He sighed. "But you are too much like your mother. You think with your heart rather than your head, Amylia."

"You need to take this Helix out of me," she said flatly, taking a sip of the water and waiting to see if it would stay down. "It's taking too much. It's going to kill me and this child."

"Ah," he said softly, patting the mound of her leg. "Now, there we have a problem. I agree, I think the stone I put in was a bit too big. I wasn't sure if cutting it would weaken it, and I could not risk it being too small. However, if I take it out, I have no doubt you will kill both me and my son before we would have a chance to take a second breath." Amylia stared back at him, and he chuckled. "Your eyes say it all, my dear. I can see the hatred there, such a shame."

He stood and walked to the window.

"You know, I have actually been wondering about what to do. The Wynters obviously will be unhappy we took you back, and if I let your mother go — I'm not an idiot — she would bring this place down. I have no doubt the first thing she would do would be remove the Helix and come back here with eleven years of wrath behind her." He glanced back at her. "It would be unfortunate if you succumbed to the Helix, my dear, but it would tie up a lot of troublesome loose ends, and if you are gone, the Wynters will have no reason to come here."

"Rayvn will come for my mother if I die. You know that," Amylia said, furious that she couldn't stop her voice from shaking.

"Oh, he might," Drakon said. "But if you are gone and we have the child, we have no real need for Addelyn. My men have informed me that your brother only inherited the healing Gifts. He alone can't hurt us here, and I'm sure Lord Wynter would see more sense in peace between the two territories rather than lose thousands of his army in a fruitless retaliation when there is nothing to gain… and by the time your brother takes over Oryx, he will be taking over a land too poor to do anything except tie with us. Everything Oryx is runs through Lylican."

Amylia snapped her mouth shut, coldness spreading through her body at his words.

Just breathe, sweetling.

Amylia almost sobbed as she heard the words, absent for so many days. She lifted her chin, meeting Drakon's gaze defiantly.

"It really is such a waste," Drakon said regretfully, still eyeing her. "But we just need you to grow this child, Amylia. After that, your job is done. Maybe once the child is not taking from you as well, the stone will be more manageable for you." He smiled gently. "Now, get some rest, my dear. You need to keep your strength up. After all, your mother's and child's lives depend on you."

Amylia rallied herself.

Don't let him see he affects you.

"You underestimate me, and those I love," she said, her voice cold. "If you break this agreement, Rayvn will see you both in the ground. He has the support of Asteryn."

Lylith slipped out of her room as the moon hit its highest, pulling her cloak around her shoulders against the brisk air.

She paused at the top of the steps, listening down to Drakon's level before taking the other set down to the dining hall. Holding her skirts up in a knot in front of her, she moved slowly. Her boots in her hand, she crept silently on bare feet. She had tried to find someone to get word out for days, but the staff had been changed around, leaving no familiar faces in the living areas of the castle.

She knew the stable boys were fond of Amylia, had seen how they smiled and chatted to her as Lylith had spied on them, unnoticed from her favourite reading spot in the stable lofts. She knew they were the best option for getting away from the keep unobserved. Knowing the servants' entrance creaked, she took the main corridor out of the hall. She stayed as close to the wall as she could, stopping occasionally to listen for movement around her. Her heart thundered in her ears, and she took deep breaths, trying to calm it.

The foyer loomed up ahead, and she ran the last few meters to the gigantic main doors, lifting the metal latch slowly as she held her breath.

"You disappoint me, daughter."

Lylith dropped the latch with a thud. Her breath exploded out of her, and she whirled to see Drakon standing in the servants' doorway, half-hidden by a tapestry.

"I'm dying to know what excuse you have for this," he said flatly, walking towards her as two men appeared from the dark behind him.

"How did you…" she began, her words getting lost as panic spread through her.

"Oh, after your last appearance, I've had you monitored." Drakon sighed. "I really hoped you were more intelligent than this, Lylith. It seems both my girls have let me down."

"Get your hands off me," she spat, as one of the men, a guard, though his uniform was different from the ones the normal guards wore, grabbed her arm.

"I think not," Drakon said, his tone sad. "Don't worry, you will not be harmed, but I will not have you causing me any more issues than I already have." He turned to the men. "Take her down to the cells. Make sure she is comfortable, mind. It gets cold down there." He looked back at her. "Wake up a servant if you need. Take bedding and her things down there. She will stay there until this child is born or Amylia is dead."

"Yes, my lord," the two men said in unison, firming their grips on Lylith's arms.

"You have gone mad!" she hissed at him, trying to throw their grip off. "Both of you have. You think this child is a miraculous saviour against the Sylvyns? They will come for her; they will come for her child. You are better to let her go and try to make peace with them."

"I have had everything taken from this family in the past, Lylith. I am merely protecting what is ours." He sighed. "And that child, trust me, that child is the key to it all." He shook his head. "Take her away," he muttered, then turned and headed back into the dark doorway.

Chapter 37

Freyja snapped at Asspyn, her beak clacking together loudly as the smaller Sylkie backed up quickly, taking out the guide rope for Silas's and Edryk's tent.

"Enough of that!" Lyrik scolded, levelling a hard stare at Freyja. Calypso slunk around the back of the tents, giving Freyja a wide berth as she went, and sidled up next to Ingryd, who chuckled, patting her tenderly.

"I know you girls are over this," she crooned. "You have done well."

Lyrik snorted. "She's the one who starts it, the minx. She baits Frey and then leaves poor Asspyn to take the blame."

Silas emerged from the tent, rubbing his eyes, and looked at the flapping guide rope. He eyed Freyja. "Are you picking on Asspyn again, Frey?" The Sylkie ignored him, curling back up in a ball and keeping her wings tucked in tight.

"They're just cranky," Lyrik sighed. She pulled the tent straight while Silas knocked the peg back in. "They're not used to having to stay put all day, and I can't risk letting them fly around this area in case they get seen. It's been weeks and that's a long time for them to stay grounded."

"It's a long time to be sleeping on rock, too." Silas yawned and stretched.

"How did last night's flight go?" she asked him, passing him a cup of steaming tea. They had moved slightly back into the mountain after the first few days, behind a rise of rock that gave them enough cover to light a fire.

"There are a lot of men down there unhappy with Drakon," Silas said grimly. "New guards have been brought in around the keep and a lot of the original guards have been locked out. I have stayed out of his sight, but Raol is making noise that will land him in hot water if we don't move soon. I think if you let me talk to him, he will help us."

"No," Lyrik shook her head, "it's too dangerous. He betrayed Amylia once, I will not put you at risk, too. Drakon would make an example of you, not to mention blow what we're trying to do wide open."

"There have been a lot of newcomers the last few days," Edryk said, groaning as he pulled himself from the tent, his hair disheveled. Settling next to the fire, he held his hands out to the flames. "I'm going to head into the camp they're setting up for the festival today; it's the only way I can get into the keep. They have deliveries arriving which they are letting in the gates, so I can see if I can find anything out."

"Don't take any unnecessary risks," Lyrik warned.

Edryk nodded. "I'll be careful. I'm going to head down tonight after dark. I can sleep rough and slip in with the workers in the morning."

"I don't like you in there with no way of contacting us," she grumbled anxiously.

"I can stay on the outskirts of town," Silas offered. "In the woods underneath the keep? I used to go there to get some peace from the rest of the men. Edryk can check in there a couple of times a day, and then we'll know if he gets into trouble."

Lyrik sighed, giving him a small smile. "Not bad Silas." She chuckled, noticing with affection how he lit up at the praise.

"I can take you down later," Ingryd said, her voice muffled as she pulled an overcoat on. "Do you have everything you need for tonight?"

"Just a blanket," Edryk answered, swallowing his mouthful of bread to answer. "Though Silas is best to take me down. I'll sleep where he wants to meet and leave my stuff there. He will need to show me where that is." Both women nodded.

"It's been a few days since we updated Asteryn," Ingryd mused, looking into the distance. "I know Cecily is getting impatient to leave. Do you want me to go let them know the plan? If I take off the far side here and loop around over the far side of the ranges, we can be pretty sure they won't see me."

Lyrik shook her head. "Not with Edryk going in. Wait until we see if he finds anything out first."

—⁂—

The day moved slowly, with little to do other than wait for the sun to go down, and even Silas was as irritable as the Sylkies by the time they were ready to leave..

"Land far out of town, and walk in the rest of the way," she reminded him for the dozenth time.

"Yes, I wouldn't risk Asspyn, you know that," he replied shortly, then cringed at his tone. She gave him a moment to compose himself.

"It's not just Asspyn, Silas. I won't see you in danger either," Lyrik said gently, patting his knee as Edryk vaulted up behind him, wedging his rolled blanket between their bodies.

Ingryd snorted, coming up to stand by Lyrik. "Padding?" she asked, her brow raised.

"I need both hands to hold on to this infernal creature," Edryk replied as he twisted his hands into Silas's heavy coat and Silas grinned sheepishly.

"Asspyn was feeling fresh last night. She cut left and Edryk stayed right."

Lyrik chuckled, giving Asspyn a look. "We need him, please don't kill him."

Asspyn clacked her beak together, shaking her head irritably as she shuffled on the spot, waiting for Silas's command. The women stepped back to clear the ground for her, and she leaped into the air. Wings scattering the embers of the firepit, she launched skyward. The faint sound of Edryk's strangled yell faded into the night sky when she cut sharply to the left, tucked her wings, and plummeted down the mountainside towards the keep. Lyrik cringed as she watched them go.

"They always pick on the ones that hate flying." She sighed.

The world spun as someone shook her awake. Amylia tried to focus on the person in front of her. She felt so exhausted, her arms like lead as she reached up to brush her hair from her face. Nausea washed over her, and her stomach heaved, rolling just in time to empty the small amount of food she had eaten into the bucket that was held for her. She felt soothing hands, cool on the back of her neck as they held her hair back. Harriet. Amylia rolled back, wiping her mouth with the cloth Harriet passed her. Her maid's brown eyes were worriedly looking over Amylia's face.

"I'm okay," Amylia began to say, but her voice cracked and rasped. She took the cup Harriet handed her, washing her mouth with the first sip, and spitting it into the bucket before downing the rest of the cup greedily. "I'm so thirsty." She refilled the cup again. "How long have I been asleep?"

Harriet held up two fingers.

"Two what? Hours?" Amylia asked hoarsely, looking out the window; she could swear it had been night when she fell asleep. Harriet shook her head and held the fingers up again, swinging her other arm in an arc.

"Two days?" Amylia gasped, horror seeping into her.

"Not quite, all yesterday and half of today," Mica said, walking into the room. "She got you to wake enough to take some soup, but you need to eat a proper meal." His eyes softened as he looked at her stomach. "I thought fresh air might do you some good today. The baby seems to be taking a lot from you."

"The Helix is what is taking from me." Amylia gritted out. "Outside?" She glanced at the windows.

"If you eat the meal that is on its way up, I will take you personally," he answered, crossing to her. "You're not going to stay strong enough for this baby if you don't eat, Amylia." He took her hand gently. She flinched when he touched her, and his face hardened slightly, but he did not let her go. "Please, Amylia, I know you won't do it for me, but this child requires you to try to eat more."

Amylia nodded jerkily, her stomach flipping in revulsion at the contact, and he sighed, his expression relieved.

"Good." He glanced away, towards the servant who walked in with a tray.

The food smelled divine. Her stomach cramped as she looked at it, but she fought down the nausea that rolled over her in waves. Tender beef in a thick, rich sauce and fresh green vegetables that steamed deliciously. Mica watched her eat every bite, patiently waiting when she paused every time it threatened to come back up.

"I can't fit anything else in." Amylia pushed the plate away, only half the food gone. "Unless you want me to throw up what I got down, and that seems counterproductive."

Mica nodded, face stony as he eyed her plate. "It will do for now, but if I take you out, you have to swear you will eat more when you get back, okay?"

Amylia nodded, looking out the window rather than meeting his gaze.

"I will leave you to wash and dress with Harriet, and I'll be back to get you in a bit," he said, patting her on the arm gently as he got up. Her skin crawled at the contact, and she pulled her arm away, turning to glare at him, her teeth bared.

He met her glare, the skin around his eyes tightening as they narrowed, but he didn't say anything, pushing his chair back abruptly and stalking from the room.

Harriet helped her undress, pulling the nightdress over her head, throwing it over a chair. Amylia looked down at herself, slightly shocked. Her ribs were completely visible now, and she was so pale, the slight scar on her thigh from Lyrik's cut — the Helix stopping the full extent of Cecily's healing — so stark against the pink of her skin before, now faded into it. She ran a finger over it, trying to remember the feel of those last moments when both Cecily's and Lyrik's arms enfolded her, and sighed. Her legs still looked relatively normal, she thought, poking them, and her arms were only slightly smaller, too.

But her stomach — she stared at it dumbly — had a slight roundness to it. She cupped a hand across the front of it, her skin sensitive against the touch of her fingers. The fine hairs rose as her hand passed and she tried to imagine the tiny life growing inside there, expecting to feel disgust, and was surprised when she couldn't feel any.

"You will be nothing like him," she said quietly, almost to herself.

The sun felt glorious. The heat of it seeped into her and warmed her core as she laid back against the tree Mica had set her against. She had detested every moment of the long trip out here, carried by him. She had kept her body rigid against him and now her back ached dully, her head swimming in time to the dull cramping of her back.

But the moment the breeze had brushed past the bare skin of her legs, her skirts hitched up against his hold, it had been worth it. Mica left her there, content with the guards stationed around the grounds, and she relaxed now with Harriet.

She dozed for a couple hours, letting the sun seep into her bones, tried to imagine she was laying on the soft grass of Asteryn's gardens. If she closed her eyes, the faint sounds of gulls from the coast sounded like home.

"I haven't seen Lylith since... you know," Amylia said, her brow furrowing slightly as her eyes came back open. "Have you?" Harriet shook her head. "How long ago was that?" Amylia asked, glancing up at the keep.

Harriet held four fingers up, then scribbled on the corner of the book she had been reading with the sharpened length of graphite Lylith had slipped from Drakon's study. It left a permanent grey smear behind her ear from where she kept it tucked and Amylia looked at it fondly.

Harriet glanced quickly at the guard before ripping it off and passing it over.

She doesn't want them to think she told you, keeping distance.

"Oh, okay," Amylia said softly, relaxing slightly. Guards called from the gate and an answering cry came from behind it. Both women looked up to see a carriage rolling in, its flat back laden with tables and boxes.

A short guard with a well-groomed red beard yelled, pointing to where he meant. "Just park up alongside the wall and unload there." The driver hopped out, taking the horse's bridle, and leading it over.

"It's not the summer festival already, is it?" Amylia asked in surprise. More men arrived through the gates with armloads of items. Two men shuffled along with a huge wooden barrel, its contents sloshing around inside. Harriet nodded, sighing sadly. Amylia reached out, squeezing her hand.

"Your singing was what I looked forward to every year," she said sadly. "He will pay for this, I swear it."

Harriet nodded, looking at her hands, her throat moving as she swallowed hard. They both looked up as Mica stalked back over.

"I did not realise they would be delivering this so early," he said, as he moved to pick Amylia back up.

She leaned back, drawing her legs up. "What am I going to do Mica? Run away? I can barely walk."

He scowled at her and scooped her up. "It doesn't matter, we're going back in."

"Not yet... please!" she said, noticing out the corner of her eye one of the men had stopped, watching them with an armload of boxes. He had his hood up, and she couldn't see the details of his face, his short stature not familiar, but something in the way he held himself, how stiff he was as he watched them, made her look twice at him.

Maybe he has an issue with Mica. But Mica stepped back inside the building, cutting off her view of the man. Dread grew the closer they got to her wing. She hated this place. She hated the huge wooden doors that marked the start of her personal jail.

She hated the silver and red tapestries, the paintings. She even hated the furniture, she thought reproachfully as he pushed open the door to her room.

She especially hated this room; even the sight of it was making her chest feel tight.

"Mica, where is Lylith?" she asked casually. "I haven't seen her in a couple of days."

He snorted. "You know what she's like. You probably said something she took offence at, and she's gone to sulk somewhere."

She glanced at him, but his face was impassive. He put her gently on the chair in the room then dragged a new plate of food in front of her.

"Eat," he urged. "I will take you back out tomorrow." He kissed her hair before turning to leave.

Amylia fought the urge to reach up and rip the hair out that his lips had touched. She glared at his back as he headed towards the door, everything about his posture irked her. So proud of himself.

She pulled the uncomfortable dress back off again, not waiting for Harriet, her head spinning alarmingly. Its fabric, even though finely made, still felt harsh against her skin, and she pulled a soft nightdress from the armoire and slipped it over her head. Her arms shook, so she braced herself for a moment against the solid wood of its surface.

Amylia glanced down as she smoothed the fabric over her stomach and sighed. "I think something is up with Lylith," she said feebly. Glancing back, she saw Harriet shaking out her discarded dress. "It's just a hunch, but can you check on her for me?"

Talking was an effort. The breath Amylia needed to form the words felt hard to draw in as she leaned against the armoire, alarm beginning to course through her.

'Just breathe, sweetling.'

She focused on those words, but they were fainter in her mind, everything was fainter. She opened her eyes again, the room swimming as she tried to take a lurching step forward. She needed to lie down, but the bed was so far away.

Harriet was suddenly at her side, clasping her with steady hands. She helped Amylia back to the bed, eyes wide, and put her hand on Amylia's forehead.

The maid hissed a breath out, got a cool cloth and placed it over her forehead.

Amylia tried to muster the strength to grumble; she felt cold, everything was cold, but she couldn't get the words out.

'BREATHE, sweetling.'

The words sounded so distant, but urgent now. Amylia fought against the darkness that rose up to claim her again, so swiftly now, as if it knew it was getting harder to resist, reaching greedy arms to pull her into oblivion.

Two days went by as Amylia drifted in and out of consciousness. Mica, in a rage, had exploded at the healer, blaming the trip outside for Amylia's turn. Harriet had barely left her side, her body numb with exhaustion as she worked to keep Amylia alive. Only venturing away for brief periods to do cautious searches for Lylith.

The nausea plagued Amylia even in sleep, and she nearly choked when she emptied what little contents her stomach held. Only Harriet rolling her to the edge of the bed and viciously thumping her fragile back while she struggled to breathe had saved her.

The maid had roused her enough to get spoonfuls of water and broth into her, but that was it, and the toll it was taking on Amylia's body was starting to show.

Harriet watched the kitchen maid pour broth into Amylia's bowl, laden with the juice of fresh vegetables and melted butter as they tried to get as much fat and nutrients into her as they could, and gulped down her own breakfast absently as another maid prepared trays of food to the side. Her interest snagged on one tray in particular bearing several candied strawberries in a small bowl.

She glanced at the guard who was waiting for it, one of the new guards that had taken a position here recently, and nodded in thanks as Amylia's bowl was passed to her. She waited for the guard to take his tray and leave before whirling to the cook and pointing in the direction he had left.

"What?" the red-faced cook asked, wisps of hair coming out from under her cap as she hurried to swing the huge roast away from the fire it cooked over.

Harriet sighed in frustration and grabbed a handful of flour from an open bag, throwing it across the table as the cook cried in outrage. She threw up a hand, silencing her as she quickly drew her finger through the flour.

Who is food for?

"What, the one the guard just took? I don't know, luv, probably Lord Drakon. He's the one who sent the request down." She wiped the grease off her hands and looked at the flour irritably. Harriet wiped her hand through the flour and wrote again.

Strawberries?

"I'm just putting in what's been asked for," the cook replied. "'Ere, you gonna clean that up?"

Harriet whirled, nearly overturning the broth. She grabbed it and raced out the door in the direction the guard had left. Drakon was allergic to strawberries, so was Mica, and they were Lylith's favourites.

She hurried through the corridors, scanning for any sign of the guard, and paused to listen when he wasn't visible in any of the obvious directions. Faint footsteps clunked down stone ahead, and she ran to the top of the spiral stairs that led down... down to the dungeons.

Harriet waited until it got dark, trying in vain to coax more broth into Amylia, bone-deep worry for her mistress gripping her as Amylia fell deeper and deeper away from her. She waited with her, rubbing her cold hand, and willing her to keep holding on, before slipping back out and making her way through the dark keep, icy fear a cold lump in her stomach. She passed a couple of guards, but they were used to seeing her come and go, especially since Amylia had been waking at odd hours and Harriet had taken any opportunity to get sustenance into her.

She hid behind a hanging curtain as she reached the lower level, waiting for a guard to pass her before flitting on silent feet to the heavy door that led to the cells beyond. It was unlocked, and she huffed a sigh of relief as it swung slowly inwards, its hinges silent. Three cells lined the side of the windowless room. The furthest was lit by candlelight. She crept up to it, scanning the sparse furniture in it, and picked out the figure lying in the bed in the dim light.

Glancing back over her shoulder, she checked the door and grunted. The figure didn't move. She frowned, stamping her foot to try to draw their attention, but only succeeded in a jarring pain going up her shin. Scanning the floor, she found a small pebble and threw it into the cell. It pinged off what she thought was the person's shoulder, and the figure startled, throwing the covers back in a billow of sheets.

Lylith.

The young woman leaped out of bed, scrambling across the cell.

"Harry, how on earth did you get down here?" she gasped, pointing through the bars. "There's a key, over there on the wall."

Harriet leaped across the room, grasping the key, and fumbling in the lock.

"Drakon locked me here before I could get out of the keep," Lylith whispered. She helped Harriet feed the key into the lock through the bars and clicked it open. "The guards down here are the same guards he has for Lady Sylvers… Addelyn… Amylia's mother. They rotate, and I have heard them talking, the fools."

If Harriet hadn't been fighting the urge to cry, she would have laughed at the offended look on Lylith's face.

"Honestly, why do men think we're idiots? They acted as if I were an ornament sitting down here without ears." She pushed the door open, cringing as it squealed slightly, and slipped out of the cell. "There is an underground cell, riding distance from the keep, with a stream below, and it's located halfway up the rise with a flat top. They all whinge about sitting up there and watching the keep at night. She is close, Harry. We can find her ourselves and take her to the Sylvyns."

Harriet stared at her with growing excitement as Lylith tucked her skirts up in a knot in front of her.

"Come on," Lylith hissed, agitation showing clearly on her face. She grabbed the maid's hand and dragged her along behind. The two women stole through the keep, taking the servants' entrances. Harriet thought the frantic beating of her heart would give them away as Lylith slouched in the shadows of a huge cabinet in the foyer as a guard passed, smiling at her. It was not uncommon for her to be walking through here at all hours, but she felt as if her intentions were written across her face.

She tapped her foot after he had passed, and they took off, running through the kitchens and out into the cold night air. Lylith snatched Harriet's hand, hauling her, half-tripping in the dark, towards the small orchard on the far side.

"I'll get you over the wall. I stashed a dagger under a tree over there. I'll get that and be over after you," Lylith whispered, putting Harriet's hands on the depressions in the wall. "Right there. Grip them and climb. It's not a long drop on the other side. I do it all the time. I will boost you up."

Harriet's arms shook as she pulled herself up the crumbling footholds, feeling Lylith boost her from behind. She lay on the top of the wall, unable to see the ground below as she waited for Lylith. Almost ghostly, the lady darted back towards a larger tree at the rear of the orchard. Harriet saw her drop and ferret around the roots of it. Harriet rested her cheek against the cold stone, fingers digging into each side of the wall, the rough stone scraping her skin. Movement caught her eye, just beyond the orchard where the light from the keep illuminated them, and her stomach went cold.

A guard.

She looked at him, and then at Lylith, willing the other woman to look up and see him, but she was too busy digging, the sound masking his footsteps as he neared her.

"What are you doing out here?" he snapped and lunged, catching Lylith by the shoulder, and pulling her roughly. Lylith splayed backwards with a yelp of shock then took off at a run across the keep, away from Harriet, leading the guard away from her.

He didn't look back; he can't have seen her, lying hidden in the shadows.

Harriet saw her turn once, as if looking over at the guard sprinting after her, and she knew what Lylith was screaming at her in her mind.

Run.

Harriet took a breath, trying to control the panic that rolled over her as the guard kicked out and tripped Lylith, the woman falling heavily onto the gravel as the guard grabbed her roughly.

Harriet threw a last helpless look down into the darkness beyond the wall and dropped over the edge, the breath exploding out of her as she hit the ground. She moaned softly as she fought to draw air into her lungs, her knees drawn up to her chest. Strong hands suddenly gripped her, sliding across her mouth.

"Amylia?" a man's voice whispered in her ear.

Harriet sucked great mouthfuls of air around his hand, a scream stuck in her throat, willing her heart to slow and shook her head, her body starting to tremble.

"I'm not going to hurt you. I'm going to let you go now. Do not scream, okay?"

Harriet nodded against his hand, her heart thundering in her ears and he slowly let her go, turning her towards him and drawing her into a shaft of moonlight to look at her. She looked at his face, and her heart leaped. His eyes glowed faintly under his hood drawn up far enough to keep the features of his face hidden in the moonlight.

"You are the woman who was with Amylia. You were sitting with her?" he asked, his voice cautious. The breath exploded out of her as she nodded, pointing to herself, to him, and then away from the keep. "You want to get away from here?" he asked, sounding confused.

Harriet nodded frantically, making the gesture again, frustration making her want to scream. He glanced over the wall. "What about Amylia? Is she okay?" Harriet shook her head, making the gesture again as she tried to push past him, tugging his arm. "Look, I have someone coming to a meeting point shortly. I'll take you there, but you need to tell me what you know," he said, picking up a bag and slinging it over his shoulder.

She grunted at him, tugging his arm again, and he raised a brow, pulling her back into the light again and surveying her face closely.

"Can you not talk?" he asked gently. She shook her head furiously again, huffing in frustration as she shoved him this time. "Okay, okay," he said, taking her hand. "Come, I'll take you to the others."

Silas was already waiting at the meeting point as Edryk slipped out of the trees. A figure tripped and thrashed through the trees behind him. A stroke of moonlight made him gasp and rush forward.

"Oh, my Gods." Silas grasped the woman's shoulders. "Harriet?" The look of relief that flooded her face tugged at his heart, and she dropped to the ground suddenly, scratching at the dirt.

"What?" Silas stepped back and stared at Edryk. "What is she doing?"

Edryk looked over the maid's shoulder. "She hasn't spoken a word," he said. "She's writing something."

Silas moved, so the faint moonlight lit her, and squinted at the words she'd scratched in the dirt.

Take me Sylvyns, know where Addelyn is.

Silas swore, crouching to pull her up to him. "You know where she is now?" Harriet nodded frantically, and he slumped slightly. "Thank the Gods." After a breath, he said, "I'll take you to Lyrik now. She's here." He frowned at Harriet, peering at her face in the darkness. "Are you hurt? Why are you not talking?"

Harriet opened her mouth, grunting slightly, and the moonlight was just enough to see into it.

"Oh, Gods, Harriet." Silas went rigid with anger, and he hugged her tightly as she shook slightly, and he wished he had extra clothes for her. "I'll get you out of here now," he promised.

Chapter 38

Lyrik looked up as the beating wings approached, feeling a curl of cold dread when the silhouette riding behind Silas was unfamiliar. She lurched forward, reaching to help the woman who trembled violently.

"It's Harriet, Amylia's maid," Silas said, his voice hard. "I'm going back for Edryk." He paused, his face pained. "Lyrik, they cut her tongue out."

Lyrik rocked back as she stared at the woman, pulling her away as Asspyn threw herself back into the skies. "They did this to you?" she hissed, horrified.

Harriet nodded, her lips tinged blue, and Ingryd strode up, pulling her cloak off and throwing it around the shaking woman.

"You are safe now," Lyrik promised, rage kindling in her belly. "I won't let them touch you again. But Amylia... is she okay?"

Harriet shook her head, her face anguished. She dropped to the ground and started writing in the dirt. Ingryd grabbed a burning branch from the fire and brought it over as Lyrik bent over the crouching woman.

Addelyn in cell in hills.

"You know where Addelyn is?" Ingryd gasped.

Harriet nodded. Not looking, she wiped it clean and started again.

Riding away from keep toward mountains, stream, cell underground, entrance halfway up hill, flat top that can see keep.

Breath exploding from her chest, Lyrik looked at Ingryd. "Go, now. Tell them to come immediately." Ingryd nodded, face ashen. She ran for Calypso, vaulting onto her back, gone in but a moment.

Harriet patted Lyrik's leg, and she looked down again, her stomach going ice cold at the words scratched into the dirt.

Amylia is dying.

Lyrik didn't look up as she heard Asspyn approaching again. She raced through the camp, gathering her weapons, and whistling for Freyja when the rumbling rasp pulled her attention away. She whirled in surprise as Falkyn, not Asspyn, landed heavily next to Freyja, her answering huff lost in the wind of his wings.

"Rayvn?" Lyrik cried as he leaped off, striding to her.

"I passed Ingryd on the way in. She filled me in quickly and carried on to take word back," he said breathlessly.

"Gryff couldn't wait any longer and sent the army a week ago. They are waiting at the edge of the forest. They made good time with the warmer weather; the river was low, and they got through it without taking the bypass. I was coming to tell you."

Lyrik's knees went weak with relief. "Thank the Gods." She looked up as Asspyn approached.

"You found where Mother is being held?" Rayvn asked, his face tight.

"Harriet did. She got out and found Silas," Lyrik answered, shielding her eyes as Asspyn back flapped, sending ashes from the fire billowing around them as she landed gently across from them.

Silas jumped off, Edryk behind him, and approached them. Face grim, he clasped Rayvn's shoulder in greeting.

"Harriet has explained where Addelyn is," Lyrik said quickly. "I would prefer to wait for backup, but…" She paused, looking at Rayvn. "There is something wrong with Amylia. I think it's the Helix. We can't wait longer than we have to." Rayvn's face clouded and Lyrik turned to Edryk. "I need you to stay here with Harriet, in case Ingryd returns with more riders. I'd prefer you with me, but they won't know where to go."

Edryk nodded. "As you wish."

Rayvn was already walking back to Falkyn, but he paused as he reached Harriet and took her hands. "I am so sorry, for everything that has happened to you. I can't take it back, but I will make them pay."

Harriet squeezed his hand, a tear sliding down her cheek, and she nodded, watching him as he turned to leap onto Falkyn's back. Silas and Lyrik followed, Lyrik bringing Freyja around to eye level with them both.

"You're looking for a rise behind the keep with a flat top that overlooks the keep; there is a cell underground part way up, and I'm guessing it will be guarded, with a stream at the foot of the hill. If you see it, whistle." She paused. "We need to find her by morning, or they will notice Harriet is missing."

The three of them launched into the sky, spreading out to soar across the harsh, jutting landscape behind the Lylican keep. They worked in a grid pattern over the vast, impossible terrain, crossing over each other's paths.

Rayvn glided low on the second pass, the moon had begun to set and panic seeped into his bones. This was taking too long. Falkyn, as if sensing Rayvn's distress, pushed faster, the tips of his wings stirring the trees as he passed above them, as Rayvn searched for any sign of the rise Harriet had described. Rayvn's peripheral picked up Asspyn's sudden drop and Falkyn banked towards her as she hovered over an area off to the side, her mighty wings near silent in the air as she waited for Silas's command.

Rayvn drew up alongside him, looking down to where Silas pointed. The slight glisten of a small stream shone through a break in the trees, and ahead, there was a hill that had a small plateau at the top. A tree jutting up from the side of it nearly hid it.

There was nowhere to land the Sylkies without getting too close to the plateau. They pulled back, whistling to Lyrik as she passed by in the distance.

Coming around, Lyrik pointed to an open bit of field between the rise and the keep to land in. They headed towards it and the three Sylkies landed carefully in close proximity.

"There's a high chance the guards spotted us," Lyrik hissed as she silently ordered the Sylkies back into the sky with a motion of her hand. "Keep watch for any movement towards the keep, the Sylkies will watch us from above."

They fanned out across the unstable terrain, following Lyrik's lead as she headed towards the sound of the stream gurgling through the trees.

Rayvn's heart thundered in his ears as he walked, watching where Lyrik stepped. He admired her near silent movements as she slunk through the trees, a wraith moving in the darkness.

The stream was small, and rocks jutted up from the water. Lyrik picked her way across them gracefully and waited on the far side at the foot of the hill for them, her head cocked towards the darkness as if alerted to something, an unearthly stillness to her.

An arrow whizzed through the trees next to them. Lyrik swore under her breath, diving off to the side as another shot past, right where she had been standing.

Silas threw himself off the rocks in the middle of the stream and grabbed Rayvn's shirt, hauling him behind a boulder as Lyrik stepped behind a tree.

"No point hiding," a rough male voice said from above them on the hill. "I've already seen ya and ya winged rats."

"Shame about your aim then, isn't it?" Lyrik mocked, motioning them to stay down, Rayvn could only just see her in the dim light and nodded to her, hoping she could see him.

"He might be a rough shot, but I'm not," a second voice sneered.

Rayvn saw Lyrik look in the direction it came from, marking the two voices. She turned to him and then nodded her head to each direction the voices had come from.

"Feel free to correct me if I'm wrong, but I don't think you could hit a fish in a barrel, to be honest," she taunted, stepping cautiously away from the tree.

A third voice laughed off to the side of her and Lyrik repositioned herself, putting a boulder between herself and man.

"The bitch has you there, Joharren," the third man said.

A branch snapped next to Rayvn, and the surrounding forest exploded in movement. He leaped up, his sword out, as a dark shape lunged at them from the side. Silas dived out of the way as Rayvn brought his sword down on the attacker, a clean cut through the man's neck. The body fell to the ground, Rayvn whirling before it had even hit the grass.

Lyrik leaped up the rise, drawing her blade, and was instantly swallowed in darkness.

Men crashed around them, and Rayvn took on the next dark shape. His blade rose to block the blow swinging towards his shoulder. Silas panted next to him, his two short swords flashing in the moonlight. His attacker was forced backwards against a tree, the whites of his eyes showing as he struggled to parry the blows. Rayvn darted forward, his blade flashing around as he saw the man's arm raise, leaving his chest unprotected. He caught the man with his sword, a deep slash across the man's chest. Shrieking in agony, the man fell. Screams ahead let Rayvn know that Lyrik's blade had also found its mark.

Silas whipped his arm around, cutting another man's throat as Rayvn pulled his sword free.

Crashing up ahead had them racing up the hill. Lyrik was holding off three men in an effortless dance of fury. One held a lethal-looking dagger, the other two swung swords, and three more men appeared from the trees behind Lyrik.

Silas threw one of his swords, sending it deep into one of the newcomers' stomach just as Lyrik felled one of hers. She whirled, so fast Rayvn could barely follow her movements, and another man fell. Dead before he hit the ground.

A beam of moonlight briefly lit Lyrik's face as she stalked towards the last.

"You!" her opponent snarled, and Rayvn saw the look of shocked recognition on the man's face as he ran to meet the other two men, Silas on his heels.

"Hello, Joharren," Lyrik purred, flipping her blade between her hands as she circled him. "Would you like another beating? Did you learn nothing from the last?"

Joharren crouched and picked up the sword of the man next to him. He rose and lunged at her.

Rayvn and Silas had reached the other two soldiers in a whirlwind of blades, swords sparking as they clashed.

Joharren met Lyrik blow for blow, snarling as she danced through the trees, mocking him.

"Oh, come on, you can do better than that!" she taunted and blocked his blade on a downstroke. Their bodies locked together. Face inches from his, she grinned slyly at him. "We missed your company in Asteryn."

"You won't be laughing when I stick this sword down your pretty little throat." He grunted as she dropped, which unbalanced him, and spun away. Her blade came down on him, but he turned just in time to block it.

"Well, I guess it's the only thing you have long enough to shove down my throat isn't it?" She laughed. Swinging her blade with lightning speed up, across, and then down, she slashed his arm. He swore, reeling back as he glanced down at the wound.

"Bitch!" he bit out, flexing his arm.

"I've been called worse," Lyrik said flatly, leaping off a boulder, sword raised. "Not very creative, are you? At least have the decency to call me something really filthy, it might get me all hot and bothered." She waggled her eyebrows at him and spun in a graceful movement, slashing with her blade at the same time.

The thing inside her prowled, screaming to be let free, aching to join in and bask in the terror it would draw from this man. She shoved it down hard, trying to ignore the scent of his blood.

Joharren blocked her again as Silas burst through the bush next to them, a stout, bearded guard prowling toward him, driving him back with ferocious strokes of his blade. As he parried, Silas slipped on a loose rock, going down heavily on his back, the breath whooshing out of him. Gasping, he tried to lift his sword against the blow aimed at his neck.

Seeing the blade seconds from a lethal blow, Lyrik faltered, her attention pulled to the boy. Recovering quickly, she lunged, blocking it one-handed, and drove her other fist into the bearded man's nose. Bone crunched and he dropped like a stone beside Silas just as white-hot agony flared up her side.

Cursing, she turned, her blade coming up and under Joharren's arm, the tip taking him in the chest. His sword dropped as he spluttered and looked at her, his face a mask of shock.

Lyrik looked down to where her sword impaled his chest, just under his left nipple, and then looked back up at him and grinned.

"You should have just shot me," she whispered. She twisted the blade, shoving it deep into his chest.

Joharren grunted, coughing blood as he fell. Lyrik's sword pulled free of him as he hit the ground. Bending, she wiped the blood on his pants, a final insult, before turning to Silas and giving him a hand up.

"Thank you," he gasped, trying to get the air back into his lungs.

"You're welcome." Lyrik murmured, wincing as the wound on her side burned. Footsteps had them both turning, swords raised, as Rayvn stepped through the trees.

"You're injured!" he cried in alarm, his eyes drawing to where Lyrik's hand pressed against her side. "How bad is it?"

He reached to lift her shirt and she waved him off. "It's okay, keep moving. Have you seen the Sylkies?"

Silas snorted, looking up. "I've seen the girls. They were hovering just above us. Falkyn snatched a man who was trying to sneak up on me and took off with hi —" A crashing sound came from ahead, followed by a meaty thud. "Ah… there he is," he finished, sounding slightly disgusted. "Remind me not to piss Falkyn off."

Rayvn grunted, catching Lyrik's arm as she stumbled, overtaken by a wave of dizziness.

"Are you sure you're okay?" he pressed, trying to look at where she held herself.

"It's been a while since I took a wound." She hissed through clenched teeth, "I just forgot how much it stings. Keep an eye out for more men."

They walked slowly up the rise, searching for any sign of an entrance, while the Sylkies hovered above.

"There." Lyrik pointed with her blade, tensing as the movement pulled at her side. Up above, there was a depression in the hillside.

Silas loped ahead, slowing as he got near. Then he waved and disappeared briefly into the hillside. Emerging again, he called in a low voice, "It's here! There's an entrance!"

Chapter 39

Lyrik pulled her arm off Rayvn's shoulders as they neared the entrance.

"There's a key, hanging on the wall there." She gasped, pointing. Rayvn reached up and took the large iron key off the nail by the doorway and slipped it into his pocket.

The narrow stone staircase led down in a spiral into the mountainside. Lyrik leaned against the entrance, her hand pressed to the wound on her side as she panted. Rayvn watched her anxiously.

"Lyrik, please. At least let me bind that... or let Rayvn heal it," Silas said.

She waved him off. "It's just a scratch. Go, I'll keep watch out here." She pulled her sword from her back, passing it into Silas's hands. "Watch his back."

Rayvn nodded to her then stepped into the darkness, pausing to let his eyes adjust and feeling for the heavy key in his pocket again. It was cold down here and a wave of anger washed over him. If this is where his mother was... eleven years in a hole in the earth. He pushed the thoughts to the side, hearing Silas's footsteps fall in behind him. Down they went, the walls feeling closer as they advanced. He could touch either side with his arms still bent, the walls slick with cold moisture.

"Feels like we're heading into the home of the dark Gods down here," Silas said in a hushed voice, panting slightly.

After descending for what felt like an eternity, feeling his way for each step in the dark, Rayvn blinked. He could see the movement of his feet on the steps below.

"It's getting lighter," he whispered to Silas. Holding his arm out, he hesitated, straining his ears, listening into the darkness. Silas, too, cocked his head to listen. Rayvn sighed. He couldn't hear anything besides his own heartbeat. Slowly, they moved forward again, the steps getting increasingly visible until, ahead, the stone arch of an open doorway came into view, lit up from an open space beyond it.

He turned to Silas, who stared at him with wide eyes. His friend gripped the sword firmly in one hand and angled away from Rayvn. He put his finger over his lips. Together, they crept forward, Rayvn leaning slightly around the corner of the door and looking first into the space beyond.

It opened up into a large room, half of which held only a table and chair leaning against the far wall and a couple of baskets.

Metal bars came down from ceiling to floor, separating the other half of the room. A small, barred door was at the edge, leading into another area.

Rayvn stepped hesitantly into the room, noticing a cot heaped with blankets, a couple of buckets next to it and... something moved against the wall on the opposite side.

"I haven't seen you before." A soft voice echoed across the space to him, and he froze, the voice familiar, yet so very different from anything he had been imagining. His eyes picked out the woman who stood from where she leaned against the wall.

"Where are my normal guards?" she asked, coming to press against the bars.

Beautiful, she looked to be in her late thirties, her pointed ears just peeking through her long dark hair. *She looked like Amylia,* he thought, except her eyes — jade green even in the gloom. She looked at him with curiosity.

Something flashed across her face as she watched him walk slowly towards her, and he noticed the slight crease between her eyes, so like Amylia when she was confused.

"Who are you?" she asked softly, her eyes locking onto his.

"Lady Addelyn Sylvers?" he asked, hearing Silas halt at the door.

"Yes?" she said hesitantly. She went motionless as she watched him coming cautiously towards her. "Come closer," she whispered. Her hand half-reached through the bars and then stopped as if she was uncertain.

He did as she asked, moving slowly so as to not frighten her. Her eyes never left his until he was just inches away, then filled with tears.

"Rayvn?" she whispered, tears starting to flow down her face. "Are you my little Rayvn?"

His own eyes prickled as he fumbled in his pocket. Quickly, he pulled the key out and jammed it into the lock. Then Addelyn was pushing the door towards him, and her arms came around him.

"Mother," he choked out. His chest felt as if Falkyn had just crushed him. "Mother, I'm so sorry. We didn't know, we didn't know… I would have come for you."

She sobbed and rocked him gently, pulling back occasionally to run her hands over his face, his hair, or grasping him by the shoulders so she could look into his face.

"No. No, you do not apologize." She sobbed, wiping her arm across her eyes. "You never apologize for this. I'm the one who is sorry. All this time I have prayed to the Gods you would both be okay." She glanced behind him to where Silas waited. "Where is Milly, is she safe?"

Rayvn shook his head. "Drakon took her back. It's a long story. We are with Asteryn now. He threatened to kill you if she didn't leave with him. That was when we found you still lived."

Addelyn's jaw set in a hard line. "I will kill him. I…" She looked at Rayvn. "He's put a stone… called a Helix stone in me. My Gifts, I can't use them. The stone makes me weak."

Rayvn nodded as he took her hand, leading her towards the door. "We know what Helix is. He used it on us. Lyrik or Gryffon can take it out."

"Lady Sylvers." Silas bowed low to Addelyn, his own eyes bright with tears and Rayvn saw his friend swallow hard a few times before speaking again. "We need to move. We don't know if any guards alerted the keep before we got to them."

Rayvn leading, they climbed the steps as fast as possible. Sword out, he guarded their exit while Silas helped Addelyn. Her movements slowed as they ascended, and her breath came in pants.

"It's this stone," she rasped, pausing yet again to catch her breath. "It doesn't just take my power, it draws from me, too."

"Wrap your hand in my tunic," Silas murmured to her. "I'll pull you up the best I can. It's too narrow to walk next to you."

It was a slow climb but, gradually, light filtered back in, and Rayvn gestured for Silas to wait as he approached the entrance, sword ready.

"Lyrik?" he called in a low voice.

"Rayvn?" Her voice strained as her silhouette came into view in the dusk light outside. He breathed a sigh of relief, stepping into the cool air.

"Was she there?" Lyrik asked urgently. Blood leaked across her hand as she bent slightly, leaning heavily on Freyja, who was clucking softly in alarm. Silas stepped out into the night air, half-pulling Addelyn with him. "Oh, thank the Gods!" Lyrik sighed, sinking to her knees, her face pale.

Rayvn swore, kneeling to pull her hand away from her side. The blood now ran freely, soaking her tunic and the whole side of one leg. And...

"Oh, my Gods..." He swore louder, put his own hand over the wound and poured his Gift into her. "You said it was a scratch!" he gritted out, horror clawing at him as he took in the deep wound. There was no way it had not hit something vital, and he poured everything he could into it. It wasn't enough, he was draining too fast and there was still so much blood.

"That's not a damned scratch!" he hissed at her.

Lyrik snorted weakly. "So dramatic. It's not that bad. I... I didn't want you to waste your Gift on it before we saw what condition Addelyn was in."

Slowly... too slowly, muscle knitted under his fingers. He felt his power drain and pushed Freyja's beak away when she nudged him, fussing over Lyrik.

His head spun as he staggered back up, looking at Silas who braced Addelyn.

"He's a healer?" Addelyn breathed to Silas in a wavering voice.

Silas nodded. "He's learning, but yes." Addelyn jumped as Falkyn prowled up next to her. "It's Rayvn's beast," Silas soothed. "He won't hurt you, m'lady."

"She's losing too much blood. Silas, I need you to get her to Cess," Rayvn said, his voice sharp with worry, glancing back down at Lyrik, her hand on Freyja's head. "I've stopped the worst of it... but she needs Cess. This is too big for me."

He hauled Lyrik up, anxiety coursing through him as her eyes began to roll shut. Going to Asspyn, he boosted her onto the Sylkie's back, eliciting a low groan from her. Silas came up behind, climbing on and folding an arm around the woman's middle, he hauled her back to lean against him. Rayvn pulled off his tunic, wadded it in a ball, and pushed it against the wound. Firmly placing Silas's hand over the top.

"Are you okay to get your mother out of here?" Silas asked, face concerned as he scanned the darkness.

"Yes," Rayvn replied. "Just get her back, as fast as you can. Frey will follow." He ran back to Addelyn, taking her hand. "I promise you it's safe, but I need you to get on Falkyn," he said urgently, leading her to the beast.

"Rayvn... I can't leave without Milly." Addelyn looked towards the keep in the distance and Rayvn felt a glimmer of alarm, worried she would refuse to go.

"I don't want to leave her either, but I need to get you back to Gryffon. I can't risk losing you again. I've only just found you." His voice cracked as he looked at her and Addelyn cupped his cheek, smiling softly.

"Now I finally have a moment to look at you," she murmured, "and you look so much like your father."

The lump in his throat that had been threatening for the last few hours was too much. He let her pull him into a fierce hug, barely believing he had her there. This woman that was stranger and home to him in one.

She grasped him by the shoulders, pulling back until she was looking into his eyes again.

"I am so proud of you, my boy, but I have spent eleven years not being able to reach my babies, not knowing what was happening to you. I will not sit back and leave either of you in that man's hands any longer."

Rayvn shook his head. "The Wynters will help get Amylia out. We can't do this without them."

Addelyn sighed, closing her eyes briefly. "This Gryffon, can he remove the Helix?"

Rayvn nodded, anxious to get her away, as far away as he could manage. "He took mine and Milly's out."

"Okay," she said, after a pause, her voice pained. "Take me to him, then we come back for her."

Falkyn shifted under them, angling himself to face down the hill as Rayvn reached behind, gathering a handful of his mother's dress. She trembled against him.

"Hold on to me as tight as you can," he said urgently. Falkyn spread his massive wings, taking three huge bounds down the hillside before pushing off and gliding into the air, as if knowing the leap would be too much for Addelyn to hold on. His mother gasped as the ground fell abruptly away and the strong wings lifted them gently into the skies. His anxiety lessened with every beat of Falkyn's wings. He had his mother, and she was safe.

Falkyn flew hard, his great wings cutting through the air as Lylican fell into the distance behind them, the stars twinkling above.

Dawn had broken by the time they reached the forest, flying high to make use of the warm thermal currents. He could see Silas and Lyrik just ahead of them in the distance, catching up and overtaking them as the camp came into view. Silas's face was drawn, his arms around the entirely unconscious woman, stiff, but he nodded to Rayvn as they passed. She was still alive.

Cecily waited for them as they landed. Rogue, trying to get a hold of Freyja who was wild with distress, was barking orders to the surrounding camp. The entire place was a heaving mass of movement as warriors gathered into groups, preparing to move on Lylican.

Falkyn landed heavily next to Freyja and Rayvn was off him in moments.

"She's wounded badly. I tried to save her," he croaked to Rogue, reaching a hand to sooth Freyja. Rogue blanched, and sprinted to Asspyn as the Sylkie descended on the camp, reaching to take her from Silas.

Cecily had her hands over Lyrik's wound before she was even out of Silas' arms, pulling the clothing that was wet with dark blood up and off her. Rayvn's stomach clenched as he peered across their bent heads. So much blood.

Rogue had Lyrik's head cradled in his lap, his hands smoothing the hair back from her face, his eyes fixed on the wound in the pale flesh of her stomach.

"Is she alive?" Rayvn asked. Freyja was nudging him, clucking softly, and circling the group.

"She is… just," Cecily said, her glowing eyes focused on Lyrik's face. "You did this healing? You saved her life, Rayvn. She wouldn't have made it back without it."

"Lady Addelyn Sylvers, I presume?" Gryffon said, touching his forehead to Addelyn as he jogged up, while throwing a worried glance to where Lyrik lay.

Addelyn returned the gesture. "Lord Gryffon Wynter," she answered, "please, formalities later." She stepped back and gestured towards where Cecily knelt over Lyrik, and he shot her a grateful glance, hurrying to the women.

Slowly, Lyrik began to move, though weakly. Her hand fluttered up to reassure Freyja, who crouched next to her head, making small urgent noises of distress, and Rayvn let out a breath of relief when Gryffon knelt and gently picked her up, Rogue going with them back towards the tents.

Cecily stood up slowly, reeling a bit, but she braced herself on Silas and made her way across to them.

"I am so very glad to meet you, Lady Sylvers," she said, touching her heart to the woman, exhaustion on her face.

"The honour is mine, Lady Wynter," Addelyn replied, echoing the gesture. "But please call me Addelyn. It's been a long time since I have been among friends."

Cecily smiled sadly. "I'm truly sorry it has taken us this long to discover you were being held. We would have come for you — for you all — had we known."

Addelyn shook her head. "We were all fooled, but the only people I hold to blame are Drakon, and the woman who betrayed me to him."

Cecily gestured to the fire behind them. "You must be exhausted. Please, come eat and rest. We have a bit of time as we will catch the troops up on the Sylkies."

"Wait, please." Addelyn hesitated, holding her hand out as Cecily went to lead her away. "Rayvn said Gryffon can remove Helix. That he did it for Amylia and him. I need to help rescue my daughter. I can't with this Helix in and I can't take it out myself. I tried. It's too deep."

Cecily nodded. "We can. But I need a bit of time before I can heal you after Lyrik drained me."

"I don't need to be healed," Addelyn said. "I just need it cut out. I can heal myself once it's gone."

"You're a healer?" Cecily asked, as Rayvn's mouth fell open.

Addelyn looked fondly at Rayvn. "I am, and it appears my son took after me." She turned back to Cecily, green eyes flashing dimly, even without her powers. "I'm a Heliacle. Help me take this stone out, so I can burn that fucking keep to the ground."

"This is going to hurt. I'm sorry," Gryffon said to Addelyn, bracing a firm hand against her knee and eyeing the heavily scarred skin on her thigh in horror. "How many times have you tried taking this out yourself?"

"I've lost count." Addelyn sighed, trying not to look at the ruined flesh, and took the piece of leather Rogue offered her to bite down on. "I always pass out before I can get deep enough."

"Well, I can see where Amylia gets that stubborn streak from." Rogue chuckled and Addelyn felt a tug at her heart, remembering the wilful, stubborn child she had last seen.

"She kept that?"

Rogue snorted. "Ohhhhh, did she ever." He turned to Cecily. "I'm leaving now, Rik is settled, and I want to stay at the head. I'm taking Athyna with me?" he asked.

"Yes, please, and Shadow, too," she answered. "Athyna will follow Shadow. I'll be coming with Lyrik on Freyja."

"Excellent." Rogue sighed, stalking off. "I think it's a good thing we will have three healers by the end of this."

Rayvn and Silas laughed softly. Gryffon heated the blade over golden flames that danced in his palm, turning it until it was red hot and then cooling it with a breath of ice.

"Your daughter's horse," he explained to Addelyn, clearly noticing her confusion as he brought the blade back to her skin. "I'm still convinced she is more Druka than mare. Brace yourself, Addelyn."

Leaning against Rayvn's legs, Addelyn took a deep breath and steeled herself. There was a flash of searing pain as Gryffon cut neat and deep through the knot of scars. The coppery tang of blood filled the air as it welled up, and the warm rivulets ran down her leg. She groaned, her head swimming, the muscles in her leg rippling as she fought to keep it still.

Gryffon cut again, slightly deeper, and she jolted, gasping as pain engulfed her.

Rayvn's hands on her shoulders tightened, his legs a solid weight behind her, and she bit back the scream of pain that was clawing up her throat.

There was silence except for her gulps for air as Gryffon gently reached into the wound, wincing as his fingers contacted the stone.

Gripping it, he withdrew it quickly until it rolled in his palm and held it out to show her, the muscles in his neck bunching and his jaw tight.

Addelyn nodded, panting, her brow sweaty. She pushed a hand to the wound to staunch the blood.

"Mother?" Rayvn asked, moving gently away from her back to cross in front of her, crouching as Gryffon threw the stone into the fire with a hiss.

"I just need a minute." She gasped, trying to flash him a quick smile as the wound under her fingers dripped steadily onto the ground.

Cecily made a move towards her, her hand reaching for the wound. There was a lot of blood, it must have nicked a vein.

"Wait," Addelyn whispered, holding a bloody hand out to Cecily. She closed her eyes, feeling the slow, tingling build in her veins.

The dripping was slowing; the tingling had turned to a rush, a flood of heat barreling through her, and she welcomed it, opened herself to it. She listened, the drips moving farther and farther apart, feeling muscle and skin knit together under her hand.

"Mother, are you ok?"

Rayvn's voice was laced with concern, and she felt his hand brush over hers. She clasped his with her free hand, rubbing a thumb over the back of his hand, soothing him as she would have done when he was a child. With a sigh, she rolled her head side to side, stretching under the tug and pull of her Gift.

She opened her eyes, holding up a hand as jade coloured flames rolled over it, curling around it like a cat welcoming its master, burning the blood on it to dust.

"Let's go get your sister back," she said in a low, deadly voice, flames winking to life in her other hand as she held it up in front of her and smiled at her son.

Chapter 40

Lyrik's eyes flew open, and she reached to where the wound had been; soft pink skin was all that was left of the deep gash that had gone through muscle and tendon, deep into her abdomen. She sat up, her head swimming as weakness overcame her, then she rolled cautiously off the bedroll she had been placed on, pushing out the tent flaps.

"Cess," she croaked, shielding her eyes against the sun that sent stabbing pain through her head.

"Easy, now. You have lost a lot of blood. Lyrik, is it?" Cool hands braced her, one sliding across her forehead, taking the pulsing headache away. She opened her eyes to jade green ones swimming into focus in front of her.

"Addelyn," Lyrik breathed, looking around as her thoughts returned to her. "No, we can't still be here. We need to be moving already!" She moaned, gripping Addelyn's arms. "Where are the boys? They got back okay?"

"They did, and I have sent Ingryd and Arya to get Harriet and Edryk," Gryffon answered, coming up beside Addelyn. "The army has already left. You have been out cold all day. We were just about to wake you so we could leave as well and catch up to them."

"We need to leave immediately," Lyrik said urgently. "Amylia… she's ill. Harriet told me when she got to us."

Gryffon's face drained. "What do you mean ill?"

"Edryk said she's lost too much weight and looks weak after he saw her last week, and Harriet," she paused, "I don't know how bad it is Gryff. They cut Harriet's tongue out! She can't talk, but she wrote… she wrote that Amylia is dying."

Addelyn choked, her hands flying to her mouth. She looked at Lyrik in horror. Gryffon stilled, looking over Lyrik's shoulder; the pain in his eyes let her know who was standing behind her. She turned and met Cecily's gaze. The lady was bone-white, her breaths coming short.

"Get everyone mounted immediately," Gryffon roared, turning to the milling riders behind him.

"Go with Rayvn, Addelyn," Cecily said, her voice shaking. "I'll be right behind you with Lyrik."

The Sylkies took to the skies as one. Asspyn, Falkyn, and Freyja streaked ahead as their riders grimly prepared themselves.

Lylican came into view just as the tail end of the army did, and Lyrik heaved a sigh of relief at the sight.

"I don't know how many fires Rogue lit under his men, but they are moving fast." She had to raise her voice for Cecily to hear, twisting to look at the woman.

"Take me down. I will move in with them. If anyone needs healing it will be the ground troops," Cecily yelled against the wind and waved for Rayvn and Silas to keep going.

They spiralled down. The rider that had Gryffon peeled off to follow them and swooped upon the army, landing in front of them.

"Stay safe, Rik," Cecily breathed, squeezing her shoulder before she slipped off Freyja. Lyrik waited, Freyja moving under her as Athyna ran to greet Cecily, howling a low tune as the woman sprinted towards Rogue and Shadow. Gryffon caught up to her just in time to swing her up into the saddle, taking another horse for himself.

"What's happened?" Rogue yelled across to them as the horses pulled up alongside Freyja.

"The Helix is killing Amylia, we can't wait any longer. We need to get there and get it out of her now," Gryffon said, tension radiating off him.

Shadow danced under Cecily as the mare pushed up next to the Sylkie, her ears flat. Cecily gave Lyrik a last look and leaned forward, her face set in grim determination.

"Run, Beastie," Cecily snarled, twining her hand into the thick mane as Shadow exploded forward.

Lylican met them on the plains outside the city and Rayvn cursed at the sight of the lines of men waiting for them.

"Drakon must have started rallying as soon as he realised Harriet was gone," Silas shouted to him as they hovered above Lylican's army, the men far below peering up at the sky, darkening with the Sylkies. The two Sylkies rumbled deep in their chests. Addelyn leaned over, her burning gaze fixed on the keep, so close now.

Rayvn set his jaw, picking out Drakon's war-horse behind the rows of assembled soldiers, the lord's red and silver armour easily visible. Mica was further back behind a line of archers, astride a large chestnut stallion, his own armour with the Lylican crest across his chest polished and glinting in the sun. With a dawning horror, he noticed the colours of other territories mixed in with Lylican's men. Solos and Credence had joined Lylican. He turned Falkyn and flew towards where Rogue, Cecily, and Gryffon led the ground troops below, Silas and Asspyn on his tail.

"Drakon is behind the mass in the middle," he yelled to Gryffon as he landed. Addelyn slipped off behind him. "Mica's further back. There are other territories there, Gryff. Drakon has used the summer festival to his advantage."

Gryffon leaped off his horse, throwing the reins to a mounted warrior. Face dark with anger, he stalked towards Lylican's troops, Rogue and Rayvn falling into step with him. They stopped, just shy of the archers' range.

"Drakon!" Gryffon bellowed, his voice carrying across the space. "It's over. Let Amylia go and none of your men will be hurt."

"Oh, I think not," Drakon called back, urging his war-horse through his men. "I don't know if you have seen, Lord Wynter, but my forces are far greater than yours, even with your Sylkies." Coldly, his eyes roamed over them, pausing on a spot between him and Gryffon. Rayvn glanced back to find Addelyn had joined them, slipping silently between himself and Gryffon.

"Not that I trust you would leave here without trying to harm me anyway," Drakon went on, his eyes roaming over her. "Hello, again, Addelyn, it's been a while."

"Drakon," Addelyn hissed. Flames danced around both her arms as she stepped forward.

Gryffon stopped her with a hand on her shoulder. "I do not wish to harm any man in this or any other territory of Labrynth, but you have one of our own locked against her will in your keep. We have come for her. And I promise you, any man standing in my way will die," he called, eyeing the rows of men.

"Amylia belongs to Mica," Drakon spat. "They are married and, as such, he owns her. Go back to your lands and your own wife. One girl is not worth the bloodshed."

His voice low and deadly, Gryffon snarled, "Nothing you can do will stand between me and Amylia."

Hoofbeats from behind them had Rayvn glancing over his shoulder and fear lanced his gut as he saw Cecily galloping towards the lines of men, Shadow barely out of the line of fire. Above, Lyrik and Freyja hurtled forwards to cover her, ready to attack anyone that moved toward the horse and rider.

Shadow halted as she got in range and danced up the line of men. The huge beast with its effortless rider cut a stunning sight.

"I am Cecily, Lady of Asteryn," she called, her voice clear and strong. "I am a healer of the line of Castarion, and I have always sworn that any man, woman, and child of Labrynth that need my healing could come to me. Asteryn does not have any quarrel with any of the territories. We battled by your side in the Great War. I healed your great-grandparents, and I would have died alongside them had I needed to. We lost many of our own fighting for what is right. Fighting for freedom. And we would do it all again." She pointed to Drakon, Shadow dancing towards him.

"But this filth came into our territory and abducted my *mate*." Cecily's eyes flashed as she snarled at him.

Rayvn startled, glancing to Gryffon and back, his mother's face echoing his own shock. Behind them, Rayvn heard the murmur of voices and a low growl from Rogue as he realised the true pain Cecily had been going through since Amylia's abduction.

"We are here to get her back, and I ask you to step aside," Cecily continued, Shadow nearly to them. "The man you stand beside is not worth your loyalty. I am not asking you to turn on him and fight for us. I'm asking you to walk away and go back to your territories and your homes and let us get our loved one in peace."

Rayvn moved up next to Cecily, Falkyn a solid mass behind him, Gryffon on his other side, as Drakon sneered across the gap between them.

"A touching speech, Lady Wynter, but we do not recognise your claim on my daughter-in-law; by our laws she is married to my son and as such, she is his property to do with as he wishes. My army won't let you get anywhere near her. Go back to Asteryn where you belong."

"What army, Drakon?" A lone horse walked out of line, and Rayvn's heart tugged, looking at the man who had as good as raised him. Drakon twisted in the saddle, glaring at the man who had moved between him and the Sylvyns.

"Raol, get back into line."

"I am in line," Raol said. "It's just not in your line."

"You treacherous bastard," Drakon hissed. "You will die with the rest of them, then."

Heliacle Rising

"You lied to us, Drakon," Raol said, his voice steely. He twisted to look at Rayvn, his face taut. "I can never apologize enough for my part in this, my boy. I thought I was protecting you both from Attica by telling him about Amylia. I didn't know. Rayvn, I would never have done it if I had known the truth."

Rayvn stared at Raol, his emotions in turmoil.

Raol turned back to Drakon. "But my wife saw who you really were," he snarled. "And you cut out her tongue, then kept her from me, locked in that keep. And you think I have any loyalty to you? You think these men have any respect for you? They see what you are!" he spat.

"Harry is safe, Raol. She is with us," Rayvn called, his voice thick.

Raol's shoulders dropped slightly in relief, and the glance he threw at Rayvn conveyed his gratitude and sorrow as he squared himself and whirled his mount around.

"Men of Lylican, to me!" Raol roared. His horse backed up as the field in front of them erupted. Over half the men turned on each other, fighting their way out of the ranks of assembled soldiers as Raol's horse leaped towards the Sylvyns. "Tell your forces the men with green armbands are with Asteryn. They will fight for you," he cried, pulling his sword, and spurring towards the mass of men beyond.

Silas vaulted onto Asspyn, shooting into the sky to warn the riders, as Rayvn turned to Addelyn.

"I will be fine." She smiled humourlessly. Her eyes glittered as flames rippled across her hands.

Rayvn leaped onto Falkyn, who shot into the air, only to plummet and rip a man from a horse that had broken the line and headed for Addelyn. His scream cut off as the Sylkie's wickedly curved beak tore through his throat, dropping him to the ground with a sickening thud.

Men swarmed towards Asteryn's forces as Rogue's men attacked, swords clashing.

Sylkies soared across the field of men, pulling away from the flashes of green or those that had laid their weapons down, trying to get away from the fight, and snatched the rest, their cries cut short as they were taken high into the skies and then dropped to the ground.

A few of the riders leaped from their mounts, drawing weapons. Their beasts guarded them from above, darting in to rake talons across those who would try to take on their riders. Silas leaped off Asspyn, pulling his twin swords from his back as he joined the men Raol led. Asspyn hovered over their heads, uttering short, angry screeches, her claws as lethal as daggers as she swooped in and out.

Rayvn paused in the skies for a moment, in awe as he watched his mother. Flames erupted from her as she worked with Gryffon, green and golden fire merging, to take out entire groups of men who rushed them. Gryffon whipped up wind from one hand to send Addelyn's spears of ice into the chest of another man. With his other hand, he threw a wall of flames out, holding back two men wielding swords. The two of them made an unstoppable force, taking out walls of men. To their left, Rogue, too, left a trail of destruction, his sword a blur, his movement almost too fast to follow as he took on multiple men at once. He was death walking, his victims barely having time to scream before he cut them down, the bodies piling up behind him. Where his sword fell short, bolts of lightning crackled from him, dropping groups of men in one blow, twitching on the ground.

White caught his eye and he looked down to see Cecily, bow drawn back, as Shadow reared, lashing out at a man in front of her. Cecily fired. The arrow took the man in the throat, dropping him. Athyna leaped over the falling body, her jaws ripping into another soldier's thigh, holding him until Cecily's next arrow took him down, too.

A horse streaked towards them, its rider's sword raised. Rayvn yelled and Falkyn dove for them, ripping the rider out of the saddle moments before he reached Cecily.

Shadow lashed a powerful hind leg at a second rider as Cecily twisted in the saddle and yelled a warning to him as, beneath Falkyn, a soldier raised his sword to slash at the Sylkie's legs. Falkyn roared in anger, darted, and grabbed the thrashing man, talons ripping into him.

The Lylican resistance faltered, split into smaller bands, and pushed back towards the keep.

Drakon's horse struggled out from behind a group of soldiers confronted by Rogue's men, panicking and lashing out as the men pushed into it. It reared, nearly overturning entirely.

Already unbalanced, Drakon was thrown, hitting the ground hard before getting dragged up by one of his men. He shouted something drowned out by the milling soldiers around him, but the group turned and retreated, running for the keep.

Rayvn pushed Falkyn towards Rogue who had been mobbed by a large group of soldiers, leaping off the Sylkie's back before he hit the ground and drawing his blade. The wind from Falkyn's wings lashed at him as the Sylkie surged forward to skittle a group of men that turned to attack.

Lyrik swooped low over Rogue to his left, Freyja snatching one of the three men he had been holding off and tossing him like a ragdoll into the air.

"You are rusty," she yelled to Rogue, drawing her bow, and taking another out with an arrow through the neck.

"Forty-seven," he roared back at her as his blade went deep into another man's chest. Pulling it back out, he wiped it on the man's shirt and glared at her, pointing to the man with his sword. "Forty-seven, Miss 'I'm-going-to get-myself-nearly-killed-and-sit-on-my-pigeon-for-the-real-fight'. What's your count then, smartass? Or are you going to come down here and fight like a real man?"

Lyrik snorted, firing an arrow past his head to take out a soldier behind him. "Fifty-two. Keep up, sweetheart!" She banked hard, flying in an arc towards the keep. Rogue flipped her off.

"The pigeon's kills don't count!" he bellowed at her disappearing form.

Cecily saw the gap in the men. They had split and left a path towards the keep. Twisting in the saddle, she made eye contact with Addelyn who stood with her back to Gryffon, the two of them surrounded by a blazing inferno. She pointed to the keep. Addelyn nodded, sending a wall of flames billowing out, taking down the last of the men who surrounded her as they screamed in agony.

Solid under Cecily, Shadow surged through the gap in the men, striking out viciously at anyone who came near. Athyna kept close to her, running next to her towards the keep, towards Amylia.

Men scattered in front of them. Sylkies dropped from the sky around her to pick up screaming men, clearing the path as she raced towards the keep. Suddenly, movement to her right caught her eye. A small knot of soldiers… and in the middle…

"Drakon," Cecily snarled under her breath, nocking an arrow. Turning Shadow with her thighs, she fired. The man directly behind Drakon dropped like a stone. He turned and cold terror filled his eyes as his gaze landed on Shadow and Cecily coming for him.

Rayvn and Rogue paused as the last of the men they had been fighting turned tail and fled back towards the keep, Falkyn chasing a terrified soldier whose piercing screams got louder as the Sylkie gained on him.

Rogue winced as Falkyn caught him, lifting him into the air before dropping him onto a group of soldiers advancing on some of Asteryn's men, the man's screams abruptly stopping.

"You know, your Sylkie has a real mean streak," Rogue muttered as they ran towards their men. Rayvn skidded to a halt as he saw Mica's huge chestnut war horse break from the bushes around the keep. Mica's armour glinted in the sun as he bent low on his stallion's back, racing for the forest towards the coast, towards escape.

"Coward!" Rayvn snarled. He whistled for Falkyn, a loud piercing trill, and the Sylkie turned and sped for him, landing barely long enough for him to leap on before hurtling into the skies again. Rage kindled in his stomach, his fingers — aching to wrap around the man's throat — crusted with ice and he curled them into fists.

Falkyn's muscles bunched and pulled under him as he screamed through the skies after the fleeing horse, then baulked, turning sharply as an explosion of ice smashed into horse and rider, sending Mica crashing to the ground.

Falkyn landed heavily and Rayvn leaped off in time to see Gryffon, roaring with rage, lunge for Mica who had stumbled to his feet.

Gryffon's fist landed a solid blow to Mica's helmet, caving the side in. He went down, crumpling to the ground as Gryffon drew his blade, his face a mask of pure hatred.

He drove the sword through Mica's shoulder, into the dirt below, pinning him helplessly.

A scream of agony tore from the crumpled helmet and Gryffon's lip curled in disgust.

"I should draw this out and make you suffer for months like *she* has suffered," he snarled. He didn't even look up as Rayvn approached, his attention focused on the man writhing at his feet.

"But I will not have her live a moment longer in a world that contains you."

Gryffon erupted in golden flames, engulfing him and the body at his feet.

Rayvn fell backwards as the heat from it billowed towards him, watching them dance and twist in a rising inferno, and then blinked as the flames abated, staring in awe as Gryffon stood untouched, panting slightly. At his feet, a pool of melted metal and dust were all that remained of Mica.

Chapter 41

Drakon ran, bowling over panicked soldiers as he careened down the hill towards the forest that hugged the side of the keep. If he could get through the forest to the coast, to the boats... maybe he could escape out to sea unnot—

Something huge slammed into him. There was a flash of white and a snarl as he hit the ground. Rolling, he tried to draw his blade. It hit him again and a vise-like grip closed on his shoulder. He screamed in pain as something stabbed into his chest. The taste of blood bubbled up his throat and cold fear bloomed in his stomach.

"Hold," a cold voice snarled. The beast stilled, a growl low in its throat.

He could turn his head just enough to see huge fangs buried deep in his skin, the beast's muzzle red to the eyes with blood. Its breath curled around them as it waited for its mistress's command.

Drakon blinked up at the rider as they approached. The huge black beast lazily picked its way towards them, stepping over a fallen soldier, its powerful muscles rippling under its coat. White scars criss-crossed the horse's wide chest gleaming with sweat, and it halted as it neared. He tried to lift his head. Pain lanced through his shoulder at the movement. He groaned, keeping his eyes on the horse's hooves.

The rider leaped off, gracefully landing with barely a sound. She stalked towards him, the horse flanking her, shielding her from the panicked soldiers running around them.

She seized a handful of his hair and jerked his head up. He gasped in pain as his eyes met her burning blue ones.

"You bitch!" he snarled and coughed as blood clogged his throat. A fleck of red splattered onto her cheek. The beast bit deeper, and a muffled snap accompanied a searing pain as his collarbone snapped. He screamed again. Her hand tightened in his hair, and she smiled humourlessly.

"I made you a promise some months ago, *my lord*. Do you remember?" Cecily's voice was low, and cold as ice as he panted.

The whites of Drakon's eyes showed as she pulled a blade from her boot with her other hand. The razor-sharp tip scraping the bristles under the chin as he stared at her. She watched his throat bob as he swallowed hard a few times.

"I remember that promise," she hissed. "You came into my home, you took my mate from me against her will, and you have hurt her in ways I can never begin to repay you for."

The tip of the dagger pierced his skin, and he held his breath, going motionless as she leaned in.

"I swore to you that you would die at the end of my dagger. And you will, but there is someone who has a far greater claim to your death than mine."

She straightened then, her hand loosening in his hair slightly.

"And I will not take that satisfaction from her."

Cecily let go of his hair as he slumped with relief. He craned his neck up, a sneer on his face as he began to talk. He stilled as Addelyn stepped up next to her, her jade eyes blazing with fury.

Cecily held her dagger out to Addelyn.

Addelyn dropped to her knees in front of him, and he flinched, the wolf's teeth sinking ever so slightly deeper, holding him in place. The edge of the wickedly sharp dagger caressed his throat as Addelyn looked into his eyes.

"I can feel your fear," Addelyn mused, speaking softly to him. "It's delicious." She flicked the knife around, the tip scraping across the stubble under his chin. "You killed my mate, Drakon. You stole my children, and you kept me locked in a cell for eleven years." She laughed mirthlessly. "You thought you could kill him, and I would accept you as my husband? Cyrus was more of a man than you ever could be."

She snarled, digging the tip in deeper. A single drop of blood dripped down his shirt. "This moment of fear is nothing compared to the pain you have caused to so many people." Addelyn leaned in, her eyes inches from his. "Know that we will not think of you after your death, Drakon. I will wipe everything away. Your son, your records, your name. You will simply cease to have ever existed. And my children? My children will live long and full lives, knowing you will never touch them again."

Heliacle Rising

Cecily watched as the realisation formed in his eyes, and settled over him as he stared at Addelyn in horror. And then she angled the weapon down with a quick flick of her hand and thrust the blade into his heart.

Blood spurted across Addelyn's hand and ran in rivulets down his chest. Cecily watched the soul leave his eyes as he let out a whimper, going limp in the wolf's grip.

"Drop," Cecily ordered. The wolf released him instantly. The lifeless body crumpled into the dirt at Addelyn's feet and Cecily extended her arm to Addelyn, pulling her up.

"Go get my daughter," Addelyn said, her eyes going to the wall of men Rayvn and Rogue still fought. "I'll end this now."

Cecily nodded. Whirling, she ran past Shadow and aimed for the entrance doors. Blades raised, two men guarded the door. She faltered, sliding to a stop just out of their reach. They sneered at her.

"Get away, Wytchling bitch," one jeered, "or we will cut that pretty head off your shoulders."

He jerked suddenly, glancing down in disbelief at the arrow protruding from his chest. Cecily twisted around and saw Gryffon running towards her, but the arrow hadn't come from him. Her gaze moved upwards, movement higher above drawing her attention just as the second arrow flew past, lodging in the second man's eye. Lyrik, pale, but with a face of stone, sat astride Freyja flapping steadily above.

Cecily spun back when Gryffon grabbed her hand. They leaped over the fallen men at their feet and into the keep beyond. Scared servants scattered as they ran in.

"We will not harm you," Gryffon bellowed. "No innocent will be hurt, but we need to know where Lady Sylvers is being held."

A young boy approached them, shaking from head to foot. "The west wing, m'lord," he whispered, pointing a trembling finger up the passageway to their left.

"Can you show us?" Cecily asked, her voice gentle but urgent.

The boy nodded, taking off at a run up the passage, Cecily, and Gryffon on his heels.

He skidded to a halt in front of two large wooden doors. "This one." He looked upset as he turned to them, shaking. "I… I don't have the key m'lord." He eyed the door then Gryffon.

"Thank you," Cecily said gently. "Run along now. You have been a big help. Find somewhere safe and hide." The boy bobbed his head, relief on his face as he vanished around the next corner.

Gryffon's Gift blasted the door into the west wing, shattering it into toothpicks as Cecily dashed through the opening. Swearing, he raced after her, eyes darting around for any threats.

"Cess, let me go first! There might be guards up here!" he yelled. She darted from room to room, ignoring him. They reached a large wooden door, bolted from their side.

Gryffon ripped the bolt completely off the door, holding Cecily back long enough to check no one rushed out at them before her released her. The room was dark and smelled wrong — of sickness and pain. Cecily cried out and he whirled to see her throw herself to the floor next to…

"Amylia," he croaked, horror washing over him as he ran to her.

She lay unconscious on the floor, frail body curled in a ball. She looked as if she had fallen from the bed, then been unable to rise. Cecily sobbed as she gently pulled her into her arms, her hands going to Amylia's pale face, feeling for the breaths Gryffon could see were far too shallow.

"Just breathe, sweetling." Cecily's voice shook as she murmured it over and over into Amylia's ear.

"It's the Helix," he said, fighting to focus through the cold disbelief that wracked him. "I need to get it out of her. Where is it, Cess?"

Cecily rolled Amylia slightly and pulled up the hem of her nightgown. Running her hand over Amylia's thigh, she stopped at a spot with a slight scar and pointed.

"There," she said, her face crumpling.

Bruises mottled the skin of Amylia's thighs. She eased the hem of the nightgown higher and then closed her eyes. Tears leaking out of them, she kissed Amylia's forehead and rocked her gently.

Gryffon was frozen as he looked down to where Cecily had pointed. Hot, fiery rage curled through him. Within the bruises, he could see fingerprints. Fire wasn't enough. He wanted to shred the man that had done this.

"Gryff, get it out," Cecily whispered.

He snapped back to himself, taking his knife out and gripping it in his hand. Fire blazed over it, heating the metal to a glowing red before he cooled it with a layer of ice and he glanced at Amylia once, checking her shallow breathing before he cut, deep and quick, reaching into the wound with a finger and locating the stone. Finally, he flicked it out with a grunt of relief.

Cecily's hand was there instantly, healing the wound. Cecily sank onto the floor behind her, pulling her up, so Amylia's head rested against her shoulder. Wrapping her arms around Amylia's ribs, she rocked her gently as Gryffon knelt in front of her.

"Amylia, wake up!" he said urgently, cupping her face in his hands and running his thumbs over her cheeks. Under his hands, he could feel the bones of her face too close to the skin. "Amylia, please!" His voice broke, and hot tears ran down his face.

"Gryff?" Amylia murmured, so quiet it could have been a breath escaping her, but her breathing was slightly stronger now, as if she was clawing her way back to them.

"We have you," he gasped, kissing her forehead. "You are safe now."

Amylia stirred, her hand fluttering up weakly to touch Cecily's arm before falling back to her side again.

"Gryff." Cecily's voice was strained, broken, and he looked up at her, noticing the expression of utter horror on her face. He followed her eyes down to where she had her hand splayed over Amylia's stomach. She was so thin that he could have missed it at first, the fabric of her top so loose over her, but Cecily smoothed her hand gently over it, showing him the rounded bump there, and his heart shattered entirely.

Gryffon scooped Amylia up in his arms, cradling her against him. Grabbing a blanket off the bed and tucking it around Amylia, Cecily led the way back out. Together, they walked out to the grounds.

Rogue ran up to them. A deep cut down his cheek oozed blood and Cecily quickly reached up to heal it as his eyes raked over Amylia.

"Is she alive?" His voice broke as he looked at her, his expression just as horrified as Gryffon felt.

"She is," Gryffon said, his voice thick. "We need to get her out of here. Where is Addelyn?"

A boom shook the ground and dirt exploded through the air to the far side of the keep.

"I'm guessing that's where she is," Rogue said, turning to look in the direction.

"Cess?" Amylia rasped, her eyes fluttering open. They all turned to her.

"I'm here, sweetling," Cecily said, taking her hand. "It's okay, we're leaving here now."

"You came," Amylia breathed, a tear slipping from her eye.

"Of course we did," Gryffon said, his heart aching at the relief in those two words. "I'm so sorry it took us so long, bug."

"You found... Mother?" Amylia was fighting to stay conscious, and Cecily's hands flitted over her, healing anything she could find.

"We did. She's here, sweetling, and she's okay."

"I'll go get her," Rogue said, turning to run towards where the explosion had come from.

Amylia cracked her eyes open, and Gryffon noticed with relief the glow, weak but steadily growing, as she looked at him.

"I thought I was dreaming again," she said, leaning into Cecily's palm as the woman cupped her cheek, healing a bruise on her cheekbone. The whole side of her face had bruised where it had hit the ground after falling from the bed. She gripped the hand as Cecily went to move to the next spot. "Cess, just stop a minute. I'm okay." She smiled weakly.

"You're not okay." Cecily's voice cracked. "Look at you. I need to heal you." She started crying silently.

Amylia touched Gryffon's arm, glancing up at him, and he hesitated, before setting her down ever so gently, one arm bracing her, as he reached out to pull Cecily in, too.

Amylia leaned heavily against them both, resting her forehead against Gryffon's chest, her arm around Cecily's waist.

'Just breath, sweetling.' The words she had clung to over the past few months had filtered to her, in the dark place she had recessed to. A light in the dark, tugging at something deep in her. She had followed them, back to the two souls that kept her firmly tethered to life.

She stood there for a while, just breathing them in, and letting the world fade away. All around them silence fell. Asteryn had won.

"Milly?" A quiet voice behind them sounded and Amylia's eyes flew open, the sound an echo of her past.

Cecily threw out an arm to brace her as she lurched backwards and spun towards the voice.

"Mother?" Amylia's heart stumbled as she looked at the woman in front of her.

Addelyn stepped forward to take Amylia's hands, disbelief on her features.

"Oh, my darling," she whispered, eyes flying over her face. "My beautiful, strong girl."

She pulled her carefully into a hug, her hand cupping the back of her head as the other rubbed her back gently. "I'm so sorry. I'm so, so sorry." She sobbed.

Amylia's stomach pressed against Addelyn, and she felt the woman stiffen, but she said nothing, squeezing the slightest bit tighter before taking a breath and stepping back, her hands on Amylia's shoulders.

"Go with them. They will take you home. I will be right behind you. I just need to help your brother finish here," she said, smoothing Amylia's hair back from her face.

Dazed, Amylia nodded. She greedily took in Addelyn's face as she buckled, and Gryffon swept her up again.

"Lylith," Amylia murmured weakly, clinging to consciousness, "and Harry. Please find them."

Addelyn blanched. "Lylith? Kestrel's daughter?"

"She was brought up with Amylia," Cecily said quietly, her hand soothing Amylia's brow.

"Go, take her away from here," Addelyn said. "I'll go find her, I promise, and we will catch up."

Gryffon nodded. "I will get the girls on their way and come back."

"No, we will be okay," Addelyn said. "Take my daughter home to Asteryn. She needs you more right now." She bent and brushed a kiss to Amylia's cheek.

Vaguely, Amylia was aware of her mother turning away, and the warmth of flames flickered to life around Addelyn's arms before Amylia fell into an exhausted sleep in Gryffon's arms.

Amylia stayed unconscious through the entire flight home. Gryffon gently placed her onto Freyja's back, Lyrik behind her, her face anguished as she wrapped an arm around the woman, drawing her tight against her.

"Are you strong enough to do this flight with a passenger?" Gryffon asked quietly, his hand on Lyrik's knee.

"Yes," she replied thickly. "Freyja's the best for this flight anyway. She will keep steady. I will flag Arya and you down if I start tiring."

Cecily had already taken off, riding behind Ingryd, casting a worried glance behind her.

They flew straight back to the castle through the night, not stopping once, and riding high on the thermal currents to gain extra speed. Amylia did not even wake when they landed in the castle gardens. Gryffon was there the second they touched down and took Amylia from Lyrik's stiff arms and carried her into the castle cradled against his chest.

He lay her in their bed just as Cecily swept in, taking her cloak off and throwing it across a chair.

"I need to check her over properly," she said, "and she needs to eat if I can wake her. The Helix has taken too much, that and… the pregnancy," she choked out. "We need to start putting some of that energy back in." She turned to Gryffon. "Can you send a maid for some food, and tea with honey in it?"

Gryffon nodded, casting a brief look over Amylia's face before striding out.

Cecily waited until he had shut the door before walking towards Amylia. She watched her breathe for a moment before bending and placing a hand gently on her shoulder. A muscle twitched next to Amylia's lip, but nothing more.

"Sweetling," Cecily murmured, rubbing her thumb over the too prominent collar bone. "I need to get you undressed. I'll go slow."

Nothing.

Gently, she unwrapped the cloak from around Amylia. The visible skin was clear, everything Cecily had gotten her hands on already healed. She pushed a hand under Amylia's shoulders, pulling her upright, and grimaced against the lightness of the woman.

With her other hand, she pulled up the nightdress, sliding it up until it was out from under her. Then she shimmied it up the rest of her body, reaching around to feed her arms through and slipping it over her head. She sucked in a breath as she glanced down, rage flooding her.

With dull rage, Cecily registered the bruises and fingerprints peppering her breasts. She could count every rib on her sides, and lower … Cecily's stomach clenched as she looked at the small, compact mound of Amylia's stomach.

The skin was clear here, as if extra care had been taken, the growing babe beneath it precious.

Cecily ran her hand over every bruise she could reach, the blues and purples fading to unblemished, pink skin, before laying her back on the pillows.

Amylia stirred slightly. "Cess?" she asked groggily.

"You're home, sweetling. We're here with you," Cecily murmured, coming up to look into Amylia's eyes as she opened them slightly. Amylia nodded, silent as she watched Cecily work.

Cecily carried on, running her hands over a deep bruise on Amylia's shin and then up. She paused at Amylia's thighs and felt the woman tense slightly when she ran a hand over them. The marks faded even as the anger in her bloomed. Finally, she tugged a sheet up and covered Amylia, and came up to eye level with her again.

"Are you in pain anywhere?" she asked. "Have I missed anything?"

Amylia shifted slightly, assessing. "No," she said, her voice faint and rasping. "I just feel weak."

Cecily smiled at her. "Gryff's getting you some food to help with that. The Helix is out already. You just need rest now, sweetling."

Amylia took Cecily's hand and twined their fingers, staring mutely at their joined hands as Cecily stroked her hair with the other.

"I thought I was dying, and that I'd never see you and Gryff again," Amylia said, barely audible. Cecily squeezed her hand gently, not trusting her voice to speak.

Amylia swallowed. "Cess... I —" She paused, as if grasping for the words she needed, before taking the hand she held and sliding it onto the covers and placing it on her swollen abdomen. She looked at Cecily, her eyes filled with sorrow.

"I know, sweetling," Cecily murmured, her thumb rubbing over Amylia's hand. "I can't begin to try unpacking the last few months at the moment, but if... if you need me to help you... make this go away, I think I can," Cecily said quietly. "It's still early, but it would need to be soon."

She kept her eyes on Amylia's face and watched as she saw the realisation of what she was saying dawn on Amylia.

"No... I... I can't do that," Amylia gasped. A wave of relief washed over Cecily.

"It's just... I understand... I understand if you both can't have me around because of it."

Cecily heard the words but had to mull them over a minute as she tried to understand what Amylia was saying. "Why ever would we not want you around?" She gripped Amylia's hand harder. "We just got you back."

Amylia grimaced, her hand moving to her stomach protectively. "It will be a constant reminder of him." Her lip wobbled slightly, and she struggled to sit up.

Cecily moved to help her, fussing with the covers until she was comfortable, then knelt next to the bed and took her hand. She levelled a look at Amylia, her eyes flicking to her stomach and back up again, and then down again suddenly. The size of it nagged at her and she paused, trying to add the weeks rapidly.

"Sweetling, did you get your courses... after you were taken?" Cecily asked cautiously.

"No?" Amylia asked, her voice hesitant. "I was sick, after the boat trip... and the Helix. I lost so much weight so fast, Lylith said it might have stopped them."

"Well... she may have been right, and the babe may be Mica's," she said, her teeth clenching at Mica's name. "But the day you... left..." Stumbling over the words, her hand twitched against Amylia's. "Sweetling, you never had time to take your brew. You were taken before I had a chance to give it to you."

Amylia looked at her, confusion etched into her face.

"There might have been a build-up, from the previous ones," Cecily said hurriedly, "but, Amylia, there is a slim chance this babe could be Gryffon's."

The breath exploded from Amylia, and she slumped back into the pillows, her hand on her forehead.

"And you would have helped me get rid of it? Even with that chance?" she asked quietly, and Cecily nodded, trying to swallow the lump in her throat.

"I only just thought of it, but even now, if that's what you needed, if you cannot take the alternative... yes," she whispered.

"But what if it's not?" Amylia asked, her voice catching.

"Any child who comes from you, I will love... Gryff will love," Cecily said urgently, sitting forward and looking into Amylia's eyes. "How could we not when we love their mother as much as we do?"

Cecily placed her hand over the small bump, rubbing her thumb across it soothingly. She could feel the flickering, tiny soul in there, nestled inside, and emotions she couldn't even begin to untangle cascaded through her. She pushed her Gift out, feeling around the tiny life, feeling for any illness or weakness after the trauma of the last few months, but there was nothing except the strong little heartbeat.

Gryffon pushed the door open, his eyes immediately catching and holding Amylia's, and a flicker of worry passed across his face.

"Hey there, Bug." He smiled. Setting the plate of food next to the bed, he knelt next to her, kissing her tenderly on the forehead. His eyes briefly flicked to where Cecily's hand rested on Amylia's stomach. "How are you feeling?"

Amylia took a deep, shaky breath and looked at Cecily, then up at him, and let it out slowly.

"Safe," she murmured.

Chapter 42

They sat together, not talking much, as Amylia drifted in and out of sleep, waking periodically as Cecily coaxed her to eat small amounts. A soft knock came at the door as night crept across the sky.

"Come in," Gryffon called, from his seat by the fire and Lyrik pushed the door open and peered around it.

"Sylkies have been spotted over the Dead Forest," she said quietly. "Rayvn is on his way back with Addelyn." Her gaze moved to Amylia, who had sat up, pushing the covers back.

"I'm so glad to have you back," she said, her voice thick.

Amylia swung her legs out of the bed, standing shakily. She took a moment for the slight dizziness to clear. "I'm okay," she protested, as Cecily went to grab her elbow and steady her. "Are you going to make me come all the way?" she said wryly to Lyrik as she began to walk across the room slowly.

Lyrik slipped in the door, crossing quickly to Amylia, and pulled her into a hug.

"Thank you," Amylia whispered. "They told me everything you did to get my mother back."

"It wasn't enough," Lyrik murmured. "I… we didn't get her fast enough. What you went thr —"

"Please shut up." Amylia sighed against her shoulder. "Don't be stubborn and just take the thanks, for once. Just this time."

Gryffon snorted quietly. Amylia heard the thump as Cecily whacked him and Lyrik sighed deeply, relaxing slightly, and rubbed Amylia's back. "You're welcome," she murmured.

Amylia insisted on coming down to the hall when the Sylkies got within sight of the castle. She hesitated as he picked her up, but Gryffon carefully carried her down and set her onto the couch by the fire while Cecily went to greet them.

Rayvn came in first at a full run, skidding to a halt in front of Amylia and throwing his arms around her neck. Hurried footsteps followed him in. Amylia looked up into the green eyes of her mother.

Addelyn stepped forward and tapped Rayvn gently on the back. He let Amylia go, wiping his eyes, and she sat next to Amylia, brushing the hair back from her face, as the people around them moved away, giving them space.

"I'm so sorry, my darling," she said softly. "You have had to endure far more than any person should ever have to, and I'm so proud of you."

Amylia stared into her mother's face, taking in every piece of it, so much like her own.

"I can't believe it's really you." She reached out to trace a finger down her mother's cheek.

Addelyn laughed. "I'd say the same, but you still look like my little Milly, even if you are grown." She pulled her into a tight hug and rocked her gently, stroking her back. A lump formed in Amylia's throat as she saw the group of people who walked in. Harriet broke from them, running across the room to lean over the back of the couch, nearly falling bodily onto her, and hugged Amylia tightly.

"Are you okay?" Amylia asked, twisting to look into her friend's face.

Harriet nodded, wiping her eyes.

"Everyone got back safely," Lyrik announced, coming in, her face drawn after the long hours of stress. "Some injuries, but no fatalities. Rogue will be back with the army. He wanted to make sure Shadow and Athyna got back okay, so he's bringing them himself with the rest of them."

Gryffon laughed quietly. "I'm going to owe him a few drinks when he gets back."

Lyrik's mouth twitched in a half-smile. "We can thank Raol for the number of men who sided with Asteryn in the fight." She nodded to Harriet. "He's on his way here with Rogue. He said to send word that he's okay as well, Harriet, and very much looking forward to seeing you again."

Harriet heaved a sigh of relief as Amylia squeezed her hand.

"What about Mica and Drakon?" Amylia asked quietly as Lyrik came towards them.

"They are dead. Your mother and Gryff saw to that," Lyrik said, nodding to Addelyn.

"Lady Sylvers?" a quiet voice asked.

Everyone turned to see Lylith. She was battered, the white of one eye was clouded with blood and she had a deep laceration from the bridge of her nose to her jawline, the cut an angry red.

"I have no right to talk of her to you. But what my mother did to your family... I have no words." Her pained gaze went to Amylia. "I just wanted to say, I'm so, so very sorry for what happened."

Harriet stepped around the sofa and crossed to Lylith, pulling her into a tight hug and shaking her head.

"No," Lylith pulled away. "You don't understand." She took a breath. "While I was trying to find information for Amylia, I found other things out." She shut her eyes briefly. "Drakon was my father." Her voice was barely above a whisper. "It wasn't just my mother, it's both of them. I'm the child of both of them." She hung her head, looking at her feet.

Amylia stared at her, shocked. Addelyn squeezed her hand briefly before standing and walking to Lylith.

"Lylith." She took her hand, reaching with the other to cup it over the ravaged eye and cheek. The eye healed, but the cut, after starting its own healing, left a light scar across her beautiful face.

"Kestrel and Drakon alone are responsible for what has happened to my family, not you. I do not hold you accountable. I have been told what you did for Amylia, and what you tried to do." She smiled sadly. "You are more than just your bloodline. Who you are is here." She touched a finger to Lylith's chest. "And how can that be anything but magnificent, with the selflessness and bravery you have shown?"

Lylith choked on a sob, her mouth wavering as she gulped in breaths. Amylia felt her trying to not let her emotions get away. It was the first time she had been able to feel anything from Lylith, and it shook her to the core. Slowly, she pushed herself up and took a shaky step towards her.

Addelyn braced her elbow as she came to stand in front of Lylith, gently taking the same hand that her mother had held. She flowed into Lylith, unable to stop herself from the pull of the strong emotions that wrapped around the woman. The anguish and hurt surrounding her, the bone-deep loneliness, loss, anger, and fear that had sunk its dark tendrils so deep into the woman, wrapping around and hardening to form an armour.

"Lylith, I'm so sorry," Amylia whispered, pulling herself quickly back out, regretting the intrusion immediately. "I never knew. Why did you help me when you were hurting that badly?" Amylia saw her warring with the wall as if aching to throw it back up again.

"I never had anyone," Lylith said quietly, her eyes starting to fill with tears. "I think I was angry at you because of that. No... not angry ..." She looked at her feet. "Jealous." She gripped Amylia's hand tighter. "But what Mica did, I couldn't stand for that."

"You are not alone anymore," Amylia said. She pulled Lylith in and wrapped her arms around her. "I can't fix the last eleven years, I wish I knew then what I know now, but I promise you are not alone anymore."

Addelyn smiled sadly, reaching out to stroke both girls' hair, and sighed, pulling them both against her into a hug.

Amylia felt Lylith slip something into her hand and looked down.

"You need to stop leaving that lying around," Lylith laughed wetly.

Amylia's necklace glinted up at her, and she looked at Lylith. "Thank you," she whispered.

Two weeks later, Rogue returned to Asteryn, his journey slow from the extra soldiers that had travelled with them. Amylia rushed for the grounds as soon as she saw the party of people and animals coming up the road to the castle.

She was outrun only by Harriet, who streaked ahead and launched herself at Raol, dragging the man off his horse with an excited squeal. He laughed, crushing her to him.

Shadow pranced across the castle garden towards her, nearly yanking Rogue out the saddle when she saw her mistress and pulled viciously against the lead rope he held. Athyna was a white blur, taking Lyrik's legs out from under her, who was unfortunate enough to get between the wolf and Cecily as they joined the growing group.

Athyna launched herself at the woman, ending up in a tangle of fur and limbs in the springy grass, as Cecily went down with the pair.

"You know, that return trip with these two psychopaths was almost worth it, to see Lyrik taken out so thoroughly." Rogue snorted as Lyrik extricated herself from the mess and hauled Cecily up after her, flipping him off with a dirty look.

"Have you grown in two weeks?" Cecily laughed, barely having to bend as she wound her hands into the excited animal's fur.

"Thank you for getting Shadow back safely, Rogue," Amylia said, leaning against the mare's chest and breathing in the familiar scent of her. Rogue looked down at her, his eyes soft, and Amylia braced herself against the wave of emotions that flowed from him.

"I'd do it all a million times over again," he said quietly. "I'm relieved to see you up and looking less dead again." He looked up and grinned as Grymes came sprinting over, two stable boys struggling to keep up with the ageing Sylvyn.

"My baby!" he cried, skidding to a halt next to Amylia as he flung his arms around Shadow's neck. The mare only fidgeted slightly and let out what sounded alarmingly close to a resigned sigh. Grymes turned to Amylia as an afterthought, concern on his face. "Should you be out of bed, my girl?" He passed a rough hand across her forehead and tutted, rounding on Cecily who threw her hands in the air in mock exasperation.

"Keeping her in bed when Shadow arrived would be as easy as keeping you in bed when Shadow arrived." She laughed.

Grymes turned and winked at Amylia. "That's because we have the hoof drums in our hearts, don't we, girl? Now go." He gave her a gentle push. "You go back and rest. My princess and I have a lot of catching up to do. Don't we, my wee beauty?" he crooned, reaching into his pocket, and pulling out an apple.

Shockingly, Shadow pricked her ears forward and took it from him. Her ears cocked towards him as he led her away, stroking her giant neck lovingly, listening as he regaled her with the improvements he had made to her stall in her absence.

"What... the... actual fuck," Rogue said flatly, his jaw hanging open. "I just dragged that ungrateful brat and her fluffy sidekick through the *damn Dead Forest,* and she bit me not twenty-five minutes ago." He turned, showing the rip in his pants on his outer thigh, the purple crescent beneath glowing through. "And Grymes shows her an apple, and she follows him like a damn kitten." He threw his reins to a waiting stable lad. "That's it, I'm done."

He stormed off towards the castle as Gryffon and Lyrik roared with laughter, following him.

Cecily took Amylia's arm, strolling after them, her shoulders shaking gently as she tried to keep her own laughter in. "Rogue, wait up," she called, giggling. "Let me heal your ass for you."

Dinner that night was mayhem. The captains and generals of Rogue's and Lyrik's forces joined them, and the tables groaned under the weight of the food. Amylia, still tiring fast, contentedly sat and listened to the buzz of the noise around her, picking at the foods Cecily placed in front of her. She glanced at

Lylith sitting stiffly towards the head of the table, Athyna's head resting on her feet.

"Athyna has taken quite the liking to Lylith, hasn't she?" Gryffon chuckled. Amylia jumped at his sudden presence behind her. He sat casually, putting a hand on her leg, and squeezed it gently.

"Is she looking like she's sitting on needles because of Athyna?" Lyrik asked, laughing softly.

"Rogue," Cecily answered, her amused voice low. "He seems to be slightly smitten."

Amylia put her hand over Gryffon's, not looking at him as she sent a half-smile to her mother across the table, who leaned in close to Rayvn and talked quietly to him.

"You two have been plotting all day," she said, feeling Gryffon's thumb rub her leg under her hand.

"It's Oryx," Addelyn said. "I don't think I can go back there. It's just, to be there all alone without your father." Pain lanced across her face. "But I do want to go and visit his grave," she said quietly.

"Addelyn, I've already said you are welcome to stay here," Gryffon said. "We would be honoured to have you."

She smiled at Gryffon and nodded. "I think I will. I would like to stay. I have many years to make up with my children, and too many years spent alone." She grimaced. "I want to be around laughter again… and… I want to be here for Amylia… for the babe."

Amylia shut her senses down quickly when she felt Gryffon go still next to her. Slipping her hand out from under his, she picked up her drink. She didn't want to feel his emotions.

"That leaves Oryx, though," Rayvn said, his face drawn. "It needs someone we trust to manage it until I can," he said. "It has not been run well over the last years and my people have suffered for it too long."

"Do you have a suggestion?" Gryffon asked.

"Harriet," Addelyn stated. "And Raol, obviously."

Amylia's head shot up as she stared at them. "Harry?"

Addelyn nodded. "What that girl has gone through, I cannot even begin to repay her for how she took care of you. And Raol's hand in Rayvn's life." She smiled as she glanced down the table.

"I'd like to give Harriet a title, and the keep at Oryx, until the time Rayvn takes it over. And after that happens, I'd like to build her her own home in a place of her choosing in Oryx, if she wishes to remain there."

"I won't be taking the keep over for a long time." Rayvn laughed. "It's still six years until I'm twenty, and even then, Lyrik and I have discussed starting a new colony in Oryx mountains." He grinned. "It will take me quite a few years to get that settled, even with Silas as my Second."

Silas's smile split his freckled face ear to ear and visibly puffed under Rayvn's claim.

"You want me as your Second?" he asked, wonder filling his voice.

"Of course I do." Rayvn punched him lightly on the shoulder. "You already are."

Amylia smiled. "I think that's a wonderful idea," she said. She looked down the table at Harriet, who was practicing signing with Raol. She smiled adoringly up at him. Amylia's heart warmed a little, the cracks filling in slowly the longer she was surrounded by her people.

"You are staring. How do I make it stop?" Lylith hissed at Rogue, irritated as he chuckled under his breath.

"I would apologize, but I'm really not sorry." He smiled, his eyes roaming over her lips and back up to her eyes. "I can't help it."

She rolled her eyes, reaching an arm down to slip Athyna a hunk of bread and cheese. Rogue noticed, glanced under the table, and groaned. "What is it with the women around me attracting deadly creatures?" he muttered.

Lylith grinned, patting the soft head. "Animals have always liked me. Maybe that's why you're hanging around," she teased, watching him from under her lashes.

"Well, I do bite sometimes," Rogue replied, his deep voice only loud enough for her to hear.

A furious blush spread up Lylith's neck. She took a drink, trying to settle the butterflies that had taken flight in her stomach, annoyed at the reaction. "You know, Amylia told me all about you." She smiled coolly at him. "But you are not at all what I was expecting."

"And what were you expecting?" He grinned, reaching his knife out to stab a tart, and bringing it across to him.

"Someone taller." Lylith snorted softly, taking the half that he offered her, and hummed in approval at the sweet little pastry. "Strawberry is my favourite." She sighed at the explosion of flavour in her mouth. "We never got fresh strawberries in Lylican. My earliest memory was picking them with my nurse. Our last decent crop was the year before I went to Lylican."

"Well, if that impresses you, come with me," Rogue said. He stood and held out a hand to her. She hesitated, eyeing him dubiously. "I swear I will be on my best behaviour," he stated solemnly, his hand over his heart.

They slipped out of the dining hall, Rogue offering her his arm, which she took, glancing around the dark halls anxiously.

"You don't need to be nervous here," he soothed, opening a large wooden door that led to night sky. "I promise you are safe in Asteryn… and anywhere else that I'm with you."

She shot him a look, and then followed him, stepping into the crisp night air. "Where are we going?"

"Not far," he answered, pushing the door closed behind her. "See that building over there?" He pointed to a large dome-roofed building, its walls reflecting the moonlight.

"Yes," she said, hesitantly.

"In there."

Rogue drew back the light door as they reached it. Earthy smells wafted out to greet her and Lylith squinted into the darkness, jumping when light flashed in Rogue's palm. Arcs of electricity rolled around it, illuminating his face and the space around them. He squatted, picking something. When he rose gracefully, he held something out to her. He brought his other hand closer as she peered at it. A fat, deep red strawberry shone in the flickering light of his Gift.

"Ohh." She gasped and took it from him. She bit into it, and she closed her eyes and groaned. "Thank you." She sighed, popping the rest of it in her mouth, before chewing and smiling shyly at him.

"You are more than welcome, Lylith," he said gently, reaching for a basket and filling it quickly for her. "Here," he said, passing her the container. "If I can get you to make those noises just by giving you strawberries, we will be going through a lot of them." He grinned, offering her his arm, and pushing the door back open for her to walk through.

Chapter 43

Gryffon swam towards wakefulness as Cecily slipped out of bed from where she had been nestled against him, hearing her murmur to Athyna. He turned his head, searching for her in the dim light, and she smiled at him as she pulled a robe around her shoulders.

"Athyna wants to go out, and I haven't seen the sunrise for a while." her voice was soothing as she leaned back over the bed, kissing him. "And I want a cup of tea."

He nodded, careful not to disturb Amylia next to him, watching her slip silently through the room as he curled back into Amylia's warmth. The scent of both Cecily and Amylia in their nest curled deliciously in his senses and it soothed something deep within him that had been so thoroughly shattered and barely pieced back together. He reached a hand out, needing her closer, and tentatively curled an arm around her, pulling her against his chest.

She stiffened, and he stilled, barely breathing as the swell of her stomach moved against his arm, her breathing rapid and shallow.

"I'm sorry, Firebug," he murmured. He withdrew his hand, placing it on the bed in front of her. His arm still encircling her but giving her room. "Would you prefer not to be touched?"

"It's not that," she murmured in reply. "It's…" She rolled slightly towards him and frowned when he pulled back. "It's because of that," she said flatly. "I don't blame you, honestly."

"Because of what?" Gryffon asked, anxiety creeping over him.

"I wouldn't want to touch me either."

"What?" he blurted, looking into her eyes in alarm as she turned her face to him.

"Well, why would you?" she said in a small voice, still rough from sleep. "I'm carrying a child who is most likely the child of another, and I'm bony, and tired all the time and…" He hushed her with a gentle kiss on the cheek, his heart aching for her.

"Is that what you're worried about?"

"Among a rather long list," she choked on a sob.

"Amylia," he soothed. "Gods, what I would give to have your Gifts right now. Talk to me Bug, tell me what you need." Cautiously, he lifted his hand and rested it on the tight little swell of her abdomen. He waited for her to relax, his hand spread wide over her belly, letting the warmth of his flesh seep through the thin nightgown she wore. "This babe is part of you, and we are going to love it mercilessly because of that. Nothing that came from you could be anything other than incredible." He brought his hand up and laced his fingers with hers. Bringing her hand to his lips, he kissed it gently.

"But you have been so… you've barely come near me," she whispered, and his eyes caught and held hers, guilt washing over him. *Gods, I made this worse for her by trying to make it better.*

"That has nothing to do with my feelings for you, except the fact that I did not want to cause you any more stress while you recovered, or for you to think I expected anything from you other than for you to rest." He turned her face to him, his stomach clenching at the dusting of tears on her lashes. "All I have wanted to do is be near you since I got you back. I thought you needed the space."

"Truly?" She looked at him and he realised with stunned surprise she really thought he had been repulsed by her.

"I want to kiss you. Is that okay?" he asked huskily. She nodded, her eyes fixed on his mouth. His lips met hers, tentative and gentle.

She jumped slightly as his cock, hard and aching for her, pushed against her hip, and he bit back the urge to pull away again, giving her a moment. He almost groaned in relief as she relaxed again, and he slipped his tongue into her mouth. She melted into him, reaching up to grasp his face between her hands.

He broke the kiss as she pushed the covers off, her skin heating under his fingers.

He leaned forward, smoothing the material of her nightgown gently over her stomach, kissing just above her navel. Very slowly he bunched the material in his hand, glancing up once to check her reaction before he pulled the gown up, exposing the swell of her stomach. He kissed the soft, sleep warm skin there again, above, below and each side of her navel, before coming back up and taking her lips again. Her sigh against his lips had his blood turning to fire in his veins.

He pulled back enough to look into her eyes. "My heart was torn from my chest when you were taken from me, all I could think about was getting you back to us. Do not ever think that I could ever look at you with anything except love, and pride at how strong you are."

Amylia stared at him, her breathing hitching slightly as her finger traced the lines of his face, over his scar, his lips.

"Bug, use your Gift and look, see what you mean to me."

"Kiss me first," she whispered pulling him against her.

He did, claiming her mouth fully as she wrapped an arm around his shoulders. He felt her then, her Gift nudging at him, and he opened his mind to her, feeling her flow into him. He didn't hide anything from her, let her feel his desperation, his wild anger, his hope, and then he showed her what he had been too wrapped up in Cecily's grief to realise himself. Until the moment he had her back in his arms and it had settled in him, so bright that he had nearly been brought to his knees, right there on the battle field.

He showed her the love, twined so deep, twisting along the bond Cecily had lodged in his soul, rooted just as deep into every piece of him. He let those feelings rise up, outshining everything, and wrap around her.

He broke the kiss as he felt her withdraw slowly. "You see?" he asked her softly, kissing the tears off her cheek as they fell. Amylia nodded. "So, you know my feelings for you. You know they will not change, Amylia. You know I will do everything in my power to protect you, and make sure no one ever hurts you, or this babe you carry, ever again. You know you are my mate, and I am yours, for as long as I live and even after?"

A tear tracked down her face and he went to wipe it away as he felt her legs hook around his waist, his body instantly responding to her.

"Don't do that," he murmured. "I'm trying to behave."

"Don't," her voice was breathless, her fingers clutching at him.

He paused, concerned.

"I need you to touch me." Amylia tugged at his shirt, fumbling to pull it off.

He caught her hands, kissing her fingers as he sat up and pulled his shirt over his head in one clean movement. Amylia's hands went to the drawstring of his pants, and he let her pull them undone before catching her hands again.

"Are you sure?" he asked, and she nodded, a small frown of frustration on her face as she sat up abruptly and tugged her nightgown over her head.

She crossed her hands over her breasts. "I— want to feel again."

He looked at her arms, the defensive gesture, and his heart clenched. He leaned to kiss her, pushing her flat again. His hand slid under hers to cup her breast, rolling the nipple gently between his fingers.

"What do you want to feel, Bug?" he asked against her lips.

"Good. I just want to feel good again." She gasped as his fingers traced across to the other breast.

He kissed her neck. Her breathing faltered as he nipped the skin gently and then moved to her collarbone, the tip of his tongue tracing the too prominent ridge.

Her skin began to crackle with heat, and she moaned, squirming under his touch. He chuckled, blowing frostbitten air across her skin in a cloud.

He moved lower, kissing under her navel as her hands twisted in the bedclothes, enjoying the mewling sounds she made as his hands brushed her thighs.

He shuffled down to lie between them, her breath exploding out of her as he kissed the sensitive crease of her thigh, and then moved across to the other side.

"Gryff," she moaned.

"Yes?" he teased, kissing down the length of her thigh and back up again. Flickers of flame rippled across her, escaping the tenuous grasp she had on them.

"Gryff, please," she moaned again, her hips jerking as he blew an icy breath over the most sensitive skin.

"More kisses?" he asked, delighting in how wet she was as his lips brushed against her.

She gasped, fingers digging into the sheets as flames crackled at the tips of them.

"Or this?" He licked right up the centre of her, revelling in the taste of her as she bucked under his grasp, a low moan coming from her. She gasped as he repeated the movement again and again and he gently held her hips down as he explored every part of her, working her closer towards the edge of oblivion with every pass of his tongue.

He pushed his hips into the mattress, trying to take the edge off as she moaned, her hand grasping his where it rested on her hip. He twined his fingers with hers just as he sucked on that bundle of nerves, and she arched off the bed with a breathy cry. His other hand moved away from her hip, sliding down between her legs and then, slowly, he slipped a finger into her.

The sound she made nearly tipped him over the edge, and he pulled out, slipping a second finger in, stroking that sensitive spot inside her that he knew made her— there it was.

Amylia arched off the bed, a ragged cry ripping from her as she wrapped a leg around his shoulder, holding him to her as fire erupted from her, the hands she had twisted in the sheets now crackling with blue flames.

He drew himself up her body, kissing her deeply. She panted against his mouth, hair damp on her forehead.

His cock pressed into her thigh, uncomfortably hard as he lay against her, one arm holding his weight off her stomach, and she reached for him.

"Bug, you don't need to —"

Her fingers curled around him then and the argument died in his throat, letting her pull him against her, realising she had turned inwards. Her breath was coming faster. He could see the war behind her eyes, her head and her heart fighting with the trauma of the last few months. He wanted to drag her to him, tuck her into himself where he could protect her, but he knew it was her fight to conquer, and waited, letting her show him what she needed.

He made love to her, letting her lead them then as she kept the bond between them open, letting him feel everything, her Gift so wide open that he didn't know where he ended, and she began.

The turmoil of her emotions hit him like a blow, and he had to brace himself under it momentarily. He took it, gratefully, awed at how she was even functioning under the weight of it, murmuring to her through the waves of anxiety, coaxing her away from the darkness that clutched at her memories until together, they found release.

"Are you okay?" he asked, scanning her face after they had caught their breath.

"Yes." She took a breath. "More than okay."

He looked across the bed and winced and Amylia craned her neck, following his gaze. Her eyes went wide at the flames that peppered across the ruined, smouldering mattress.

He patted the nearest flames out, sending ice across to suffocate the ones he couldn't reach.

"Whoops," Amylia cringed, looking mortified as she surveyed the destruction, and Gryffon snorted.

"It's been a while since we needed a new mattress." He kissed her on the tip of the nose. "At least I know you had fun." He chuckled as his eyes followed the blush that rose up her neck.

They both looked up as Athyna pushed the door open and prowled in, stalking to the cushion Cecily left for her by the fire as Cecily walked in, holding three cups of steaming tea.

She grinned wickedly at them. "Redecorating, sweetling?" she teased and sat on the edge of the bed, passing Amylia a cup, and then his, before settling in against Amylia, carefully avoiding a large burnt patch with a snort of laughter.

"She got a bit hot and bothered when I told her she was my mate," Gryffon said softly, returning Cecily's smile.

"Ahhh," Cecily said. "It does tend to have that effect." She put her cup down, gently taking Amylia's free hand. "I want to show you something, too." She put Amylia's hand on her chest. "Look," she said softly.

"I don't need to," Amylia replied, her voice wavering slightly. "I felt it, Cess, when you were holding me, after Gryff took the Helix out. It's what brought me back. I think… I think I may have been dying, but you were calling me back. Not letting me go." She swallowed hard. "I heard your voice the whole time I was gone, telling me to just keep breathing. It kept me alive."

Cecily swallowed, her eyes overly bright. "I realised the second they took you what you were to me." She looked at him. "Gryff was so focused on my feelings for you, and how broken I was, that he didn't realise his own until we had you safe."

Amylia leaned across and kissed her. "I love you," she whispered. "I love you both."

Amylia and Cecily walked along the beach the night of the feast, their feet bare, and Amylia dug her toes onto the cool sand, listening to the surf crash against the sand next to them.

They looked up as Gryffon lithely jumped down the bank, a bottle and three glasses in his hands as he came up to them.

"Good plan, coming down here," he grinned. "Between Grymes and Rogue, they have everyone running around like headless chickens."

Cecily snorted, dropping into the sand, and holding her hands up to accept the glass he held out to her. He dropped next to her and lifted his arms cautiously up to Amylia, who folded herself into his lap, leaning against his chest as she watched the seabirds wheeling above in the dusky sky.

She took the glass he handed her, listening to his heart, and hearing his sigh of contentment as he leaned back against the bank.

"We had a question for you, sweetling," Cecily murmured, running a finger down the length of Amylia's forearm, and stopping at the tip of her ring finger.

"Hmmm?" Amylia asked, drawing her gaze from the birds.

"Gryffon and I… when you were taken," Cecily started.

Amylia stiffened but then Gryffon pressed a soothing kiss to the side of her hair.

"It broke us. We never want to feel the loss of your absence again," Cecily continued, glancing at Gryffon.

"What Cess is trying to say," Gryffon murmured against her hair, "we want you in every way possible. As our mate you are recognised amongst the Sylvyns, but mortals don't understand those ties. We would be honoured if you would marry us so the whole of Labrynth understands who you are to us. When you are ready, of course. We can wait for as long as you need."

Amylia looked down at her glass then looked back up at them, tears blurring her vision. "Yes," she whispered. "I can't live without either of you, too."

"Yes?" Cecily said, a smile creeping across her face.

Amylia half-laughed, half-sobbed at the expression. "What else would I say?"

She squeaked as Cecily shot forward, upsetting both their drinks over all three of them. Cecily kissed her, climbing into Gryffon's lap with her, so he held them both. His laugh rumbled up his chest as Cecily looked sheepishly at the red stain across his white shirt. He snorted, taking the glass from her, and chucking it aside as he pulled them both to him.

The dining hall was full as the Asterynians and their guests piled into it, the huge glass doors open to the night sky beyond, letting the guests wander in and out as braziers were lit for people to mingle around.

Gryffon wandered over and carefully draped a blanket over Amylia's shoulders as she stood near a brazier with Lylith and Lyrik, talking quietly. He brushed a finger along her shoulder, and she smiled at him, turning back to Lyrik, and looking at the blade the small woman had pulled out to show Lylith in the firelight. Amylia glanced up over the flames and watched with a smile as Raol stood with Harriet, his arms wrapped around her, murmuring something into her ear that made her smile softly.

Someone touched her arm and she turned to her mother, the woman's eyes warm as Cecily moved up on her other side, her arm slipping around her and her head on Amylia's shoulder.

"Your colour has come back," Addelyn said, brushing a lock of hair back from Amylia's forehead.

"I'm feeling much better," Amylia agreed, leaning into Cecily.

Rogue strolled over to join them, holding his hands to the flames.

"Ah, so this is where all the beautiful ladies are hanging out." He grinned, batting his eyelids at Lylith.

Lyrik snorted.

A sharp ringing sound echoed across the room, and Gryffon appeared, stepping up onto the side of the garden fountain, so everyone could see him easily. The brazier next to him lit him with soft golden light and made his eyes glow brighter as his gaze swept the crowd, pausing on Cecily and Amylia with a quick smile.

"I wanted to take this moment to make a few announcements," he began, his voice strong and clear. "First off, I want to say how proud I am to be the lord of such people who reside in Asteryn, with everything you did in the last month."

Cheers rang out across the gardens and from inside the hall, and he raised his glass to them.

"Secondly, we are formally recognising Lylith Drakon, Amylia's adopted sister, as the new Lady of Lylican, and announce that Lylican, under her rule, will become the second sister territory to Asteryn." He smiled at Lylith, raising a glass to her. "I believe under your hand, Lylican will flourish."

More cheers rang out, the news of Lylith's sire having already spread through Asteryn, and Lylith ducked her head, her cheeks going red.

"Thirdly," he called, silencing the crowd. "Lady Harriet and Sir Raol have been named to manage Oryx while Rayvn and his Second, Silas, work to settle the new colony of Sylkies into the Oryx mountains."

A louder cheer at this came from the group of riders situated towards the back of the crowd, and Lyrik laughed softly, raising her glass to them.

Gryffon grinned broadly.

"The alliance between these three territories is bound in blood and kinship," he boomed, holding his glass high. "And with the three pillars, we will stand strong. With our shared resources we will make a home for all our people, where no one hungers or has to live wanting and with time, we can unite Labrynth back together as it once was — human and Sylvyn together."

Rayvn emerged in their group, grinning fiercely as Amylia smiled warmly at her brother and Rogue clapped him on the back.

"And lastly," Gryffon said after the crowd had died down. His eyes glowed as he looked to where Amylia and Cecily stood together. "Cecily and I are honoured to introduce you all to Amylia Wynters, your new Lady of Asteryn."

Epilogue

Mica glared up at the woman in front of him. The guard's hand fisted in his jacket, pinching painfully as he forced him to kneel.

"I caught him in the forest snooping around," the guard said, his voice cold.

"I have already told you, I was not snooping," Mica spat. "I was trying to reach the palace for an audience with Queen Imogyn."

The woman in front of him raised a delicate brow, her jade-green eyes scanning over him. "Well, you have my attention. What is important enough for a human to risk his neck in the Wytchling lands?"

"I wish to trade information for a favour." He studied the woman. She was stunning. Black hair with skin as smooth as a babe's and fine features that while lovely, didn't soften the hardness of her eyes.

"I know where your daughter is," he said coldly.

Imogen started slightly. "My daughter is dead!" she snapped, her green eyes flashing. "Do not come here with your lies. Her grave was verified by one of my most trusted guards."

"The grave in Oryx was put there by my father," Mica said coolly. "When he took Addelyn and her children for himself."

She laughed, a cold, lethal sound that sent a tremor down his spine. Flames tinged with green swirled around her head like a crown as she stood and glared at him. "My daughter was a Heliacle Wytchling, born of one of the greatest lines of Wytchlings there has ever been, and you try to tell me a human captured her?" She scoffed.

"My father," Mica interrupted blandly, "infected Addelyn and her mate Cyrus, with Helix.

After he killed Cyrus, he had Helix embedded into your daughter and into your grandchildren. This is why you could not find them." He brushed a speck of dust off his filthy clothes. "My father was quite the genius, until your daughter killed him a couple of weeks ago and placed my territory into the hands of my half-sister."

Imogyn glared at him, the flames rippling down her arms to pool in her hands. "I should just kill you where you stand for your insolent tongue," she mused.

"Now, now, my Queen. I'm already dead. Or at least they believe I am," Mica drawled. "The... man," his lip curled in disgust, "responsible for taking my wife thinks he killed me. It's amazing what a quick change of armour can do... though, I admit it worked far better than I had planned, such a temper on him. I only meant to buy myself enough time to get away and regroup... instead I'm now a ghost and have had time to rally the men still loyal to me."

He looked her up and down, a slow, insolent look. "You won't kill me. I'm not an idiot, you see. I do still have loyal men, split up along the coast, waiting to go back to Lylican if I do not return unhurt, *with* a blood oath from you that I will remain that way." He grinned. "Oh, I know about those blood oaths. They are unbreakable. My men have orders to return to Lylican and warn Addelyn and her children of your intent to find her. There is no way you will get to her if she knows you are coming."

Imogyn shook with rage, fire dripping from her fingers onto the floor and pooling at her feet. "So, you're trying to blackmail me," she hissed.

"As a matter of fact, yes," he said. "You and I are family, as it turns out." He grinned widely at her shocked face. "Your granddaughter, the Heliacle Wytchling, Amylia Sylvers... now Amylia Drakon, is my wife. She is pregnant with my child... and she has been taken," he said, his voice like acid. "If you help me retrieve my child, and restore my territories to me, I will tell you where your daughter is hiding out."

"You want me to leave my blooded great-grandchild in your hands?" she hissed, flicking her long obsidian hair over her shoulder.

"Yes," Mica said tightly. "The child is the heir of the Lylican territories, Lylican has strong ties with all the major territories in Labrynth, which is currently split with no ruler. I know Labrynth is a country you have been trying to get for years. You failed to secure it in the Great War and have failed ever since with your spies and your schemes. My father knew this and worked towards securing our lands against a future invasion by Attica by tying our lines together." He smiled. "My child would be raised to acknowledge you as the rightful Queen, and with our support... Lylican's support, you can take over as Queen of Labrynth with barely any resistance."

Imogyn glared at him. "And what is it you want from me?" she hissed, her eyes glittering jade.

"Help me retrieve my child and land and kill those who are in the way of that and leave me enough guards that will help me retain those lands until my own forces grow again," he said. "Simple."

Imogyn was silent for a moment. "And my granddaughter?"

"You can keep her. I have no use for a wife that cannot stay where I put her," he said coldly. "Though I will allow her to stay with the child if she cannot bear to leave it. I wouldn't separate a child from its mother." He smiled coldly.

"And you know exactly where my daughter is?"

"I do," he replied, looking at his nails as if entirely bored.

Imogyn growled softly.

"Andromachy," she snapped, holding her hand out to the tall, dark-haired man who appeared by her side. He pulled a blade from his belt, glancing up at her once with grey eyes as she nodded to him.

He cut neatly across her palm, snagged a chalice from next to the throne, and held it under the wound, catching the drips into the cup.

"Tell me where my daughter is then, boy," Imogyn snarled, drawing a bloody finger down the bridge of her nose. "And I will grant you the lands back."

Gryffon kneaded Amylia's lower back, working at the bunched muscles there. Another pain started, clutching at her abdomen. She moaned through it, rocking back against his fists. She felt the anxiety flow from him. It surrounded her and her anxiety reared to meet it.

"Gryff, you're not helping," she hissed as the pain receded slightly.

He began rubbing his thumbs either side of her spine again, his hands warm and soothing against her skin.

"Sorry, bug. I'm trying to keep my feelings to myself."

Cecily smiled at Gryff as she sat in front of Amylia on the bed, holding a cup to the labouring woman's lips.

"This is natural, Gryff. It's all going fine. Stop worrying."

He sighed, his hands tracing lines of ice across Amylia's forehead, as he pushed the damp hair away from her forehead. "I hate that you're hurting, and I can't stop it," he said in a low voice.

Everything felt tight. Her skin felt stretched over her bones as yet another pain rose to grip her. Hissing through her teeth, she arched her back to try to get some relief from the steady ache that pounded there. She pushed off the bed, swaying slightly as she stood, and braced herself against the post at the foot. The pain crested before she paced across the room from one side to the other.

She felt Cecily's eyes following her across the room, her taut belly outlined against the soft glow of the fire behind her, and Athyna whined low in her throat as Amylia paused for the next one. The wolf approached the woman slowly, who was bent over, her hands on her thighs and Amylia reached up, straightening to wrap her arms around Athyna's neck.

She buried her face into the thick fur as the contraction ripped through her and let herself flow into the wolf.

The wolf's simple emotions surrounded her, soothing her as if a cool cloth had been placed over her mind and her body faded away slightly. Calm washed over her, and she let herself stay there with Athyna, her breaths slowing to match the beast's.

Athyna's interest flared suddenly at a new scent. Then she jolted, ripping back into herself as she felt water gush down her leg.

"Cess!" she gasped, panicked.

Cecily was there instantly, her hand soothing on Amylia's back.

"It's just the babe's waters, like I told you. It's okay, sweetling. Let's keep walking for a bit."

They walked slowly through the room, Cecily bracing Amylia every time a contraction took her. She gasped through them as they got stronger and stronger, unable to stop the low growl that ripped from her.

"Are you sure you don't want me to get your mother?" Cecily murmured.

"No." Amylia groaned as the next wave of pain washed over her. "She's the only thing stopping Rayvn from bursting in here."

Gryffon watched from the fireplace, his face creased in anxiety as his eyes followed them.

"Gryff!" Amylia gasped and doubled over. Her stomach bunched in a tight knot in front of her as Cecily braced her.

He strode to her. "I'm here, Bug," Her flames were escaping her grasp. Flickers of them danced across her skin and then vanished again as she grappled with them.

"Don't let me burn Cess." Amylia moaned, leaning her forehead against his chest as his ice chased the embers on her skin. Wisps of it caught the flames and eased them out with a hiss, cool against her burning skin. Cecily reached down from behind Amylia, feeling between her legs as another contraction surged through her, straight after the last.

Amylia growled low in her chest, her hands clutching the fabric of Gryffon's shirt.

"Let's get you to the bed, sweetling. The babe's not far," Cecily murmured.

Gryffon guided her to the bed, letting her go only to settle himself onto it first. He held his arms out to her and she eased herself backwards, sliding between his knees, her back braced against his chest. He continued to cool her, every flame that escaped getting put out gently and a cool kiss to her temple eased her clammy skin again.

Pressure was building fast, low in her abdomen. She cried out when the next contraction swelled up to meet the last. The need to push overwhelmed her. Cecily knelt in front of her, rucking her nightdress up and bending Amylia's legs, bracing her feet against her own knees.

She kissed Amylia's knees gently, thumbs stroking the skin on the sides of them. When the contraction passed, she reached down to check her progress again.

"I can feel the babe's head." She smiled at Amylia. "You have done so well, my love. Now on the next contraction, I need you to take a deep breath and push."

Amylia nodded, panting. She took each of Gryffon's hands in her own, leaning back into him. She bore down, her muscles straining, her fingernails digging into his palm. Pressure, so much pressure. Waves of white-hot pain rippled through her as her muscles contracted and Athyna whined softly from the hearth.

"Good!" Cecily encouraged. "That was good. Push again with the next contraction, sweetling."

It was rising fast, and Amylia gasped a breath, groaning as she bore down with the next one, feeling as if she were slowly ripping in two. She felt a rise of anxiety from Gryffon and blocked it out, focusing on Cecily's voice coaxing her through the pushing. Her voice calm and steady, her hands resting gently on her thighs. "Another big push and I'll be able to see the babe's head," Cecily soothed. "As soon as the babe's out, I can take all the pain away, sweetling. I just need you to push hard."

Amylia nodded, feeling heat and cold ripple over her hands in turn as her flames vied with Gryffon's ice.

"I've got you," he whispered to her. "Just focus on our babe."

The next contraction gripped her, and she screamed. Pushing with everything she had, she felt a shift, her muscles popping inside her, stretched to the breaking point. Distantly, she heard a choked cry from Cecily that the woman muffled quickly, and she looked down in panic.

"What's wrong?" she gasped, panting as pain tore through her, the burning feeling of skin stretching making her feel lightheaded. Tears rolled down Cecily's cheeks and an odd look of wonder crossed her face as she smiled.

"Nothing at all, sweetling. I can see the babe's head. You're nearly there. One more push and the head will be out."

Amylia groaned as the next contraction built. She pushed hard, feeling herself tear slightly. Cecily leaned forward, her hands cupping the babe.

"Stop now," she soothed. "Just breathe. The shoulders are out. That's it."

Amylia felt sharp, burning pain, and then the pressure eased suddenly as Cecily moved to catch the babe.

A mewling cry curled through the air. Gryffon stroked Amylia's hair back and kissed the back of her head.

They both watched as Cecily grabbed a cloth. She curled a finger into the babe's mouth to clean out the mucus and wiped the infant's face tenderly before she lifted the babe onto Amylia's stomach.

"She's perfect," Cecily murmured, smiling through her tears at Amylia.

Amylia stared down at her daughter, feeling Gryffon's breath hitch in a sob as he saw the same time as her.

Tiny golden eyes with a delicate ring of silver around the edges blinked up at them, her little face devastatingly perfect as she quietly took in the world around her. Her hands, so delicate, opened and closed against Amylia's skin. Gryffon trembled behind her as his emotions overtook him, and she opened her senses entirely.

The feeling of his wonder and fierce protectiveness mixed with Cecily's, a mirror to her own emotions. Gryffon reached out and cupped the baby's tiny head, running a gentle thumb over the wisps of white-grey hair that had started fluffing out delicately as they dried.

Gryffon pressed a kiss to Amylia's temple as tears ran down her face.

"Hello, sweet girl," Amylia whispered to her daughter, her hand cupping over Gryffon's. "You have a lot of people waiting to meet you."

The end

Made in the USA
Monee, IL
08 May 2024